TIME RENEGADES

BOOK ONE

KIM ALLRED

STORM COAST PUBLISHING, LLC

TIME RENEGADES
Book One
KIM ALLRED

Published by Storm Coast Publishing, LLC

Print edition April 2025
ISBN 978-1-953832-39-9

Come what come may, Time and the hour runs through the
roughest day.

Macbeth - William Shakespeare

Los Angeles Region - Central Sector - 2172

THE TRANSPORT HAULER bumped over the uneven asphalt, jostling the team. Sergeant Rowan Lockwood grabbed hold of the strap hanging from the ceiling to prevent knocking into the sweating squad member sitting on either side of her. A total of twenty guards jammed the two benches that ran down the sides of the hauler. She ignored them and stared at the glass imagers above their heads. The imagers currently displayed an aerial map but were unreadable with the rough road, but once they stopped, each team member could review maps and other pertinent data regarding the pending raid. The jittering screen gave her double vision, and she lowered her gaze to study the man across the aisle. His helmeted head rested on the hard metal side of the transport, eyes closed. She envied anyone who could nap on the way to a raid, but she'd been tasked with leading the squad that evening. Barely five years since graduating from the academy, this would be her first command. What a cluster. The butterflies had been playing roller derby in her gut since the team had entered the vehicle.

She tugged at her braid and played with the band that held it together. On instinct rather than thought, she reached into the pocket of her black tactical pants and wrapped her fingers around the old timepiece she'd found on a reclamation run. The guy at the pawnshop in the Yards had told her it was over a century old, maybe two, and though it no longer worked, she liked looking at the old-fashioned black numerals and the delicate arms of the minute and second hands. After tucking the watch away, she double-checked her sidearm and both knives. One blade was kept in her light-armored vest, the other in a holster above her combat boot. She would grab a high-velocity pulse long rifle from the armory cage when she exited the transport.

Without warning, a wicked pain pierced her head as if she'd been struck by a crossbow bolt. She blinked back tears and bent over, elbows on her knees, head lowered as she attempted to rub away the headache. She'd had these blinding headaches before, back when she'd been a kid. They came with visions—images from a child's imagination. From what she could remember, the headaches and visions both stopped sometime after puberty. Now, she'd had two crippling episodes in as many months. Fortunately, the pain should stop in a minute or two.

"Here, Rowan. Take one of these."

At the gruff voice, she slowly turned her head to glance at Dozer, who held out a bottle of stims. He smiled, his perfect white teeth glowing in the dim darkness of the hauler, accentuated by the dark grease covering his face. Her own teeth must cast the same eerie vision, emphasized by her pale-green eyes. Cap had once told her she looked like a Valkyrie when she swooped into a barrage of smugglers—braid whipping around, teeth bared, eyes wide as saucers, her long rifle primed.

Dozer nudged her arm. He was a grizzly old man, not old enough to have been around for the Climate Wars that changed the world, but young enough to have fought during the two years of the Uprising. That had been twenty-five years ago, and the old man was just as quick and lethal as the younger hotheads in the unit. But his face showed his age, emphasized by the deep crevice of a scar that ran from the left side of his mouth, across his chin, ending somewhere under his jaw. In the dim green light of the transport, his steady glare could make a full-grown man piss his pants.

Unwilling to shake her head, she managed an "I'm okay." To prove it more to herself than him, she sat back and closed her eyes to clear her vision. When she opened them, the pain had receded.

"Hear you passed on the earlier call." Dozer studied her.

"Yeah." She yelled over the noise of the thrusters sliding into reverse as the hauler made a one-hundred-eighty-degree turn to get into position.

"Take a stim. It'll clear away the alcohol." His expression turned soft, though his tone sounded more like a command. The old man had taken her under his wing when she'd first joined the unit, and his bluster didn't scare the shit out of her anymore.

She grabbed the bottle and fumbled the handoff. The canister rolled down the aisle, and she swore as she unclipped the safety harness and stood. The quick movement made her head swim and legs shake. Between the hangover and the remains of the piercing headache, she waited a heartbeat before she was steady enough to walk, then made two attempts at retrieving the bottle before one of the guards picked it up and tossed it to her. After settling back and re-engaging the harness, she shook out a pill, dry swallowing it before placing the bottle back in Dozer's hand. The bitter taste was a minor payback for ignoring the earlier call.

As if he'd read her mind, Dozer said, "It's okay to pass on a call when you're off duty. That's not on you."

"I know." Yet, she couldn't kick the guilt. Zach had taken the call, and now his squad was pinned down, waiting for them to bail him out.

Dozer grunted, and after all these years, the best sense she could make of his grunt was confirmation he had her back—just one more of his cranky charms. Tonight, she latched onto it like a lifesaver.

Cap, dressed in the same combat gear as the squads, walked into the cargo area from the driver's cage. The hauler idled, its heavy engines vibrating the vehicle.

Dozer elbowed her. "You need another stim?"

She shook her head. "No. I'm already buzzing."

"Lockwood," Cap yelled.

Rowan jumped up and met him at the central display console, tucked into a corner of the wall dividing the compartments. There were three squads on this raid, and tonight, they'd follow her commands. She sucked in a breath. "What we got?"

Cap frowned and shook his head. He punched keys until a map lit up the console and the two rows of imagers for the other guards to follow along. "Our team is pinned down on the backside of this abandoned building." He zoomed in on the interior shot, then moved the pointer until it hovered where a barricade had been set up in front of the back wall.

She could make out movement behind what looked like part of the crumbling ceiling. Abandoned buildings were commonplace in the Yards. That ceiling could have come down yesterday or twenty years ago.

"The team received a call about an illegal tech sale. The informant was either misinformed or it was a setup. We have an unknown crew of suspected contraband runners directly across from them, pinning them down on three sides."

She studied the image as Cap split the visual, adding a map from the outside of the building. "How thick are the walls?"

"At least a foot."

"A single pulse grenade should take care of it, but..." She pushed her helmet up to scratch her temple. "Have the team move to the west side, as far as they can go. It wouldn't hurt to put a couple sharpshooters in position over here." She tapped the left side of the screen, outside the range of the image. "They can provide cover fire."

"A grenade could take down the whole wall."

She nodded and gave him one of her know-it-all grins. "We'll have to be careful."

He nodded. "Let's round 'em up."

Five minutes later, after taking the long way around the building at a fast jog, she placed six of their team around Hernandez, who used a laser GPS scope to pin her target. Rowan typed into her wrist unit and waited for the response. Ten seconds later, a single word came onto the screen. "Green."

She knelt next to Hernandez. "Make it a nice clean hole about head high."

Hernandez nodded, and within seconds the grenade hit the wall. Chunks of cement and layers of dust filled the air. Rapid gunfire followed. That would be the cover teams laying down suppressing fire as the trapped team moved toward their escape.

When the dust settled enough to see the expanded hole, she gave Hernandez a questioning glance. "I thought I said head high. That hit wasn't more than five feet."

She shrugged. "I'm short."

Rowan snorted as she watched the first of the pinned-down unit crawl through broken scraps of the hole. The second person had to be helped through. They dragged their leg, a field dressing leaking a dark stain. As another guard climbed over the dusty rubble, she noted movement from the right, outside of the building where the exterior wall had crumbled away.

A single-person Airborne Vehicular Unit, or AVU, was positioned alongside the building. It hadn't been there when they'd run a patrol around the building, nor had she heard it land. It must have come in when the grenade went off. A dark figure, feminine in movement but difficult to identify in the dim lighting, slid along the farther side of the vehicle until they stopped where the windshield leveled off to meet the hard surface metal. They leaned over the AVU, and several seconds ticked by before Rowan understood what she was seeing.

The person had a scoped rifle, and Rowan tracked where the muzzle pointed, directly at the crumbling wall where the team was evacuating. The person currently climbing through had their arm clutched to their chest and stumbled on the debris before one of their squad moved in to assist.

Zach, as the team's commander, was the last to emerge. She turned her back to him and stood as she drew up her long rifle, shouting a warning to the team. "Rogue shooter!"

"Zach. Drop!" someone else yelled.

The shooter was quick. They'd already tossed the rifle in the AVU before jumping in behind it. Rowan zeroed in on the driver's compartment and released three rapid-fire shots as it began to lift. The shots went low, one hitting a wheel, the second piercing the back panel of the AVU, and the last one disappearing into the night sky. The vehicle moved so fast, she wasn't able to catch the identification tag. It would have been a miracle in the low lighting.

She spun around as the "all clear" command was given. Guards stood in a loose circle around the med unit. A knife twisted in the middle of her chest as she ran for the growing group, skidding to a stop but still managing to barrel through two burly squad members. Two people hovered over Zach—one pumping on his chest and another trying to staunch the bleeding from a neck wound.

No. No. No. She froze, searching his face.

She didn't need anyone to call it to know her brother was already gone.

ONE

L*os Angeles - Six months later*

THE LIGHTS from the imagers cast a blue glow within the command transport. Rowan listened to the chatter in her earbuds, still thirty minutes until the mark was due to show. Dozer and Mahoney played cards in silence. The two old-timers wouldn't be needed until the target's vehicle entered the net—the area between where the deal was going down and where the team had surrounded the area. The size of the net depended on the raid, and this one was narrow, barely a block in circumference.

She leaned back, her combat boots resting on a console—the cool squad leader showing no worries. But her outward demeanor didn't reflect the tingling of excitement before an imminent raid, the light sheen of sweat along her spine, or the crickets jumping around in her belly. If this raid failed, it could end her short command of the squad. Cap had said as much before they'd left the barn, the name long ago given to the garage of the Internal Security Agency, or ISA.

The ISA was a worldwide agency, a mixture of the old world's police, military, and international investigative units rolled into one. The agency cared for internal Earth issues ranging from simple property disputes to murder to corporate espionage. They were the unseen force that people subconsciously knew was there, took comfort from it, but rarely saw, except through occasional video feeds in the media. Lately, at least in the L.A. Sector, the ISA's primary focus had been on the Yards.

Topside—a moniker derived long ago from the Terrestrial Origination Project and where seventy percent of the world's population lived—enjoyed the utopia of the new world order after the global destruction wrought by the Climate Wars a hundred and fifty years ago. The Yards was its underbelly. When Topside was being built, railyards circled the city, and the workers lived near them. Now, almost all the railyards were long gone, but the term Yards remained, as did the housing. Most of the people had moved to the mainstream Topside, but others hadn't wanted to leave their culture-driven neighborhoods. Life in the Yards was now driven by the old world's phenomena of sex, drugs, and rock and roll.

Rowan preferred the Yards on most days. The grit made everything seem real, rather than the almost too-sterile Topside.

"Hernandez?" she whispered into her headset. "What do you see?" She didn't expect anything yet. This guy, whoever he was, she'd never been able to get a name or a face, was too slick, a professional who timed everything with exacting precision. She'd learned that, if nothing else, in the last two failed attempts at catching him.

"Nothing, boss." Her voice was smooth and steady. "Wait."

Rowan sat up, swinging her boots to the floor, and caught

the quick glances from Dozer and Mahoney before they went back to their cards.

"There's a single-person AVU rolling through. Might be a lookout." Silence, except for the humming of the radio signal. "A woman. Looks like she might be lost." A few seconds ticked by while Rowan tapped her fingers on the arm of the chair. "She's parked on the far side of the lot, behind a small shed."

"Marco," Rowan whispered. "Keep an eye on her."

Two clicks from the radio said he heard.

Ten squad members were spread around the net. Two were marksmen: Marco and Jess. Jess was the better of the two if the mark was on the move. She had a natural flair for timing movement with her shot. The other eight would rush in commando-style, weapons hot. Sometimes Rowan would call for a larger backup team, but this was a small meetup based on what little intel she'd scraped together. One commercial cargo transport with the contraband and one AVU with the target.

A quick buzz sounded, and the dispatcher's voice filtered through from a secondary feed. "Sarge, you have a call. It's on the command channel."

Damn it. This wouldn't be the first time Cap called during the last minutes before a raid to shut the whole thing down. It was annoying, and while it wouldn't be a mark against her leadership, it would be weeks of work for nothing.

She caught the two men's glances again. They'd be just as disappointed. Once the raid started, they were the cleanup crew. They'd run toward anything going haywire and mop it up. The whole team was lethal, but these two could crawl up behind someone while they stood stock-still in the middle of an empty field. They were scary crazy.

She nibbled at a nail. Better to get this over with. It would be easier to pull out now before the target showed up and destroyed any chance of moving on them in the future. She tapped her earbud. "Go ahead, dispatch."

"Rowan?"

"Kendra?" For fuck's sake. Her sister-in-law. Rowan's chest tightened, and she turned her back on Dozer and Mahoney.

"I'm sorry, Rowan. Your mother gave me the link to contact you."

She blew out a breath and ran a hand over her hair, cut short after that horrible night, and was now a messy mop of untamed auburn reaching her shoulders. Only command personnel should be calling on this line minutes before a raid. Her mother could only have gotten the link from her father—General Thaddeus Lockwood—known lovingly by some as Bear, an old academy nickname, known in terror by others as the Grizzly. Her name would be listed under the terror column.

"I'm in the middle of a raid, Kendra." She held her tone level. Whatever this call was about had nothing to do with her sister-in-law. She'd been through enough these last six months, now trying to raise her two kids all alone. And it was Rowan's fault.

The silence was deafening. The two could sit for long moments with just the silence. Kendra had a heart of gold. This particular silence swelled with apprehension, and they both knew it hadn't been her choice to call.

"What do they want?" Rowan couldn't stop the bitterness from leaking out.

Kendra sighed loudly. "They've called a family dinner. It wasn't my choice. I tried to tell them it wasn't necessary."

"Don't tell me. Mother is intruding."

Kendra let out a shaky laugh. "You have no idea."

"Hmm. I have some."

"I suppose you do." Another pause. "Listen, Rowan. They

called it for tomorrow. I'll understand if you discover you have... I don't know...maybe another raid?"

She snorted. "Will one of my drunken binges do? They'll believe that."

"Oh, Rowan. You need to stop beating yourself up for something you couldn't prevent."

"Do you really want me to find an excuse? Or would it be easier to just get this over with?" She hadn't seen her parents for weeks. Kendra had been to their place numerous times with the kids, but it required an official family dinner before Rowan would be allowed in the house.

"Zach would never blame you, and your parents are asses."

She laughed, mostly to cover the first part of Kendra's statement that would always sting. But her sister-in-law could turn into quite the tiger when she had her back against a wall.

"Message received, Kendra. Could you pass a message to my loving parents that I have a previous engagement and require more notice next time?" She was happy to take the hit for Kendra. God knows the woman deserved whatever break she could get.

"Thank you, Rowan." There was a brief pause before she finished. "Zach is watching over us. I believe that with all my heart."

Then all she heard was static until the air she'd been holding rushed out, releasing the clamp around her heart. She blinked, then turned to the second imager, getting her head back in the game. The center of the net was the parking lot of an old warehouse that opened into an old-fashioned farmer's market on the weekends. The team had become rigid, and the chatter had quieted.

"Talk to me, Hernandez."

Hernandez was tucked into a high-level nest in a nearby building. She used to be the sharpshooter of the squad, one of the best in the unit, but her true talent was as a techrat. There wasn't a computer she couldn't tame into submission. Right now, she would be watching several cameras—the team's eyes and ears.

"Nothing, boss."

Rowan's heart sank. She checked the clock on the console, less than five minutes until the meet.

"Game time." Hernandez's voice had moved up an octave. This was the real deal.

Dozer and Mahoney dropped their cards and stood. They checked weapons and moved toward the door, their bodies tensing for the order to be given.

"Everyone, hold back until you hear my command." Her voice was calm and controlled. "We wait until after the exchange." The squad knew that, but everyone got jacked up, eager to jump into the fray. The words were meant to keep everyone settled.

"Here comes the cargo transport. I see the driver but can't see the passenger side." Hernandez would call out everything she saw to advise the squad where the players were and how many.

"We don't know the size of the team traveling with the package. Be prepared." She continued her mantra with the same calm voice she always mustered up, having learned long ago how to keep the nervous shake out of her tone.

"The AVU is coming in from the north. It looks like the right color and model."

"Marco, you have eyes on that first AVU?" Rowan asked.

"No movement." His voice was nothing more than a whisper.

"Keep on her." She leaned toward the imager, the camera confirming Hernandez's report. "Patience." The AVU was a flashy green, easy to spot, but down here in the Yards that meant nothing. Flashy AVUs were all the rage, especially for the street races held outside the Yards, away from prying ISA security monitors. The races could be picked up by satellite if they were worth ISA's time. They weren't.

The cargo transport was commercial grade, the type that could be found on any street during delivery times. In Topside, delivery times were in the early predawn hours or late at night to prevent hampering traffic during the day. In the Yards, delivery was whenever.

The two vehicles stopped ten feet from each other, each parked slightly toward the right, making for an easy escape.

"Tighten the net. Slowly." Her command brought the squad in closer, erasing the target's comfortable exit.

"Boss, another vehicle. A rammer." Hernandez's voice was urgent. "They're coming in from the east side alley and moving fast. They'll pass our lone woman."

Rowan leaned toward another imager to get a better angle of whoever was approaching. Was one of the players breaking the rules, or had they missed something? Maybe this was someone in the wrong place at the wrong time. But with a rammer? A rammer was a street-modified, four-seater AVU rebuilt like the old armored vehicles before the Climate Wars. They were illegal and only had one purpose, as the name suggested. Having it show up in the middle of their raid screwed with her plans, but the squad could adapt.

"Dozer, Mahoney, grab the pulse grenade launchers on your way out."

They smiled as they opened lockers, grabbing weapons that could launch grenades up to three hundred yards. One grenade would be enough to take out the rammer, but they might as well play it safe.

They were out the door before the rammer reached the spot where the marks had parked.

"Hold steady." She scooted up in her seat, her right leg bouncing. She nibbled on a nail as she watched, partially wishing she was down there, waiting for the signal to go in.

When the rammer was almost to the center of the net, a female voice shouted, "Go. Go. Go."

Who the fuck was that?

"Hold your positions," Rowan screamed into her headset. "Hold your positions. I said hold." She jumped up, hands twisting in her hair.

It was too late.

The squad was moving. Shouts and weapon fire prevented her screams from reaching anyone. The occupants in the AVU and cargo carrier hadn't even gotten out of their vehicles. Tires screeched as they each took off in different directions. The squad might have stopped them, but the rammer surged into the fray—weapons fire streaming from the windows.

Then everyone was firing and all she could do was yell, "Weapons down. Weapons down. The op is scratched."

Either Dozer or Mahoney released a grenade that missed the rammer circling the parking lot, still firing. The grenade took out one corner of an abandoned building, but it wasn't enough to take it down. Thank god for small favors. Squad members were everywhere as they pulled back, returning fire on the rammer. She had no doubt another pulse grenade would be released. The raid had taken on a life of its own, and everyone wanted a piece of that rammer. No one wanted to walk away empty-handed.

Before pushing back from the console, the last thing she noticed was the tiny AVU with the lone woman that raced past everyone as it screamed down the alley. She caught its taillights as it lifted off toward an open fly zone but missed the opportunity to track it. Their only hope would be to review the security monitors spread throughout the Yards, though most of them were constantly stolen or destroyed by the locals.

She grabbed the closest thing not nailed down—a coffee mug—and threw it against a locker. It crashed hard, but the only thing the metal cup did was bounce off the locker and slam into a holo-monitor before falling to the floor. They'd had them. The target had been in their hands. As much as she wanted to know where that rammer had come from and who the hell that woman was—it wouldn't matter. Three strikes on this one, and Cap would have her ass for breakfast.

TWO

Rowan fiddled with the buttons of her dress uniform, staring dully at the rows of pictures on the wall outside Captain Jiang's office. The images honored ISA guards who'd earned special accommodations in the line of duty. First, she counted them. Twenty-two framed pictures with smiling faces and firm handshakes. Impeccable in their dress whites, their eyes shining with determination to go out the next day and do it all over again. Next, she scanned the faces, recognizing many of them. Cap had only been there two years and hadn't hesitated in filling the wall. He was proud of his squads.

Her last captain, now Major Jolanda Taylor, had been just as fierce in her devotion to her unit. It was that loyalty along with her brains and no-shit attitude that got her promoted to Special Investigations, a hybrid team operated by ISA agents but within the purview of the Global Science Ministry. GSM was the political power around the globe. No more countries with their individual leaders. Instead, seven Regions across Earth encompassed multiple Sectors that supported smaller Districts. Each Region had its own level of governorship that worked within the framework of GSM policies. Bottom line—

science, medicine, math, and the arts were king. After the Climate Wars, the world needed engineers, scientists, and chemists to stitch everything back together. But everything came at a price. She'd hated to see Major Taylor leave but rarely did anything remain the same.

She scowled when her gaze stopped at her own face on the wall. The picture had been taken a year ago. Back when life had meant something. Before it had all gone to hell. Unable to stop, her gaze shifted to a photo two down from hers. It still hurt to look at his face. It was bad enough when she glimpsed his image in his six-year-old son and his eyes in his three-year-old daughter.

A fist squeezed her heart, and she pushed back the tears. She snorted. It had been a helluva two days since the ops, and she had to stop letting the past sneak up on her whenever she let down her guard. Six months—and it stung like it was yesterday.

"Sergeant Lockwood? The captain's ready for you."

Rowan took a deep breath before standing and turning to Terrance. She smiled, testing the waters, and immediately got her answer. His expression was all business, as it was whenever someone was called to Cap's office. When everyone knew someone was going to have their ass chewed.

She nodded, tugged on the edge of her sleeves, then strode into the office to take her beatdown. She had expected it, deserved it, and planned for it. Right down to her prepared speech about how she'd do better, gather more evidence—blah, blah, blah.

Cap had his head down, reviewing a tablet that might hold her incident report, yesterday's Jonga ball scores, or a letter from his daughter at university. One could never tell. He was younger than her father, but there were slices of gray in his dark hair. He wasn't a tall man, but he was lean and scrappy and stood unbeatable in the unit's annual fight match. Although, she'd come close to beating him last year. Her martial arts training had significantly improved after finding a new sensei when her first one moved back to Tokyo Region.

"Sit down, Sergeant." He continued to scan the screen.

She recognized the incident report as she sat on the edge of the chair. Her empty stomach lurched, and her prepared speech evaporated. If Cap wanted to chat, he would have smiled and directed her to the sitting area that looked out over Los Angeles, the capital of Earth.

After several agonizing minutes, Cap sat back and stared at her. She refused to look away, and he shook his head. She pretended not to see the disappointment in his eyes. "Can you tell me what happened out there?" His voice was soothing, deep, and rich. A voice that could calm a person or, with a slight change in pitch, make them shake in their boots. So far, he'd kept the tone somewhere in the middle.

She shrugged. "Bad intel."

When she didn't elaborate, his brows drew down. "Second time in a row?"

She stopped the second shrug that turned into more of a shudder. "This group is wily. I think they're using the same supply route as the Sons Syndicate to disguise their shipments and runs."

"That doesn't match up with the other reports."

She tipped farther out of the chair, leaning toward him. She reined in her rant, knowing in her gut what was going on. But she had to pull back—force herself to shut it down. "I know other squad commanders aren't convinced, but I think there's a new syndicate in the Yards. Someone we haven't seen before. I found similar profiles in two other Regions before they grew cold. Maybe someone has their sights set on a larger target." Everyone knew more money ran through the Yards in the Capital Sector than in any other Region.

Cap shook his head. "There's no evidence of that unless you're holding something back."

Cap knew her well. She did sometimes hold stuff back—but not this time. She wished she had something intriguing, if not substantiated, to reveal. "I have no firm evidence."

"But you approved the raid anyway."

She fidgeted. Her hunches had always paid off in the past, and she was positive this wasn't any different. Yet, thoughts of Zach had haunted the last few weeks. Had it thrown her off her game? A niggle of doubt refused to go away until she shook her head. "I knew there was a meet going down. I had everyone in place, and the players showed up. Just like the intel said."

"And yet you knew nothing about the other two vehicles. One of them a rammer."

She stiffened. "No. I don't know where they came from."

"We have three injured soldiers and two dead civilians."

Civilians, her ass. "The two dead came from the rammer."

The captain shook his head. "No one can remember seeing anyone getting out of the rammer before it got away. According to the IDs, the bodies were a young couple visiting the city."

"Visiting in the Yards? Besides, the team swept the area beforehand."

"Not well enough. It's not on the dead to explain their whereabouts. It's about you doing your job right."

She straightened her back as her gut churned. With no proof that the two bodies were part of a syndicate she couldn't prove existed, this would go down as a bad shooting. Which probably meant another suspension.

"Look, I know the last few months have been difficult." He stopped when she glared at him. After a second, he sat straighter, and his face became a mask. This was a man she hadn't seen before. "I'm moving you to Lin."

The churning in her stomach froze into a solid brick of ice, chilling her to the bone. "A desk job? You're taking me off the streets?"

"You need more time."

"Bullshit."

Cap raised a brow. "Here's what I know. You've been off your game since Zach's death." He raised his hand when she opened her mouth. "No. I don't want to hear any more excuses or gut instincts. Right now, I can't trust your instincts. That's the sad truth of it. In a year..."

"A year?" She couldn't stop the shrill in her voice or the fear flooding her veins. A year trapped at a desk for an entire shift. The monotony of it all. Claustrophobia crept in.

"Or..." Cap picked up a second tablet, and Rowan's skin itched like ants were crawling over her. He'd set her up, and his wicked "I'm an asshole" smile appeared. "I have a request from Major Taylor."

She perked up. Her old captain. A lifeline.

"She's started a task force in the Investigation's unit. I'm not familiar with all the details, but she'd like your assistance with a homicide investigation."

Her excitement over possible salvation died. "I'm not an investigator. I would think that was obvious by my last two incidents."

Cap surprised her with a chuckle. "I agree, but a change of scenery will either get your head in the game or prove you're done in ISA."

That sobered her. Somehow, she'd missed how close to the edge she'd been walking. Or maybe she hadn't and didn't care. Which seemed to be the point Cap was trying to kick into her thick skull.

"Not really a choice, is it?"

His expression changed to the one they used to share. His

softer side, his "let's sit back, drink a few, and figure this out" expression. The one she rarely saw these days.

"Maybe working Topside will chase your demons away."

Topside. Most people thought all the crimes happened in the Yards. They'd be shocked by the truth. There was just as much crime Topside; it was just packaged differently—prettier and neater for the media but just as ugly under the tidy bow. Mostly white-collar crime with domestic abuse and unsightly murders mixed in.

"When do I report?"

Cap checked his wrist unit. "Now. The major just sent her team to the scene. The address is on your pad. You have time to stop and change."

"Change?"

"The major prefers her investigators to be out of uniform. Something about blending in and making the witnesses more compliant."

"Of course." In the Yards, the ISA insignia tended to make the innocents more cooperative. Topside was more arrogant. ISA agents were acceptable as long as they weren't seen. She stood but stopped at the door. "How long is this assignment?"

Cap studied her for a long moment until she fiddled with the buttons on a sleeve. "Until the major and I are both satisfied you're ready to return."

"Will I be turning in my sidearm?"

"No. You're still on active duty, and your new assignment will require it. You just won't have access to the armory." He smiled, which allowed her shoulders to ease.

She attempted a return smile but couldn't seem to raise one. Instead, she just turned and walked away from the only home she'd known for the last five years.

THREE

The stop home took less than thirty minutes. It wasn't like Rowan had an extensive wardrobe of acceptable clothes to choose from. Of the two decent dress pants she owned, one had a stain, and the other was wrinkled from being stuffed in a drawer. A quick run through a clean and press cycle was the best she could do. She had better luck with the shirt and jacket, but it was apparent she'd need to ask Kendra to help with more appropriate attire. The thought unnerved her, but a single shopping trip was better than a year at a desk.

She took the monorail, jumping off two blocks from the incident address, which gave her time to cool her temper and readjust her thoughts. This was a critical moment. She couldn't blow it. Her life was ISA. It wasn't like she couldn't be transferred anywhere in the world at a moment's notice. Dozer had been stationed in every Sector at least once during his long tenure, mostly in his early career when the ISA was still building and lacked skilled resources. Forced transfers were rare these days and were primarily disciplinary actions.

She could only blame herself. If she'd spent another day gathering intel. If she could have found a single informant who had a name. Just one name. She straightened her shoulders. Her short-lived command was over. The best she could do now was prove she was a team player. The fact she had no skills in investigating homicides was an opportunity to learn. Right? That, and the fact the major believed in her enough to have her reassigned to Investigations.

The small group of ISA agents stationed near the front door confirmed she'd reached the correct address. Responding to a murder Topside was nothing like the Yards or the old days she'd seen in video clips before the Climate Wars. No yellow tape, no large crowds of nosy neighbors waiting to catch a glimpse of a dead body, and no media. Homicides and other crimes committed Topside were orderly.

An ISA armored transport, which probably housed a handful of bored soldiers, parked a block away. The transport would return to the barn without a single guard setting foot on the street. There would be no one to chase, but protocol required them to show up. A nondescript body wagon would be waiting in the underground garage. Any one of the AVUs on the street could be an unmarked ISA vehicle.

She craned her neck to stare up at the height of the tower. Not one of the tallest, probably just under a hundred floors, but its shiny surface sparkled under the balmy sun and clear blue skies. She checked her wrist unit to confirm the housing number then reviewed the updated incident report. Data direct from the crime scene would be uploaded to the master report within seconds of entry. It took her a moment to scan the limited information. No name. Even if forensics hadn't finished, they should have the victim's name. The body would have been immediately identified, and the fact it wasn't on the report made her pause before going up.

There were only two reasons a name would be missing. The victim hadn't been chipped, or the GSM was holding this one close. A jolt of excitement ran through her. This might be interesting after all.

No one asked for identification as she strolled through the lobby and entered the elevator.

"Floor 24."

The elevator accepted her command, taking seconds to reach the correct floor. Her boots made a whooshing sound as she traversed the upscale carpeted hallway. The first sign of ISA was a single officer standing in front of housing unit 2412. He didn't bother asking for her identification. Another twist in working Topside. Everyone was so trusting.

She stopped five feet into the unit. This was how many of the Topsiders lived. The spacious quarters opened to an inviting living room with a dining area next to a long counter that separated the kitchen from the living space. The carpet was pristine white, and the walls were painted a light silver. The only splashes of color were the bright turquoise, dark browns, and bits of orange found in pillows, drapes, and decorative artwork. And, of course, the large splotch of crimson that pooled underneath the victim.

There was no blood splatter, something that would have been quite noticeable on the white carpet. So the victim, who appeared to be an older gentleman based on his thinning gray hair, had either been shot, stabbed, or accidentally fell on a butter knife. She snorted. Wouldn't that be something for all this fuss?

The forensic unit was still at work, and someone came over and sprayed the bottom of her shoes with a sealant that would prevent any trace from marring the scene. Her squad rarely required anything like it in the Yards, but she was familiar with the practice. When she stepped closer, she waited for the woman, dressed in black slacks, pink shirt, and a tailored jacket, to glance up from where she squatted by the body.

Major Jolanda Taylor hadn't changed in the two years since Rowan had last seen her, but she hadn't expected her to be at the incident. This was way below her pay grade, which confirmed this was a high-profile victim. Another tingle of anticipation prickled her skin. At least she wasn't considered a complete dolt if ISA assigned her to this task force.

The major's hard stare made Rowan hesitate until she noted the slight twitch of the major's lips. She relaxed and gave her what she'd hoped was a humble smile. "Sorry, I'm late, boss."

Taylor stepped around the dead guy and held out her hand. "Good to see you, Lockwood. I'm glad you were able to join us."

Her handshake was as firm and steady as Rowan remembered. "Looks like an interesting party." She inwardly sighed, grateful the major wasn't going to mention why she was now part of her team. She glanced at the body before turning back to Taylor. "I didn't think you'd be here."

"Normally, I wouldn't. I believe Captain Jiang told you I'm running a new task force. We have a strange one here and could use your skill and knowledge to round out the team. The majority of the team are back at headquarters running data searches and reviewing video feeds, but we have our lead investigator here." She paused and glanced over her shoulder toward the floor-to-ceiling windows overlooking the Los Angeles basin and reservoir. A beautiful sight with green parks surrounded by more glass towers encircled by crisscrossing monorails.

A man with raven-black hair stood facing the window. He wore a tailored dark-gray suit that stretched over broad shoulders and tapered to a trim physique. For a moment, she wondered if it was hard muscle or flab that filled out the sleeves.

"You'll be working with a partner." Taylor eyed her, waiting for a response. The woman knew her too well.

She wrestled with her immediate irritation, then nodded

and gave the major a wide smile. "Great. I'm obviously not in my comfort zone, so someone needs to show me the ropes."

Taylor lifted a brow. "Mr. MacGregor isn't with the ISA, though he's worked with us before."

Mr. MacGregor. No ISA grade. This just got better and better. It seemed best to hold her tongue.

"He's with a special unit in GSM." The major paused again, which almost made Rowan laugh. Major Taylor hadn't forgotten her hot temper and propensity to open mouth and insert foot, so she'd decided to feed Rowan one nugget at a time before dropping another bombshell. If the GSM was involved, she was playing in a whole new league. Her earlier excitement of a juicy op just got spiked with cold tendrils of fear. The GSM wasn't anything to fool with.

She forced her shoulders to relax. "Well, that just dropkicked me into the outer edges of reality. I've never worked directly with GSM before." Her calm response seemed to satisfy the major for the moment, who was quite aware Rowan saved most of her tantrums for behind closed doors.

"Mr. MacGregor works within the gray areas of GSM, so you won't be dealing with the bureaucratic nightmare you're thinking of. I think the two of you will get along. Eventually." The last word was said with a wider grin, which sent hackles up the back of Rowan's neck. In other words, this was going to be a challenge. The major turned toward the window. "Mr. MacGregor? When you're ready."

Time moved on without a response from him. At first, she assumed he was on his earpiece, but no words floated her way. Another minute ticked by before he turned to them, hands in his pockets. Her stomach dropped like she'd jumped out of a hopper. He was the most gorgeous man she'd ever seen. His brooding brows dropped low, and their color matched his midnight hair. But it was the eyes—a gray that reminded her of a stormy winter sea. And those lips? Somehow emphasized by the short stubble, they might be full if they weren't pressed into a hard line. He hadn't been on a call, and he didn't seem happy to see her.

The major nodded. "This is Sergeant Rowan Lockwood. She'll be your ISA investigator."

MacGregor glanced at her like she was yesterday's Chinese takeout left on the counter overnight. She was tempted to sniff her armpit to see if she was giving off an odor. His slow perusal took in every inch of her before landing on her face. His grim smile was a surprise until she realized she'd been performing her own perusal. She had no doubt her expression was as equally irritated as his.

"I'm sure we'll get along fine." His deep voice held a bit of an accent that reminded her of Galway Alley, one of the districts in the Yards. The fact it rolled over her like a warm ocean wave only increased her annoyance. He gave Major Taylor a nod and a slight smile. "We can take it from here. I'll provide a report later this afternoon."

"Excellent." The major stopped before her unexpectedly quick departure. "Rowan, did you bring an AVU?"

She hadn't expected the major to be there but had assumed she'd be working with an ISA investigator, not dumped with some GSM hard ass. Her aspirations of being a quiet team member, getting the job done, and scurrying back to her squad were slowly deflating.

When she shook her head, the major glanced at MacGregor. "Do you mind if she rides with you?"

She was pretty sure he wanted to say something else, but what came out of those magnificent lips was, "Fine."

Once the major was gone, she turned to MacGregor. "She told you I'm not really an investigator, right?"

He turned to the body where the forensic team was taking

their last samples and readings. "My understanding is your squad runs dozens of operations each year."

"That's right."

"I would think some level of investigative work is required before receiving a green light."

She sighed. "Yes, but that's different than working homicide."

He squatted next to a man spraying a sealant over the victim to protect any evidence on the body. The forensics man pointed at something, and MacGregor nodded.

"What is it?" She moved closer, bending over to get a better look.

"A tattoo."

Intrigued, she squatted next to MacGregor. "I've seen something similar. Down in the Yards." She thought about it but couldn't remember what she'd been doing. It had been a couple of months ago. "Maybe the African Quarter."

"More likely Galway Alley. This is a Celtic design." MacGregor took out his data pen and took a picture of it.

"I can think of one or two places Topside that might be able to identify it." Although she wasn't too hopeful.

He glanced at her. The broody look was still there, but his pinched lips had relaxed. "See. You already took part in the investigation."

"I wasn't exactly correct."

"No. But it was enough to put me on the right track." He stood and handed a silver image disk to the forensics man. "Here's some additional data you might want to add to the report. Once you're done, send me a complete medical workup, including a full drug panel." MacGregor stood and strode toward the door.

She hurried after him, feeling lost in whatever just happened. Weren't they supposed to prowl the residence looking for evidence? Ask more questions of the forensics team, like when did the victim die? With all the blood, she still didn't know if he'd been stabbed or shot.

He waited at the door for her, holding out his arm to wave her through. Then he dropped the next bombshell. "And our job isn't homicide. This man was one of my informants."

FOUR

Rowan increased her stride to keep up with MacGregor as he exited the tower. If they weren't on a homicide task force, what the hell was his mission? If she had dozens of questions before, they'd just doubled. "What is your operation if it isn't a homicide task force?"

He ignored the question, and she was ready to ask again in case he hadn't heard her when he stopped in front of a dark-jade AVU.

"I didn't know this model was out yet."

"It's not." The doors automatically slid up, and he got in.

Since the passenger door was open, she assumed that was an invitation. She laid her head against the seat and sucked in a deep breath. There was something about the clean smell of a brand-new AVU. But she also detected another deeper scent—some type of vegetation and the hint of rain. The effect was calming. She closed her eyes, forgetting the man in the driver's seat, and indulged in the first peaceful moment she'd had in months.

By the time she opened her eyes, they were speeding through Zone 1 airspace. Within each sector, the airspace was broken into four zones. Zone 1 was just above street level, and other bands increased in elevation until Zone 4, which topped out at the airspace reserved for passenger carriers, ISA personnel carriers, and GSM security drones. Each band had its own speed limit, and MacGregor's speed was well beyond Zone 1 limits.

"Where are we going?" She assumed they'd head back to the GSM towers, but the AVU was flying in the opposite direction. The ISA Sector offices were next to the GSM towers, so they weren't going there, either.

"Another informant," he mumbled.

"Are you going to bring me up to speed? I didn't have time to meet with the major before arriving at the victim's residence."

He kept his eye on the midday traffic. Most people programmed their AVUs for automatic navigation. There was little need, even in busy airspace, for manual control, but MacGregor seemed to be old school, his hands resting gently on the steering column as he maneuvered around the other AVUs. They must be close to their destination, or he would have climbed to Zone 3, which was more appropriate for their current speed.

He brooded for so long, she assumed he'd ignore her question and was startled when he finally spoke. "Let's set the ground rules."

Here we go. This was where he would tell her she wasn't needed. That she should just sit back and mind her business. Well, bullshit on that. "By all means."

He flashed her a side glance, picking up on her belligerent tone. At least he was observant. "My operation, as you call it, is under Global Security Protocols, and unless you're cleared, there will be items I can't discuss with you. So, if you're frustrated now, it will only get worse."

Global Security Protocols rang colossal warning bells. This

was some deep shit she'd been thrown into. Any mission that impacted Global Security Protocols typically meant it was for GSM Council ears only. He was right. She wasn't cleared for anything that secret. What had the major thought she could do here? Or was she being shelved somewhere to spend her disciplinary time out of everyone's way?

"I wasn't expecting to have someone from ISA tagging along," he continued. "You'll have to wait until I decide what you need to know and whether you're allowed to know."

"Then why am I here?"

"I don't know. It appears we'll both have to make the best of it."

"Great," she mumbled, then turned her attention to the passing landscape. GSM, Global Security Protocols, and a dead guy. Not one of those things worked in her favor. "Can you at least tell me how your informant died? I assume, by the amount of blood, it was either a knife wound or a point-blank shot with an old-style handgun, perhaps with lead bullets."

He swiveled his head toward her for a couple heartbeats before turning his focus back to the airspace. "Why would you say that?"

She shrugged. "There are dozens of laser-style weapons, most not available to the common citizen, and while they leave a hole, the heat of the blast would cauterize without leaving a pool of blood. A high-velocity GR would have cut his body in half. Even if it had clipped him, it would have left a distinctive odor for hours. That leaves either a knife or an old-fashioned combustible, which carries its own scent, but modern deodorizers would have dissipated it by the time I arrived."

He kept his gaze on the traffic, but she caught the slight upturn of his lips. "It appears you have better skills than you thought."

The compliment surprised her and warmed her cheeks. She turned to the passenger window. "Just common sense."

"Well, your common sense was correct. It was a knife wound. Best guess until the lab confirms it was a six-inch, single-edged blade."

Silence descended, and when she glanced down, she noted they were skimming along the Edges, the narrow strip of land that separated Topside from the Yards.

"Are you worried someone might have killed your other informant?"

He appeared to consider the question before shaking his head. "There's no connection between them."

"They both worked for you."

His scathing glance made her cheeks warm again, but this time in annoyance. She'd thought it made sense.

"The victim didn't work for me."

Okay. A bit touchy on that topic.

He sighed at her apparent confusion. "The dead guy, who didn't tell me his name and apparently didn't have a body chip, called me yesterday in a panic. Said he had information that hinted at a global security issue. I was there to meet with him and hear what he had to share."

"But you never got the opportunity." Her voice faded as something familiar slipped over her for an instant before it was gone. She ignored the shiver that passed through her. The memory would either return or be lost forever. She rubbed her forehead, irritated by the fleeting thought.

"I found the body and immediately contacted GSM."

That snapped her thoughts back to MacGregor. "Not ISA?"

He glanced at the display that reflected traffic behind them, then looked over his shoulder to the air traffic on his left. "I have a contract with GSM. They would be my first call. It would be their decision if they wanted ISA involved."

She couldn't argue his reasoning. "And who's this other informant? If you can tell me." So far, he'd been forthcoming. No reason to stop asking questions if he was willing to talk. He seemed the type that once he clammed up, that would be it for the day.

He lifted a shoulder. "He's someone I keep in touch with. His business takes him on both sides of the Edges."

"He's running skinners?" Criminals who worked between Topside and the Yards, usually passing illegal contraband or information. They were hard to catch.

MacGregor gave her an actual grin. "Something like that."

"And you've been running him a while."

His silence confirmed her suspicion.

"When did GSM decide to get ISA involved?"

He dropped the AVU into a slow spin as he landed between a utility service vehicle and an old street roadster. Directly in front of them was a six-story building that appeared to be in surprisingly good shape for its location. When he shut the AVU down, MacGregor turned in his seat and looked her in the eye when he finally responded. "Your agency was called in moments after I found the body. They're a little more difficult to ignore."

"Yeah, no one cleans up dead bodies as quickly as ISA." Her edged tone was more in response to her disapproval of ISA than of his condescending tone. ISA moved quickly to remove anything that would appear messy in the public's eye, some-times before sufficient evidence could be collected.

"I don't make the rules, Sergeant."

When he didn't make a move to get out, she surveyed their surroundings. The Edges was a mercurial area, a section of community that hovered between the new world order and the past. It had always made her feel itchy, but it was a more comforting border between Topside and the Yards than a fence.

Today, the streets were quiet. The surrounding area appeared residential, so most people would be at work.

MacGregor performed his own quiet surveillance. She calmed her restless legs, which wanted to bounce with anticipation. When on a stakeout, she was typically the one in charge, staying busy by monitoring surveillance cameras and reviewing intel. But sitting next to this man, who filled the interior with his sheer presence, and not knowing her place in his secret mission, left her jittery. After reviewing their surroundings three times, there wasn't anything else to look at except MacGregor.

She perused the fit of his jacket over his broad shoulders, then the bulge around his upper arms where muscles seemed to strain at the confinement. He rested his arm against the middle console, which pulled up the sleeve of his pristine white shirt, revealing the edges of a tattoo. That was interesting. She flashed on what he might look like without his shirt—his chest and arms sprinkled with muscle and ink.

She blinked, erasing the mental image. "Are we waiting for something?" She desperately needed to get out of the AVU or find something else to think about.

Her impatient tone spurred him out of wherever his mind had been. Those piercing stormy eyes bored into her, which only increased the need to put some distance between them.

His lips twisted into what might constitute a smile or indigestion—she hadn't been around him long enough to tell the difference. But an image came to mind of her nephew squirming when something made him uncomfortable.

"Horatio should be home from work soon. It's best to catch him before he gets carried away with his after-hours activities."

"Ah. He works in the Yards?"

"No. He works for Stoker Industries and spends his off time in the Yards."

That made her speechless. Stoker was the primary worldwide supplier of weapons for GSM and ISA. "What does he do that he lives in the Edges? Concierge services?"

"He's the brains behind Little Sister."

She choked at his response. Little Sister was the basis of the planet's internal security net. In a nut shell, it was a set of complex algorithms that connected all public and private security systems together including street sensors, building security systems, private housing security, GSM drones, ISA monitors, and more. It correlated data to provide security threat risks and alerts to GSM and ISA employees based on their clearance level. It also provided a variety of research parameters to dozens of worldwide agencies. And now, she'd discovered that Little Sister had been created by a human and not an advanced computer.

"Are you frickin' kidding me?" Her breath hadn't returned when she croaked that out. And for the first time, she discovered what his smile truly looked like. Whatever air was left in her lungs gasped out of her. Then MacGregor was patting her back and commanding the AVU to lower the windows.

She pushed his arms away, and he held them up in self-defense, his smile growing more disarming. She had to look away, wishing he'd become disagreeable and say something that would irritate her.

"I didn't mean to shock you."

"Right." Her throat burned from the coughing, which made her voice sound sultry. "Is it okay for me to get out?"

MacGregor glanced around, then nodded. "It looks like our prize has arrived. Give him a minute to get in the building."

She caught a glimpse of a scrawny dude wearing a baggy, nondescript black suit closing the door behind him. What stuck with her were the lime-green runners and bright-blue hair. That made sense for the Yards, but not Stokers. Within seconds, she was out of the AVU and sucking in deep gulps of air before choking again on the horrific smell coming from the building next door. Her eyes watered from the foul odor that had to be a broken reclamation unit. Why hadn't someone called it in? She had half a mind to stop everything and give them a citation, except she couldn't catch her breath.

She doubled over, hands on knees, and within seconds she felt the hard slaps of MacGregor's hand on her back again. She staggered away. "What is it with the backslapping? Do you really think that helps?"

He shrugged. "It has in my experience."

She didn't want to know what type of experience required that skill. "Do you enjoy dropping bombshells like that?

His smile turned to a grimace. "It's not typically me with the surprises. But I have my moments. Come on."

She trailed behind as he strode toward the front door of the building.

"You're not worried this Horatio fellow won't say something I'm not supposed to hear?"

He turned on her abruptly, forcing her to step back before she landed in his arms. "I assume Major Taylor assigned you to me because you can keep your mouth shut."

There was his disagreeable side. She sighed with relief as the hairs on the back of her neck rose. "We all sign the GSM waiver as a condition of employment." The waiver basically said if an assignment intersected with GSM, the information became classified with the severest of penalties. "My word has never been questioned." She maintained a light tone, but based on his squint, her newfound irritation had been received.

He turned and entered the building, not bothering to hold the door open for her. They were finally on a level playing field.

FIVE

The interior of the six-story building looked like any other stump tower, a moniker for any tower with less than ten floors. For being in the Edges, it was surprisingly clean. The housing in the Yards and most of the Edges were challenging to maintain. Many of the buildings were leftovers from before the Wars, remodified where possible, but even a fresh coat of paint couldn't hide some of the odd smells ingrained in their walls.

The oversized lobby was light, airy, and carried a pleasant citrus scent. The glassed-in section immediately to the right housed security boxes for deliveries. The first floor would also contain the common areas—health facilities, entertainment areas, conference rooms, and such. The remaining five floors would average ten units per floor. If standard housing rules had been applied, each floorplan would be different. Some floors could have fifteen single units, while another floor might have two massive apartments.

A secured door made of high-tensile glass—impenetrable by any weapons the public could get their hands on, but not enough to stop ISA—blocked anyone from reaching the stairs or elevators. The door, like most towers, could be opened either by facial recognition, a retinal scan, by code, or a silver data disk similar to the one MacGregor had handed the forensic guy. MacGregor entered a disk she assumed Horatio must have given him.

Once through the door, MacGregor ignored the elevator and took the stairs. He moved fast, and she stayed on his six, prepared for any abrupt stop on his part. He turned down the hall on the third floor. She'd been right. Peering down the hallway past his formidable shoulders, she noted several doors on each side. This floor would house single units—a simple living room, one bedroom, and a kitchen. A handful might have an office nook.

Without knocking, MacGregor used the same disk to enter a unit at the end of the hall. The apartment was sparse, even for its cramped size. One couch faced a digital screen used for news, entertainment, and communication services. Even the housing units in the Yards had these conveniences, though this particular model appeared to be a few years old. The kitchen was bare except for a combination food station and reclamation system. A table with two chairs sat empty of any debris. MacGregor opened a closet door and walked inside. She followed, unsure what he was searching for, and was surprised when he exited through another door.

She paused, glancing around the empty storage pantry when he poked his head around the doorjamb. "Keep up." Then he was gone, and she raced to catch up. How was she supposed to know the closet turned into a passageway?

They exited into a short hallway that led to another staircase. Another two floors up emptied them onto the fifth floor, which had three units—one halfway down on the left and two doors on the right. MacGregor stopped at the first door on the right. He knocked three times, followed by two short raps.

He'd been overly cautious running them through a dummy

unit. Who would have seen where they went in the building? It was rare to find that level of security in the Edges but, keeping her head down, she checked the hallway. She didn't see any scanners, but that didn't mean there weren't any, and it was too late to ask.

A display screen on the door, which had remained blank on the first unit they'd entered, sprang to life. The blue-haired man, or in this case, someone who looked barely old enough to be out of university, stared at them as he stuffed chips in his mouth. "Hey, Keene."

Keene? So that was his first name. She was beginning to think he didn't have one.

"Horatio."

The door clicked open and, before the screen went dead, Horatio turned, waving a hand to come in.

Keene barged through the door, bypassing Horatio, whose head swiveled to watch him disappear into the back of the unit before swinging back to give Rowan a who-the-hell-are-you look.

When she brushed past him to follow Keene, his vocal cords kicked in. "Hey, who are you?"

The lime-green runners pounded behind her. "Hey, man, where are you going?" Horatio pushed past her as she slowed, uncomfortable racing through someone's home without permission.

Keene had reached the far side of the spacious room, ducking behind a freestanding partition with a gargoyle printed on it. She recognized the image, if not the name, from a gaming program.

"Hey, I told you not to mess with my setup," Horatio shrieked as they reached the silk-screened partition.

They'd definitely discovered techrat headquarters. Several imagers were mounted around the communication center. Each displayed something different. One screen scrolled computer code. Two screens held floating 3D images that looked like blueprints. Two others were tuned to a news station and a shield soccer game. A desk stretched around three sides, cluttered with various keyboards, a gaming stick, and a hologram imager. The only other person she'd seen with this much tech in their home was Hernandez from her squad.

"This is touchy stuff. Most of it isn't even on the market yet. You have to know what you're..." Horatio froze, his eyes going wide. "Oh. Cool. Try increasing the linear parameters. Yeah, a touch more. Stop." He stepped next to holo-imager, pushing MacGregor out of the way. "Let me." MacGregor—or Keene—handed Horatio the interface stick. Instantly, Horatio's arm waved through the air as if he were conducting an orchestra, his moves magical as the picture cleared and became a 3D image, its color darkening to shiny ebony, and he left it spinning in a slow rotation.

The image was the tattoo from the dead guy—minus the arm.

"Have you seen this before?" Keene stepped to his left as if he wanted to follow the rotating image but had to stop at the edge of the desk.

Horatio squinted and began to sway to some internal tune. His nod was slow, and Rowan wasn't sure if he was focused on the tattoo or was mentally somewhere else. "I think I have." He moved his arm up and flipped the image.

"Where?" Keene kept a cool, even tone.

Horatio stepped closer, reaching out a finger to trace the Celtic pattern. "Maybe the African Quarter."

Keene glanced at Rowan, and she shrugged, holding back a smug response. She refused to behave like a five-year-old, but the desire to say she told him so burned through her. She did have skills.

Either Keene refused to believe Horatio's statement, or he was testing him. "You mean Galway Alley, right?"

Horatio sighed and gave Keene a withering glare. She got the impression the kid wasn't used to having his knowledge questioned. "Celtic knots are a dime a dozen in Galway Alley. But this..." He pointed at the image. "Something like this? This would stand out in the African Quarter." He closed his eyes. "The ink was on a man's wrist. His sleeve had slid up." Horatio shook his head. "I only saw a portion of his face. I don't remember a name, and I haven't seen him since."

"How long ago was this?" Keene asked.

"I don't know. A few weeks. Maybe a couple of months." Horatio scratched his head then moved to his keyboard. "Let me store this, and I'll make a few copies."

Keene's storm-gray stare turned her way. "When did you remember seeing it?"

It took her a moment to register the question. She shook her head. "About the same time as Horatio, at least a month ago, maybe six weeks. I remember seeing it as more of a flash. Something about the ink stuck with me. I don't know why." She rubbed her forehead. "I know it was a man, but I didn't see a face. His robe had wide sleeves. Satin, I think. With fine embroidery."

"Yeah. I remember that now." Horatio handed an image disk to each of them, and she slid hers into an inner pocket. "I was thinking kimono."

"Or maybe a martial arts robe," she suggested.

"Do you remember enough of his face for a sketch?" Keene's voice seemed more urgent this time.

Horatio shrugged. "Two months is a long time." He ran a hand through his hair as he stared at the ground. "I can't be seen going into GSM with you."

Keene started for the door. "Get your bag. We're going somewhere else."

"I need to grab a few things. I'll meet you in back."

Rowan followed Keene out the door, and when he took them back the same path they'd come, she had to ask, "Why are we going through all this trouble? If there's a scanner, it would have seen us at his door."

"The only scanner is in the lobby. Once you get past the security door, there's a sensor, but it only monitors who enters from the lobby."

"That's old tech. Security should be running internal scanners and sensors throughout the building."

"This is the Edges. There might be private homes with current tech, but these community stumps only get upgrades with a major renovation."

"Even with Stoker's brightest employee living here?"

They broke into the sunshine, each of them squinting from the glare. The street remained as quiet as when they'd first entered the building.

"No one knows he lives here. He has another apartment about twelve blocks from Stoker. He stops there on his way back and forth from work for appearances. The kid doesn't trust many people."

Yet, he seemed to trust this man. Why?

Keene had turned toward the AVU when she heard the release of a pulse-generated crossbow bolt. If there had been the slightest hint of traffic, she wouldn't have heard it. Keene fell back, grabbing his shoulder. He dropped and rolled as bullets sprayed the sidewalk.

Rowan pulled her sidearm and ducked behind the old roadster parked in front of Keene's AVU. Someone ran across the street, but she didn't shoot, not knowing who was foe versus friendly. She kept her weapon out as Keene pulled her toward the AVU, allowing her to cover them both.

He shoved her through the passenger side then forced her over the console into the driver's seat. He crawled in behind her, and the door dropped into place.

She started the AVU, pushing buttons for extra rotors that kicked up dirt. It wasn't necessary for lift-off but would provide cover until she could get them in the air.

"Turn right. There's a back alley. We need Horatio."

They found him racing down the alley in a zigzag pattern as he tried to slip on his backpack, his blue hair flying in the breeze.

She passed him, then yanked the controls to the right as she turned the AVU to face him. The kid held up a hand as if in surrender, his other arm stuck in the straps of his bag. When he noticed who was staring at him through the windshield, he raced for them as she turned the AVU and hit the button for the back door to open. No bigger than a cramped storage area, the kid barreled into the space, his bag tucked against his chest.

When she glanced over, Keene was sweating, his jaw clenched. And that's when she noticed the blood seeping through the fabric of his suit jacket. He held a med kit in his lap while he tried to apply a quick-gel tourniquet that didn't seem to be doing anything to staunch the bleeding.

"Just follow my directions." Keene bit out each word. "And don't ask questions. Not until we're safe."

She was good with that, for now. But global security or not, someone was trying to kill them, and that had just drop-kicked her onto the "need-to-know" list.

SIX

After picking up a hysterical Horatio, Rowan drove down the alley, slowing for the intersections, before fully lifting to Zone 1. Despite Horatio's screams to fly higher and get out of the Edges, she circled the area, searching for any sign of who'd been shooting at them. She anticipated Keene barking out some command, but he stared out the passenger-side window, performing his own scan. He gripped his left arm, heavy drops of blood seeping over his fingers.

"Do you see anything?" She yelled to be heard over Horatio.

He shook his head, and she flew up to Zone 2. Whoever shot at them was either hiding or was long gone. She took one more slow pass at the higher elevation until she spotted the hopper.

"We have an ISA hopper coming in from the north. Should I signal them?" Her initial reaction urged yes, but she waited for Keene.

"Yes!" Horatio screamed.

"No," Keene barked at Horatio. "They'll ask too many questions and keep us locked down for hours. We need to clear the area."

She understood his reservation. Even though she was ISA, and they were performing a legal investigation, she reluctantly agreed. ISA wouldn't just keep them locked up for hours; they would drill them until GSM showed up. And if Horatio was an informant, they couldn't blow his cover. Not yet.

She kept her head down as the hopper approached, keeping the AVU to the legal speed for Zone 2. The last thing they needed was someone recognizing her. The hopper passed by, and through her peripheral vision, she noticed two guards checking them out. Fortunately, Horatio's fear subsided enough for common sense to take over, and he quieted, staying low.

Once the hopper passed, lowering to scan the area, Rowan took a leisurely turn past two towers as they moved into Topside.

"Where to?" she asked.

"Just east of the Biodome."

"The Biodome? I didn't know there was a GSM facility out there." GSM preferred to keep their facilities in the center of major cities. They used district ISA offices if required, but that was rare.

Horatio twisted around until his head stuck through the space between the front seats. "Sweet ride. You have the upgraded nav system and, oh, cracken, is that Bertha?"

"What's Bertha?" she asked, glancing over the dashboard.

"That's just the working name. This is so new, GSM is still working on the official name." Horatio reached out and touched a button.

Blue and red lights lit up, and she slapped his hand away. "Do not touch buttons while I'm driving if I don't know what they do."

"Relax. Bertha is the new multiplexed coms and tracking system. It works from a combination of inputs—heat sensors,

GPS, body chips, coms systems, ISA alerts, and more. But it's still GSM proprietary software." Horatio almost crooned as he reviewed the information scrolling over the imager. Then he refocused his attention on her. "Who are you?"

"Sergeant Lockwood with ISA." She paused. "You can call me Rowan."

She glanced over at Keene, who'd grown silent. His eyelids fluttered, his pallor turning gray. That wasn't normal for an arm injury, even if it wouldn't stop bleeding. "MacGregor? You with us?"

"Yeah." His tone and lethargy contradicted that.

"Hey, partner, you need to stay awake until you get us wherever we're going."

"Maybe we should have stopped for ISA." Horatio sounded worried. "If we go to a hospital now, it will be worse." He wasn't wrong.

"Not far now." Keene leaned his head against the window. His hand slid down, no longer strong enough to grip his wound. The bleeding had grown to a free-flowing trickle.

She lifted them to Zone 3 and increased speed, sticking close to Zone 4 and the major transport routes. When she spotted the Biodome, she took them back down. The Biodome was similar to versions created more than a century earlier. This particular one housed an enclosed community simulating conditions of the moon as part of the Earth's revised focus on interstellar travel.

"Five miles." Keene pulled in a ragged breath. "East of Biodome...small town." Another short breath. "Mostly deserted...barn silos." Keene shook his head and pulled himself up straighter, trying to stay awake.

She spotted them. Any other time, she wouldn't give them the time of day. The silos were barely noticeable behind large trees that circled what was left of the town. A few cars parked around an old diner. A block down, a fuel station looked open. That made sense as the city gave way to rural communities where co-ops and crop test centers remained. Most agriculture districts were centralized within the Sectors, but small farm zones had taken root on the outskirts of major cities.

When they drew closer, Keene pointed toward a grassy knoll near another grove of trees a mile from the diner.

"Bring it down...behind the hill. Garage in back." Keene slumped back, giving in to the pain now that they'd reached what appeared to be some type of bunker.

When she brought the AVU down to its wheels, gates opened automatically as she drove towards a building. Huge bay doors also opened as they approached and lowered after they passed through.

She'd been expecting a dark parking garage, not a well-lit, high-ceilinged room. Vehicles were parked in a row at various angles, all facing the entrance door as if ready for a fast departure. Nothing curious here. She glanced at Keene, but if he was worried about what she was seeing, the injury to his arm removed all his earlier precautions.

Dumping her list of questions into the it-can-wait file, she slammed the button to open all the doors of the AVU. She could have used voice commands but had to admit she was too worried about Keene and was running on adrenaline and instinct. She all but fell over the top of Horatio, who still clutched his bag as he rolled onto the gray-painted floor. She raced around the front of the vehicle in time to catch Keene as he tried to exit on his own.

Strong hands moved her aside and grabbed Keene around the waist. "Sir, no one said you'd been injured." The man was broader than Keene and had no difficulties half dragging him away. Horatio followed while she slowed to glance around.

Four elite AVUs were parked on the right-hand side of the spacious garage, similar to Keene's though all in different colors. Two armored rovers filled out the other side of the area, partially blocking a room sectioned off by mesh glass, which was highly resistant to most firearms. A high-velocity GR might put a dent in it. Only a portion of the inventory was visible but what she gleamed was impressive enough—long rifles, PT5 armor, titanium-piercing rifles, and what looked like a newer gen-phased rifle, something that was still on GSM's drawing board. Who knew what else lay beyond? The room could be five feet in length or twenty. She couldn't tell from where she stood.

The man half-carrying Keene was almost to the elevator, and she jogged toward them, noting the micro-cameras set in the exact positions where she would have placed them. Everything was hi-tech and top-of-the-line. Why would GSM have a bunker out here? And why hadn't the major briefed her on whoever this team was? Something didn't feel right, but one thing she trusted was that Major Taylor wouldn't have assigned her to someone without confirming the intel.

She slid next to Horatio as the doors shut. The security guard, if that was his role, glowered at her, and she smiled in return. But her smile faded when she noticed Keene's pale face. He slumped against the bigger man, his eyes closed as the elevator dropped. She'd expected they'd be going down since there wasn't a building over them, but the speed made her replant her feet. The stop was abrupt, and she reached for the wall to prevent knocking into Horatio, who used the corner to stay upright.

When the doors opened, confusion hit her. She'd expected white walls and floors of concrete gray. Instead, the walls were green with murals of forests and soft rolling hills dotted with hundreds of purple-flowering plants. Various sizes of planters, overflowing with live plants, were scattered down both sides of the hallways. The entire place smelled of earth and a fragrance she couldn't place.

Running feet pounded down the hall on a floor painted to resemble a well-worn path in the middle of the forested walls. Another broad-shouldered man and a petite woman raced toward them, both with grave expressions. Were all the men built like giants? The man took a moment to notice Horatio and then her. His gaze registered recognition before turning blank. Had they met before? She would have remembered the golden god with hair the color of fire. His blue eyes held a touch of humor behind his current concern. Then his attention snapped back to Keene.

The woman's hair was strawberry blonde, and her gray eyes were pinned on Keene. A pang twisted Rowan's gut at the urgency in the woman's intense gaze. He might be worse than she'd already feared.

She followed the group as they raced down the hall, making a left and then a right before shoving their way through the door to an infirmary. The forest decor stopped at the entrance, giving over to walls of pale blue with cabinets, tables, and beds of stainless steel. The two large men helped Keene onto one of six beds spread around the room.

The first man, who she'd pegged for security, gave her another glower before leaving the room, probably to return to his post. The other man began cutting away Keene's shirt while the woman pulled bandages and bottles out of cabinets.

When she glanced back at Keene, her breath caught. His shirt had been removed, and she couldn't decide what was more impressive—his muscle-bound chest leading to delightful abs that spoke of hours in the gym, or the intricate scrollwork of ink that started on one arm, wove up his biceps to solid shoulders, across his chest, then down the other arm. From where she stood, she couldn't tell if his back was tattooed, but tendrils of ink that snaked from behind, similar to the vines painted on the hallway, hinted at the possibility.

When the woman stepped toward the med bed with her handful of supplies, the unusual scent from the metal bowl she carried broke Rowan's slow perusal of Keene. The smell might be unexpected, but it wasn't unfamiliar. It was common in parts of the Yards, created from some mode of herbal medicine.

The man, who'd positioned himself on the other side of the bed, lowered his head across Keene toward his injured arm. "I smell hemlock."

"Aye. And turmeric, too." The woman laid her supplies on a wheeled cart and bent over the injury. "That's why the bleeding won't stop. Turn him a bit." The woman glanced at Keene, who opened his eyes when she began washing out the wound. "Is it an ache or a burn?"

"Burn." Keene's raspy voice slurred. Seconds later, he began to shake. Whether from blood loss or shock, Rowan didn't know.

"Shouldn't he be in a hospital?" Rowan stepped closer to get a better look at the wound. "If there's still a bullet, it needs to be removed."

"They wouldn't know how to treat this. And it's not a bullet wound. My guess is some type of arrow." The woman stopped to stare at Rowan. Her gaze moved between the large man and Keene. Something unspoken passed between them, and Rowan assumed the woman wasn't sure how much she knew. "My name is Lanis." She tilted her head to the large man holding on to Keene as the shaking increased. "That's Conall."

Names. That was safe enough. "I'm Sergeant Rowan Lockwood of ISA, and this is Horatio." She gave her own head tilt toward the kid. He'd found a stool, his focus on a pad that must have come from the bag resting safely between his feet.

"Ah, Horatio, it's good to finally meet you," Lanis said while she wiped the wound. He never looked up at Lanis's greeting but mumbled something unintelligible that must have been a form of greeting because she nodded.

The wound still bled, but between wipes, it was obvious it couldn't have been more than a flesh wound. The arrow, which made sense having heard the crossbow, must have taken a hunk of skin as it skimmed his arm. A painful injury, to be sure, but nothing that should have created the symptoms Keene was showing.

"What's hemlock and turmeric?" After five years working in the Yards, Rowan had never been interested in the herbal concoctions sold in many of the stores.

"Hemlock is a poison," Lanis explained. "Turmeric has several properties, one of them being a blood thinner which is why the bleeding won't stop."

"Crossbows with poisoned arrows? A long rifle would have been more effective."

Lanis gave Conall a glance, and he shrugged. "I can think of a few reasons, but only the ones with the weapons can tell you why. But if they're using herbs, then it points, rightly or wrongly, to the Yards."

Which was what she'd been thinking ever since Lanis pulled out her own medicine.

"Are either of you injured?" Lanis laid a thick pad of gauze over the wound for Conall to hold. She turned to them, waiting until they both shook their heads. Satisfied, she returned to the cabinet filled with dozens of bottles and jars in various sizes, shapes, and colors. They weren't the typical bottles one would find at a hospital.

The collection reminded Rowan of the apothecaries in the Yards. Yet everything else about the place screamed hi-tech when she noted the computer station on a side desk complete with two holo-monitors.

"Can I plug into your system?" Horatio asked.

"Yes. But you'll need to run on your own network," Conall replied. "Nope. Stay upright, brother. Just until Lanis is done."

Brother? That could mean almost anything, and though they were both big men, they were as different as night and day. Except they were both what Hernandez would call tasty appetizers. The hot guys you had fun with before settling down with the more predictable main course.

"What exactly do you all do here?" She stepped closer as Lanis applied a thick paste to the wound.

At first, the brown mixture turned darker as the blood seeped through it. Lanis wiped away anything that dribbled down Keene's arm. After several minutes, the brown paste turned a deep green, the blood slowing to a trickle before stopping altogether. She waited another couple of minutes before prying the glob of green paste from Keene's arm. The paste had turned hard and fell with a clunk into the pan, which Lanis set aside.

"Hand me the yarrow." Lanis took another small bowl from Conall. She applied a yellowish paste to Keene's wound before wrapping a bandage around his arm. She patted Keene's shoulder. "You should be feeling yourself in a few minutes."

Conall helped Keene lie back, then placed a thermal blanket over him. The covering could be programmed and remotely controlled for any temperature setting—either cooling or warming the body. Within seconds, Keene's eyes closed, softening his rugged features.

Lanis returned supplies to the counter and nodded at Conall. "You might as well show them what we do here. I can see the questions spinning away in Rowan's head." She smiled at her for the first time. "It's all right if I call you Rowan, isn't it?

Sergeant seems so formal. And well, since you saved our brother's life, first names seem more appropriate."

Rowan nodded, stuck on the brother comment. Before she could ask, Horatio slung his bag over his shoulder and stared at her while bouncing on his lime-green runners.

Conall waited by the door and winked. "Follow me."

<h1 style="text-align:center">SEVEN</h1>

Keene's muscles relaxed under the warmth of the blanket. The pain in his arm had receded, but a headache tapped on his skull with an offbeat staccato rhythm. He remembered something sharp slamming into his arm, his instinct driving him to drop and roll. Then Sergeant Lockwood covered them on their run to the AVU.

From there, his recollection was dicey. Horatio running in the alley. Panic seized him. Worry for the kid clenched his gut until he remembered Horatio pushing buttons on the AVU's dash. Then the bay doors opened, and Jericho caught him. Conall held him still while Lanis prodded and poked.

Something stabbed at his good arm until he understood it was real and not a memory.

"Wake up."

Keene rubbed his forehead, wishing she'd go away.

Lanis poked him again. "You can sleep after we talk. They won't be gone long."

That got his attention. She must mean Sergeant Lockwood —Rowan if he remembered correctly. Rowan. Her name spoke of the color of her untamed auburn hair.

He sat up, struggling not to topple over. "Horatio?" His voice sounded thick, and he clutched his head.

"Headache. I assumed as much from the hemlock." She handed him a glass. "Drink this."

"They poisoned me?" He gulped it quickly before he could smell it. Her concoctions were always nasty.

"Do you know who they were?"

"No. Someone caught us coming out of Horatio's place in the Edges." The drink tasted like pond scum—and he would know—but the potion dulled the ache and cleared his head.

"So Horatio's place has been compromised."

"Not sure. They might have been waiting for us in the Edges. Maybe they followed us from the tower where I was supposed to meet my new contact, who happens to be dead."

"Where did you pick up a sergeant from ISA?"

He sighed, pushed the blanket down, and swung his legs off the table, giving Lanis his back. "The major overseeing the task force. I didn't have a choice."

Lanis cleaned off the cart next to his bed and scooped the blanket over one arm. "Interesting."

"There's nothing interesting. She's with the ISA, and I'll get rid of her as soon as we find out who the dead guy was and who killed him. Before that, if I can think of another assignment to send her on." Keene circled the room. "Where's my shirt?"

"In the reclamation unit." Lanis glanced around the room, seeming satisfied everything was spotless. She'd always been fastidious, even as a child. "It might be in our best interest to see what she has to offer."

This was an old argument, and Keene should have known the minute he saw the redhead in the apartment that he should keep her away from the bunker. Thank the gods she seemed just as irritated at being stuck with him. That should make it easier to shake her loose. He wasn't about to spur Lanis's crazy notions. "Not a word to Conall about this."

Instead of agreeing, she changed the subject. So like her when she refused to swear an oath. "Were you able to find anything in the apartment before ISA showed up?"

"No. The unit either belongs to someone else, or he uses it for other purposes. He doesn't live there. There was something I found on him, but I'd rather wait for Conall, so I only have to go over it once."

"What should we do about Horatio?"

Keene rubbed his face. The headache was gone, but he felt like he'd been running for days. His bones ached, and he was losing focus.

Lanis laid a hand on his arm. "You need to get some rest, then we'll figure out what's going on. I can keep Horatio occupied, and we have plenty of rooms for him to stay."

She studied him, and his irritation grew. "I'm fine."

"Was Rowan of no help at all today?"

He stepped away from her, needing space to think. "Her ISA training got us out of the thick of it." He recalled her standing in the apartment, looking lost and out of place like she'd wanted to be anywhere else but there. But the dead body had intrigued her, at least the mystery of it. And how the hell had she remembered a tattoo from weeks earlier? She must see hundreds in her line of work, especially if she spent time in the Yards. He shook his head.

Lanis walked him to the door. "Well, if that's all she did, it was enough. You're alive, and, after a good night's rest, you'll be good as new. In fact, why don't you get some rest now? I'll see to our guests."

Keene watched her walk away. He should have told her about the tattoo and Rowan having seen it before. But she'd know soon enough. God's blood, of all the times to saddle him with a partner. Didn't they have enough to deal with? He walked to the elevator, not realizing he was humming.

———

CONALL WALKED CLOSE as he escorted them down the hall. Close enough for his masculine scent to wash over Rowan. When she put some distance between them, he grinned as if he knew the effect he had on the opposite sex. She doubted many women said no to him. If the circumstances had been different, and this had been a year ago, he might have been one of her conquests. But she wasn't that woman anymore. And after her first day on her new assignment, she barely recognized herself.

"How far underground are we?" She peeked through opened doors, seeing nothing more than conference rooms, lounges, and empty labs. They'd walked down several hallways, turning seemingly at random, with Horatio trailing several steps behind until she had gotten turned around. She eyed the big man, considering whether he was supposed to confuse her or simply waste time.

"The infirmary is on the first of three lower levels, and the first floor is approximately ten floors down from the garage."

"Why all the secrecy?"

Conall's hearty laugh made her smile. It was one of those infectious laughs that started deep in the belly before rumbling out and ensnaring anyone in a ten-foot radius. "There are no secrets here, though we store many priceless artifacts that require secure facilities."

He led us down a staircase, the walls a warm green, before turning us down another hallway painted with the same forest theme as the upper floor. She guessed the murals were only for the hallways. "Why did we take the stairs and not the elevator?"

"You rode the bloody thing. It gives my stomach a good toss."

They walked through more hallways, many of them appearing to be the storage areas he'd mentioned earlier, before passing the elevator.

"What is it you do down here?"

He paused at a set of double doors, giving her a quick perusal as if determining how much to tell her. Then he opened the door and waved them through. She took a hesitant step, then several more, staring at what appeared to be a central command center. Dozens of imagers lined a wall and displayed an assortment of news feeds, meditative reels, and streams of running code. Several workstations held individual terminals, visual interfaces, holographic imagers that could record and display, and other pieces of equipment she didn't recognize.

"Rowan wants to know what we do around here." Conall's statement made Lanis glance up from her tablet.

She sat at a small conference table, studying her pad, and held up a finger as she typed, giving Rowan time to absorb everything in the room.

If she didn't know better, she'd think she was in a hi-tech version of the Yards. This was a group that used herbal medicine for healing yet surrounded themselves with all the modern toys.

"We're anthropologists." Lanis stood to greet her.

"Right." Her flippant response was returned by a snort from Conall. She searched the room again when it dawned on her that Lanis hadn't been joking, and that she must have missed something.

"Did you expect we'd sit by candlelight and scratch away in leather-worn ledgers?" Her tone matched her amused expression, making Rowan feel like an idiot.

"It just seems like a lot of tech for researching old things."

Her statement made her cringe. Maybe she should keep her mouth shut.

Horatio, who'd found a spot in the corner, laid down his pad and jogged over to one of the consoles.

"Don't touch the spectral analyzer. I have an experiment running," Lanis shouted at him before he gave her a wicked grin. "We study more than objects, but we'll start there. Come see one of my current projects." She led Rowan to one of several holo-imagers that made the ones at ISA look outdated.

A 3D image appeared on the display pad. "With this holographic model, we can analyze almost anything, regardless of size, and transmit data from the image to other programs for further analysis. Let's take this ninth-century crown for example." She pointed to a golden crown currently rotating on the pad. "If this were a building, we could view the entire building scaled down to a smaller version that fits on this display pad. Or we could use the larger pad we have in the adjoining room. With that, we could study the entire structure or dice it into sections for a more detailed analysis."

"Why would you do that?" Rowan couldn't take her eyes off the crown that looked so real she could touch it. The fact the image was so lifelike wasn't anything new. It was the crown itself that tempted a further look. She couldn't explain her attraction to it. She'd grown up enthralled by the old, curious about the history—who had owned the piece, what their everyday life was like, what happened to them, and who owned the artifact after them. Curiosity was one thing; making a career out of it was another.

"Many buildings, especially when you go farther back in history, carried etchings and ancient text that we decipher and catalog. There are various fields today, like cryptography or linguistics, that use what we discover from a single slice of a wall."

"You said this piece was ninth century? Did someone just excavate this?"

She laughed. "No. Wouldn't that be amazing? This piece is one of the recovered."

"Recovered?" Horatio had shuffled over and peered over her shoulder.

"This particular piece was found about four months ago, lost from the British Museum during the Climate Wars. It had been stashed in an old metal locker with several other interesting pieces. A team discovered the locker in a reclaimed building in Turkey."

Literally millions of buildings had been destroyed during the Climate Wars. The government and political system that grew from the aftermath—the early days of GSM—decided to rebuild society from scratch in various hand-selected cities around the globe. The older cities that weren't rebuilt were blocked off until resources could scour them for explosives and other armaments. Once cleared, licensed salvagers could enter to reclaim lost tech, art, and other items.

"So, what are you looking for in this crown?" It was a rustic piece. A miracle it hadn't been melted down as scrap metal during the Wars. As she studied it, she pictured some bearded warrior, his crown askew, sitting by smoky firelight as he sharpened a dagger.

"We're validating the age. Before the Wars, the age of artifacts was determined by measuring carbon isotopes. We have better technology now, so the first stage of any analysis is to validate the original dating."

"This particular crown was said to have been owned by a Scottish king. Something our family is quite interested in." Conall joined them to stare at the image.

"Because MacGregors were originally from Scotland?" she asked.

"Something like that," he replied. "See the etchings?"

She bent closer, not noticing them before. "It looks like a hunt. Maybe a royal hunt considering this is etched on a crown. The lead man seems to be wearing some type of medallion. I can't make out what type."

Lanis clapped her hands. "Marvelous. You're a natural."

Her cheeks warmed at the acknowledgment, and she shuffled her feet. "It seems obvious with the deer and men with bows."

"Perhaps." She gave Conall a quick glance, and he shrugged.

Before she could consider what the quiet signal meant, the scent of wild meadows and rain mixed with an herb she'd smelled in the infirmary floated in the air. She turned to find Keene strolling in, who was now dressed in a black T-shirt that showed off his toned biceps and black leather pants that fit snugly around his hips. His clothing choice was a far cry from the tailored suit he'd worn earlier. If she had to guess, with the stubble on his face and his broody expression, this was the real Keene MacGregor.

"Is Lanis boring you with treasures from her scavenger hunts?" He let a slight grin escape, but it didn't reach his eyes, which squinted with residual pain.

She pushed thoughts of him aside, attempting to make sense of everything she'd seen for the last couple of hours. Were they all truly family? And why would GSM contract with a family of anthropologists?

"I'll have you know, Rowan was quite interested in King Malcolm's crown." Lanis's defensive tone made it sound like this was an old argument between them. Maybe Keene didn't have anything to do with his anthropologist kin. If that was true, his contract with GSM made more sense.

"I'm sure Sergeant Lockwood has better things to do with

her time." With that, he turned to her. "I thought you might need a ride home. I think it's best Horatio stay here for a day or two."

"Sergeant Lockwood, is it?" Conall bellowed. "She's Rowan to us, now and forever."

Keene rolled his eyes with obvious irritation. "Aye, when we're off the clock, it's Rowan. And you can call me Keene."

"Sure." She glanced around, squirming under three steady stares. "Horatio, are you okay staying here for a day or two? ISA could put you up somewhere."

Horatio stood in front of a console where he was running a program being displayed on a wall imager. He took over a second imager with a grid of housing units which he immediately narrowed down to a single block—the one with his tower unit. The place looked quiet. Any ISA agents that might have stayed to investigate were long gone. "Nah. I'm good here."

"Then we should be going. We can pick up the investigation tomorrow." Keene took two steps before Lanis stepped in his way.

"Oh, no, you don't." Lanis pushed him out the door. "You're not deceiving anyone. I can see you're in pain. If you have any hope of being released from the bunker tomorrow, you'll get your rest. I'll give you a potion to help you relax."

"Not to worry, brother. I'll see Rowan home safe and sound." Conall stood and grabbed a jacket from a hook by the double doors. He winked at Keene, who scowled in return.

Keene managed a low growl. "Behave."

"Model behavior, brother. Ironclad."

Keene shook his head, apparently another old squabble, this time between the brothers. It was still hard to believe they were related. Conall was pretty-boy handsome with a square jaw and pouty lips. He was obviously the charmer with his lightly tanned skin, hand-tousled red hair, and pleasant smile. She'd have to keep an eye on him.

As Conall led her out, Keene shouted. "It will be an early morning. I'll pick you up at eight sharp."

Conall leaned down. "Don't let him bully you. He's just jealous it's not him driving you home."

Oh, yeah. She'd definitely have to keep an eye on this one.

EIGHT

Rowan's housing unit was close to the Edges and one of the four main entrances to the Yards. She was also far enough within Topside to give the appearance of respectability to satisfy her parents, which, of course, she failed miserably. Since they considered her a rebel for following her brother, Zach, into the ISA, she was expected to toe the line in everything else. To appease her mother, she'd leased a comfortable unit in a well-sought-after location. It was close to an entertainment center consisting of upscale shopping, restaurants, and gaming theaters. Not that she'd ever been there. Her off-hours were either spent at home or in the Yards, adding to her black stain of shame.

Conall was as skilled with an AVU as Keene, knowing exactly where to flaunt the air zone speeds and dropping them between two other vehicles with only inches to spare. Once the wheels touched, he jumped out of the AVU to run around and open her door before she released the seat restraints.

He bent with a mock bow and an impish grin as she stepped out, waving a hand for her to proceed to the tower. His gaze scanned the area before he followed her into the building, and his surveillance continued in the lobby even after she nodded at the security guards, who gave Conall a long stare as he followed her to the elevators.

She was too tired to put up a fight when Conall followed her up the elevator to her tenth-floor unit, halfway up the tower. Her unit had a view of the park, making the small balcony worth the extra price.

"I could never get used to living in these towers," Conall mumbled as they approached her unit.

"Too shiny."

He shook his head. "I don't like elevators."

She stared at him as she stood in front of her unit. "You mentioned you didn't like the one at the bunker. But you never use it?"

He shrugged. "Rarely."

"You always take the stairs?"

"Usually. It's only ten flights down. But there are other ways out of the bunker."

Before she could ask what those ways were, he barged past her as soon as she disengaged the security locks. He worked his way through her two-bedroom unit as if he was on a raid. She wasn't sure whether to be offended by his assumption she couldn't take care of herself, embarrassed by the mess, or comforted by his concern for her safety.

"All clear?" she asked as she dropped her sidearm and holster on a side table before stepping into the kitchen. "Can I offer you something to drink? I have beer."

He opened the door to check her balcony then met her at the counter that separated the kitchen from the living space. "Nice place."

"If messy." She opened a beer and slid it across the counter toward him.

He picked it up and assessed the label. "A brown beer. You don't usually find these Topside."

"Nope. I get it from a place in the Edges, but the brewery is hidden in the Yards."

Conall took a swig, and his eyes widened. "That's good. I'll need to get the name of the store."

"Something tells me your family doesn't have a problem finding anything you need or want."

"True enough."

She opened a beer and took a seat next to him. "So tell me, what else do you do in that bunker of yours?"

He grinned. "Always the ISA agent."

She bristled, and her cheeks burned. How many times in just one day had she found herself blushing around the MacGregor brothers? It must be their masculine charm—or their gentle intimidation tactics.

Rather than answer her question, he asked one of his own. "How is it, working with my brother?"

She shrugged. "It's only been one day, and we ended up running for our lives. Not your typical day at ISA."

He laughed. "Keene always knew how to show a woman a good time."

"You act like this is a typical day for him."

He leaned back, considering her statement. "My brother has spent most of his life working in security. He's always had a penchant for trouble."

"Unlike you."

He grinned, his twinkling eyes only enhancing his perfect features. "I prefer love over war."

She couldn't help but match his grin. "So, you're the light to Keene's dark."

Something flashed in his gaze, but it came and went so fast she might have imagined it. "My brother had a more difficult road to travel." He shook his head and swigged his beer. "But it's more pleasant to talk about me."

Of course, it was. Either Conall was quite proud of himself, or it was an act. "Which gets us back to my original question you ignored earlier."

"Oh. Right. What else do we do in the bunker?" He rubbed his chin as he studied the label on the beer bottle. "What bothers you the most? The hi-tech or the fact it's a bunker?"

"And why do you always answer a question with another question?"

He laughed deep and low, his dark blues glittering, and his hands held up in surrender. "Not everyone likes to live in glass towers. We prefer being a little closer to nature."

"Deep in the earth."

"That's about as close as one can get." He gave her a teasing look. "You didn't see everything in our little tour. You judge too quickly. No wonder Keene has a problem with you."

She choked on her beer. "What do you mean by that?"

He rubbed his face, and his earlier cheer disappeared. "My brother has worked alone for a long time. Now, he has a partner thrust on him. One who judges everything before understanding it." He shrugged as if that explained everything.

"He can't expect to work with an ISA agent without questions being asked."

Conall set the beer down and nodded. "True enough. But maybe the questions should be about your case and not our life choices."

He stood, and she trailed him to the front door, knowing she'd upset him, but she couldn't take back the questions. He opened the door before turning back to her. "Sometimes watching and listening are more effective than running in and kicking doors down." He glanced around the room. "Somehow, I was expecting more color." He flashed his smile and bowed his head. "Since we'll be seeing more of each other, I'll share a bit of advice. In Scotland, it was always considered good luck to bring a gift on your first visit to someone's home. Some of that brown beer wouldn't be turned away."

And with that, he was gone.

She grabbed her beer and fell on the couch, suddenly bone-tired. He was right. The only reason they'd gone to the bunker was Keene's injury, and she spent the entire time suspicious of who they were and what they were up to. Was everything always suspect with her? Apparently so. She'd promised herself before ever walking into the homicide scene that she would be a team player—whether Keene was or not. She had to stay focused on the case, not the MacGregor's. She needed to talk to the major.

She plugged in her earpiece and requested Major Taylor over her wrist unit. The major's assistant brushed her off, stating that the major had meetings all day before traveling to Sydney on another assignment. He assured Rowan the major would return her call when she could and that she had every confidence in her.

In other words—figure it out herself. She threw the earpiece across the room and finished her beer before stretching out to stare at the ceiling.

When she opened her eyes, the room was dark—the lights from the city the only illumination. She checked her wrist unit. Three hours since Conall had left and no calls. Not a peep from her old squad. She rubbed her face, feeling more alone than she ever had. Things could be worse, though she wasn't sure how.

She sat up and did the one thing she knew how to do. Focus on the case. The tattoo was a clue to Keene's dead informant, and someone wanted either Keene or Horatio dead.

She had her arm through one sleeve of her jacket when she stopped. What if she'd been the target? No. Who could possibly want her dead? She wasn't a threat since she was no longer on a squad. There must be another explanation, and they simply didn't have enough information to sort it through. However, she found it strange that whoever had been shooting at them didn't have enough sense to have all the exits covered. Otherwise, Horatio could have been snagged exiting into the alley. Maybe Keene had been the target.

She shrugged the rest of her jacket on, stuffed a beer in an inside pocket, and slammed the door behind her. The walk to the bridge took twenty minutes. The bridge over the Los Angeles River was wide enough for vehicles but was used mostly for foot traffic and recreational vehicles. It had been her quiet place since she'd been a teenager. It was a safe place where she could escape from her parents' constant complaints about her studies, her friends, or any one of a dozen things she always seemed to do wrong. Back then, it had been a good forty-minute hike from the elite towers they'd lived in.

After her brother's death, spending time at the bridge had turned into a daily habit. Now, she visited at least once a week. The MacGregor's had their bunker. She had her bridge.

She climbed the rough stone base of a support beam until she reached a small platform twenty feet up. It was three feet wide and circled the stone base where it gave way to steel. The bridge offered two amazing views—one of the city, and the other of the great Pacific Ocean. L.A.'s landscape was quite different from the days before the Wars. At that time, much of the city had been overcrowded with people, traffic, and unhealthy air, with sporadic areas of urban renewal and upscale neighborhoods. Today, it was a shiny conglomeration of glass towers, expansive parks, two levels of monorails, and four transport zones. During the day, the clear sky filled up with AVUs, commercial transports, and ISA hoppers. The bright colors of the Yards could be seen from this vantage point, the thin strip of the Edges a clear buffer from the rest of the city. But at night, Topside was the clear winner. Colorful lights shimmered from the glass towers, along the streets, and from the lit paths in the parks.

She turned her back on the city and tiptoed to the far side of the platform before sitting down to dangle her legs off the side. It was irrational, but sometimes she became disconnected from the place where she'd grown up. Times when the city seemed to have turned its back on her. When she was more an outsider than part of the fabric of its existence. Like today, when she'd been stripped of a job she loved and tossed into the unknown.

She pulled out the beer and swallowed a quarter of it before leaning her head back, breathing in the brine from the ocean. Against the silence of the evening, she heard the distant waves crash against the barrier walls that kept the sea at bay. She could always rely on this place and the sense of unfettered freedom to settle her wild nature.

Though tonight, instead of peace, cloying tendrils of memories pressed on her. The blistering hot day, standing at parade rest in her dress uniform, sweat running down her spine. The frown of disappointment in her father's eyes and the dull stare of her mother's as they exited the limo, surrounded by color guards. Kendra, dressed in black, her back ramrod straight as she strode to the bleachers holding the hands of her two small children, their eyes huge as they stared at the crowd.

A black AVU drone, hovering three feet off the ground, its doors removed, led a motorcade that included command transports, armored rovers, ISA AVUs, and, finally, fellow ISA guards on foot. A parade that stretched seven blocks. Inside the drone AVU, a banner of silver and navy blue, the colors of ISA, covering a single personnel pod. A solitary white calla lily resting on top. Onlookers filling both sides of the immaculate sidewalks. A hero's funeral.

In these days of peace and prosperity, it was rare to lose an ISA officer in the line of duty anywhere in the world, so each one was honored in a similar fashion as if the fallen hero belonged to the world and not their family. Parading the family's grief for all to see, the funeral broadcasted over the global net. Hoorah for being such an enlightened society.

Tears had threatened that entire day, but she'd held them back. She stood like a statue, unwilling to meet anyone's eyes—not those of her parents who blamed her, not Kendra, who forgave her, and never to her fellow guards who saw Zach's death as a risk of the job. But she knew her parents had finally been right about one thing—it had been her fault. It should have been her in that pod, not her brother.

She shook off the memory, swallowing the rest of the bottle in one long pull. She didn't know which nightmare was worse, that one or the one where she'd seen Zach fall. The memories had lessened the last several weeks, so why come back now? It had to be the turmoil at work. The one mistake that dumped her into an unwelcome job with a partner who'd just as soon get rid of her.

The ocean wouldn't bring her solace tonight. She tucked the empty bottle in her pocket and climbed down the stone pillar, turning for home. Out of the corner of her eye, she caught the flicker of someone disappearing behind one of the other stone encasements farther down the bridge. There was little illumination, and a light fog had kicked up, so she might have imagined the figure. She kept to her usual pace as she strode home, but she couldn't shake the feeling she was being followed. The sigh of relief when she reached her building surprised her. Her knife and sidearm were all she needed, though it had been overkill taking both to the bridge. She hardly used either, except on a Yards raid, but they seemed a wise precaution after being shot at earlier in the day.

The only thing was, as she considered her stalker on the way up the elevator, something about the shape was familiar. It clicked the second she walked into her unit. The shadowy figure disappearing into the fog had an outline similar to the one and only Keene MacGregor.

———

KEENE STARED AT THE CEILING. He'd slept for a couple of hours while Lanis's salves pushed the poison out of his system, then spent the following hour mentally reviewing the mishap at Horatio's building. He hadn't seen the crew that shot him, and with the number of bullets and crossbow bolts flying, there had to be more than one person. He hadn't seen anyone suspicious at the dead informant's tower.

He'd been appalled to discover the major had assigned him a partner. Then Lockwood—Rowan—had surprised him by her accurate evaluation of the scene. Between mixing her obvious skilled experience with his irritation at having to babysit someone who couldn't be told half of what she'd need to know to be useful, he'd ignored everything else. Like having a tail. A rookie mistake.

Nothing to do about it now.

If the crew that attacked them had used laser weapons rather than crossbows, he wouldn't be worried. Someone was always trying to kill him. It came with the job. But they'd used arrows spiked with old-world poisons, making this a whole new ballgame. One that put his new partner at risk. Without the knowledge she wasn't cleared to have, she would be in danger, unschooled on how to protect herself. That burden now lay at his feet.

Too restless to sleep, he slipped on his jacket and crept down the hallways, his senses on high alert. Lanis had exceptional insight, and he expected her to pop out of a doorway at any moment to herd him back to his room. But he made it to the stairs without incident and jogged up the twelve flights, their individual rooms being on the lowest floor. He nodded at Thompson, the night guard, before jumping into his AVU. He barely made it past the garage doors before taking it straight up to Zone 2 as he sped toward the city.

He parked a block from her tower, walking the rest of the way and keeping to the shadows. Conall had given him a quick surveillance recap when he'd returned from Rowan's. Tenth-floor unit, hallways and stairs monitored by cameras and sensors. Security on-site. He shouldn't worry, but he wouldn't be able to sleep without seeing for himself that all was well. He'd made that mistake before and swore to never let it happen again—no matter how long ago that had been.

An hour. That's as long as he'd wait to be sure. Thirty minutes into his self-imposed watch, he groaned. Rowan strode out the front doors of the tower. Wherever she was going had to be close if she was walking. Or maybe she'd take the monorail. The major had suggested Rowan didn't own an AVU. Many people didn't, not bothering with the expense when public transportation could take you anywhere in the capital—or the planet for that matter.

He followed at a distance, finding it easy to match her stride. She didn't glance around, either too focused on her thoughts or comfortable with the safety within Topside. When she turned for the bridge, he sped up. It would be more difficult to follow across the bridge with only the stone buttresses to hide behind, leaving a lot of space in between where she might spot him.

She stopped at the second stone pillar, and without glancing around, climbed up. That was interesting.

He slipped behind the first buttress and watched her shimmy around the platform to sit. He smiled when he noted the bottle. Probably some of that brown beer Conall had crooned over. When she dangled her feet off the side to stare at the dark ocean, he understood.

This was her place.

He leaned against the rough stones and watched her. What was she thinking? What dark thoughts drove her here? He snorted. Maybe she was devising ways to find another assignment. He had the impression she was equally unhappy to be tied to him, but for the moment, he didn't know how to get her transferred. His GSM contact had made it clear Keene would need to play nice with ISA after he'd discovered his dead informant. He'd made several calls to Major Taylor, but they'd all been blocked by her guard dog, who'd used the excuse of her traveling to another sector.

Until she returned, Keene was stuck with the willful sergeant who asked too many questions. He still might find some task to send her on, but would he be putting her in more danger if there was a crew out there, their intentions unknown?

Twenty minutes passed before Rowan climbed down and returned the way she'd come. He followed her back and was relieved when she turned into the lobby of her housing tower. She'd hesitated for the briefest moment before going through the door.

Damn. He was pretty sure she'd caught her tail. She was good. Did she know it was him? He'd find out tomorrow, assuming she'd mention it. Rowan seemed the type to hold her cards to her chest until the appropriate moment. He smiled. At least she had skills.

NINE

The next morning, Keene was early. Rowan was advised of his arrival by the bleep on her wrist unit, not a knock on the door. He waited in his AVU. No suit today. Instead, he'd dressed in black pants and a long-sleeved tee that accentuated his muscled physique. He was apparently anxious to hunt for the tattooed man. She didn't have a chance to grab coffee or breakfast, and it required fifteen minutes of her best grumbling before the AVU slipped into a drive-through convenience station where she grabbed two coffees.

Once a couple of sips had cleared the cobwebs, she considered her new partner. Had he been her mysterious shadow from the previous night? She doubted he'd admit it one way or another.

"How's your arm?" She glanced out the side window, noting the increase in foot traffic in this part of town. Three different monorails converged at the transportation center, unloading hundreds of workers going about their typical day. Before the Wars, L.A. was a city of multiple forms of industry. Once the newly established GSM declared Los Angeles the earth's capital, several industries moved out to the surrounding Sectors.

The mammoth scientific complex of GSM, including laboratories, research centers, contractors, and new universities, filled the city.

The only area of science that wasn't melded into this metropolis was the Houston space program headquartered in the New Orleans Sector and the St. Petersburg satellite site in the Oslo Region.

Keene stretched out his left arm, and she glanced over in time to see his grimace. "It's fine."

"Doesn't look fine."

He grumbled something under his breath that sounded like, "Damn, woman."

She ignored him. "Did you have a chance to do any further investigating? Background checks, that sort of thing?"

"Lanis shut the command center down so we could get Horatio settled."

"Hmm. Conall mentioned there were several ways out of the bunker, not just the elevator and stairs."

He didn't respond right away, and when he did, he turned the tables on her. "So, you and Conall got cozy, sharing secrets and tall tales."

"We didn't get cozy." She hadn't meant to snap. He was testing her as much as she was pushing him. "I was curious about the bunker, that's all."

Silence returned, and it was apparent that Keene wasn't a talkative man or simply had nothing to say.

"Did Horatio go to work today?" She would have been surprised if he had.

Keene snickered. "He can work from anywhere. It's not the first time he's worked from home. When I checked on him this morning, he was monitoring the surveillance systems on both of his housing units."

"Paranoid much," she mumbled.

Keene dropped the vehicle to Zone 1, resting the AVU in a parking complex near the entrance to the Yards that included two monorail stops. The narrow streets in the Yards made parking a nuisance. Even during the week, hundreds of people visited the unique street markets that couldn't be found Topside.

They entered the Yards close to Galway Alley, where Keene had insisted they begin their investigation. The Yards had five large districts similar to pre-war cultural boroughs. European, Asian, African, British Isles, and Latina cultures had marked their territories back when the Yards were filled with rail yards and mixed housing.

Most of the Yards was safe to walk, even at night. Crimes against the population itself were as rare as Topside or the Edges. Crime here was the typical illicit trade—drugs, sex, and rock and roll, as her brother used to say.

Keene grabbed her arm as he turned down a narrow alley, disturbing her musings. "Pay attention."

"Sorry," she grumbled and tossed her empty coffee cup in a nearby reclamation unit.

Galway Alley was a blend of the British Isles culture—Irish, Scottish, Welsh, and English. Like most of the Yards, there were multi-storied homes tucked here and there between apartments. No building was taller than five stories, and while most were well-tended apartments, the age of the structures reflected their time-worn and battle-scarred histories.

Keene appeared relaxed as he strolled through the streets that worked like spokes radiating out from a center court. Within the court was a two-story building that used to be a library and museum. The library was partially functional. The artifacts in the museum had been removed years earlier, and that section of the building housed the civic center. The other four districts carried the same basic structure. The only difference was the type of building they'd commandeered for their headquarters. Each district elected a council that determined policies that aligned with the overarching rules of the Yards set by the GSM. It wasn't an easy line to walk, and she had to give each council credit for making the attempt.

They wandered through the outdoor market stalls, and she kept an eye out for the symbol Keene's mysterious informant had on his wrist. Although she noticed similar designs, Keene shook his head. Several times, Keene stopped and spoke to a shopkeeper in a language she didn't understand, but he simply shook his head as they left each shop. Women watched him before their gazes fell on her—curious rather than hostile. When they stopped at one shop close to center court, a shopkeeper handed Keene a pin. It was made of interlaced silver strands that Keene explained were Celtic knots, similar to what they were searching for. The middle of the silver pin appeared to be made of enamel in a plaid design of red and black.

Keene thanked the man and pinned the trinket to his shirt just above his heart.

"An interesting pattern." She gave him a side glance as they walked past food vendors with fresh fruit and vegetables from the community gardens.

"Aye, they're one of the colors of the clan MacGregor."

"I thought those types of monikers were discouraged."

He nodded and gave her an odd look. "They still persist in the Yards. When you're huddled with people of your own culture, you tend to remember more of the old traditions. I'm surprised you haven't noticed it before."

With the amount of time she'd spent in the Yards, she was ashamed to admit she hadn't spent much time considering the mixed cultures. The districts were obviously separated by it, but she'd never looked deeper. She shrugged. "My focus has always been on the illicit trade. I can tell you all about that culture."

He just nodded, and for some reason, she sensed she'd somehow disappointed him. The thought irritated her. Before the silence grew to awkwardness, three young boys, barely past mid-school age, barreled to a stop in front of them.

"Keene, Keene, have you seen Chester?" They were all talking over each other, their expressions flushed with excitement, spittle flying from one of them.

"Gross, Charlie, wipe your mouth," one of the kids whined.

The one who must have been Charlie slid a dirty sleeve over his mouth and grinned sheepishly.

Keene rubbed his head. "So, what's all this excitement about Chester?"

The boys kept elbowing each other to be the one closest to Keene, who patiently waited for them to settle and answer his question.

The boy who'd yelled at Charlie was the winner. "Chester won the Regional tournament. Beat those Topsiders well and good." He glanced at Rowan and turned beet red. "Uh, sorry." He checked his shoes. "I didn't mean anything by that."

Keene squeezed the boy's shoulder. "Now, Michael, don't apologize. There's nothing wrong with a little healthy competition. Be proud of where you're from."

Michael stood tall. "Right." He lifted his chin and stared back at her, a fire in his gaze. "Chester is the best winger in the Region."

She didn't follow sports, no matter how many times Zach had tried to explain them. Only a handful of sports were played globally, but that still didn't help narrow down what a winger was. She smiled at Michael. "That's a pretty upright title."

The street slang was challenging to follow—especially between Topsiders, the Edgers, and those in the Yards all having their own. She hoped she was close.

The boy gave her a long look, then smiled. "You're a little strange. But if you're part of Keene's clan, you're all right by us."

"Well, thank you, Michael."

Keene squeezed Michael's shoulder. "So Chester must be on his way to New Rochelle. I hear that's where Global Titles are this year."

The boys' grins faded. Charlie finally answered. "No. His parents took him down to Mexico City to work with their team. Something about trying to help them win their Regional title."

Keene's jaw clenched. "You mean they won't let him compete in the Global playoffs because he's from the Yards."

The boys glanced at their shoes again, and Keene shook his head, mumbling something to himself. "I can't promise anything, boys, but I have a friend who might be able to help." He raised his hand. "By Dagda's word, you won't tell a soul, especially Chester, until I know whether I can help. Promise?"

They nodded their heads, but she could tell they thought it was all in vain.

After the boys ran off, Rowan and Keene hopped on a trolley, jumping off at the edge of the African Quarter, where Keene directed them to a small group of food carts. This section of the Yards had been replicated from what had once been called the French Quarter in the New Orleans Sector. The district was known for its food, jazz and blues clubs, textiles, and gem markets. Of all the districts, it hired more workers than any other.

They grabbed lunch from one of the food vendors and found a table. Keene had eaten half of his sandwich before he began grumbling. "Nothing ever changes."

Not knowing what he referred to, she kept her mouth shut, using chewing and slight nods as her response. When she glanced at him, his brows were knit in contemplation, or maybe it was irritation. In an attempt to change whatever was upsetting him, she asked a question that had bothered her since leaving Galway Alley.

"You said you could help that boy get to the Global Titles. Who do you know that high up?" From what Zach had told her, Global Titles was a big deal, and just being on a Regional team could write a player's ticket for a lifetime contract. He and their father argued all the time about overlooking players from the Yards. Edgers rarely made it on a team.

"I have a friend or two." He gave her a look somewhere between angry and offended as if it was unthinkable he had any friends.

"That's pretty impressive. I thought I was cool knowing the major." She hoped to add levity to ease his mood. It partially worked.

His grin didn't quite temper the storm in his eyes. "Those boys give up most of their childhood training to be the best. The games should be based on merit, not what side of the wall you were born."

"It's the nature of the game. The Regional teams set a Global impression that relies on more than just skill."

He looked at her as if she was whackers. "Are you daft?" He leaned closer so he wouldn't have to shout in the public space. "It's a sports game. The only thing that should matter is skill." He took a breath, but his tone was still heated. "When you don't include all the people in your Region, you create a divide."

It seemed as if he blamed her for the situation, making her one of "them," whoever that was. "Everyone knows it's a long shot at best for someone from the Yards to make it to Globals. The teams are expected to be from Topside."

"Is that so?" His lips formed a thin line, the muscle in his jaw pulsed, and he bounced his foot, his knee gently tapping against the table. He pushed his hands through his hair before scooting closer.

She caught a whiff of wild meadows and spring rain and realized he was the scent she'd been smelling. It distracted her for a second before his next words snapped her back.

"When this great altruistic society recreated the world and carved out who fit where, what skill they would learn, where they would work, and then got down to the few who either couldn't or wouldn't conform, those people were pushed into the Yards. And they had to learn to fend for themselves. And because Topside forgot about them, they became alienated and unwanted."

"But they didn't want to be governed by Topside."

He rolled his eyes and gave her one of those "how naive can you be" looks. "They weren't given a choice, Sergeant."

His brusque tone should have flared her temper, but his passion for the people in the Yards showed a deep concern for others she hadn't expected from his usually cold exterior.

"I've seen it a hundred times." His voice grew so soft she had to lean forward to hear him. Or maybe it was his intensity that drew her toward him and the scent of wildness. "People mashed together under the hopes of colonization, industrialization, and civilization. But there are always people who fall through the cracks, marginalized and forgotten. The Regions would be stronger if they allowed players from the Edges and the Yards to compete. It would show how united the Earth truly was. Divisions breed contempt, and that grows to discontent. After that, any little match could ignite disaster."

She'd heard versions of this before. Rumblings and other political rhetoric at Duster's. Mostly from old-timers tossing back their fourth or fifth shot of the evening. But she'd never heard it from a Topsider, and Keene had to be a Topsider. Right? That would be the only way he could get a contract with GSM.

"A hundred times?" She couldn't help but smile, trying to

defuse the conversation. "You look great for your age to have seen that much."

His mouth slammed shut so hard she could have sworn she'd heard his molars rattle. He breathed deeply for a few minutes. "My kin are anthropologists, remember?" He glanced at his wrist unit and stood. "Toss your garbage. I don't want to be late." Keene dumped his food basket in the reclamation bin, took a long sip of tea before dumping the cup, then bumped into a lanky kid who looked like a university student before he stormed away.

TEN

Rowan scrambled to toss her trash before jogging to catch up and match Keene's stride as they strolled the streets of the African Quarter. They'd walked three blocks before he stopped at a jewelry shop. He held the door open and waited for her to enter. His quick mood changes never ceased to amaze her.

He showed the image of the tattoo to a tall, raven-haired beauty behind the counter.

"I haven't seen anything like that. Have you tried Galway Alley?" Her tone sounded sincere, but the hardness in her eyes told a different story. Rowan had seen the look countless times during raids. The woman had seen too much in her life and would do anything not to see it again. They'd get no help here. Keene sensed it as well because he smiled before glancing down at the display boxes.

After a minute, he pointed. "How much for the bracelet?"

Rowan stepped closer. It was a single strand of glass beads the colors of a rainbow. In between each bead was a small silver box with varying designs of interlaced silver. The piece was stunning, and Keene surprised her when he haggled in earnest with the shopkeeper. Who was he buying a bracelet for? Or was it simply a ruse to gather information?

A twinge twisted in her chest with a flare of irritation at Keene's flirtation with the shopkeeper as his accent thickened. While the bartering continued, she averted her gaze, deciding her annoyance wasn't with the wide, engaging smile he gave the woman but at their earlier conversation. Somehow, the MacGregors had her questioning everything she'd taken for granted in the world, or at least her piece of it.

She turned her back on them to wait by the door and people watch. Across the narrow street, a man leaned against a stucco building, his arms crossed over his chest as he surveyed the crowd. He was a big man, but there were lots of them in the Yards. He could have been waiting for someone, yet there was something about his posture, his awareness of everything around him that made the hairs on the back of her neck rise. She'd seen him before. Had he been at an earlier shop? His gaze flickered to the door of the jewelry shop several times, and she stood motionless, unsure if he was able to see her.

After the cash and bracelet exchanged hands, Keene tucked the bracelet in a jacket pocket, and they continued their stroll as if they did this every afternoon.

"Did you notice that big guy across the street from the jewelers?" She pointed at flowers at one of the outdoor carts, enforcing their ruse as shoppers.

He shook his head and pointed to another stand across the street, wrapping his arm around her shoulder to turn her in that direction. "I noticed him a few shops ago. Maybe we should see why he's so interested."

She instinctively ran a hand over her jacket, comforted by the feel of her sidearm. "I'm game."

His arm slid down and snaked around her midsection. She

stiffened at the feel of his hard muscles when he pulled her close.

He bent his head to whisper in her ear. "Relax. We need to look like we're going off to have some personal time."

This wasn't the first time she'd worked undercover, pretending to be someone's lover, but she'd never considered she'd have to play that game with Keene. Somehow, it seemed too intimate, but she wrapped an arm around his waist and leaned her head on his shoulder. His chin grazed the side of her head, her hair ruffling under his breath.

They walked half a block before Keene turned them down a narrow alley. Although they were out of sight, Keene kept her close. "This looks like a dead-end, but there's an exit on the left, behind a large piece of sheet metal. Or there was the last time I was here."

"How long ago was that?" She knew the street crew that ran this area. They were smart and had given ISA the slip too many times to count.

"A couple months ago."

"That might as well be years for how often they change their routes."

"It's the best choice we have."

They'd only walked twenty yards before the heavy sound of boots grew close.

When Keene turned to confront the man, they dropped their loving pose and stepped away from each other, giving each of them room to react. Keene's eyes widened momentarily, as surprised as her to discover there were four men, not one, who had followed them.

The men also spread out, leaving no escape to maneuver around them. The bulges in their jackets weren't just muscle. They were carrying. And if these men were regulars in the Yards, they would know every hidden exit.

She waited for Keene. This was his mission. If it had been hers, she would have called for backup when she first spotted the big man and suspected a possible threat. And right about now, she'd have her sidearm out with a clear call to cease and desist, knowing a hopper would be a couple minutes out. Not that a lot couldn't happen in that time, but the men would know satellites had begun tracking her signal, and everything was being monitored. But now, she was exposed out in the open with no backup coming.

Keene's posture was relaxed, as if he was meeting someone he hadn't seen for years and was surprised to find more of his old friends waiting for him. When it was apparent the other men weren't going to say anything, Keene smiled at them.

"Hello, mates. If you were hoping for expensive trinkets, I'm afraid we'll be a disappointment. All I have is a simple bracelet." He reached into his pocket, but what he brought out looked nothing like the bracelet he'd purchased. This one, though colorful, appeared to be made of paper.

The men looked disinterested. Everyone knew they weren't there to rob them. When one of the men reached into his jacket, Keene pulled a small string from the bracelet before tossing it at them. Then he spun around and grabbed her arm. "Run."

Seconds later, multiple explosions filled the air along with the acrid scent of sulfur. She cringed, waiting for the hit of shrapnel. It never came.

They raced for the hidden exit, hoping like hell it was still there. Keene stopped long enough to pull back the sheet metal, but it wouldn't budge. He stepped back and stared at it.

"What are you doing?" she yelled, looking over her shoulder to see if the men had advanced yet. It was difficult to tell with all the smoke, but she heard boots.

"I know it's here." He tried the metal panel again without success.

She scanned the area, her heart pounding, one hand on her sidearm though she hadn't pulled it yet. An old vintage door, stained with various paint colors, leaned against a wood fence. It couldn't be that simple. Yet, for some reason, she knew without a doubt that was the literal doorway out of there.

When she tugged on Keene's sleeve, he pulled away, and she left him where he was. He could either follow or not, but she wasn't waiting around. She raced for the door, which covered an opening in the fence half the size of the door. She ducked and was halfway through when Keene bumped into her, pushing her faster. He replaced the door while she continued running down an alley. Within seconds, he caught up with her.

They broke into a street crowded with people, several already deep into their drinking based on their loud singing and swaying pace. After running a block, he pushed her into an empty doorway, and then she was falling, her legs knocked out from under her. Keene grabbed her on the way down, his arm moving around her in what she assumed was an attempt to protect her head, but in doing so, he fell on top of her.

His weight was heavy.

Solid.

"Get off me." Her voice squeaked as she tried to catch a breath under his weight. His only response was a slight shift so she could suck in air.

Footsteps. Coming fast.

Then his nose pressed into her neck. His scent washed over her like a spring morning, as it had that first day in his AVU— meadows of woodsy plants, wildflowers, and rain. How strangely intoxicating. The smell of rain was so strong, she could almost feel the first drops of a shower on her shoulders. This wasn't the rain from the Yards, mixed with filth and oils from the battered streets. This was the fragrance from the first rain of the season. Something she would connect with her bridge, of open sky and sea. A fresh breeze as if heralding in a time when everything was new again.

He rolled off her, breaking the spell. There had been someone coming—a group of someones.

"They're gone." His voice was gruff. His charming personality snapped back in place.

Already? "They didn't even slow down."

"They wouldn't expect us to stop for a quick one." He stood and brushed off his pants, scanning the area to make sure no one returned.

"That's what I like about you, MacGregor. Always the gallant one." She scrambled up since it was apparent he wasn't going to assist. She followed his lead and brushed off the dirt. "I take it we're done here for the day."

"Let's go back to the bunker. Maybe Horatio has something."

She followed him. And try as she might, she couldn't keep her gaze off his backside.

ELEVEN

The departure from the Yards had been uneventful, but it wasn't until they'd settled into Keene's AVU that Rowan relaxed her vigilance. They hadn't raced back, but they hadn't kept to their casual stroll either. Heads down, they fell into a comfortable rhythm, Keene monitoring the left side of the street while she covered the right. After two close calls in the same number of days, they'd both learned a little about each other—they knew how to get out of a scrape.

Neither of them spoke as Keene weaved them through Zone 1 at a leisurely pace until he gently lifted the AVU to skim Zone 2. When they rolled into the garage of the bunker, Rowan considered asking him if he had a GSM office but decided to hold her tongue.

If either of them hoped to find time to recover and analyze what had happened in the African Quarter, it was wishful thinking. The command center was a firestorm, and she had to give the three souls in the room credit for their ability to create such a disastrous scene.

Horatio paced the stretch of floor that ran along the wall of imagers that shimmered with blank green screens. His hands gripped his hair, and the reflection from the displays cast his blue hair in dark mossy tones. Every few steps, he stopped, stared at an imager, shouted some profanity, then continued his pacing. Lanis followed behind, leaving plenty of distance. Rowan was too far away to hear her murmured words which she assumed were meant to console and calm. Conall picked up pieces of broken items—remnants of a mug, data pads with shattered screens, keyboards dangling from consoles, a holo-monitor flashing sporadic images.

No one noticed them enter.

Keene stopped to survey the mayhem. He took a step toward Lanis and Horatio, hesitated, then turned toward Conall. The big man stood with the remains of a tablet that would never be used again. Half the display dangled from a broken casing as if it had arms and legs and someone had tried to rip them off. His eyes widened when he noticed Keene, either in shock from the destruction or confused to see them back so soon.

He shrugged. "We've had a bit of bad news." He tossed the broken display into a large trash receptacle that looked two-thirds full. "Did you find the tattooed man?"

"No. But we're either getting close, or the crew that shot me yesterday somehow followed us to the African Quarter."

Conall's expression turned serious, and he gave them a more thorough perusal. "You weren't injured?"

They shook their heads, which seemed to mollify him. With the disarray around them, and Lanis trying to calm a crazed Horatio, this seemed the best time to ask the question bothering her since they'd run from the men in the alley. She pushed Horatio's occasional keening off as white noise and planted her hands on her hips to face Keene.

"What was that explosive you used to distract the men? It looked like a bracelet, but it wasn't the one you bought."

Conall grimaced. "Explosives? We told you not to use those."

Great. They had a license for explosive materials? The major owed her a complete explanation. If she ever bothered to return her calls.

Keene gave Lanis and Horatio a quick glance before he brushed debris off a desk to perch on the corner. He pulled another paper bracelet out of his pocket. He tossed it in the air, caught it, and tossed it again as he gave his brother a wicked grin. "Not an explosive."

Conall squinted, assessing the item as it flew up and down in the air. Then he smiled, and his deep belly laugh filled the room. "Firecrackers?"

She swiveled her head to Keene. "That's contraband." And she realized how stupid that sounded after they'd admitted to having explosives.

Fireworks of any type had been on the GSM's long list of illegal items since the end of the Climate Wars. Any material used to make an explosive item carried heavy restrictions, but unlicensed incendiary devices were strictly prohibited except for ISA or select GSM units. Even though Keene was contracted by GSM, he dealt with informants. Why would he require explosives?

Before anyone could respond to her statement, a new silence filled the room. It took several seconds to realize Horatio had stopped his intermittent crooning and was striding toward Keene, his eyes sparkling with interest at the bracelet Keene continued to toss. When Horatio reached Keene, he snatched the fireworks during a midair toss and turned away, investigating his new toy.

"Is that such a good idea?" Conall asked, his smile fading as he kept an eye on Horatio. "Don't pull the string. You'll blow your hand off."

"I know," Horatio snapped with the tone of a petulant kid.

Lanis stood with fists on her hips, duplicating Rowan's posture. "If I'd known that was all it took to distract him, I would have given him one of our handmade decoy devices and sent him outside." When they all stared at her, she added, "In case he blew himself up. Though that would have been a shame. He's a whiz at data retrieval and encryption." When she caught Rowan's open-mouthed stare, she shrugged. "It would have been a waste of talent."

Rowan rubbed her forehead. A headache was coming, and she didn't know what had induced it: the unsettling notion that an unknown crew was tracking them, that some unpleasant news had triggered Horatio into a destructive frenzy, or that they let the disturbed kid wander off with firecrackers. Which brought up another question.

"Did you have those with you the whole time?"

Keene shook his head. "No. I thought we were being followed since we left Galway Alley."

"Really?"

He nodded, then must have noticed her discomfort. "Don't worry. It wasn't anyone I saw, so you didn't miss anything."

She hated that he could already read her expressions.

"Keene has worked undercover for years. It's just a feeling you pick up." Conall went back to cleaning, finding another display pad that he must have considered fixable since he placed it on a table with other salvaged items.

She accepted the statement because she'd experienced the same insight on numerous missions. It was something she had a knack for, and she blamed her inability to sense it as Keene had on the fact she knew little of what they were doing. The operation was like a confusing puzzle, pieces strewn around with no idea what the whole picture looked like.

"I picked them up on the edge of the African Quarter."

"I was with you the entire time and never saw you buy anything like that."

He leaned back on the desk, his legs swinging in a slow rhythm, his biceps straining against his sleeves. "Let's just say I bumped into someone after our little spat at lunch."

She traced her memory to that moment. He'd walked off, leaving her to catch up. He had bumped into someone, but she hadn't noticed any handoff. Not that she'd been looking for it.

Conall laughed at her bemused expression. "Don't fret, lass. Even I have a hard time spotting his exchanges, and I know all his tricks."

"Most of them." Keene released a heart-stopping smile.

Both men laughed, and Lanis waved a hand at them. "Enough with the both of you. Neither Rowan nor I want to hear about your conquests. But thank you, Keene, for distracting Horatio."

"So what bad news could have created such destruction?" Keene asked.

"We traced the dead guy back to who he worked for," Conall supplied.

"And?" Keene prompted when no one continued. It seemed a natural response, as if he was always dragging information out of the other two.

At first, she thought it might have been because she was there, and neither Conall nor Lanis was sure how much information should be shared. But no one gave her a furtive glance or even seemed to remember she was in the room. A pattern emerged between these three. Each of them had developed a systematic approach, divulging portions of information to assimilate before moving on to the next item. It spoke of years of teaming.

"Your dead informant was Elton Sodowski. He worked for Stoker Industries." Lanis pulled up a chair, pulling her strawberry-blonde hair over one shoulder, finger brushing the long strands.

When no one responded, Rowan put the pieces together. "The same place Horatio works."

Lanis nodded. "More than that. They both worked in the same department, though on different projects."

"Did Horatio know this Sodowski?" It would explain the rampage. She wasn't deeply familiar with Stoker Industries, only that their main business was in defense systems—internal and external. If she correctly remembered conversations from family dinners, they also had their fingers in other areas like bio-research. Each department could be running hundreds of worldwide projects, each involving dozens to hundreds of employees, so working in the same department meant nothing.

"We were trying to figure out if they'd worked together when the kid started tearing the place up." Conall chuckled. "Reminded me of the times when Liam would go berserk."

Lanis and Keene shot each other a look before glancing at Rowan. She considered asking who Liam was when Horatio skirted the group, his head down, hands in his pockets—a school kid knowing he'd done something wrong and unsure how to make amends.

"Come sit down and tell us what you know of this Elton Sodowski." Keene nodded toward an empty chair next to him.

Rowan was too jazzed to sit but not comfortable enough in her surroundings to pace. What she really wanted was to find a working console and run her own data, then contact the major or maybe her old squad. Instead, she moved farther from the group and leaned against a wall, her arms crossed, her fists gripping her shirt. After sucking in a deep breath, she swallowed down the thickness developing in her throat.

Horatio plopped down in the chair, the wheels allowing him to glide back and forth. She wasn't the only jittery one in the room. He picked at a fingernail, one knee bouncing. "I didn't really know him, but we'd spoken a few times over the last year. We were both using an experimental fusion technology in our projects, and we shared notes." His head remained low, and when he lifted it to measure our responses, he focused on Keene. "Am I next? Is that why that crew was at my place?"

That silenced them until Keene asked the first thing that had popped into her head. "Why would you think that?"

He shrugged. "He's the third person from related projects that's recently died."

"The third? Were they all killed?" Rowan couldn't help blurting it out. It was the ISA agent in her, but no one seemed to mind, probably all wondering the same thing.

He shook his head. "One was a car accident. I think another had an allergic reaction or something."

"They seem natural enough." Lanis didn't appear as convinced as she sounded.

"Worth checking out," Conall suggested, and he flipped through the tablets on the salvage table. He fussed with one until the display lit up. "Give me their names."

Horatio mumbled a couple of names as Keene kept a watchful eye on him. "If you didn't know Elton Sodowski all that well, why the freakout?"

The kid shrugged. "You said he was an informant, and I'm your informant." He paused, bit at his nail, then shrugged again. "And I didn't bring my meds."

"You're on meds?" Rowan shook her head. What else was this kid hiding?

"Just to calm me down when I'm surrounded by too much stimuli."

"You're autistic?" Lanis asked.

"ADHD."

"Well, we're not going to get much done with what's left of

the equipment." Lanis turned to Conall. "Is there another working pad? I'll need to make a list of supplies."

"I'm sorry." Horatio sounded like he was close to tears. "I can fix some of it."

"We have someone who might be able to help, but he's—" Lanis stopped, glanced at Rowan, and finished with, "away on assignment."

Rowan ignored whatever Lanis wanted to keep from her, her thoughts swiftly moving to her own solution. "I know someone who could have this place operational within twenty-four hours."

Everyone looked doubtful.

"There are optical as well as spectral analyzers that require specific calibrations." Even with doubt in her tone, Lanis looked hopeful.

"No problem. I don't know everything you have here, but there isn't anything my specialist hasn't been able to fix or jerry-rig." She raised her hands. "Sorry. This isn't my ops, and I know this assignment is top secret. Hernandez is ISA and works on my old squad. I don't know if she's on another mission or can even spare the time, but it's your call."

Keene didn't look at anyone other than her. "This Hernandez wouldn't be able to divulge anything she learns here. And it seems whatever is going on, someone thinks we're getting too close."

"I've been thinking about that." Conall continued to stab at the pad. "We assumed you were the target because you were the one shot. If that's true, then maybe someone's after you for another reason."

"Or there's something else at play here." Lanis glanced at Rowan.

She nodded and stepped away from the wall. "Someone

could be after me. I've taken down some large organizations. I wouldn't rule it out."

Lanis nodded. "Which just confirms we have little to go on without more information."

"Once Hernandez gets this place back in shape, I think she'll give the kid a run at who's best at digging up intel."

Horatio laughed as if he'd like to see anyone try. He appeared to be snapping back to normal.

Keene jumped up and slapped his hands together. "We're not going to get anything done until we get the lab back in shape. Lanis, let's see what backup equipment we have, then give Conall your list." He turned to Rowan. "When will we know if Hernandez can join our merry band or if we need to pull our man off his current assignment?"

"I can let you know in a couple hours." First, she'd need to see if she could swing having Hernandez assigned to her or, worst case, work off-book. After seeing the lab yesterday compared to how it looked now, the techrat would beg to get her hands on this stuff—specifically the items that were more advanced than what was available at ISA.

"Good enough." He grabbed Horatio by the shirt and dragged him to a standing position. "Let's go get your meds."

"We're not going back to my place, are we?" Horatio's tone sounded like he might be getting jacked up again.

"That would be a bad idea. I know someplace we can go where it won't be traced." When he walked past her, he said, "Come on, Sergeant. I'll drop you off on our way. There's nothing more we can do for now."

She followed Keene to the garage, annoyed she didn't have a method of transport without him, and the bunker wasn't close to any public transportation. She would need to fix that.

TWELVE

After Keene dropped Rowan off at her housing tower, she made a stop at the front desk. She didn't recognize the woman behind it, but it was midday, and she was rarely in the building at this hour. The woman, olive-toned, eyes black as night, and a smile that could warm you on a cold day in the Arctic turned her smile up a notch as Rowan approached.

"Sergeant Lockwood, isn't it?"

Her question startled her. "Yes."

She caught her hesitation. "I'm Verlene. I work the split shift. It's nice to put a real face to the name." She chuckled when she noted Rowan's confusion. "I make it a practice to review pictures of all the tenants. We wouldn't be much of a security service if we didn't know our clients from strangers."

Rowan shook her head. Of course, she would have. It would be standard procedure for security. Her brain didn't seem to be working at full throttle these days. "Call me Rowan."

"Rowan it is. What can I help you with today?"

"I was hoping to speak to Gunther."

Verlene checked her wrist unit. "He's at lunch for another

thirty minutes. I'm not sure you know, but the day shift has a lovely two-hour midday break since they work longer hours."

"I did know that, though I'm rarely home to see it."

Verlene glanced around, then leaned toward her. Considering what Rowan did for a living and always enjoying a bit of cloak and dagger, she moved closer.

"Gunther is down in the garage."

Understanding dawned, and Rowan smiled in earnest. Exactly what she'd hoped for. "He's working on that old AVU?"

Verlene snickered. "I don't know why he bothers. He'll never get that thing running. I doubt they have parts for something that old."

"You'd be surprised what you can find on the net. There are dealers whose entire business is specializing in old things. Even parts for old AVUs."

Verlene shook her head. "Why anyone would be interested in that old stuff, I'll never understand. Well, I'm sure he'll be happy to see you if you want to go down."

Rowan nodded and wished the woman well.

Gunther was inside the old AVU, and after giving it a quick scan, she understood Verlene's point. The vehicle was one of the first AVUs off the line thirty years ago and had seen better days. But if anyone could get her flying, it was Gunther, who had a magic touch. He was also a fan of old movies from before the Climate Wars, which had given him an idea. Not one to let it go to waste, he started racing his AVUs out at the old storage facilities, away from the monitoring eyes of the ISA and GSM. No one went to the Barrens, which was nothing but a desert wasteland with no street or air traffic. Perfect for AVU races.

She was still ten feet away when Gunther called out, "Rowan. Get your sweet backside in here and let me show you what I've done."

She chuckled. "If anyone upstairs heard you say that, your job would be toast."

He gave her a look that said different, and she didn't argue. Gunther had to be over fifty, considering he'd fought in the Uprising, and his craggy features and fake eye showed the wear and tear his body had taken. But his energy and personality didn't seem hampered by whatever past experiences he kept carefully guarded. Gunther was a solid friend.

"Take a look at this." He punched a few raised buttons and flicked a couple of switches—definitely old school—but she whistled when the display popped.

"Sweet." The imager was as crisp as a new model. "You must have changed out the interior housing to connect with Little Sister." The earlier AVUs wouldn't have the necessary technology to support something as sophisticated as GSM's latest security net.

He grunted. "I had to strip the entire electrical chassis."

She cringed. That was a lot of work. "It was worth it."

"Yes. Yes, it was." He set his laser drill down and sat back. "So, to what do I owe the honor?"

"I need an AVU. Nothing fancy. In fact, it would be better if it didn't stand out."

"I heard you got reassigned."

"That was fast."

"It's been two days, and you have strangers picking you up and dropping you off at odd hours."

She shook her head. ISA would have advised the tower's security on her reassignment. "And that would be the reason for needing a temporary ride."

"You sure it's temporary?"

"I'm trying not to think that far ahead."

He nodded and fiddled with the wire connections. "I can't

blame you." After a few seconds, he gave her a side glance. "Your mother was by earlier."

That left her speechless. Mother rarely came by, and if it had been an emergency she would have called. Then it hit her. Father's birthday was coming up. Was it that simple? She rubbed her forehead. Her father would have heard about the reassignment.

"Did she leave a message?"

He shrugged. "Don't know. To be honest, I'm not sure why she'd think you'd be home."

"What about the AVU?"

He typed a note on his wrist unit. "I just sent you the location and code for the perfect AVU."

"Uh-huh."

"Now look, Rowan." He turned in his seat so he could look directly at her. The tug he gave his right brow told her he was serious about whatever was coming next. "You don't spend much time behind the wheel of an AVU. This one might look like nothing, but it'll do circles around anything on the street or in the air."

"I don't need anything that fast."

"Have you forgotten that I listen to the ISA bands?"

She had, at least momentarily. Listening to ISA bands was considered illegal but difficult to prevent, especially with Gunther's skills.

"So, you heard about the shooting in the Edges and somehow put me at the scene." Maybe another reason Mother had paid a visit.

He smiled. "I only know what I hear. It seemed you could use something with some zip to it."

She laid a hand on his arm. "You're the best."

After getting out of the AVU, but before she took two steps, Gunther called out, "Not one scratch on her. And I'll know."

She waved goodbye, positive he'd see it on the imager, which was how he'd known about her initial approach before she walked into his line of sight. The man was top-notch when it came to security.

When she entered her housing unit, she made a quick sweep. Conall and Keene were making her paranoid. The activity from the last two days was making her paranoid. Once she cleared the unit, she stopped at her communications center and located Hernandez.

The noise on the other end of the com was loud and drunken. Hernandez was at a bar, probably with the squad. She checked her wrist unit. A bit early. The team must have had a successful op.

"Hey, boss." Her words weren't slurred, just loud, no doubt trying to talk over the crowd.

"I need a few minutes," Rowan yelled back as if it would help.

"Hold on," came the muffled reply. Background noises floated by—clips of speech, music, a grunt or two as she elbowed her way through the crowd. She wasn't tall or beefy but solid muscle in the tight package of a small tornado. One of her best strengths in a takedown, besides her incredible tech skills and marksmanship, was her size and speed. She rarely lost a target.

With a rushed breath, Hernandez whispered, "Okay. I'm clear."

All she heard in the background were the sounds of children, probably in a nearby park. They must be at Safety Zone where most of the local ISA guards hung out. It was technically in the Edges but borderline to a park that was considered Topside. Close enough to not get any bullshit from the top brass.

"I was wondering if you were interested in a side gig."

Rowan preferred to have her reassigned, but she didn't want to make her feel obligated if asked.

"Something to do with something you have on the side, or is this part of your new assignment?"

She sighed with relief. Hernandez wouldn't have asked if she didn't want to be part of the game. "You want in?"

"Oh, yeah." No hesitation.

"Look, I have to warn you..."

"You got shot at your first day on the job," she finished for her.

"How did you know?"

Hernandez waited patiently until she caught up. "Oh, yeah. You're a coms specialist." The woman had many mad skills, but she was the second person to have heard of the shooting. How had ISA put her at the scene in front of Horatio's building? Maybe Keene had put it in his report and had forgotten to tell her. She snorted. She doubted he would have even thought of telling her.

"So when do I start?"

"I'll need to make some calls. I didn't want to presume."

"I appreciate that, but presume away. You know who the brass sent to fill in for you?"

She had an idea and immediately understood Hernandez's desire to get away. In a meek voice, she offered, "Lingetti?"

"Yeah. I think we all put transfers in as soon as Cap made it sound like he might be permanent."

"Ouch." That didn't bode well for Rowan or the squad.

"Yeah, so anything you could do would be appreciated."

"I'll make the calls now." Before she hung up, she added, "And don't tell anyone."

Hernandez snickered. "And take the chance of losing the spot to someone with more years? Not a chance. Besides, my lips will be sealed around a cold brew of Menchkins, and probably a couple more after that."

"Cheers, my friend."

She made two more calls and patiently waited on hold while people on the other end made calls. When she was done, she followed Hernandez's idea and grabbed a cold beer out of the fridge. Thirty minutes later, Hernandez was miraculously added to the team. She'd expected more of a fight. Although the major was still unavailable to talk to, she must have given her approval. Not hearing from Cap on stealing his best tech specialist sent a twinge down her spine. Instead of questioning why fate had blessed her, she chalked it up to name recognition, at least her father was good for something, and that Cap couldn't overrule the major.

Her afternoon activities had spurred an appetite, and she dug through the cooler, coming up with enough ingredients to make a small salad and some pasta. She had enough cooking skills to boil water and wait for noodles to cook. She was putting the dirty dishes in the wash unit when a headache slammed into her like a bolt from a pulse crossbow.

She dropped to her knees, the heel of her palms pressing into the sides of her head in a vain attempt to ease the horrific pain. Darkness blurred her vision, then a flash, and an image appeared. It was like an old celluloid film—two men raced across a grassy, rock-strewn landscape, barren of any structure or landmark. The men turned, their faces masked with concern, but they continued to run. Then she was on her ass, squeezing her eyes shut and rubbing them. She couldn't have just seen what she thought she'd seen.

She hadn't had visions since she'd been a child. Her hands shook, and she stared down at a broken cup on the floor next to her, though she couldn't remember holding it. When she'd been a kid, the visions came first thing in the morning, like REM sleep, where one remembers bits of a dream just before they woke. She'd never been fully awake when they'd happened.

Maybe this wasn't a vision. But what else would have her on her knees—nauseous, weak, and ready to throw up dinner?

What really hit home wasn't the fact that this was the first vision she'd had in almost twenty years. It was what she'd seen.

The two running men had been Keene and her dead brother, Zach.

The light chime that signaled a visitor was on their way up woke Rowan out of her stupor. The front desk had given whoever it was a pass up the elevator. It would have to be someone on her list of approved visitors. Mother. It was the only person who made sense since she'd been by earlier. Why hadn't she called?

Rowan crawled toward the door, then froze. She didn't want her mother to see her like this. She knew about her childhood visions. She'd been the one to teach her how to stop them. Horror filled her at the thought of her mother ever discovering she'd seen Zach in one. They never spoke of him. Hell, Mother still blamed her for his death.

At least she was walking, albeit on her knees, by the time she made the foyer. She clutched the nearby doorframe and hauled herself into a standing position, prepared for the headache to increase. But it was receding, leaving her whipped. Her legs shook as she stumbled to the door.

She pushed her hair back, surprised to find it damp with sweat. Maybe she could convince her mother she was coming down with something. The more plausible cover story was a hangover. That was something she'd believe, having seen it often enough.

The next tone, this time with a pleasant melody, meant the visitor was at the door. She took several deep, slow breaths before opening it, ignoring how heavily she leaned on it. Then her stomach heaved when she met the eyes of her visitor.

Keene caught her as she sank to the floor, a hand over her mouth.

Her head spun as she was lifted off her feet as if she weighed nothing. Her first thought was how glad she was she had to throw up. Otherwise, her thoughts would be tangled with how good his muscled arms felt as he held her close. But she didn't have to worry. A second later, the dizziness came back.

"Where's your bathroom?" Keene moved through her apartment, and she waved a hand in the general direction. She clenched her eyes shut against the harsh brightness of the room as it tilted. Maybe that was her.

He cradled her head as he set her down by the toilet with only seconds to spare. She dumped her dinner. A cool cloth was placed on her neck. A warmer one swept the sweat from her forehead and the sides of her face.

"Let me wet these down again." The washcloths disappeared, and she huddled against the door to the shower, her body trembling from dry heaves.

He pushed her head forward to place the refreshed cloth around her neck, then wiped her forehead again before handing her a towel. "Take your time. I'll wait for you in the kitchen."

When he shut the door behind him, her head fell against the shower door. He'd been her partner for two days. In that time, he'd been shot, chased, and had cleaned her up after hurling. Partners didn't get much closer than that. His actions surprised her. He'd been running hot and cold at her tagging along, yet underneath that rough exterior was a man of conviction. But what else could he have done when she all but collapsed, ready to vomit in the entryway? He could have just grabbed the closest reclamation bin. Or maybe one of the fake plants her mother had insisted on buying. She used to grow beautiful plants before joining the ISA. Before her schedule belonged to the job.

She rubbed her arms, forcing the chill out of them, then found her legs. Shaky at first, she made it to the sink and took the time to rinse the towels and wash her face. She dried the tips of her hair and patted at the wet spots on her shirt.

Keene was in the kitchen, and it looked spotless. He'd picked up the broken pieces of the cup and other remnants of her meal that she'd crawled through. He sat at the table reading something on a tablet while nursing a beer.

He glanced up and lifted the bottle. "Hope you don't mind."

She shook her head. "I might join you."

"Hair of the dog?"

She stared at him, and he chuckled. "It means chasing a hangover with more alcohol."

She smiled. "I like that."

"It's an old phrase." He squinted as he looked her over. "Are you all right?"

She sat across from him and waited for the first taste of beer to slide down her throat and hit her empty stomach. When nothing happened, she took another swig, then nodded. "It must have been something I ate."

"Remind me to say no if you ever invite me to dinner." When she began to respond, he raised a hand. "Don't try to convince me it wasn't your own cooking. I've seen the evidence."

On one level, it irritated her that he thought she couldn't make a meal without poisoning herself. Her cooking skills were at least one step above that. On the other hand, since it had only been a few hours since he'd seen her, it couldn't be a hangover. There was no way she'd mention the vision. He was already having reservations about working with her. He didn't need validation she was a basket case outside of work.

"Something must have been beyond its recommended expiration date."

"That must have been it."

"So why the house call?"

"I tried calling, but you didn't answer." He looked a bit contrite. "With the excitement of the last two days, I thought I'd better check in."

She glanced down and confirmed her wrist unit was gone. It must still be at her coms station after she had Hernandez reassigned. "Sorry. I took it off and must have forgotten to sync to the house communications."

"It doesn't do that automatically?"

That would be standard practice. The wrist unit was most people's lifeblood—health monitor, appointment schedules, personal contact information, access to their AVU, or other transit systems. It connected people to everything. As soon as someone entered their housing unit, the wrist unit uploaded to the house coms system. Everything on it could be displayed on any media unit with a verbal command.

"It used to." This topic would take them too close to the last op with her brother, and that was dangerous territory. "I rarely remove the wrist unit. But with my job..." She winced. "My old job, anyway. I sometimes need to get away from the constant chatter."

He leaned back and seemed to consider her answer. Now that she was an ISA agent, rather than a guard, she had no excuse not to have the coms unit on at all times, even off-duty. "We'll set up a schedule. It would be wise to have safety checkpoints, even if it's just a message. At least until we know who we're dealing with."

"That makes sense. I didn't think."

"We seem to have an unusual situation at the moment."

"On that note, I was able to find us some help."

"Your tech expert?"

She nodded. "She'll be reporting to me tomorrow. I thought she could meet me here, and we'll drive together so she gets familiar with the area. I didn't think you'd want a lot of traffic in and out of the bunker."

His gaze lit up. "That was fast. And how do you plan on getting to the bunker?"

"I worked out a ride. I didn't see a reason for routine babysitters."

"We'll have you added to our security system so you can come and go as needed. Conall will work out the details. That's his area."

"I thought you were security."

"He handles the technical stuff."

She took her time sipping her beer as she considered his words. If Conall handled the tech stuff, then Keene must be the muscle. A flash of those arms of steel as he carried her to the bathroom suggested he was probably very good at that. He'd already demonstrated his quick thinking the two times they'd gotten into a jam. She hadn't seen him in hand-to-hand combat and had to admit was eager to observe his skills. Conall might be the tech guy, but with his buff physique, she assumed he would be just as lethal as she suspected Keene was—but everyone had their specialty.

She was about to ask a question about their mission when she noticed Keene fiddling with her old timepiece. She'd dropped it on the table after removing her sidearm. Her first instinct was to grab it, but his curiosity as he analyzed it stopped her.

"It was an odd find. I don't know why I bought it."

"You like antiques?"

She laughed. "For some reason, mostly just timepieces. The good ones are hard to find—even in the Yards. And most of the time they don't work. I found someone who thinks they can get this one working, but—" She shrugged. "I would hate for someone to damage it. You know, mar the surface or something."

He nodded. "I can fix it."

She stared at him. He squinted, his entire focus on the watch as he turned the knob on top, then appeared to be looking for a place to open it. She reached for it, but he swatted her hand away. When she reached a second time, he grabbed her hand. She felt the callouses—a man used to hard work. Interesting in these times—unless you were a laborer.

"Aren't partners supposed to trust each other?" he asked as his gaze locked with hers.

"At work." What a weak reply.

"And the trust stops there?"

Before she could answer, the chime went off for the second time in less than an hour.

KEENE STOOD. "ARE YOU EXPECTING SOMEONE?"

Rowan shook her head and grabbed her sidearm. "They won't let anyone up that isn't on my approved list. Wait. How did you get past security?"

"My GSM ID."

Of course. She hadn't considered that. Her brain really hadn't recovered since getting pulled from squad. Then she remembered who might be on their way up, sighed, and laid her weapon on the table. "It's probably my mother."

Keene picked up his empty beer bottle and placed it in the reclamation unit. "Let's be sure, then I'll be on my way."

She tossed her bottle after Keene's and surveyed the room, checking for anything out of place that would result in a glare of dissatisfaction, assuming it was her mother on the way up.

He didn't say anything as she went through her usual routine of racing through the apartment, picking things up, stashing them in drawers, and nudging other items into place before scanning the results with a slight panic. She ignored his smirk.

When the second melody played, she ran a hand through her hair and grimaced at the damp spot on her shirt. No help for that. She gave Keene a quick glance, and she could have throttled him when his smirk changed to a wry smile. He seemed to be enjoying the show, not at all bothered by how unnerved she was about a visit from her mother. Maybe she wasn't the only one who panicked from unexpected family visits.

She opened the door to find not only her mother but also Kendra. Her mother scowled at her while Kendra rushed in to wrap her in a bear hug. She instinctively squeezed back, not wanting to let go. Six months since her husband's death, and not once had she ever placed blame. She loved Kendra all the more for it, as misguided as it was.

"We're sorry about the surprise visit." Kendra rushed to explain, attempting to be a buffer. "It's your father's sixtieth birthday in a couple of days, and we're planning a party. Almost everyone from his command has been invited." She couldn't seem to stop her chatter, which meant something was coming she wasn't going to like.

Rowan glanced at her mother, still poised at the door. After she'd attempted to surprise her at home, now the woman hesitated. Her mother made two tentative steps, then stopped and peered past her.

Keene.

She turned to find him studying the family drama. He wore his bland expression, but there was a slight uptick to his lips. He was amused. Only two days, and she already recognized his expressions.

"Are you coming in, or should I drag some chairs over?" She couldn't stop the snappish tone. She understood why her mother was angry at her, but it seemed she'd been mad at her since forever. Yet, maybe that wasn't entirely true. She'd always assumed her mother's indifference was because Zach had been her favorite. But after the vision she'd had earlier, a new realization popped. Her mother's behavior toward her had changed from a doting mother to one who always found fault right after her visions had stopped. Why hadn't she remembered that?

"And you are?" Her mother had marched passed her and now stared up at Keene, her tone as commanding as her father's.

She couldn't help but cringe at her mother's rudeness. A quick glance at Kendra revealed she was just as appalled.

Before Rowan could intercede, Keene stepped forward, hands in his pockets. "The name is Keene MacGregor, and I'm your daughter's partner."

A brow lifted as her mother studied him. Rowan tried to force the heat in her cheeks to abate, realizing her mother must have thought he was one of her one-nighters. Great.

She stepped in. "This is my mother, Mrs. Grita Lockwood, and Kendra." She'd stopped calling Kendra her sister-in-law ever since Zach's death. Not that she wasn't and wouldn't always be family—it was just one more reminder of what she'd lost.

Kendra appeared confused but adapted quickly. "You work for ISA too?"

"No." His abrupt response made Rowan cringe again. At least he'd delivered it with a charming smile that Kendra instantly returned.

"I see." Kendra nodded toward her but focused on Keene. "Well, this wouldn't be the first time Rowan has been on a secret mission." She hadn't skipped a beat, but it didn't prevent Mother from keeping the conversation stilted.

"Well, I hope she does a better job than on her last missions." Mother's stern tone made her want to crawl under a rock.

"I'm quite confident that Sergeant Lockwood has my back." Keene hadn't hesitated in his response, and she mentally counted how many cases of brown beer she'd need to buy to satisfy what she owed the MacGregor brothers. "And that's my cue." He turned to Rowan, ignoring the other women. "I'll see you in the morning. Oh eight hundred."

"Sounds good."

He strode toward the door with a smile for Kendra and a brief nod for Mother. "Ladies." And then he was gone, taking what little hospitality remained with him.

Mother ignored her and strode through the apartment like a drill sergeant. Kendra trailed behind, murmuring words too low for her to hear. She assumed Kendra was attempting to settle her—an impossible task.

"I think this kitchen is the cleanest I've ever seen it. Have you been eating out?" Her dig didn't go unnoticed, and Rowan's cheeks heated, knowing it was Keene who'd been the one to clean it. Mother turned, finally giving her the once over. And that brow went up again. "Your shirt is a mess. Is that how you dress for a meeting with your partner? And why did you get transferred from the squad?"

She ran a hand over her shirt, remembering Keene's tender care as she retched in the toilet. Then her mother's words hit her, already aware that Father would have heard about the transfer. She dropped into a chair at the table, reflexively reaching for her timepiece, the one item that always soothed her. She straightened. The table had been cleared of everything but a vase of fake flowers. The watch was gone. *Damn him.* Her anger at Keene temporarily buried the irritation with her mother.

"I have a lot of work to do before tomorrow." What a lie. "Am I actually being invited to the party?"

Kendra glanced at Mother. It was going to be worse than she thought.

"It would be unseemly if you didn't attend such a grand celebration. There would be talk."

Of course. It was all about appearances.

Mother took a seat across from her, and Kendra took the chair in the middle. Their mediator. Naturally.

Mother pulled out a holo-monitor and, with the press of one button, an image floated above it. If she had to guess, she'd say it was the Strand Hotel, her father's favorite hideaway. His gun club met there once a week for lunch, and the hotel's lounge was his favorite watering hole for the days in between.

She kept an eye on Kendra, who no longer met her gaze. Mother moved images around until she found one of a banquet room. "We thought it best if you made a quick showing just before his speech."

A speech. No occasion would be complete without listening to Father's bluster. The image zoomed in on a long table that sat on a three-foot dais where Father could stare down at his command. Good grief.

Mother circled a seat at the end of the table with her finger, the one closest to the exit doors. "You can come in once the speakers start. Everyone will just think you popped in from work."

While Mother droned on, she glanced at Kendra, who smiled and nodded along, but under the table, Kendra grabbed her hand and squeezed.

She pushed back the tears and settled in for the unpleasant visit. Her mother's words became white noise as she focused her anger on Keene.

If he damaged her watch, she'd kill him.

———

KEENE JOGGED down the stairs to the third level of the bunker, heading for the kitchen. He'd reviewed his visit to Rowan over and over during his return home. Her dinner had been a simple fare—pasta and salad. Nothing that would have caused her to be as sick as she'd been. Her squinted eyes had suggested a headache. A bad one. That could have initiated the vomiting. Completely plausible. It meant nothing. And he mentally filed it away as nothing more than that.

What he couldn't push away as easily was how she'd felt in his arms. A strong, muscled body. Lean and well-proportioned. A warrior's body. Her red hair had been soft and smelled of lilacs, right up to the point she'd tossed her dinner.

"There he is. What took you so long?" Lanis strode in from behind him with Conall in tow. "Horatio said you dropped him off well over an hour ago."

"Sorry, Mother, if I'm a bit late." He'd meant it as a tease, but it came out a growl as he dropped into a chair. Some days, he wouldn't mind a place of his own after living for so long in what was basically a commune. At times, his quarters, as expansive as they were, became confining. There were days he'd have been happy with a tiny tower unit similar to Rowan's where he could see the sky.

"No bickering." Conall placed three sandwiches on the

table then pulled two beers from the cooler before sliding one to Keene.

"He's two days late on the team reports. And he needs to contact Boris so he can prepare to come back early." Lanis pulled out her worn journal where she kept notes on everything. He'd snooped once and swore never again. She was the only one who could make heads or tails of her chicken scratch.

This might be the technology age, but each member of the team was required to keep a written journal, especially when on assignment. The most critical information was later transferred to the bunker's primary and secondary data crystals and was instantly available for research. The journals, once filled, were archived in the bunker's ever-growing library.

"We won't need Boris." Keene bit into his sandwich and followed it with a swig of beer.

"Why not?" Lanis looked doubtful.

"Rowan was able to get her tech resource reassigned to her. They'll both be here in the morning."

"That was fast. Did she call you?" Conall set a bowl of nuts, dried fruit, and cheese on the table before sitting across from Lanis.

Keene shook his head. "I stopped by, and good thing. She was sick as a dog." The minute he said the words, he could have slapped himself. "She swears this Hernandez is as good as Horatio." He kept his gaze averted and took another large bite. With any luck, they hadn't caught what he'd said, but he noted their quick glances and swore through his mouthful of food.

Once he washed down the bite, he shook his head and spoke again without thinking. "Don't say it. She simply had a migraine that must have upset her dinner." *Damn.* What was wrong with him? He hadn't wanted to mention her headache.

"Keene. You should have mentioned her headache right away." Lanis laid down her pen, her gaze unfocused.

"It could be a coincidence." Conall didn't sound convinced, but at least he wasn't ready to jump on the crazy train.

"That's exactly what it was." Keene kept his tone even. Getting upset would only make this worse. "People get headaches, even in this day and age. It could just as easily have been food poisoning. She doesn't keep a well-stocked cooler, and what's in there was probably well past its expiration."

They didn't appear to believe him, but he wasn't going to let them go on about it.

"One headache doesn't a prophecy make. The two of you are as bad as the Celts. Superstition and nonsense." When Lanis opened her mouth, Keene swept a hand across his throat. "Enough. We won't speak of it again. Those are my final words on the topic."

Conall laid a hand on Lanis's and gave her a stern look. "Keene's right. Redheads get headaches just like any other. Don't read too much into this. Not unless we have more proof."

Lanis glared at them, but her shoulders finally sagged. "Fine. But I'm making a note of this. We'll see how it plays out."

Keene sighed. He wouldn't have expected anything less. At least the two of them had gotten his mind off Rowan's body.

FOURTEEN

The two things Rowan loved about Hernandez was her ability to think three steps ahead and her uncanny ability to get into the heads of her targets. Once she hacked the system of a target, she monitored their communications for more than just their words. After listening to hours of recordings, she understood how the target thought and how they reacted, and immediately put together a cause and reaction ratio. She could determine what the target would do, almost before they knew it themselves. Both ISA and GSM had AI analyzers that did the same thing, but Hernandez did it in her head, which gave her an immediate advantage in time and human experience, resulting in a better accuracy rating.

She'd never considered she was a target in Hernandez's mind until that morning. Upon doing a bit of snooping, Hernandez discovered Rowan's unexpected family visit from the housing unit's security files. She arrived an hour early, knowing Rowan would have been up late drinking after spending time with her mother.

Rowan slept through the initial door chime and the next melodic ring, only waking to the pounding of fists on her door. After she stumbled around for a cup of coffee, Hernandez pushed her into the shower and ordered her to stay put for fifteen minutes. Pretty bossy for someone who'd admitted she'd hacked into Rowan's visitor log—for her own good.

She had to admit, the hot sonic blast made a reasonable effort at removing the cobwebs. Twenty minutes later, fully dressed and appearing sane, if not feeling it, Hernandez forced her to eat a two-egg tomato and cheese omelet.

Three more cups of joe later, the two of them searched the garage for her newly borrowed AVU. Gunther had provided the exact location, but the old clunker sitting in the marked space couldn't have been the one he meant.

Unfortunately, it was. The paint had dulled to a muddied patina of silver, rust red, and what had either been a green or blue a decade ago. There were two large dents on the admittedly sleek design—one on the driver's side passenger door, making her question if the door would open, and one on the right back fender. The windows were new. A small blessing. The AVU would fit four, but the back seats weren't meant for long rides if comfort was a concern.

The wheels were passable, but whether it was safe to attempt a jump to Zone 1 was anyone's guess. Hernandez stayed several feet away and gave her a hesitant look.

"I hope you didn't pay for this piece of shit, boss."

Words couldn't quite reflect what she was thinking as she shook her head. "It's a loaner."

"You did mention it needed to fly, right?" Staying a good fifteen feet away, Hernandez circled the vehicle like it was some wounded predator that might attack at any moment.

She sighed before mumbling, "Gunther has a way with vehicles." She opened the door, expecting the rotten smell of death and decay, and smiled at the citrus scent that permeated the interior. Then she backed up and waved a hand in front of her nose.

"Something dead?"

"Lemon."

Hernandez busted up and moved a step closer. Everyone knew Rowan's aversion to lemons. "And this Gunther likes to keep these wreckers around?"

After Rowan got past the cloying lemon smell, half preferring the scent of decay, her gaze locked on the dash. She almost wet herself with excitement. It was obvious Gunther had poured money into the tech. While the AVU had to be ten years old, the tech was top-of-the-line. The seats oozed comfort. She could spend hours on a stakeout without any complaints about her backside.

The passenger door opened with a grating sound that made Hernandez squint and hunch her shoulders, blocking whatever she was mumbling. Then she released a long whistle as she slid in and ran her hands over the slick glass imagers, not wasting any time punching up various programs. They spent fifteen minutes familiarizing themselves with every inch of tech and updating their ISA identifications, allowing the AVU to connect to both ISA and GSM networks.

For an AVU that had seen better days, it felt solid as Rowan drove out of the garage. They were overdue at the bunker, so she immediately punched it to Zone 1, knocking them both back in their seats. Once they were clear, she glanced at Hernandez. They both laughed and pumped their fists. They were still grinning when she dropped them to ground level to approach the bunker. Hernandez bent low to peer through the windshield, then pointed up toward the trees. Security monitors tracked them to the garage bay doors.

Once through the doors, she turned towards Keene's AVU. He sat on the back of the vehicle, and a quick glance at his wrist unit confirmed they were late. Hernandez scanned the garage, her expression dreamy when her gaze landed on the armored rovers. Her eyes twinkled when she spied the armory. A kid in a candy store.

Rowan ignored Keene's glower. "Sorry for being late. Completely my fault. This is Corporal Maya Hernandez, the best coms specialist in ISA." She turned to Hernandez. "This is Keene MacGregor." She paused a second before adding, "My partner."

Hernandez raised a brow before nodding at Keene.

"Corporal," he returned the nod.

"I prefer Hernandez." Her tone was matter of fact.

"All right." Keene led them to the elevator. "Conall's finishing up your security clearances. Your..." he turned back to stare at her vehicle, "AVU will be tagged before you leave."

She winked at Hernandez, who hid her smile by focusing on the floor.

"It got us here." She saw no reason to tell him what her crap AVU could do. He'd figure it out eventually.

They traveled down to the first floor and met Conall in the room across from the elevator. It could be a security room in any ISA tower. Banks of imagers displayed views from an array of inside and outside cameras. He'd definitely watched them drive up. The feeds were probably accessible from wrist units and terminals throughout the bunker.

After introductions, Conall added their fingerprints, palm prints, ear images, DNA samples, and retinal scans to the system. They were given ID chips to transfer to their wrist units, then added their individual security passwords to prevent anyone from stealing the information should their wrist units be stolen.

Once completed, the four of them took the stairs to the command center, which looked remarkably better than the day before. The only remaining evidence of destruction was the missing tech on the desktops and blank spots on the wall between the still-functioning imagers. A lone table held the remains of tech that might be salvageable, the pieces laid out in three neat rows.

Lanis, whose heavy mane of hair had been tied into a thick braid that hung down her back, pushed up the sleeves of her shirt and smiled, giving Hernandez a quick once-over. "Welcome. I trust Conall added you to our security system."

Hernandez and Rowan both nodded.

"Excellent. Then you'll be able to access our system straight away." She spread her arm wide. "As you can see, we're in better shape than we were yesterday. The system is fully operational, and most of the imagers survived. Fortunately, the holo-monitors were undamaged."

Lanis led them to the table of broken tech. "We haven't had a chance to do much with this stuff. Conall knows someone who might be able to fix them."

Hernandez stepped next to Lanis and picked up a tablet from the top left row. She looked it over, turned it on, made a few adjustments, then shut it off and laid it down. She went through all twenty items in five minutes, tossing two imagers and one pad into the reclamation bin next to the table. "Those don't have a prayer of being fixed. I know someone who can fix the rest. Two days at most." She stood at ease, her hands clasped behind her.

Lanis peered into the reclamation bin. She seemed tempted to retrieve the items Hernandez had dumped.

Conall grinned and clapped his hands. "Amazing. Horatio identified those same objects as damaged beyond repair." He tilted his chin toward Lanis. "She refused to throw them out." He winked at Lanis. "I guess you're outnumbered."

She did a passable imitation of the MacGregor brothers'

scowl before calling out, "Horatio. Quit hiding and come help Hernandez get acquainted with our system. She has full access."

Horatio crept out from behind a partition separating the workstations and banged his knee on a chair before shuffling over to meet the team's newest member. He winced as he hobbled over, lifting his leg every few steps to rub it. He stopped at a center console with dual imagers and waved Hernandez over. The rest of them followed, keeping a few paces back as they watched the two work.

After several minutes, Horatio leaned over. "Hey, what are you doing?"

When Hernandez didn't respond, Horatio took a step until they were shoulder to shoulder, blocking everyone's view. "How did you do that?"

Hernandez shrugged. "Something I picked up a few years ago. I don't use the trick often, but the security in this system will require a little more finesse."

Horatio stepped back to his keyboard.

This time Hernandez glanced over, and her brows stretched toward her hairline. "I didn't know that was possible."

Horatio grinned. "That's not all. Watch this." The wall imagers lit up with layers upon layers of code.

Keene pushed between them. "You're not playing around in Stoker's systems, are you?"

"Only the first level." Horatio sounded bored. "There's no real security at this level. Just basic stuff like temperature and lighting controls for non-secure areas and screen feeds for public areas. No one will notice."

"Maybe you should stop until we know what we're looking for." Conall probably didn't want a repeat of the kid's antics from yesterday.

Yet, Horatio appeared calm. His previous emotional breakdown had stretched their tolerance, but they had to consider he'd known the murder victim and two others who'd supposedly died from natural causes. He'd also forgotten his meds in their mad dash to flee the tower amid flying bullets. But playing around in Stoker's systems could prove dangerous if someone traced the hack back to the bunker.

Hernandez, known throughout the sector for never leaving a trail, shook her head, keeping her eyes on the display. "No. It's better if we practice. With two of us in the system, it's simple to leave false tracks and dead ends. On this level, no one will ever know we were there." Then she stopped, her brows scrunching together as she gave Horatio a side glance. "What did they say your name was?"

"Horatio."

She tapped a few more keys, then stepped away from her console to stare at him with admiration and something akin to awe.

"You're Teo."

FIFTEEN

Horatio grimaced before he slowly backed out of Stoker's system. Little bars in the top corner of the imagers began to wink out as layer after layer of code disappeared. When the imagers faded to green, he turned to Hernandez, his cheeks pink.

"You're pretty cracken." He shoved his hands into his pockets, his gaze dropping to the floor as he rocked back and forth on his heels. Then he glanced up, peeking through strips of bangs that fell over his forehead. "Almost as good as me."

Hernandez clapped her hands before performing a small fist pump. "I knew it was you." She could hardly contain her excitement as she eyed the rest of them. When no one shared her excitement, her expression turned to exasperation. With a hand on a hip, her tone reflected her disappointment in them. "Does no one here know who Teo is?"

Rowan racked her brain and came up with nothing. Then it hit her like a fast-moving monorail, but Lanis beat her to it.

"The Underground hacker?" Lanis stepped closer to Horatio, giving him a once over as if seeing him for the first time.

"It couldn't be. The kid works for the bloody GSM." Conall

sat down, scratching his head and probably trying to knit together the last two days.

"Of course." Keene seemed the least fazed by the pronouncement, giving Rowan a slight twinge. Had he known all along?

Everyone turned to him. With an unfocused gaze, similar to Conall's, he appeared to be replaying past events. Then he slowly nodded. "The intricate exits from your apartments in Topside and the Edges, all the time you spend in the Yards. You must have a third apartment there. That's where you do all your hacking."

Conall smiled. "Damn brilliant if you think about it. Who's going to suspect someone with such a high-security clearance at GSM of being Teo?"

"No one would ever consider the creator of Little Sister to be an Underground hacker." Rowan's grin matched Hernandez's, whose constant ogling made Horatio, or Teo, blush brighter as he examined the tips of his shoes.

"Why?" Keene's question was one of her own.

A question that required a decent answer before he could be allowed back into any system. One obvious reason for his hacking was disillusionment with GSM, and this was his way to fight back. Or, he was working on GSM's behalf, trying to sabotage and finally dismantle the growing Underground, an unidentified and impossible-to-find group that nipped at Topsiders, Edgers, and the Yards equally. The Underground stirred up division and, if not managed quickly and succinctly, could drive Earth to a second Uprising, or worse—another world war.

By now, everyone except Horatio had found a chair. With an encouraging smile from Hernandez, he paced in front of the wall of imagers, hands shoved in his pockets. He shrugged as he curled into himself, and his pacing increased.

"It's okay, Horatio. You don't have to tell us everything, just the basics." Hernandez's gentle tone slowed his pace until he hopped on top of a nearby counter, cleared since the previous day's carnage. He swung his legs, his lime-green runners almost neon in the glow from the imagers.

"It's mostly personal." His voice was so soft, Rowan leaned toward him. "But there's another reason. One you might understand. Maybe not." He glanced up, surveying them as if testing the waters. He seemed to accept their curiosity and current lack of judgment.

"On the whole, GSM's strategy to recover from the Climate Wars was sound. And they rebuilt the world in an amazingly short time, considering the destruction. But some of its tenets leave holes for manipulation. I believe that's what has kept the Yards and, to a minor degree, the Edges split from the mainstream."

"That's huge speculation." Conall's tone was casual, an opposing opinion, and Horatio took it as such, nodding enthusiastically.

"Agreed. But when a group of friends and I started hacking around the net, we found stuff that, on the surface, seemed normal, or at least not overly problematic or inconsistent with GSM's tenets. But there was only one way to really find out."

When no one spoke, he stared at them as if they'd missed the punchline.

Hernandez opened her mouth, shut it, then tried again. "That's when you decided to apply to Stokers."

"Wait." Lanis rubbed her forehead. "You're saying you were hacking GSM before you went to work for one of their most illustrious contractors?"

Horatio shrugged.

"How did you know you'd get hired?" Keene asked, but his tone suggested he already knew the answer.

"I gave them just enough information on Little Sister to make them wet their pants. I was hired the next day."

Keened nodded. "And that's when you leased the apartment Topside. You're from the Yards. Not the other way around."

"Technically, I leased the apartment before I applied, along with a credible fake background to allow me enough security to be effective."

Conall whistled. "It's been a while since I've seen anyone play such a long con."

"What's that?" Rowan asked. She had a vague notion but wanted to be sure.

"It's a con game. You make it look like you're giving your target something of value, but you're setting them up, so you're the one receiving the benefits. But instead of it happening in a few days or even hours, you've laid out an elaborate plan stretching for months, even years."

Lanis shook her head. "But they got Little Sister. That's not something without great value."

"But his little group is receiving much more." Rowan kept her tone even, but the ISA guard buried deep within her wanted to tackle the little shit. She'd bet half her ops, especially those that didn't go so well, had been his doing. "He's running most of the contraband in the Yards." It was a hunch but a decent one.

Horatio shook his head. "I admit there was a little of that over the years, but only to initially fund the operation."

"What operation?" Conall's pleasant smile at the kid's ingenuity faded.

"We give people from the Yards new identities so they can get better jobs Topside."

"What about their training and experience?" Hernandez perched at the edge of her seat, hanging on his every word.

Maybe it wasn't such a good idea to bring these two together. GSM might never be the same.

"That's where we start. We get the Upsiders into the right schools, then find openings where they can gain the required experience. Sometimes we have to falsify data that goes beyond their new identity. It's one of the trickiest areas. But then it's clear sailing if they pass the interviews, which is on them."

"Upsiders?" Rowan asked, but when she thought about it, it made sense. And Horatio only shrugged.

"Where do you get the housing?" Lanis's question was fair. Finding housing in the cities was difficult. You had to validate steady income within Topside or have grown up there to snag a unit. That was part of the growth issue and why so many ended up in the Edges and the Yards. But it proved to be a two-edged sword. Once you fell into the Yards, your employment opportunities became limited.

Keene grunted, running a hand through his hair. "A few years ago, it was easier to advance to higher-paying jobs, even if you lived in the Yards. That stopped with updates to a few of GSM's tenets. Now, for higher-paying jobs, you have to live in Topside. Anyone can still work Topside, but there's a ceiling on how far you can rise if you're from the Yards."

Conall whistled, and he leaned back, hands resting on top of his head.

"I don't remember that," Rowan said. Distant conversations from family dinners scratched at the surface, but she'd been living a different life at the time. She didn't pay much attention to Earth policy changes. Her life focused on the missions and having a good time afterward. Then Zach. Then nothing.

Keene continued, focused on the ideologies Horatio had touched on. "GSM was concerned about all the new children being born Topside and having available jobs and housing. With their attention turning to space travel, money for enlarging the regions slowed. The population growth hasn't."

For some reason, it surprised her that Keene was well-versed in Earth's politics. It didn't seem to fit with his security role. But he knew people at GSM, so he must hear things. Everyone in the bunker appeared more knowledgeable on the topic of GSM's tenets than she did. But with her cavalier lifestyle that continually irritated her family, she'd gotten used to her father and brother being her primary source for Topside information. Now, she recalled the heated discussions between Zach and Father. The two had very different opinions on the expanded reach of GSM.

Conall stood and clapped his hands. "I think we got a bit off track. We now seem to have two of the best hackers here. What do we do with them?"

Keene also stood and shrugged on his jacket. "First, we need a thorough background on Elton Sodowski. Personal and professional. I want to know what he ate for breakfast, who he was sleeping with, his specific roles in GSM projects stretching back five years, his hobbies, and associations."

Hernandez nodded. "Full history. We'll also pull familial relations, finances, and investments." She glanced at Rowan. "Three levels?"

"To start. Let's see what that gives us."

"Three levels?" Lanis asked.

"Think of it as an organizational tree," Hernandez responded. "We gather all their main connections, take those connections down a level, dig into those people, then see if we scrape up any new names. The second and third levels give us a basic outline. It's not nearly as deep as the first level but can kick up connections we wouldn't otherwise find."

"Perform as much of the first level as you can in the open," Keene added. "We need to show a trace that we're doing a proper investigation. But we don't want GSM or ISA to know how deep we're digging until we know what and who we're dealing with."

"No problem," came from both Hernandez and Horatio, the two of them already in sync.

Keene's smile appeared predatory. "When that's done, tell us how our dead guy connects with Horatio. There has to be more than an occasional chat. That information is only between us. And let's remember, Teo is his hacker name. He's Horatio to us. Absolutely no slips."

When everyone nodded, Keene pinned his gaze on Rowan. "And what shall we do today?"

She had one idea. One that his firecrackers had shaken loose. "We go back to the Yards."

SIXTEEN

Keene's mood turned amiable as he flew them toward the Yards. Rowan became more pensive. Hernandez's discovery that their prodigy wasn't just Horatio but Teo, a well-known but untraceable hacker, put a different spin on things. While the team seemed enthralled by the new dynamic tech duo, she had her reservations. She had to take Hernandez's word that the kid was trustworthy, at least for now. Horatio claimed he only had brief conversations with the dead guy. Yet, they were both informants, though Keene claimed he'd only talked to Elton once over the phone before he turned up dead. That seemed to put Keene in the thick of the mystery. A coincidence?

"Who's this contact of yours?" Keene had sunk down in his seat, his grip on the stick light. Even with a mundane flight, he refused to put the AVU in automatic drive.

She tapped her fingers against the metal casing of the side door control panel. How much should she tell him? It was best to share only what was necessary. Nothing more. "His name is Kai Li. He helped me out on a case."

After a long pause, Keene asked, "What made you think of him now?"

She had to laugh. "Your firecrackers."

When he lifted a brow, she shrugged. "I'd forgotten about him. He runs the West coast distribution of Xendran from Asia Town." Xendran was on the contraband list but for reasons other than the drug's primary purpose. The prescription drug was doled out in small doses to alleviate several mental disorders like schizophrenia. Combined with other known uncontrolled substances, the drug created hallucinogenic effects similar to the drug LSD made centuries before. "Or he used to."

Keene slid her a side glance, and the slight tic in his right eye showed the first indication of irritation. She'd picked up on that tell rather quickly over the last three days. "What do you mean used to? Shouldn't you know with all your agency contacts?"

She glanced out the window, unwilling to share how old her intel was. Let him connect the dots, which he did with amazing speed.

"How long has it been since you've spoken with him?"

"About three years, but he should still live in the same place." She gave him one of her stunning smiles. "Unless he's dead."

The tic moved to his jaw, but he didn't say anything. His charming mood seemed to have quickly disappeared, and not being in a talkative mood herself, she let the conversation die. Unfortunately, he had his own game to play.

"Does your mother live close?"

Her head spun around so fast, she could have given herself whiplash. She studied his rugged features, looking for some ploy, some little game he might be playing, but the tic in his jaw and the twitch in his eye were gone.

"My parents live in Decker Heights." It was a posh village in Topside that catered to the ISA brass.

"I presume it's your father that's also in the ISA."

"Why would you presume it's my father?"

He shrugged. "I would agree your mother could be an effective inquisitor, but she doesn't carry the ISA aura."

She had to grin. Her mother hadn't been kind to him, and he wasn't wrong. She could worm a confession out of a snake as well as her own children. "I'm sorry for how she treated you. Her rudeness was directed at me. She's long past caring who might get in the way of her barbs."

"Based on your sister's reaction, it seems like it happens a lot."

"For as long as I can remember." She surprised herself by admitting that out loud. It had been nothing more than a whisper that wasn't meant for his ears. She avoided his gaze as his complete statement hit her. He assumed Kendra was her sister. She was, but he wouldn't know she was her sister-in-law and not direct blood. She decided to leave it at that.

"I remember when my sister and mum didn't get along. We'd clear the room when they both got their dander up."

"It certainly cleared me out of the house when I was old enough."

"Your sister must take after your da." His accent grew heavy when he spoke of his family, and she shook her head to clear the warmth of it.

"What's with the family hour reminiscing?" She forced an edge in her voice—anything to get him off the topic of her family. She didn't talk about them to anyone.

His tone became flat. "I heard it was what partners did. Chatted about things in between interviews and running from bad guys."

The comment should have made her smile, but there couldn't be small talk between them—at least not the personal stuff. She turned toward the window, grateful to see they'd arrived at the same place they'd parked yesterday. This time, Keene parked under a large sycamore tree that would shield them from the public cameras.

She jumped out of the AVU the minute it stopped, not waiting for him to shut it down. When he caught up, he passed her, taking a different path from the day before. Once they were well into the Yards, she gave him the shakedown.

"I'll do all the talking. Kai Li is selective with who he speaks with."

"Yes, ma'am."

She sighed. If he was going to become petulant because she didn't want to talk about her family, so be it. Distance was a good thing. This was, after all, a temporary assignment. If one could hope.

After their experience from yesterday, they stayed on high alert while appearing to be spending another sunny day in the Yards. They'd arrived earlier than the day before, and more street vendors were out with their fresh vegetables, cut flowers, and trinkets. A few streets were impossibly crowded, but they worked their way through the throng of people, hoping to shake loose anyone who might be tailing them.

The streets thinned as they left Galway Alley and made a left turn down a side street that would lead them to the center of Asia Town. The one constant throughout all the Yards on Earth was that each district held the same monikers. With the high-speed transports that were available to every citizen worldwide, regardless if they were Topsiders, Edgers, or from the Yards, anyone could reach another part of the world in a matter of hours. Asia Town or Galway Alley could be found in Paris, Mumbai, or Rio. The unity showed promise to her, but after a short time with Keene, she might have been deceiving herself.

The street vendors were just as thick in this district, the only difference being the inventory sold. At this time of day, just like in Galway Alley, most carts were stuffed with their own varieties of vegetables, baked goods, and silks. When they entered the courtyard of a block-wide, three-story building, she noticed several possible sentries —two young men on a corner, an older woman by a flower cart, and a man and woman sitting on a bench. She gave Keene a side glance, and he returned a slight nod. He'd seen them too.

They didn't meet resistance until they entered the pristine lobby of the Lotus Hotel. Built in the style of ancient Japanese buildings, the interior spoke of past centuries. The expansive lobby was made of marble floors and columns, accented by dark woods. Japanese silk prints of cranes, dragons, and pagodas dotted the walls. Buddha sculptures of various sizes perched on tall, wooden pedestals that lined the edges of the room.

Low couches and tables surrounded what used to be the registration desk and was now a bar. From what she recalled, first-time introductions were made there during the day, while in the evenings, the men and women employed by Li could meet at the bar for drinks and relaxation while still guarding the front door. An elevator, the doors painted with flying dragons, was hidden to the right behind large ferns.

Two men, who bore the size and shape of Sumo wrestlers, sat in front of the registration desk. They were impeccably dressed in custom-tailored black suits that fit their irregular shapes. One of the Sumo twins stood and met them before they reached the desk. He had two inches on her, so she gazed up and studied his features. He looked familiar, but it had been too long for her to remember a name she'd only heard once. Did he remember her?

"I'm Sergeant Lockwood from the ISA. I was hoping Kai Li was in and could spare a few minutes to speak with us. We worked on a case together about three years ago. I don't know if you remember."

He studied her as intently as she had him before giving Keene a short perusal. "I remember. Do you have weapons?"

She nodded. "A sidearm in my left harness and a knife in my right boot."

"I have a knife in a leg holster, two throwing stars in my right inside jacket pocket, and a sidearm in my left holster." Keene's posture never changed, but he kept his gaze lowered.

The man shook his head, but she caught the turned upper lip of a possible grin. "Keep the weapons where they are. You should be advised you are on a security monitor."

"Understood." She nodded and held out her hands. "This is a friendly visit."

The man bowed and spread his left arm toward the elevator. "His office is still on the third floor."

She bowed in return, and Keene followed her to the elevator. They remained silent, knowing there would be listening devices in addition to the camera feeds. No one stayed in business long without tight security, no matter how relaxed and accommodating everyone seemed.

The hallways were quiet, probably due to the early hour. She should have called ahead or come later in the day. Some of these exporters worked into the early hours and would still be asleep, though she wasn't convinced Li ever slept. When they reached the outer doors of his third-floor office, two more security guards waited for them. This time they were tall, thin women impeccably dressed in black slacks and white shirts, dark-haired, and of mixed Asian descent. Regardless of the different districts, almost everyone in the world these days came from mixed heritage. While distinct cultures might exist and be nurtured in the Yards, one improvement from the Climate Wars was that no one cared about one's skin color or religion anymore. That was something.

The women moved with a languid grace as they each

reached for one of the double doors, opening them wide. Li enjoyed a grand entrance for his visitors. Rowan didn't let the women's sublime movements fool her. Their elegant poise hid skills that could easily overtake her and Keene if they didn't pay attention.

While the lobby was sleek and elegant, Li's office was warm and welcoming. The floor was covered with a multitude of Persian carpets. Dark-cherry bookcases covered most of the walls and were filled with books—many aged with time. More silk prints covered the limited wall space. The room offered two large seating areas. The one to the right circled around an old-fashioned fireplace. The other was positioned in front of an entertainment center with a bank of imagers, each displaying something different—a stock report, global news, a soccer match, and a shopping channel. The furniture was a mix of modern and ancient, some pieces probably centuries old.

Kai Li sat behind an immense mahogany desk, decorated with carved dragons. The desk held an imager, a holo-monitor, a dark jade Buddha, and a tea service. He stood and walked around his desk when they entered, a serene smile on his angular face. He wore his long raven-black hair tied back in a queue. He was dressed in black pants and turtleneck covered by a red kimono that he wore open. The long sleeves hid part of his hands, but they fell away as he reached out to take both her hands in his.

He gave a gentle bow. "I was so sorry to hear about your brother. He was a good man."

SEVENTEEN

The shock of his greeting had Rowan blinking back unexpected tears, completely unprepared for Kai Li's condolences. She hadn't known he'd met Zach, and was equally surprised he even remembered her. Though considering Li's illegal trade business, he probably had a dossier on all the local ISA guards. His expression revealed nothing, but she thought there was genuine sorrow in his gaze. It could have been a trick of the light.

"Thank you, Kai Li." She didn't want to be rude, but the topic made her uncomfortable with Keene standing behind her. "I'm sorry to bother you, but we hoped you might be able to help us with a case we're working with GSM. This is my partner, Keene MacGregor."

He dropped her hands, his soft smile replaced with an interesting twinkle in his gaze when he glanced toward Keene and bowed in his direction, receiving one in return. She waited patiently and let out a slow breath when his smile returned. "I understand. Come, let us sit in comfort and as friends."

He strolled with a stately posture toward the bar, a king in his domain. He waved them toward the sofas in front of the fireplace. "May I offer you something to drink?" He lifted a bottle from an ice bucket. "This is the finest sake in the world."

"We're on duty." It was the only way to refuse without offending him.

His smile grew wider. "Of course, Sergeant Rowan." She winced at the use of her first name with her rank, having forgotten he'd done that the first time they'd met. He turned to Keene. "Something else then?"

"Perhaps another time when we can truly savor the sake as one should." Keene took a seat on the sofa.

She sat next to Keene and leaned back, leaving plenty of room between them. An appearance of casual discussion would go further with Li than a direct interview.

Li poured a glass of sake and sat in the tall-backed mahogany chair that was polished to a high gleam by the hundreds who'd sat in it over the centuries. He swept the kimono aside, the sleeves falling to his elbows as he lifted the sake and took a graceful sip. His eyes closed for a moment as he savored the taste, then turned his gaze to her.

"So, what can I do to assist the lovely Sergeant Rowan?"

"We're trying to locate a man with a unique tattoo on his hand. We suspect it will be his right hand but could be on either."

"I see. And this is some form of Asian symbol?"

The question surprised her, but it shouldn't have. Most Asian languages used glyphs and the unique characters were often used in tattoos.

"No, but I can understand why you'd think that. This tattoo is some form of a Celtic knot." She noticed he had a second holo-monitor on the low table between them. "If I may?" She pulled out a small silver disk and held it up.

He nodded and leaned forward as she slipped the disk into place. The monitor instantly turned on, and the image of the tattoo lit up, floating eight inches from the base. She hit a second button, and the tattoo turned in a slow clockwise circle.

Li scooted closer, waiting for the image to make two complete turns before sitting back. He took another sip of the sake, rolling the liquid around before swallowing. "The majority of my enterprise is focused within Asia Town districts all over the world. But I occasionally trade with a few local districts, including Galway Alley."

She glanced at Keene, expecting him to jump in with his own questions regardless of her request to remain silent. However, he seemed more interested in one of the wall tapestries, so she nodded at Li. "We've spoken with several contacts in Galway Alley, but no one seemed familiar with it."

"Ah, which is why you thought to come to me?"

She shrugged and gave him a knowing smile. "It's no secret you trade locally, and while I know this is a long shot, I thought you might have seen the tattoo before. If not, then you might be able to provide some direction."

Li leaned his head back, eyes closed, his fingers wrapped tightly around his glass. She gave Keene a second glance, but now his attention had turned to one of the bookcases, his fingers doing a slow tap dance on the arm of the sofa. He appeared utterly disinterested in the entire discussion, probably thinking all of this a waste of time.

She hadn't provided much assistance since joining his mission other than suggesting a possible connection to the African Quarter and perhaps bringing in Hernandez. Of course, the two of them had never sat down to discuss the actual mission, assuming there was a deeper operation than finding Elton Sodowski's killer. Maybe that was why GSM retained Keene as a contractor—someone to flush out individuals attempting to divulge corporate secrets or, worse, GSM secrets. Maybe they used Keene to make problems go away.

She shook her head. GSM didn't do that, did they? Nothing like that happened in ISA, but she knew little of internal GSM politics, and what she did know came from her father during family dinners. At this point, she only had Keene and the major's word that GSM was even involved.

The quiet rustle of Li's kimono and the clink of his glass settling on the table snapped her out of her musings. Li's hint of a smile matched Keene's. Apparently, she'd been the only one daydreaming.

"Sorry. I guess I was lost in thought."

"Of course," Li replied. "Perhaps wondering where to go next if I had nothing to share."

She smiled. Li might rigidly follow specific tenants in life, but he always saw through subterfuge and other bullshit. "It's a never-ending struggle for ISA agents."

"No doubt." He clasped his hands together and held them in his lap, one finger tapping in time with a distant clock. "As I said, I do very little trade outside of Asia Town. Any local trade has been primarily with Galway Alley, Little Europe, and Hispana. But I once had an occasion to do business with Alaitheia in the African Quarter."

Alaitheia was a Creole and current leader of the African Quarter. The Quarter wasn't organized like the other districts, which were run by councils voted in by their constituents. The Quarter had no ruling council to speak of. Officially, to keep within the tenets of GSM, there was a council, but they weren't elected and had no vote. Council members were hand-selected by a single leader, who fought their way to the top. Alaitheia had ruled the Quarter for over a decade, and as odd as it might seem, the district ran like clockwork.

Li paused after admitting he'd done business with Alaitheia, and his face wrinkled with displeasure. "The Quarter can be quite unscrupulous." He had his own questionable business rules, but she decided this wasn't the time to point it out. "We had a common business partner, the Spider, who suggested a meeting that would provide a mutual benefit. She planned for more than one opportunity and introduced us to another person in the hopes of creating a triad. We had a single meeting, but nothing came of it. It was this man who had a tattoo quite similar, if not the same, as this one." He nodded to the holo-monitor, where the tattoo continued its slow rotation.

"Do you remember his name?"

He shook his head, and Keene appeared as disappointed as she felt. "He had little to say, but he wore a hooded cloak, which was one of the reasons I had no interest in pursuing the opportunity."

That made sense. Li would want to look his prospective business partner in the eye before making a deal. Most would. A hooded partner doesn't shout trust, and Li insisted on a personal connection with his partners, which was why he didn't do business in the Quarter and kept most of his trade within the other Asia Town districts.

"But you remember a tattoo?" This was the first time Keene spoke, and it startled her.

Li nodded with obvious distaste. "With his face hooded, it was all I could remember of the man. His cloak was unimpressive, other than the odd red fabric."

"Red?" Keene's one-word question seemed to be nothing more than a confirmation, but she noted his clenched jaw that lasted the briefest of moments.

"A shimmering fabric of deep blood red. His sleeves, which covered his hands, would occasionally slip back, revealing the tattoo. I haven't seen anything like it since." He pinned his gaze on Rowan. "I probably wouldn't share this with you if I hadn't heard that the Spider closed her deal on the triad. Alaitheia remained involved, though I don't know who their third party was other than they were someone from the Edges."

This last piece of information told her a great deal. If Li couldn't find out who this third party in the Edges was, it was a well-guarded secret.

Li stood, and she and Keene followed him back to his desk. He picked up his tablet, and a second later, her wrist unit lit up.

"You now have the Spider's information should you wish to question her. I would use caution when approaching, Sergeant Rowan. I don't do business with her anymore."

That spoke volumes, and she wondered why ISA hadn't known about the Spider. Or, if they did, why the local units hadn't been updated. Another task for Hernandez.

She held up her wrist unit as he walked them to the door. "I don't have anything to trade for this information. At least, not until I'm officially back with my squad."

"Perhaps I can help with that." Keene opened the door before smiling at Li. "I can offer two cases of Scotch whiskey for one case of your finest sake."

Li considered the offer, then countered. "Three cases of your Scotch Whiskey for one of sake."

"Two cases of Dalmore for one sake."

Li's brows lifted with delight. "Agreed. Our usual arrangement."

"Agreed." Keene held out his hand, and Li shook it before turning back to her.

"Always a pleasure, Sergeant Rowan. And you shouldn't make yourself so scarce."

Stunned by the exchange of liquor, she forced a smile and pretended not to hear the soft chuckle as they left Li's office.

Neither said a word as one of the female bodyguards walked them through the lobby, past the Sumo twins, and bowed before closing the outer door on them.

Their silence continued until they reached the first empty alley she could find. She shoved Keene down it before grabbing his arm to spin him around, pushing his back against the wall. He appeared confused, but it was his grin that notched up her anger.

"Why didn't you tell me you knew Li?"

"This was your lead. I didn't want to influence it."

She wasn't expecting that answer and could only stare as she fumed. What would she have done in his position? Probably the same damn thing. Neither of them knew each other well, and this had been their first interview together. She would have wanted to know how much he knew about a shared contact, and what better way than playing dumb and seeing where it went? Damn it. It still made her want to punch him. Although she mainly wanted to smack him because of that grin that turned into a gorgeous smile. He knew she couldn't argue with his tactics.

"And what did you do with my watch? I want it back."

His smile grew wider, making her insides churn. "It's in my pocket. If you'll let me retrieve it."

"Why the hell did you take it in the first place?" She took a couple steps back. "I told you it was important to me."

"Aye, and I thought you might want it to work." His brogue slipped out, and he cleared his throat. "I spent some time with it last night and cleaned the gears."

He dropped the timepiece into her hand, and she turned it over. The second hand ticked smoothly. She glanced at her wrist unit and mentally calculated the conversion to the old-time system. Keene had even set it correctly.

She blinked. Rapidly. Then stuffed the watch in her pocket. "Next time, ask first."

She stormed away, heading back toward the gate they'd

come through, unable to thank him and feeling off-kilter. She still wanted to punch something.

EIGHTEEN

Rowan strode through the streets of Asia Town, her vision blurred as she walked off the anger that clawed to get out. Anger at Keene. Anger at Cap for giving up on her because of one bad call—a call she still believed in. She fumed at her parents for moving her around like a pawn on a chessboard, using her when it was convenient for them before shoving her back in a box until next time. She was even furious at the major for still believing in her. Most of all, she hated herself for not taking that call six months ago. The one mistake she could never take back.

She brushed the tears away, infuriated by her weakness. At the edges of her anguish, the constant pounding of boots never faltered—Keene staying with her but not trying to stop her, following like a good partner. And she cursed him all over again.

By the time they left Asia Town, the vendor carts had changed from silk tapestries to homespun scarves and silver-smithing.

She ran out of steam before they reached the gates, and Keene forced her to stop at a table that skirted a food vending area filled with colorful carts. After dropping onto the hard stool, she hung her head in her hands, afraid to look at Keene. Would he be angry, or would his eyes be filled with pity? Several minutes went by before she noted the silence—but not of Galway Alley. The street was full of raucous laughter, shouts of friends, and the chatter of street urchins running from cart to cart.

No. This was the quiet that came when she turned off the world—like flipping a switch and being pulled into a different dimension. One where she could still see those around her, but they were out of focus, untouchable, and there wasn't anyone to help with the pain. If only Li hadn't mentioned Zach.

She sucked in a breath, ready to face reality when a cup of coffee appeared in her peripheral vision. The heady aroma gave her a lift she hadn't expected. Keene found a seat across from her. He leaned back on his stool, sitting sideways so he could people-watch, a steaming cup in his hands. His gaze was hidden behind sunglasses, and her stomach did a little flip.

"If I remember, you like your coffee black." He blew on his cup before sipping.

The scent of bold coffee made her grab the cup. The first swallow provided instant relief, and the building tension began to seep away.

"Thank you."

She should have said more but didn't have the words. Her emotions had messed her up and wouldn't be easily soothed. They sat in silence and drank coffee until the sounds of Galway Alley slowly returned, removing the stone of anger that had weighed her down.

She fished in her pocket and brought out her timepiece. The silver casing had been polished to a shine, the tarnish removed as if never there. She stared at the etchings, rubbing a finger over them. The tick of the second hand vibrated with each movement.

"I'm sorry I got mad about the watch. Thank you for fixing it." She wasn't sure he'd heard over the roughness in her voice.

"It was wrong of me to take it without your permission."

She snorted. "I would have never let you take it."

He grinned, though he still watched the crowd. "I know."

She tucked the watch back into its pocket. "Should we track down this Sheila Cross?" Li had sent the real name of the Spider to her wrist unit.

"Aye. The business and home address are both in Topside."

"Really? That in itself seems suspicious." The scent of a lead pushed her personal baggage into their respective closets with the doors firmly slammed shut.

He nodded. "I know it's backtracking, but I thought we could take a stroll through the Quarter."

She smiled. "Living dangerously?"

He shrugged. "I'm curious if we receive the same reception."

She stood and grabbed her empty cup. "Do you have your firecrackers ready?"

"That and my pulse gun." He stood and took her cup, dumping both in a nearby reclamation bin.

They strode through the Yards, jumping off and on the trolley to shake any tails. After the last trolley stop, just before the Quarter, they didn't slow to look at trinkets or the daily fresh fruit—no one mistook them for a couple. They fell into a familiar pattern as he monitored the left side of the street while she scanned the right. If anyone was looking for them, they wouldn't have to search hard. They almost shouted ISA, and people moved out of their way.

When they reached the center courtyard, Keene stopped at a natural herb dealer across from the five-story brick building that survived the Climate Wars and the Uprising. It had once been a courthouse but was now the central hub of the African Quarter.

No one bothered them. No one appeared to notice them. When Rowan glanced at Keene, he was speaking with the herb vendor, which seemed odd. No one spoke to anyone who even smelled of being an ISA agent. Not in the Yards, and especially not in the Quarter. When she listened in, he wasn't asking questions—he was negotiating a price. She rolled her eyes. He shopped more than Kendra—firecrackers, a bracelet, and now little bags of herbs.

After he finished his haggling and stepped next to her, she had to needle him. "Anything else on your shopping list before we leave?"

He shook his head. "No. But if Lanis knew I walked past a vendor with feverfew and chervil, she'd skin me alive."

"Well, we wouldn't want that." If it wasn't chamomile or lavender, one herb was as good as another. She scanned the courtyard for a second time. "We don't seem to have anyone's interest today."

"Which makes me question whether the crew that chased us were sent by Alaitheia."

"You think someone else?"

He released a long sigh. "I don't know. Maybe Alaitheia hadn't realized we were on official business and is now thinking better of her order. It's not her usual style, but it's equally difficult to believe another crew would step into the Quarter."

Rowan would prefer the first possibility, but without a sit-down with Alaitheia, they'd never know. But it was premature to call on her, and any meeting would require a trade. Rowan wasn't prepared to be beholden to the Queen of the Quarter. Not without good reason. Although, after his exchange with Li, Keene might have something to trade. He knew more people in the Yards than she'd previously thought.

She snorted, which caught Keene's attention. She'd let him wonder about it. The last thing she wanted him to know was how resourceful he'd become.

After ten minutes of people going about their daily business, she rubbed a hand over her face. "I have to be honest. Other than grasping one lead at a time, I'm having a problem seeing the big picture."

"Let's see if we can find the Spider. I have a suspicion that whoever our mystery man is, if he's operating in the Quarter, he either has Alaitheia's backing or she's completely in the dark."

They took the long way back to the AVU, walking along the outer limits of the Yards, where a diverse collection of wire fences, brick walls, and open fields separated the Capital from the open countryside. No walls kept people in or out of the Capital city, but there were outer perimeters marked by electrical-field grid sensors and satellite imagery. No one entered or left a region or sector without GSM knowing it. A friendlier way of keeping up with the citizens.

Exhaustion flooded her by the time they made it back to the AVU, any remnants of her earlier irritation long gone. Keene shot them up to Zone 2, heading to the business address they'd been given.

"We're heading toward the GSM campus."

"I don't think we're going to like where this takes us."

He circled the block twice. Any more would signal ISA, and while they might be on GSM business, with everything they'd learned so far, secrecy was their best ally.

When he set them down a block from the address, they stared at each other before turning their gazes to the glass tower. The offices of Stoker Industries. The place where Elton Sodowski had worked, where Horatio still worked, and now, apparently, the home office of Sheila Cross—the Spider.

"Does this seem a bit coincidental to you?" She strained her neck to glance through the front windshield to scope out the top of the building.

"The meeting with Kai was three years ago."

"Yeah. That doesn't make me feel any better. Maybe it was just a business arrangement about shipments of sake." Keene's grunt said he didn't believe that any more than she did. "Or it's someone with a long game."

"And that makes it worrisome."

"Should we go in or see if Hernandez and Horatio can pull some intel?"

"Let's be more discreet this time. I don't want our pictures on their surveillance records until absolutely necessary."

"They probably have the AVU on their long-range cameras."

"They can't trace this vehicle."

That seemed odd and added one more item to her list of questions regarding Keene and his bunker team. She held back the obvious question as to why the AVU couldn't be traced but had a strangely sick feeling she might get the answers she sought, whether she wanted to know or not. "Let's see what progress Hernandez and Horatio have made."

———

THE BUNKER GARAGE was peacefully quiet when they returned, and Rowan noted her newly acquired AVU was where she'd left it. She'd given Hernandez permission to use it if she decided the job wasn't for her or if she needed to get some headspace. The fact the AVU hadn't moved was a good sign, though the real reason Hernandez was still there was more likely an insatiable desire to be near her idol—Horatio.

She rubbed her head as they stepped into the elevator, wondering how she would explain Horatio to the major. Maybe it was best not to mention him at all. Any information they found would have to be linked to a legal search, which was one of the reasons Rowan had brought in Hernandez.

When the doors opened to the second floor, she stepped back, reaching for her weapon until Keene pulled her arm away.

"It's all right," he said, but he pushed her behind him as he stepped out to peer both left and right down the hallway.

Melodic music blared from the communication system. Though loud, it carried a soothing tune similar to the songs she'd heard played in Galway Alley. But all she could think of were antiquated cinema flicks where music played in a quiet home with bloodstains on the wall. Her focus instantly turned to the colorfully painted walls reminiscent of woodsy forests, searching for any dark stains that could be blood spatter. It would be hard to discern without brighter lights, but the browns of the painted trees could hide the evidence.

Her gaze was so intent on the wall in front of her, she hadn't noticed Keene step away from the elevator. His head popped back in with a wicked smile. "Are you going to stay in there all day, or should we find out what the music is about? Though I have a good guess."

Her hand rested on the butt of her sidearm still tucked in its holster as she took a step into the hall.

"What's wrong with you?" Keene's question made her spin toward him.

He stood, hands on hips, and she had to admit, other than the loud music, nothing appeared amiss. The lighting was the same. If there were blood spatters, they were confined to the wall murals. The grayish-tan floors gleamed, and the potted plants were undisturbed.

She straightened, letting her hand fall to her side. "What's with the music?"

"You've heard music before, haven't you?"

She scowled. "Not in the halls and not this loud. Is it playing everywhere?"

"Probably. When Lanis is in a mood, she likes to broadcast the music bunker-wide. Though usually at a quieter level."

"So that must mean something is wrong, right?"

He folded his arms across his chest and leaned against a wall. "I can understand why you might believe that and then become alarmed."

"You think I'm overreacting?"

That damn grin returned. "What do you think?"

Instead of giving him a snappy comeback, she analyzed the situation and her reaction. She nodded, only partially satisfied. "You know the building, the security, and the occupants better than I do. And while the last few days would give anyone the right to be cautious, I should take your lead in this instance."

"Very good. I imagine that's basic ISA procedure."

Her scowl returned, and he raised his hands in an offer of truce, yet his cool gaze held a hint of humor. Then his eyes refocused on something behind her.

She turned as someone stormed out of a door—any one of a dozen doors leading to unknown rooms. Her training and instincts didn't wait for her common sense to catch up. She drew her sidearm.

"Rowan, no!" Keene's shout could barely be heard over the music.

Conall dropped a tray as he rolled to the ground. Her arms were grabbed before she could lower her weapon, and she was dragged against Keene's hard chest.

Keene yelled, "Clear."

A moment later, Conall stood and brushed himself off. He looked pissed. "Woman. For all that's holy, what the hell was that all about?"

His brogue, when he let it slip, was typically light. Now, she could barely understand his words. But she'd heard the first word well enough, annoyed that Keene used the same tone when he called her woman. It was beginning to sink in that it wasn't a word of endearment.

She relaxed against Keene, her head bowed. She should have stayed in bed that morning. Her emotions were all over the place. If only Li hadn't mentioned Zach. When was she going to stop using her brother as an excuse? Maybe she should have taken Kendra's suggestion to continue seeing the company shrink.

Conall stared down at what must have been his lunch strewn across the floor. A bottle of beer lay in bits, a heady foam bubbling under the shards of glass. The salad greens already appeared wilted, the meat from the sandwich huddled in a lump against the wall.

Keene shifted and shouted above the music. "I think we need to review the security protocols with Rowan."

Conall muttered under his breath and turned an irritated glare at her.

It took her another few seconds to register that she was leaning against Keene's hard muscles and wrenched away. "I'm sorry." And the next words were even more difficult considering what Keene had said only moments before. "I might have over-reacted."

"Overreacted." Conall's voice rose an octave. "That was the last of me homestock beer."

She cringed, not really knowing what homestock beer was but understanding its importance by the look of dismay hidden beneath his scowl.

He shook his head and released a long sigh. "Sorry, lass. It's been another Horatio day."

"What happened?" Keene held an attachment for the kid. Whether it was his concern for Horatio getting hurt before his usefulness was complete or a wayward affection for the boy, the worry in his voice couldn't be mistaken.

Conall left the mess on the floor and walked closer so he wouldn't have to shout. "Let's go to the command center. It's best if you see what they found. It upset the kid, and Hernandez suggested music. Lanis turned on her Celtic music, and he immediately calmed down."

His brogue had disappeared, and she wondered if Conall's accent only came out when he was angry. She'd heard Keene slip into a light brogue. Perhaps strong emotion brought it on. If so, she was mildly disappointed she hadn't gotten Keene angry enough to hear more of it. She smiled. She'd have to try harder.

"Why does it have to be so loud?" she yelled. As melodic as it was, how could anyone find it relaxing at this volume?

"Problem with the communication system," Conall shouted. "Something about special programs Hernandez and the kid are running and needing the extra power. They bled some from the coms system, which cut the individual room controls."

That didn't explain the high volume, but she followed the men to the command center. Hernandez and Horatio were at the same consoles, both consumed by whatever they were tracking. The wall imagers reflected data whizzing by, confirming they were on to something.

Lanis spotted them and stopped at another console on her way over, dropping the volume to a more tolerable level. "Sorry about the music. I've found it takes fifteen minutes at that decibel range to calm Horatio down, but I have to admit, total immersion is difficult to walk away from."

"Says the musician." Keene handed her the bag of herbs he'd bought in the Yards.

Lanis opened the bag, whiffed the contents, and her eyes glowed with excitement. "I didn't think you'd remember."

He kissed her cheek. "Of course, I remembered." He gave a

nod toward the two at the console. "What got our young hacker in an uproar this time?"

Lanis steered them to a table where two data pads had been placed by a holo-monitor. Everyone sat, Keene in front of one of the pads, leaving the seat with the second pad for Rowan. It activated when she touched it, and an image of a conference room instantly floated into view. Keene made an entry on his tablet, and the conference room began a slow rotation until he seemed satisfied with the view. The holo-monitor received commands from both pads and would process the sequences in order of receipt.

She selected a command, and the image turned into a playback of a recording. Twenty people sat around a long table where the woman at the head of the table was talking. The sound had either been muted or was unavailable. The discussion couldn't have been riveting and reminded her of dozens of mind-numbing meetings she'd attended in the past. A few people listened, their gazes locked on the speaker, others fiddled with their data pads, some were taking notes, and others stared into space. One such individual sat at the edge of the image, his head down, his fingers rapidly moving over a larger tablet. A red circle appeared around this person, and since neither Keene nor she had touched their pads, the auto-command must have been added earlier by Lanis or Conall. It wasn't required. The lime-green runners were all that was needed to identify Horatio.

Next, a green circle appeared around a man on the other side of the table, two seats to the speaker's left. Keene selected a different camera angle to reveal the man's face. Their dead guy. Bingo. The recording must have been a meeting at Stoker Industries, but it might have been an off-site location. Wherever it was, and whenever it had occurred, this was their first validation that Horatio and Elton had been involved in more than idle chitchat.

Then a third circle appeared. This person lurked in the shadows, seated in a row of chairs against a wall where one would assume the person was of no interest and certainly had no power. The person wore a crimson robe which in itself wasn't uncommon. Robes were fading out from the fashion scene, but there wasn't a visible timestamp to determine the significance. Many people in research facilities preferred the robes over the drab lab coats. This robe was a bit unusual in the length of sleeves. The person was completely hidden within the robe, only the tips of shoes protruding from the hem. For a brief instant, the right sleeve slipped down the person's arm. The image zoomed in and froze.

A Celtic knot had been tattooed on the hand. The same tattoo they'd been chasing.

NINETEEN

"What are we looking at?" Keene asked. The holographic conference room began a slow, methodical clockwise turn as, one by one, the image zoomed in and out on each face in the room.

"A meeting that took place at Stokers about three years ago. The meeting was an hour long and gave us a clear facial image of everyone except..." Conall leaned forward and pointed at the robed man. He waved his hand through the image, temporarily disrupting it before it reformed from a colorful cloud of light particles back to the conference room image.

"Our mystery man." Keene gave Conall a glance Rowan couldn't interpret. But if she had to guess, the two of them knew something they weren't sharing. Maybe it was just a brotherly look of disappointment. Either way, her skin itched.

"What was the meeting about?" Rowan leaned toward the image. They would be extremely lucky if there was sound, but few meetings were recorded with audio. Most corporate offices had cameras mounted in hallways and various rooms for security, not for eavesdropping on meetings.

"No audio." Connall glanced over at Horatio, who seemed

oblivious to the group. "But the kid remembers the meeting quite well. That's what shook him up. That and seeing the mystery man in the shadows."

"So he saw his face?" Her excitement was short-lived when she caught Lanis's brief shake of her head. "How does a man keep himself completely covered while walking around a secure facility like Stokers?"

"As long as he had the proper clearances, no one would question him." Keene zoomed in on the tattoo. "But that also means all of the people in the meeting should have been logged with security." He was citing the standard security protocols. All GSM facilities and contractors kept records of employee and visitor ID chips, including their movements throughout the buildings—all in the name of security. Once they left the facility, the recording stopped.

"He was listed as a guest of Sodowski." Lanis took the data pad from Keene and pulled up the image of the dead guy. "No name was provided."

"And that's damn strange." Conall scratched his jaw.

"Aye," Keene confirmed. "There's something wrong with that. How important was our dead guy?"

"The meeting listed him as the sponsor, but he didn't appear to be leading the meeting." Another image replaced the dead guy. "Sheila Cross was listed as the team lead."

Rowan stared at the face before glancing at Keene.

He leaned in, recognizing the name Kai Li had given them for the Spider. "And now our mystery woman has a face." Keene shook his head. "And wasn't it about three years ago that Kai Li had been asked to meet with our mystery man?"

"An interesting coincidence." Rowan filled Lanis and Conall in on their morning meeting.

"Well, it appears we're circling in on them." Conall gave

Keene that look again, but this time Lanis turned her watchful gaze on Rowan.

The itch between her shoulder blades returned. Something was up with the three of them, and it didn't appear they were in the mood to share.

Before she could decide the best approach to dig into their secrets, Keene shut the image down and stood. "We need a background on every person at that meeting."

"Horatio and Hernandez are working on that now." Conall leaned back and stretched, lacing his fingers behind his head. "And we need Horatio to tell us what happened at that meeting. He was too hyped to discuss it earlier."

Lanis nodded. "For now, he's focused on gathering data, but we need to get him out of this room and into some sunshine. Somewhere less intimidating. Since it's past lunchtime, and apparently, Conall missed his meal—" She gave Rowan a smirk that made her cheeks heat. How did she know about the hallway misunderstanding? "Why don't we gather everyone in the garden?"

"You have a garden?" She hadn't seen anything outside the bunker during the flyovers.

"Yes. You've seen some of its bounty strewn along a hall corridor." Conall's firm voice said he hadn't quite forgiven her.

She was pretty sure it had nothing to do with the salad and everything to do with the broken bottle of beer. But she had overreacted and felt foolish enough. She stood. "If you show me where the cleaning supplies are, I'll clean it up."

"Right you will," Conall replied.

Keene motioned her to the door. "I'll help. We'll meet you in the garden."

She followed Keene out, happy to get away from Conall's glowering. When they stopped to gather cleaning supplies, she chewed on a nail. "How long will I be on the outs with your brother?"

She was surprised when Keene pulled out an old-fashioned broom, dustpan, and trash bin. He shoved them toward her, then retrieved the portable reclamation vac and led her back to the scene of the crime.

"Until you find a way to make amends."

She stared at the mess. The salad had wilted into dark-green slime, and the sandwich pieces almost made her cry. It would have been a delicious sandwich. Thick crusty bread lay limp on a shattered dish. The thin slices of roast beef were beginning to turn gray, and the cheese appeared stuck to the floor.

"Do you have any recommendations on how I do that?" She started toward the broken glass first until Keene stopped her and pointed to the spoiled food.

"Food waste goes in the trash can. Lanis prefers to make her own compost. I'll get the broken glass and dishes."

When she started sweeping up the food remains, Keene answered her question.

"Making a Scot happy is fairly simple. A good Scotch whiskey, a finely rolled cigar, or a buxom lass will usually do the trick."

She snorted. "The cigar is contraband, a buxom lass would probably earn him a punch in the eye by said lass as well as some time in harassment therapy, and I wouldn't know a good Scotch whiskey from Irish."

"And that right there tells me you don't get out much."

"You have no idea how much I get out, and my personal time is none of your business. Or did your previous eavesdropping into my personal life not teach you a lesson?"

He chuckled. "I don't need a lecture from you to understand how an ISA guard lives."

She bristled but said nothing. Their disagreement would

end up in a war of words neither of them would win. "So, basically, he'll be angry with me until the mission is over."

"Now, I didn't say that. You asked what you could do, and I answered. Barring any of that, which I understand could be difficult with the contraband laws, I still have a trick or two that will smooth his ruffled feathers."

Once the hallway was clean, they walked down to the third floor. Conall's initial tour hadn't included the third subbasement floor, but he'd mentioned it held the living facilities, including private quarters, the central kitchen, and recreation rooms. Keene led her to a room down a short hallway some distance from the elevator. She noticed a door to the stairway across from it.

"This is my unit." Keene punched a code on a keypad but could have used the retinal scanner or inserted a disk. And suddenly, the location made sense. The stairwell would give him quick access to the other floors. No one wanted to depend on an elevator during an emergency.

She expected a room with gray cement walls and minimal furniture. When the door opened, and he waved her in, she looked around in wonderment. The comfortably furnished room, complete with an entertainment center, two sofas and side chairs, a small bar, a simulation fireplace, and a large dining table, could have been any housing unit found in the finest glass towers. A single imager encompassed an entire wall and displayed a wooded forest complete with a babbling brook. The scent of firs and earthy loam made the immersion into the scenery complete.

An arched doorway led to a kitchen with a long counter that sectioned off the dining area. A hallway led farther into the quarters, which she assumed led to his bedroom and communication center.

"I'll just be a minute."

She waited as Keene disappeared down the hallway, unsure why they were there. Noises traveled down the hallway that sounded like he was moving furniture. A couple minutes later, he reappeared with two brown bottles in his hands that looked similar to Conall's broken beer bottle.

He handed her the bottles. "This should heal Conall's broken heart and have him panting after you once more."

She gingerly took the bottles but scowled at his comment. "Nothing personal, but I think your brother would prefer it the other way around."

Keene gave a short chuckle. "Perhaps you're right." And she was left to wonder at his half-hearted response.

She held up the bottles. "Is this more of what he called homestock?"

Keene nodded. "He doesn't know I still have a supply. So I'd kindly appreciate it if you tell him you begged for my last two bottles."

She gave him a wicked grin. "So, there are secrets among brothers."

For the first time since they'd returned from their earlier outing, he gave her his heart-stopping smile, and she ignored the heated tingle that swept through her.

Then he winked. "Of course."

She was the first out the door, needing to escape the intimate setting of Keene's quarters. If she had a clue where the garden was, she would have outpaced him to it.

Instead of returning toward the main elevator, they strode down several hallways leading to a different one. She didn't remember seeing the second elevator in the garage, but she never got a complete look at the space.

"Does this go to the garage?" She noted the elevator had the same three floors as the bunker and a button that read G, which she assumed was ground level. Yet something was different. The forest murals on the elevator walls were the first indication. The second was that the other elevator used an M, which she assumed meant the main level, which also happened to be the garage.

"No. This can only be used between the lower three floors and the garden. There's a third elevator on the other side of the bunker that goes to the garage. This is the only lift that goes to the garden."

"What is the garden?"

He looked at her as if she might be an idiot. "You've never heard of a garden?"

His smile irritated her, once again making her feel one step behind. "Of course, I know what a garden is."

"Well, you're the one who asked."

She crossed her arms over her chest and leaned against the wall, refusing to play his word games. She could wait.

When the doors opened, she threw her arm up to shield her eyes from the glare of the bright sunlight. She followed Keene out, stepping onto a real stone path that didn't lead down a hallway but through a maze of genuine trees and bushes. The vegetation was so dense they could have stepped into the National Arboretum. This wasn't a garden. It was a forest.

The trees were so thick in places that dappled light peeked through the leaves like miniature spotlights and was the only indication the sun might be above them. The path weaved through the trees for several yards before breaking into a luscious meadow. The verdant grass was ankle-high, bending with the tiniest of breezes, and she lifted her head to feel the sun and fresh air on her face. White, yellow, and lavender flowers dotted the meadow, but what drew her gaze and made her mouth drop open was the immense oak tree growing in the middle of it all. She'd seen oaks and other rare trees when she ventured to the arboretum once a month, seeking solace like other visitors. But nothing could compare to the symmetrical beauty of an oak.

Two long wooden tables, several chairs, loungers, and hammocks were spread haphazardly under the fully leafed branches. To one side, a short distance from the tree, a ring of chairs surrounded a fire pit. Lanis, Conall, Horatio, and Hernandez sat at one of the tables where several platters of food and two pitchers had been placed.

"How is this possible?" She circled, taking it all in, until Keene grabbed her shoulders and steered her toward the table.

"Lanis has a green thumb." Keene's flippant reply wasn't going to deter her.

"I'm not in the mood for bullshit."

When they traipsed through the meadow, she got her first glimpse of what appeared to be the sky. A glass dome covered the entire garden. "Am I seeing the real thing?"

"In a sense. The outside of the glass are holo-imagers that reflect a large grassy knoll to anyone flying over."

"Or seen on satellite imagery," she added.

"Exactly. But with the imagers, direct sunlight can't get through, so we use mirrors to reflect the sun during the day and stars in the evening."

"Why go to all this trouble?" But he didn't have to answer. She was stepping into their personal business. "Never mind. But someday, you're going to owe me an explanation for all the secrecy here. This isn't just some convenient bunker to live in, and you're not just anthropologists recording history."

"We didn't lie to you. We are anthropologists, scholars of history if you will, but we also have contracts with GSM." He grinned. "We have to have some way to pay for our toys. Now, enough about this." When he saw her protest coming, he raised his hands in surrender. "For now."

TWENTY

When Rowan and Keene were several yards from the table under the large oak, she couldn't stop her curiosity. "Those holo-imagers must take up a lot of power. No wonder Hernandez was siphoning power from other systems. What type of energy runs this place?"

Keene picked up his pace as if he couldn't wait to pawn her off on someone else. "I think it's some form of cold fusion."

"Cold fusion? I heard that was barely in prototype."

He shrugged.

"And that's why Keene's role is in security. We use a combination of geothermal and solar energy." Lanis's soft voice spoke with the confidence of a subject she knew well, and her practical explanation almost masked her irritated glance at Keene.

"Huh. Too bad it isn't cold fusion. I'd heard rumors of something like that being tested at GSM." She studied Keene, but his expression remained blank, so she filed it away as one more secret.

The others were well into their sandwiches, and Conall's brows lifted when he spotted the two bottles in her hands. She gave him a wry smile before placing them in front of him. "My way of apology."

He grabbed both bottles and turned them over in his hands. He shot an accusatory glance at Keene. "You've been holding out on me, brother."

Keene shook his head, taking a seat across from Horatio. "You started with four cases to my two. The fact you've run out and are now holding the last two bottles from my stores is a testament to your squandering."

"It's meant to be drunk, not squirreled away and preserved. You've never shown any respect to the profession."

"Enough." Lanis stomped her foot in the grass, and though it made no impact, it didn't slow her down. Her irritation grew, and Rowan suspected Keene's earlier slip about fusion hadn't lit the flame but only fueled it. "We have more important matters to discuss, so eat while it's still fresh."

Conall went back to his sandwich, though he pulled the beers closer to his plate and out of reach of others, as if anyone was brave enough to take one. While they ate, Conall entertained them with stories about Lanis and Keene, each retaliating with their own memories of silly Conall stunts. The camaraderie between the three and laughter from the rest of them eased the earlier tension.

When everyone picked at the remains of their lunch, Keene placed a holo-monitor on the table and waited for the conference room to appear.

"We need to understand the intent of the meeting and who the players were." Keene tapped his finger in front of Horatio's plate.

The kid was gorging on the remaining cheese cubes. How long since he'd last eaten, or was this normal? When he focused on Keene, he looked exhausted and a bit like a trapped wild rabbit like the ones she'd once seen in the Barrens.

"Tell us what you can remember." Keene's voice maintained a smooth warmth. Dark chocolate melted by the sun. "I'm not interested in the people right now, just the topic of the meeting." He let some of his brogue slip out with a melodic rhythm that could hypnotize anyone stupid enough to gaze into his eyes. If he had been a detective, criminals would confess everything. Thank the stars she had more control.

Hernandez squeezed Horatio's arm for encouragement. "Can you remember who invited you to the meeting?"

Horatio's head bobbed. "My boss. She said it was mandatory." His leg bounced, either from pent-up energy, anxiety, or sheer terror. It was too early to tell. He ran a hand through his hair before lifting his head. His leg slowed as he sucked in a breath. "I get called into meetings a lot, mostly to listen and report whether I thought the project had merit. You know, like if it was realistic, not too far out there. I wasn't part of the teams. I was more of a truth monitor. We worked out a rating system."

"Like a temperature?" Rowan asked.

"Exactly. Is the science valid? Was the right team assembled? That one was tougher because I usually don't know the teams. Many were from other regions, hoping to grab some of the annual budget. So all I could do was see how they worked together. Whether their part of the project fit. I think she just wanted to know if the team lead was padding the project."

"Ensuring no one was getting money that could be better spent elsewhere." Keene nodded along with Horatio, whose bouncing leg had slowed to an occasional tic.

"Right." Horatio sat up, finding comfort in a safer topic. "There's a lot of waste. If you can get one project funded that won't take as long as originally forecasted, you can sneak in pet projects that wouldn't normally get approved. Once a project is funded, they monitor the spending but not how the money is applied to the project."

"Because until recently, they haven't had to worry about where the money was coming from." Keene appeared disgusted, which she found interesting. Maybe he was more ethical than she'd originally thought.

"I'd heard that was changing." It had been one of the last dinner arguments between her father and Zach.

"I'd heard that too." Hernandez squinted, a sign she was trying to recall where she'd heard it, but she shook her head. "I didn't hear it. It was in a coms message I'd read. But that was months ago."

"It started way before that, but just a project here and there." Horatio hit a button on the holo-monitor, and the image began its slow rotation. "This was one of the first pilot projects where GSM would provide more oversight." His leg bounce returned, picking up a steadier rhythm. "The tension in the room was high. More so when three other people joined us after the meeting started."

"Is this your boss?" Keene pointed to Sheila Cross.

Horatio shook his head. "No. That's the project leader. They call her the Spider."

"Why?" Lanis popped a handful of grapes in her mouth, appearing somewhat bored.

Horatio shrugged. "Not sure. The rumors say she brings in specialists to get through the initial budget meetings to make the projects sound realistic, then she cuts them after they get their funding."

"That's an old trick that's been going on for years." Rowan remembered her father laughing about it, though he found the practice distasteful.

"And the reason for the political shakeup up top." Conall tapped his finger on the second bottle of homestock. The first bottle had disappeared in three swallows. He seemed to be savoring this one. Then his words sank in. She hadn't pegged

Conall for someone interested in politics. "The new blood wants to clean up the wasteful spending. Especially with the new space program well underway."

"What was this meeting about?" Keene refocused Horatio down his original path, keeping his tone soft.

"They wanted to fund a project developing a new material called XR454."

Lanis gasped. XR454 was a recently discovered, unstable byproduct that had decimated a small research station in the Nairobi sector. If used in small quantities, it proved to be a reliable energy source, reducing the footprint of energy requirements a thousandfold—assuming nothing blew up in the process. But neither the gasp nor mention of the explosive material had caught Rowan's attention. It was the furtive glance between Lanis, Keene, and Conall. She was getting tired of their secrets. They knew something about this product, and their worried expressions made her gut clench.

"What are they up to?" Lanis rubbed her forehead.

Horatio assumed it was a literal question and provided the answer. "According to the Spider, the material was to power the sleeping pods required for long-distance space travel, cutting down the weight of the space shuttles."

"It makes sense if you don't care that you're sleeping next to a ticking bomb," Conall muttered.

Horatio shook his head. "The current energy protocols for the sleeping pods aren't that heavy. If they want to use XR454, they could find a better use for it."

"Okay, let's not get buried in what they want it for." Keene tapped the monitor to stop the rotation. "Chances are it was a ruse for their true intentions." He zoomed in on their mystery man. "Can you tell us who this man is?"

Rowan wasn't convinced the project's true intent wasn't important, but Keene was right to keep Horatio focused because the bounce in the kid's leg increased as he studied the image. But Horatio wasn't really looking at the holo-monitor. His head had turned toward it, but the minute he saw the man in the robe, his eyes dropped just a fraction. She could be wrong, but she'd watched hundreds of people in interviews. Interpreting body language was a skill. One she'd gotten good at over the years.

Horatio wanted to curl into a ball, but he was fighting it. He was scared, and Hernandez must have sensed it too because she touched his arm as she'd done earlier. His leg bounce decreased, but he didn't answer the question.

Keene shut down the monitor and leaned back. "My guess is that he was never introduced. He slipped in after the meeting started, then left before the meeting ended."

Horatio's leg bounce stopped, and his head popped up. His features relaxed into a small smile as he nodded agreement.

When she glanced at Keene, his entire focus was on the kid. He seemed to read people as well as she could—and that was saying something, all modesty aside.

"That's exactly how it happened." Horatio became more animated. "We were about fifteen minutes into the meeting. I don't think anyone heard the door open. You know how when someone comes in after a meeting has started, someone always looks up. But no one did. The guy was stealthy, even with two guys following him. He was almost invisible. And it wasn't like the Spider was any type of motivational speaker. The first part of the meeting was about budget and finances, which bore most people. Once this guy showed up, she started on the purpose of the project. He left once the Spider finished the presentation and everyone began asking questions."

"Did you ever see his face? Even a bit of it?" Hernandez asked, her hand resting on his arm, a smile that seemed only for him.

At first, Horatio shook his head, then he glanced up at Keene. "Can you run the image again? Keep it on a slow rotation."

After the image played twice, Horatio asked, "You didn't get the whole recording?"

"That was all there was," Conall responded.

Horatio shook his head. "No. The protocol is always the same. Meetings are scheduled in advance. When the meeting time comes, the recorder automatically starts and continues until the end of the scheduled time. If the meeting runs long, you can manually extend the time but can't stop it early. That's to prevent tampering or hiding something because you know you're being recorded. This meeting ended right at the hour mark." He pointed to the time indicator at the bottom, which Rowan hadn't noticed before. "You're missing five minutes."

"How could they have modified this recording, and why?" Lanis asked.

"This is where I'd seen the tattoo for the first time." Horatio's excitement increased. "I tried to get a look at his face, but the hood was in the way. I thought maybe the cameras might have shown us more. Since he left before the end of the scheduled meeting time, we should see him stand and leave. But the recording ends before then. Someone cut that piece out."

After a few seconds, Hernandez suggested a possibility. "If they copied the recording, modified it, and then reloaded it…"

"The editing would have to be perfect, but it's not impossible," Horatio finished for her as they both began speaking rapidly.

"It would leave a ghost where the recording was edited. But that would only prove it was edited not tell us what was cut."

"We need the original."

"They would have copied over the backup too."

Horatio's leg bounced again, but this time for a different

reason. He wanted his hands on a keyboard. "But they might not know about the vault."

"That really exists?" Hernandez's eyes glazed with that furor she got just before a mission.

Everyone turned to Horatio. He grinned at Hernandez while the rest tried to keep up with their rant.

"What the hell is the vault?" Conall finally asked.

"I've heard of it," Rowan said. "But I thought it was an old tech tale from the Climate Wars." Something else she'd learned from her father, although that conversation wasn't meant to have been overheard.

She hid a lot while growing up. It was her way of avoiding the commands and shouting when she'd done something else wrong. She had several hiding spots where she could squeeze in with a book or her music and ignore the world. It hadn't been her fault Father had come home early and hid in Zach's room to make a secret call. She often used Zach's room to hide because no one ever questioned him, and it would be the last place anyone would look for her.

She would have ignored the entire conversation if Father hadn't spoken in whispers she had to strain to hear. He kept saying, "Bury them in the vault." At the time, she thought he'd been talking about dead bodies. It was years later when she'd heard the rumor of the vault that the memory resurfaced.

Horatio turned to the group, eager to share his knowledge. "The vault was used by the military when the Climate Wars broke out. A place to hide secret files, videos, documents, whatever. After the war, part of GSM's mission was to restore what they could from before the Wars. That's when they discovered the vault."

"How do you know so much about this?" Lanis asked.

"They make new employees take the GSM history tour at the Capital's visitor center. It was one of the side exhibits."

"And you think they're still using the vault?" Keene asked, but his head turned toward Lanis and Conall, and she couldn't read his expression.

"I know they are. About six months after I started, the project I'd been hired for was shut down. They had another project lined up, but it was delayed for three months, so they put me in the records department helping to reorganize data files. It was a temporary assignment, but it gave me access to GSM's filing system and the network, which is pretty massive. They didn't know how boring that would be after the first couple of days." He chuckled, and Hernandez snorted in agreement.

"I started digging around, performing the secret research I'd originally planned when applying to work at GSM. It was pretty simple to get past most of the security protocols. Then I remembered the history of the vault. The exhibit made it sound as if it was just a historical footnote, but I wanted to know if it still existed."

Rowan snorted. "And you discovered it did." The Yarders should thank whatever spiritual gods they believed in that Horatio was on their side. He was proving to be quite the formidable resource.

Horatio shrugged. "It wasn't that difficult to find once you looked for it. I mean, not for someone like Hernandez or me." His cheeks turned a slight pink when he glanced at her, but she seemed too starry-eyed by his brilliance to notice.

"That's your next task." Keene stood, picked up his plate, and placed it on the tray. "We still need a complete background on everyone at that meeting, but let's see if we can find the original recording first. We need to confirm this mystery man has the tattoo, and maybe we'll get lucky enough to get a glimpse of his face."

Hernandez picked up the empty cups before Conall

nudged her aside. "You two get started. And if you find the vault, copy the whole blasted thing if you can."

"If they were copying everything into the vault, that would be a lot of data." Hernandez sounded skeptical.

This time, Conall smiled as if he had his own secret. "Lanis will show you the library and where the extra data crystals are stored." He turned to Rowan. "Let's help with clean up, and then you'll get the full security tour. No more drawing a weapon on me in my own house."

TWENTY-ONE

Rowan sighed with relief when she slid onto the torn seat of a back booth in Duster's bar. Hernandez dropped into the opposite seat, her excitement still bubbling. She'd spent the rest of the afternoon with Horatio searching for, then finding, the vault.

Conall and Keene had dragged Rowan through every inch of the bunker. While there were only three underground floors, each floor was as spacious as two tower floors combined. A quarter of each floor housed the utilities, air scrubbers, generators, and such that made the bunker livable. She and Hernandez had been given their own guest housing unit. A place to rest or find solitude, something Lanis insisted on. Rowan doubted she'd ever use it, but with the number of hours Hernandez spent staring at imagers, she would need a place to rest and clear her head.

They ordered two mugs of dark brew. Neither spoke while they waited. Hernandez laid her head back on the seat, eyes closed, her breathing slow and steady. Rowan scanned the place, not looking for anything particular other than making sure nothing appeared threatening. It was an instinctual maneuver for any ISA guard and possibly a residual after-effect of being chased twice in the same number of days. Hernandez's head popped up a minute before the mugs arrived like she could smell them coming. Fat creamy heads gave them foamy mustaches, and they grinned like teenagers.

"Thanks for hooking me up with this assignment." Hernandez's expression was earnest, but Rowan ignored the gesture. She needed to say it, and now she had.

"Did you have any problem finding the vault?"

"No. Horatio went right to it. I think he's been dipping into it since he went to work for Stokers. But I don't think he's gone very deep—only the second level." Hernandez tapped her fingers on the sides of the mug. "Our first problem was getting to the third level." Her gaze glittered with humor, and she tweaked her lips into a half-smile. "I was the one that cracked it."

Rowan blew out a whistle before taking a swig of beer. A twinge in the back of her neck made her question whether Horatio had only gotten to the second level. Maybe he was being truthful, or maybe he'd gotten deeper and just wanted to give Hernandez a win. Mostly, she wanted them to find something that would connect the dots that told them what was so important it required killing people. She decided for one night, while Hernandez was on a high, to keep the train rolling. "I've always said you've never given yourself enough credit. What did Horatio say?"

Her cheeks flushed, and she dropped her gaze, the foam on the beer apparently more interesting. After a few seconds, she mumbled, "He thinks I'm the best he's ever seen."

"Ha!" Rowan slammed the table, which caused heads to turn. "I told you."

"He was just being nice." But she lifted her chin, her grin wide.

"Why do you think I asked for you in the first place?"

That gave her pause, and she shrugged. Then Hernandez blindsided her, deftly moving the topic away from herself. "I saw in the news that your dad is celebrating a birthday."

Rowan slumped in her seat, pulling the mug to the edge of the table so she wouldn't have to reach so far. After several gulps, she released a small burp then fell back. "I can't believe something like that would be in the news."

"It was in the entertainment section, if that helps."

"Not really."

"Have you figured a way out of it?" She winced. "Sorry. Were you invited?"

Rowan laughed, and suddenly the whole thing was nuts. "Barely. Mother and Kendra ambushed me at home last night. Not only did I get an invite, but I've been given the exact time to enter stage left, get myself noticed as the attentive, hard-working daughter, then exit stage right. All quite proper and well-organized. Mother would have made the perfect logistics officer."

Hernandez lifted her mug, only a quarter of it remaining. "To family we can't choose."

They clinked mugs, and Rowan raised an arm toward the bar to signal another round. "What's it like in the bunker when Keene and I are gone?"

Hernandez gave it some consideration, draining her mug as the next one arrived. "Conall comes and goes. Likes to tinker with stuff when he's in the command center, which isn't very often. And then we have Lanis, who never leaves the command center. At first, I thought it was to keep an eye on us, and maybe it was. But she typically has her head buried in her journal or wears that ocular piece when studying the holo-monitor. I think there were times I could have raced out of the room screaming, and she wouldn't have noticed. She gets pretty focused on her work."

"Do you know what kind of work?"

"No. Don't you?"

Rowan shook her head. "Not really. They told me they were anthropologists."

"That seems to fit with what Lanis was doing. Studying old things."

She gave a short grunt and drank. "I know they seem like nice people." She thought about Keene and his hot and cold temperament. "Most of them." Hernandez gave her a knowing grin. "Anyway, it wouldn't hurt to keep an ear open. The major didn't give me any background on Keene or his mission, and she's been impossible to track down. Other than this dead guy Elton, I have no idea how Keene's connected with GSM or why they would call him in."

"How did he find Horatio?"

"From the way Keene explains it, Horatio has been a long-time informant. I don't know how long or why he needed an informant in the first place. Maybe that's something you could discuss with Horatio."

Hernandez stared into her beer again. What Rowan asked could jeopardize her growing relationship with the kid. She shrugged. "It's a fair question to ask how he knows Keene. I'll test the waters." Then she locked gazes with Rowan, her chin jutting out like it did when she was getting her stubborn on. "But if he doesn't want to talk about it, I'm not going to force it."

She softened her expression. "Understood."

Hernandez finished her beer and checked her watch. "The squad should still be at the Zone. I thought I'd meet up with them and see what they're hearing. If anything."

She nodded. "I don't have to tell you."

"That everything we're doing is classified? The team knows not to push."

"I know. It just makes me feel better to have said it."

Hernandez stood and punched her arm. "You've done your due diligence. Will you be okay?"

She glanced up and laughed at her friend's wicked smile. "If you mean am I okay to drink myself silly, maybe get laid, and still make it home in time for your early morning wake-up call—consider it just another day." She lifted her mug, still half full, and winked.

Hernandez strutted out of the bar, several eyes following her backside. Once she was gone, Rowan moved to the bar and chatted with the bartender before going home.

It was early, not quite eight, and she buzzed around the city in Zone 3 to let the AVU stretch itself. Still smiling and patting the dashboard, pleased with her new ride, she parked the vehicle in the special spot Gunther had reserved for her. More likely, he'd selected the space to ensure his AVU remained safe. She'd consider buying it if Gunther would sell it. She had money saved up, and it would be worth every credit.

When she strode into the lobby, she'd missed Gunther by minutes, and though a little disappointed, she shrugged her shoulders. Tomorrow would be soon enough. A few steps from the elevator, someone called her name.

She turned to find Kendra rushing up, her face friendly, but it was easy to see the worry reflected in her honey-colored eyes.

"Kendra. What's wrong?"

Kendra hugged her and whispered, "Let's go up first." She smiled and grabbed onto Rowan's arm as they stepped into the elevator. Once inside, her words tumbled out. "I'm so happy I was able to find you. I wasn't sure how late you might be working, and I know I should have called, but I just needed to talk to you. It's been so long."

She didn't respond, somewhat startled by Kendra's words. Since they'd just seen each other the previous night, she had to assume Kendra was being overly enthusiastic for the security system that monitored the lift and hallways.

She led Kendra to her unit, rubbing her back as if encouraging her to talk.

Once the door shut, Kendra's entire demeanor changed. She released Rowan's arm and strode into the kitchen. By the time Rowan entered, she had pulled out two small glasses, added ice cubes, and moved to the opposite counter. She searched through Rowan's limited supply of liquor, checking labels before deciding on vodka. She filled both glasses to the brim.

Without a word, Kendra glided to the living room, where she set down the second drink before falling onto the couch, somehow not spilling a drop of her own. She drank a good quarter of it before Rowan sat, feeling obligated to at least take a sip.

"Where are the kids?" They were too young for Kendra to have left them home alone. But since she was acting wildly abnormal, the question seemed fair and the safest place to start the conversation.

"They're with your mother. I told her a friend was in town for the day and wanted to have dinner. I thought I'd have a better chance of finding you after work." She sipped the vodka. "I hope you don't mind."

She studied her sister-in-law. Her hands trembled, and her voice was shaky, all hidden behind false bravado. "What's wrong?"

Her meager smile matched her tired gaze. "I'm sorry about yesterday. I told your mother we shouldn't have ganged up on you. She was being silly with all her restrictions and demands. You're still their daughter."

"They'll never forgive me for Zach." She stared at the floor. An automatic response so she wouldn't have to see the pity in Kendra's eyes.

"That's on them. It wasn't your fault, and we've been over this." Kendra flopped back in her seat, and Rowan grimaced as she gulped rather than sipped her drink. "I'm here for another reason."

"When did you start drinking like a fish?"

She quirked a brow. "You noticed?" She let out a long breath, took a small sip, then another, then laughed. "I guess it's connected to the reason I'm here."

"Don't make me ask."

Without pause and with a hysterical chirp, she said, "It's your mother."

Rowan had no idea what she'd expected Kendra to say, but she'd caught her off guard in the lobby. She'd had a good reason to drink since Zach died, but she'd handled her grief in her typical fashion—calmly, generously, and privately. Being driven to drink wasn't her style. But that simple word—Mother—said everything as the tumblers fell into place.

"She's smothering you."

"Oh my god, Rowan." She leaned toward her, tears glistening, and set down her glass before grasping Rowan's hands. "We've always had a connection. The two of us. Zach always said that. You've been my bedrock since his death."

She pulled away, stunned, but Kendra wouldn't let go of her hands. "That's crazy talk. I've been doing my best to ignore you."

Kendra laughed, pulling her in with a tighter grip. "You've been there when I needed you. And that's what matters. But your mother?" She shook her head, and her voice dropped to a whisper. "I can't take it anymore."

She understood. There had been a time when Mother smothered her with attention, but that was long ago when she was still young. Before the headaches. Before she began to rebel against the strict rules and heavy punishments for stepping out of line. Then Mother's attention focused on Zach. It wasn't all the time.

Mother had her friends and hobbies, but when she was thrown for a loop, her world unsettled, the smothering began. Zach would come to Rowan, hoping she could deflect some of it. Since Mother no longer lavished her affection on her, Rowan stirred the pot so both their parents would be so consumed with anger at her latest stunt, Zach would be free. It stopped after he joined ISA. She assumed Father had put an end to it. It would be unseemly for Mother to visit the training barracks like Zach was a six-year-old. Mother relaxed when her grandkids were born. Not that she wasn't in everyone's way, but it was a more natural response than her fear-based need to control everyone else's life.

Then it hit her. How Zach had gotten away from the smothering. She twisted out of Kendra's grasp so she was the one gripping arms. "You're leaving."

Her smile was sad, and tears rimmed her gaze. "Just for a little while. Your mother needs time to grieve, and she can't do it with me here."

"Where will you go?"

Kendra didn't have family. Her parents died a year before she met Zach, and she'd been an only child. She had distant relatives, but they lived on the East Coast.

"I have a friend who will see me established in a safe place."

By safe place, she meant something untraceable. A place like the Yards.

Kendra laughed and pulled out of her grip, wiping her eyes. "Don't give me that look. It's not what you think. It's not a secret lover or some shack in the Yards. Well, I guess it is connected to the Yards, but I can't tell you which one. We'll be well cared for."

"I don't like not knowing where you'll be. You know I wouldn't tell anyone."

"I know. And I trust that, but I don't know the exact location myself. I'll only be told the next leg of the journey after I complete each one."

That didn't make her feel any better. She was traveling over the contraband highway where no one knew the continually changing route. Whatever it took to stay off GSM's radar. Until Mother learned to process Zach's death, she'd never leave Kendra alone. So, Kendra would have to stay hidden. Anywhere she went, Father would attempt to track her.

"Don't worry, Rowan. As soon as I arrive, I'll contact you with my information. We'll only be out of touch for the time it takes to travel."

It was difficult to breathe. She hated what had become of her family. Of their family. How much impact could one missing person have? Turns out, quite a fucking lot. That constant pang of guilt beat louder, impossible to turn off.

She wiped at her eyes, her voice thick. "Okay. What do you need me to do?"

"I'm leaving your mother a message. In fact, I've already recorded and scheduled it to be delivered four hours after we leave tomorrow morning. If she asks if you've seen me, tell her I was here this evening. The security recordings will validate that. I told you I was taking the kids to the Alberta sector for a couple of days to meet an old friend and her kids. I planned on being back by Monday."

"So when Mother's first call comes in, I'll ignore it like always because I'm on a case. I'll call her after my shift ends. By then, you've gained another couple of hours, maybe more."

She smiled. "You always were the smart one of the family." She kissed her cheek. "I promise the kids and I will be back before you know it. Neither of them can be away from their Aunt Rowan for very long."

They couldn't hold back the tears and when they reached the door; they hugged for a long time. Rowan finally pushed Kendra away, wiping her eyes. "Dry your tears. You don't want security picking them up. Not until you're walking out the doors of the lobby and at least a block away."

Kendra dotted her eyes with her sleeve. "I always loved your theatrics, Rowan. Don't forget the children will be expecting a gift when they return."

She laughed. "I thought they were supposed to bring me the gift. They're the ones on an adventure."

"You know who's to blame for that."

They replied in unison with "Zach." But they both knew she'd be away for longer than either of them would admit.

TWENTY-TWO

The following morning, Rowan was primed to track down the Spider. With any luck, they could tie up the loose ends and solve the mystery of the tattooed man and his connection to their dead guy. The only mar in her day would be Kendra putting her plan in motion to take the kids and disappear. It would be hard on Mother, but she'd done it to herself. The fallout would land on Rowan, but after the last six months, what was one more guilt to lay at her door?

A chat with the Spider would take her mind off the drama that would unfold once Mother discovered Kendra was gone. Until then, she'd have enough to keep her occupied. And it started with an argument after the morning briefing. She wanted to take her AVU, partly to show it off, the other because Keene's AVU was too flashy and might be tagged by security.

Keene refused. This was his mission, and technically, while not working for him, she was assisting on behalf of ISA. That meant all decisions were his and, unfortunately, his argument had been sound. But she wouldn't let it go and continued to be disagreeable once they were in his AVU.

"We're going to the GSM campus. I'm a GSM contractor, and the major, who you work for, has an office in the east tower. That's too far away." Keene rolled off his reasoning with maddening assurance, which only came across as arrogant.

"It's still on the same campus." Her response was weak at best, and any more rebuttals would come across as whining.

"We'll park between the buildings, though I'd like to be closer to the Projects Tower."

"In case we have to run?" Her tone was sarcastic, but to be fair, it had been their experience every time they traced a source.

"Exactly."

At least he understood the stakes as well as she did.

"You don't trust my AVU."

He never took his eyes from the airspace, even though they'd elevated to Zone 3, which had minimal traffic for this time of day. When he didn't answer, she sat a bit taller, her suspicions confirmed.

"That's what I thought."

"It's not that. Hernandez mentioned how—what's the term? —how fly it is."

She snorted. "I think the term is jack."

He grunted.

"Then what's the problem?" When the silence continued, she got snappy. "Just tell me. Partners, right?"

After another short pause, he sighed and mumbled, "I reviewed your driving record."

"What?" She winced at her shrill tone.

"If I'm going to leave my safety in the hands of someone else, I need to know they can get us out of a jam."

She stared at him, open-mouthed. He'd checked her records. The asshole.

"There's nothing wrong with my driving, and I'd have a better shot of getting us out of trouble with my AVU than this flashy piece of trash." She wanted a better response, but a scathing one didn't come to mind. Instead, her temperature soared to combustible levels. Sure. She had a few incidents that Cap had no choice but to write up. Some personal property had been damaged, and paperwork had to be submitted. To ensure GSM would compensate the individual citizens appropriately, the truth was occasionally stretched. All ISA guards took a hit on their driving records at some point. It was a well-known game that no one questioned and was an archaic practice. One that had made sense when society was being rebuilt.

He seemed to be mulling over her response, his own irritation climbing if the mad pulse along his jawline was any indication. Served him right.

"Then why does your record say differently?"

She could have explained, but what would be the point? She didn't owe him anything, and if he wanted to play chauffeur, so be it. Besides, she hardly ever got to watch the city's landscape and turned to take in the view from her side window.

But she couldn't let it go and muttered, "I didn't hear you complaining when I got you and Horatio out of that little scrap where you almost died."

His mumbled response was almost too low to hear. "A point to you."

He dropped down to Zone 2 when the glass towers of the GSM complex came into view, finally setting down in the parking complex, closer to the Projects Tower, owned by Stoker Industries. Once they left the AVU and neared the front doors, he pulled her aside to sit on a bench near a massive bed of roses. The different aromas tickled her nose with a mix of sweet and pungent. They stared straight ahead.

"I want you to take the lead on this one," Keene said.

Avoiding another opened-mouth response, Rowan glanced at a bed of perennials across the expansive walkway leading to the Tower. This guy never failed to surprise her.

"Why?"

"I think she'll be more threatened by another powerful woman than she will be by me."

She turned to him, and it required every bit of control not to look glassy-eyed stupid. Had that been a compliment? Too many words popped into her head, and she shoved them back as she considered his words. Of course, she was a powerful woman. She was a sergeant in the ISA. It was a hard-earned title now. Commissioned officers versus non-commissioned didn't exist anymore. The ISA was primarily a civilian protection service, and she could climb as high as she wanted, assuming her questionable behavior and big mouth didn't sabotage any such dream.

"Is there a particular approach you'd like me to take?"

"I'm open. My first thought was to ask about the meeting. Since our dead guy was in the meeting, it makes sense we might be checking up on his acquaintances."

"And why would we be interested in a meeting held three years ago?"

He smiled, though he never turned in her direction. "Excellent question. Since he was murdered, we're checking into all of his high-profile projects—whether they were approved or not. We're going back five years."

She nodded. That made sense, and no one would question it. Though she doubted that would give them their mystery man.

"Or you can go for broke." He turned toward her, his expression unreadable. "You can ask why she was meeting with Kai Li and the tattooed man."

"Right." When he didn't respond, she laughed. "Are you kidding? Do you enjoy having to run for your life?"

He rubbed his jaw, checked his wrist unit, and stood. "Then play it by ear. I'm good with that." He followed behind her, committing to the appearance that she was in charge. He even waited for her to sign them in at the front desk.

Security scanned their GSM and ISA credentials and made a note in the file about their sidearms. Once that was completed, they were given directions to the Spider's office.

The first clue something might be wrong was when they exited the thirty-fourth floor to a silent hallway with only a handful of people scurrying past. The floor should have been a high-traffic area with the number of project teams housed in the tower. They followed signs for the correct hallway and entered the office number they were given.

The waiting area was the typical setup for senior project leaders. Three closed doors surrounded the empty reception desk. One would lead to the Spider's personal office, one to a lab room, and the last to a conference room.

Rowan glanced at the empty desk, then at Keene, who responded with a shrug and a raised brow.

She checked her wrist unit. "Too early for lunch. Maybe a meeting?"

"Security should have told us if either the Spider or her receptionist wasn't available."

"True. Maybe something critical came up after we checked in." She opened the first door on the right. "Conference room is empty."

Keene went to the door on the left, knocked, then stuck his head in. He walked in and returned after a minute. "The lab and a supply closet. Immaculately clean."

She knocked on the middle door and shouted through it. "Ms. Cross? I'm Sergeant Rowan Lockwood with ISA. I have a few questions about Elton Sodowski. He worked on one of your projects."

She waited for a beat, knocked again, then opened the door to a spacious and nicely furnished office. Keene gently pushed her aside so he could enter. Before she suggested contacting security, her eye caught the tablet on the floor next to the desk. She sidestepped to get a better look and, when she saw the tip of a shoe, raced to peer behind the desk.

Keene bumped into her, not prepared for her quick stop.

She wasn't sure what registered first—the pool of blood or the Spider's face. Her right leg lay across her left. It appeared that she'd been grabbed from behind, twisted around, then jerked off her feet, but forensics would confirm. The shoe she'd spotted had fallen off a few inches away. The opened flap of her navy-colored jacket exposed a pink blouse with a large red stain. The blood had seeped through the blouse, spreading hazy lines out from the center. At first blush, the image appeared to be an unfurling flower against a tapestry of pink and blue. A horrible picture of death and rebirth.

Keene stepped around her and checked for a pulse, but the dead stare of Sheila Cross told Rowan all she needed to know.

"She's still warm." Keene pulled his weapon and scanned the room.

Trusting he could take care of anyone returning, she moved closer to determine what killed the Spider. She pushed the jacket aside and lifted the blouse. The blood-soaked garment pulled away with a sucking sound. She'd definitely bled out from something. When Rowan pulled the blouse up far enough, the clean edge of a knife blade was apparent, even though the heavy red stain marred the copper skin. She leaned forward to confirm there weren't burnt edges in the wound which would suggest a laser weapon, but with the amount of pooled blood, it would be unlikely.

"We need to get out of here." Keene pulled her up by the elbow.

"We need to call ISA."

"We'll do that after we get out of the building."

That made her pause. "You think someone would think we did this? And then, what, decided to sit around and wait for security to show?"

"Where is everyone? The assistant, the people who normally cram the halls?"

She shook her head. "We need to call it in."

He held her gaze, his expression stern. But beyond his stare, she sensed his concern. "Something is going on here. I don't know if someone expected us or if we're unlucky enough to be players in their game. But I don't think it would be good for anyone to find us here."

Logically, it didn't make sense to run. She was an ISA agent. They'd signed in at the front desk. Yet, as his brows furrowed, a sense of unease crept through her. "Back the same way or the stairs?"

"The stairs."

They kept to a brisk pace as they left the office, taking a right toward the end of the corridor and the stairwell. Thirty-four sets of stairs, but if they heard anyone coming, they could escape through another floor.

They made it down six flights before they heard doors slamming above and below them.

"They've boxed us." Keene stopped at the next door and tried it. Locked. He pulled a laser pen out of his pocket and, using the narrow beam, cut through the lock.

They'd know what floor they were on, but there were dozens of corridors, offices, three other stairwells, and the same number of elevator banks. If they could make it to the twentieth floor, they could escape over the connecting bridge to the GSM tower. Their pace quickened when a door slammed behind them. Their progress could be tracked through the security sensors, but this floor was crowded, and they dodged between the workers.

When they reached the other side of the building where a service elevator and staircase should be, the halls became deserted again. Seconds later, six armed men raced onto the floor from the stairwell. They carried long-range pulse weapons that could fry every nerve in their bodies. Nerves that might or might not regenerate to full functionality. Their first shots went high and wide, which she assumed had been on purpose. Did they only want to take them into custody, or slow them down to make better targets?

Keene wasn't falling for whatever game was being played. He pulled his sidearm and returned fire as he turned them back the way they'd come. Rowan took the lead, dodging down the first intersection they came to. She ran, turning down corridors —right, left, another left.

More pulse weapons fired—they were closing in.

The next turn brought them to a short corridor. A dead end.

If she'd only reviewed the floor plan before they got there. But honestly, there had been no reason to assume they'd be chased inside a GSM facility, whether owned by Stoker or not.

Keene pushed her along as he watched their back. She read the plaques beside each door. Rooms 2820 through 2826 ran down the left side of the hallway. Four labs and two conference rooms were on the right.

They stopped at the end of the hallway at a door marked storage, and he stared down at her.

She shook her head. "They'll look in all the rooms, even the storage closets. This won't help us."

She couldn't pull away from his gaze. He appeared to be

making a decision—fight or give up? Whatever he was planning, she was reasonably certain she wasn't going to like it.

In one swift movement, as the sound of racing boots closed in on them, he opened the door to the storage closet and pulled her in with him.

The door slammed shut behind them—plunging them into darkness.

TWENTY-THREE

Rowan tripped over something in the darkness. Keene grabbed her arm to keep her from falling, though she managed to knock into a standing shelf unit, rattling god knew what.

"Help me with this." Keene pulled on something, the scraping sound piercing the stillness of the small space, and she clapped her hands over her ears. The rattle of bottles and containers knocking against each other confirmed what he was doing.

"I can't see anything." But she found the other end of the rack and began pushing.

Her eyes grew accustomed to the darkness from the diffused light seeping under the door. The rack had five shelves and was filled with cleaning supplies and storage boxes, yet somehow, it inched its way across the floor.

"I can see how this could slow the security team down from entering, but where did you plan on us going?"

Once the rack was in place, Keene leaned against it and pulled out a handheld device no larger than a deck of cards. It was made of a molded transparent material, and colorful lights sparkled within the case, seeming to move to their own internal music. He punched buttons on the screen, stopping occasionally to refer to his wrist unit. At times, he entered information into the wrist unit, then typed what she assumed was the response into the device.

"What is that?" When he didn't respond, she tried again. "What are you doing?" She couldn't see how the device could help unless he was calling for backup. But why not do that on his wrist unit? Besides, no one would arrive in time to be of any help.

"Let me concentrate. This is a little trickier with two."

That told her nothing.

The doorknob rattled, followed by banging. Either fists or weapons slammed into the door, but other than shaking it, the rack held.

After several seconds, Keene ran a hand through his hair, his eyes squinting as he continued to read the display while tapping and mumbling something she couldn't hear. Then he glanced down at her.

"I'm ready."

"Great. Did you decide to leave your last-minute thoughts with friends and family?" When his brows furrowed into a question, she nodded toward his device.

"I wasn't sending messages. I was making calculations." His voice was a fine mixture of annoyance and concentration as he pushed his finger around the display in small circular motions. "Are you ready?"

"For what?" She had to yell over the increased pounding on the door, but she stepped back until she ran into the wall.

Without another word, he wrapped his arms around her so her back was against his chest, her arms caught in his tight grip. He held the device in front of them.

"What are you doing?"

"We're going to transport."

"What?" she shrieked. "No. I mean, I've heard GSM was testing something like that, but I wasn't aware they had any positive results." When he didn't respond, she began to struggle. "I don't think I want to be a test subject."

"Hold still. I still have a few numbers to add." His grip tightened in an attempt to stop her wiggling.

He ran his fingers counterclockwise as he mumbled again. She couldn't decipher the words and didn't think they were in English. Shouting came from the other side of the door. She guessed security had grown tired of pounding.

The lights that had previously been flashing stopped as they turned a single blue color. Then she noticed the small groups of lights formed symbols. She didn't recognize them, but something tugged at her to run as they began to pulse. She didn't have a chance to give it any more thought.

The symbols went dark, and the room fell away.

One minute they were standing in the dark storage closet, then she felt like she'd been shrink-wrapped as the floor disappeared. They were in some form of vacuum surrounded by a rushing sound. The g-forces sucked her tighter to Keene. She could barely breathe. The lights were back, but rather than displaying on the device, they floated all around them. This time in brilliant colorful symbols that meant nothing to her.

As quickly as it started, her breath came whooshing back, her body seemed to expand, and her feet touched solid ground. Unprepared for the arrival, her legs went limp, and she fell onto a hard-packed surface.

Not the cement floor of a storage closet, but dirt. And not darkness but bright sunlight. She squeezed her eyes shut. Had they transported somewhere outside the towers? Her breathing was shallow, and she wondered if she'd busted a rib until she realized a large body lay rather comfortably across her.

The body was warm against the chill in the air. The intoxicating scent of rain and wildflowers invaded her senses, and her body grew warm. She felt safe, secure—protected. Her eyes snapped open when she remembered who must be lying on top of her, cutting off her air. Somehow they'd ended up facing each other.

"Ugh," she moaned and shoved Keene. "Get off me."

"Give me a minute, woman." His bark matched his scowl as he rose up on his arms. His storm-gray eyes bored into hers, his expression growing soft before he moved aside, turning over to sit.

Rowan pushed into a sitting position, performing an internal body check to make sure nothing was broken or bruised. The chirp of a bird made her glance around. They were surrounded by soft rolling hills, purple wildflowers, and a rocky ridge not far away. The soft murmurs of a stream came from somewhere nearby.

They weren't in Los Angeles anymore. Where the hell did he transport them? She checked her wrist unit, but the screen was dark. It didn't appear busted, but she couldn't get it to work.

Keene held his device. His brows furrowed as if he was working out a problem. He typed something, then flipped through other screens so quickly they were nothing but a blur, stopping for a brief second to tap something before scrolling again. Then he tucked the device in his pocket.

"Where are we? Couldn't you just transport us back to the bunker or your AVU? Or do you have to transport us to a specific location?" She scanned the sparse landscape. "Like out in the middle of nowhere."

Keene stood. "Let's go. We have a mile or so to hike before we're safe."

She got up and turned a complete three-sixty. Not a building, AVU, hopper, or person in sight. "Safe from what? Mother Nature?"

He grabbed her arm and tugged her until she followed on her own. "I'll explain later. For now, just follow and try to keep your voice down. Or better yet, don't talk at all for the next thirty minutes."

She didn't understand why he should be angrier than her. He wasn't the one who had been blindly whisked away in some strange new-age invention that, to her knowledge, had never been successfully tested. She clearly had more right to be pissed than him. "I have to keep my mouth shut because someone might hear us out in this deserted place? Or are you already tired of my wondering what the hell just happened?"

When his response was to increase his pace, she shut her mouth until she caught up to walk by his side. She kept her voice low in between puffs of exertion. "Can you at least tell me where we are?"

"Scotland." He kept walking while she stopped to stare at his back with what was most likely that dumb open-mouthed expression. Then she ran to catch up with him.

"Isn't that a bit extreme? I didn't know the transport devices could send someone that far."

He increased his pace again, and when she caught up, tugging at his arm, he stopped and turned on her. Annoyance marred his features, and she took a step back. She'd pushed too far. But really, didn't he understand how frustrating it was for her?

He must have realized it because he blew out a breath as he scanned the desolate landscape. His expression changed from irritation to concern. She'd seen that face for the briefest of moments when they'd been in that alley in the African Quarter and four thugs threatened their lives. He'd been focused, a smile on his face, but she'd seen a glimpse of his apprehension. One she'd seen in other ISA guards. The one that questioned if they would survive the mission. Was that what made her stomach tighten?

His voice softened. "I know you're confused, and as I promised, I'll tell you what you need to know as soon as we get out of the open. You need to trust that I know what I'm talking about. Just twenty more minutes." This time he waited for her response before moving forward.

She had no idea where they were, other than the land that, before the Wars, had once been called Scotland. They were probably far north by the looks of it, meaning the closest town with a monorail could be a hundred miles away. The logical choice would be to agree for now. But she'd followed his leads since meeting him in Sodowski's housing unit, agreeing to play by the rules and be a good little ISA agent. They'd just broached those lines with the impact of a cargo hauler running over a scooter.

She folded her arms across her chest. "No."

"Excuse me?" His concern morphed back to anger as the tic in his jaw grew. His rather nicely shaped brows turned down, drawing her attention to the storm raging in his eyes that should have scorched her with their heat.

"You heard me. I don't know what just happened or why we're in Scotland, but you're going to explain it now. Not later. This is as good a place as any. And maybe if it was only coping with transporting from a supply closet in the middle of Los Angeles, compressed like trash in a reclamation unit, then dropped in the sunny barren hills of Scotland, I would be willing to wait another few minutes. But the crease in your forehead when you reviewed your little transport device didn't give me a warm feeling. So we're going to do this now."

He fisted his hands several times, and his chest heaved with whatever pent-up emotion he was riding. After a minute, he shook his head. For someone in a hurry to get someplace, he seemed to have forgotten about it. And that told her more than she wanted to know. Perhaps she should have waited the twenty minutes.

"Did you not expect to end up in Scotland? Is that it? Did something go wrong, and now no one knows where we are?" She pointed toward the pocket where he stored the device. "You do know how to operate that thing, right?" She began to pace in a tiny circle, focusing on the ground as she rubbed her temples. "We weren't supposed to arrive in Scotland. Wait. If that was true, then how do you know this is Scotland?"

"Christ, woman, give it a rest." With hands on hips, he stared at her, and to her surprise, might have been trying to suppress a smile. "You're worse than Conall with all the outlandish questions and idle thought."

She wasn't sure if that was an insult, then decided it most likely was. He tended to smile when he tossed them around. But it was time for him to talk, not her, so she kept her mouth rigidly set. She couldn't trust herself not to dribble out more questions.

"I see you've figured out my confusion, but it isn't what you think. And the reason I wanted to wait until we were in a more secure place is that you're not going to like, or quite possibly believe, where we are."

He seemed satisfied when she didn't respond, but that was only because it was difficult to catch a breath. It was all she could do to hold her anger at his tone. But he held her gaze until her breathing settled.

"Our problem isn't that we arrived in Scotland. That I planned for." He hesitated, then released a sigh so deep, she doubted there was any air left in his lungs. That might explain why she had to take a step closer to hear his next words. "The question I've been pondering is *when* in Scotland."

She must have been lightheaded from the transport and couldn't have heard that right. "What does that mean?"

"What I mean is that I'm concerned something was off with the calculations. I'm not used to someone harping at me while stuffed in a dark closet with armed men trying to break in to kill us. You might have jarred my hand."

Her anger flared. "You're telling me you sent us all the way to Scotland, but somehow it was my fault because I bumped you."

He stared off into the distance, his hands and jaw clenched again. As irritated as she was, she couldn't stop staring at him. The breeze blew the hair from his forehead, his profile one of strength and beauty. Even with his compressed lips and squint as he faced the wind, he was a handsome man. And somehow, it registered that whatever problems she thought they had, it didn't touch the surface of the real issue.

Keene finally looked at her. At that moment, she instinctively believed that whatever he was about to share, no matter how unrealistic, was the unvarnished truth. "What I'm saying is that I planned on Scotland, but I might have missed a calculation which means I'm not sure which year we arrived."

TWENTY-FOUR

She'd lied. What Rowan heard Keene say couldn't possibly be the truth. "What year? You're joking, right? You thought this would be a good time for some of that MacGregor humor?"

"You can believe it or not. You'll see the truth of it if we ever get to the mountain." And with that, Keene turned and continued his quick pace, leaving her to either chase after him or stay where she'd planted her feet.

She was well-versed in survival skills, but with only her sidearm and knife and no knowledge of where the closest city was, she could die of dehydration or exposure before anyone found her. So she buried her pride and disbelief to chase after him.

He kept a brisk pace over the hilly terrain as they moved up the side of the mountain. With nothing to do but follow, she took the time to survey her surroundings. The air seemed fresher. She supposed it was being away from the city where the flowers and grass gave the air a unique smell, not unlike Keene's scent.

She marveled at the moss and lichen growing on the rocks

they passed. The climate in Los Angeles was too warm for the tiny plants. To her left, a small creature, brown and furry, scampered away at their intrusion in its daily life, and she idly wondered if there was a predator that liked the taste of the tiny creature.

A loud shout sounded from her right, and as she turned to see where it came from, she found herself falling, slamming into the ground with Keene's heavy weight on her again. But this time, her face was planted in the dirt.

"What the..." she began.

"Quiet. Like your life depends on it." His hushed voice was firm, and she stopped squirming. He shifted to the left, and she sucked in air.

So far, she wasn't enjoying Scotland.

Then she heard it. Screaming. No. Not quite screaming. She lifted her head, searching for where the yelling was coming from. She glanced at Keene, who was peering over a boulder, and he allowed her to crawl over to see what he was looking at.

In the valley from where they'd just come, a dozen men with long hair and beards crested a ridge and ran down the hill, arms raised with what appeared to be swords. Or were some of them axes? They ran in skirts, their shirts billowing in the wind. Another group of men advanced up through the valley to their right. They wore similar attire with the same type of weapons.

The two groups came together with swords and axes raised. Was this some type of reenactment? In the middle of nowhere? Then sword met sword. When the blades sliced flesh, the spray of crimson convinced her this was no game.

Keene grabbed her arm and hauled her up. "We're going to run the rest of the way while they're busy. Keep your head down."

He didn't have to tell her twice.

They were huffing by the time they reached a cave. The

entrance required both of them to duck, but the space opened up once inside. She stopped short, not willing to enter the darkness beyond. Keene had turned to watch the skirmish. She stepped next to him, trying to make sense of it, but the battle had stopped. Both groups appeared to be gathering their injured, or possibly dead, comrades.

"Can you tell me what the hell is going on?" She wasn't sure what she'd just witnessed, but it felt like some dark nightmare. And somehow, as unhinged as it seemed, Keene knew precisely what was happening.

He nodded. "Aye, lass. Follow me."

He sounded tired, so when his hand device emitted a beam of light, she stayed two steps behind as he led them into the cave. She didn't like it, but what choice did she have? She wasn't going to chase after the men with swords to see if anyone felt like talking.

The deeper they went, the cooler the air grew. After several yards, she was about to complain, but he took a left when the path split. After another thirty feet and another fork, he turned left again. When she was thinking they should have marked the turns, he stopped. She couldn't see much beyond him other than the path continuing into the darkness. He ran his hand along the left wall, his fingers running over the stone as he mumbled strange words. She began to worry he hit his head on their landing and might be a bit delusional.

When a portion of the wall moved with a loud grinding noise, she jumped back. Keene pried at the edges and pulled open what turned out to be a door, revealing more darkness. He motioned for her to go first, but she hesitated.

"It's all right. I'm right behind you." His light swept across a room that appeared to hold furniture, so she stepped inside.

She swore at her stupidity when his light went out and the door closed, pitching them into complete darkness again. A second later, light seeped from the floor and spread upward, lighting the chamber, or more accurately, a room about forty feet square. The walls weren't the expected rock but a smooth cement painted a soft green with a single door on the far side. Stacks of books and odd knickknacks sat on a low cabinet that ran the length of one wall. On the far wall, near the door, two bookcases were filled with more books and neatly labeled containers. In front of the bookcases were two short couches and a couple of stuffed chairs. Against the third wall was a single-person bed. And in the middle of it all was a wooden table with four matching chairs. A hideaway with modern furnishings inside a cave. For what reason?

Keene strode to the closed door, and light appeared moments after he entered. He returned a minute later with a liter of water and two metal mugs, then motioned toward the couch. When she hesitated, he shrugged. "We can do this at the table, but I thought we'd make ourselves comfortable until the clansmen are gone."

When he produced a flask, taking a sip before passing it to her, she waved him off, but he kept his arm outstretched. "With what I'm about to share, you'll need a bit of reinforcement."

She sniffed the container and smelled whiskey. Not her drink of choice, but she took a swig to pacify him. It went down smooth, and her expression must have conveyed her surprise.

The corner of his eyes crinkled, and it was the first time she noticed the fine lines that come from years of smiling. "That's Conall's favorite. They don't distill it anymore."

Her interest piqued, she took another sip. "So he decided to carve out a room in a deep dark cave to store his secret stash of rare and limited-supply whiskey."

He allowed a small grin to escape. "Not any whiskey, but good Scotch whiskey."

"Of course. Because we're in Scotland."

"Aye, lass." His brogue thickened, sounding more like Conall. Yet, there was something deeper and more musical in Keene's voice. "But the whiskey, though non-existent in our time, is not in limited supply everywhere."

She nodded as if she understood what he was saying. She let the words sink in as she passed the flask back to him. She'd considered the idea of time travel. Hadn't everyone? It was in thousands of books and movies. But if time travel was real, how could this have been hidden? Word of it would spread like wildfire no matter how hard they tried to lock it down. No. Strange men battling with swords and the fact they weren't in Los Angeles anymore didn't prove they were in a different time.

"What do you mean by not limited except in our time?"

"We can transport through time to any moment, any year we wish to. For the most part. It's not as easy as that, but with the right conditions, it can be done."

A slashing pain hit her, and she doubled over, gripping her head. Not now. A vision on top of this crazy notion of time travel would be more than she could handle. She was walking a thin edge as it was. Any other day, she'd be screaming and racing back through the tunnels, probably getting lost. Four days with the MacGregor's was more than anyone should have to deal with.

"Do you need a bag?" Keene knelt in front of her.

She glanced up, taking deep breathes in an attempt to ease the pain. "A bag?"

"To breathe in. You're hyperventilating."

Not quite, but close enough. "Just back off a minute."

He moved back to his seat, and she closed her eyes until the pain passed. She sat up and rubbed her temples. "Is this time travel stuff sponsored by GSM?"

He studied her, and she averted her gaze, making an effort to glance around the room again, thankful the headache was slipping away. He sipped from the flask and handed it back to her. "Go ahead." He waved the whiskey at her, and she grabbed it, gripping it tightly but not drinking.

"This is where I'm going to ask for your oath."

"Oath?"

"There are only a handful of people outside of the bunker that know about time travel, and it's imperative we don't stray from that."

"But you're telling me?"

He refilled the mugs, pushing one toward her. She sipped the cool water. It helped. After giving her another long look, he stretched out his legs and rested his mug on his stomach. "I can't travel, or what you call transport, within the same year. In fact, I can't travel within a ten-year period from our current time." He shook his head and gave her one of those heart-melting smiles. "I can't tell you why. Not because the answer isn't known, it's just too scientific for me to follow all of it."

"And if I don't give you my oath?"

There was a brief flash in his eyes, so quick she might have imagined it. But he never looked away when he admitted, "I guess I'll have to trust your better nature that having other people know, at least for now, wouldn't be in the best interest of Earth. We take care of our secrets."

She wasn't sure what his last words meant, and she shivered, guessing now wouldn't be the best time to ask. "Okay. I give you my oath I won't say anything. Does this mean you can answer some of my questions?"

This time he pinned her with a stern gaze that reached her soul. Whatever he saw must have satisfied him because he nodded. "I'll answer anything that is considered safe for you to know."

Always with the stipulations, but she'd learned a thing or two about Keene MacGregor. If she didn't push, he'd divulge more than he probably would otherwise. "Okay. Why do you time travel?"

"What Lanis explained when you first met her was true. We are anthropologists who study the past. You can only learn so much from books, memoirs, and personal artifacts. But living among them, you get the entire story."

"Living among them? Is that what you do?"

He shrugged and reached for the flask. This time, she took a longer sip before returning it to him. "It's not my primary responsibility, as I'm not a qualified archaeologist. But I do spend time in different periods of history whenever a team member needs me."

"Security?"

He grimaced. "Security is my current job. When I travel, it's typically to clean up anything that might have jeopardized the timeline."

He did not just tell her he was an assassin. She pushed it aside. It was a rather drastic leap in thought, and there were other ways to get at the truth. "What about this place? I'm guessing, based on the bits of tech I see, that this doesn't fit with whatever year we're in."

"You're right. This room isn't impacted by time. For every day that changes outside these walls, everything inside these walls remains constant to our normal time."

"Why?" Although she hated to admit it, she was as naive as he was with most science and wasn't prepared to hear the how. She'd wait to see if Lanis could explain how a room could exist inside a mountain and not be impacted by time moving around it. The headache was returning, and it had nothing to do with visions.

"We need a safe room. A place to store items of our time in addition to clothes and personal items serviceable for different centuries. And with the supplies in the next room, we can stay here for as long as needed."

"And you always come to Scotland?"

"No. We go to many places, and for each location, we have a room like this."

"And why, if it was such a secret, did you bring me here?" And this was the secret of a lifetime. How did this small group of people figure out time travel and not share it with anyone? Were they getting rich off the artifacts they brought back with them? Great. She'd ended up in the middle of thieves.

"I didn't see us getting out of that supply cabinet in one piece."

She didn't either. They had been moving fast, and she'd only gotten a glimpse of the armed security shooting at them, but she hadn't seen ISA insignia. Worse, they never called out who they were. But she wanted to validate her thoughts on the topic. "And how would ISA, or whoever was chasing us, explain the death of a GSM contractor and an ISA agent?"

"Easy. Whoever killed the Spider hadn't expected our inopportune visit and decided not to take a risk on us talking. Our running helped them. Who else would run except guilty people? It would all be filed away as a horrible mistake."

That was an answer she could believe. "Why didn't you just take us back ten years? You said that was the closest time period we could go back." She considered her statement. "Can you go forward in time?"

He stood, picked up his mug, and emptied the remaining water in hers. "Drink up. We have more walking to do." He stuck the flask in a back pocket. "We can go forward, but it's not as easy because there are more variables." He waved for her to follow, and she almost stepped on his heels, eager to see what was in the other room.

It was a supply room the same size as the first room. Everything appeared neat and orderly, with three of the walls filled with wardrobe closets, bookcases, stacks of labeled bins, and several floor-to-ceiling cabinets. She spotted a sign for the armory, a galley kitchen in a back corner, and another small room that probably answered the call of nature.

"I considered traveling to the first possible year but decided anywhere I took you would require your oath. So, why not make the best of it?"

She wandered to the bookcases. In addition to dozens of books on various topics, none of them on Scotland or time travel, three shelves held tech games, and two shelves stored the hand-held devices required to play them. Although there was only a single bed, she guessed there were times when more than one person used the room. This room, buried deep in a cave, didn't feel like living among them. Nor was it much of a living space.

"Then we're here as a side trip for your anthropology business?"

"It's not really a business, but yes, this has nothing to do with GSM."

"Okay. I'll play along since I'm guessing my other choice would be to stay here until you return."

His smile was predatory. "I was impressed by your intelligence the first day we met. You never fail to disappoint."

"Why is it you always make a compliment seem like a poor behavioral trait?"

"We all have our talents." He opened the third wardrobe closet from the left. The cabinet was split. One side had a single bar across its width for clothes to hang. The other side held shelves and drawers. She stepped behind Keene and noted the clothing was for males and females.

He pulled out tan-colored pants that had seen better days. They appeared clean, though stained, and several spots had been stitched to cover a rip. A yellowed work shirt came out next, and she noted it had to be pulled over the head with nothing more than a string at the neck to tie it closed. No buttons, zippers, Velcro, or the more common self-adhering strips. Worn leather boots followed the rest as he laid them on the table.

Then he studied two plain dresses made of rough fabric similar to the men's clothes. They also appeared to be stained and mended. He pulled one out, along with undergarments and shoes.

"You're a bit taller than Lanis but about the same size. This will have to do for now. Let's hope the shoes fit."

"I'm not wearing that."

Keene turned to her. "We're going to a small village about five miles from here. You will be foreign enough with your speech, and hopefully, they won't think you to be English. That would not be good, but I have another cover story, just in case. So, you can wear what I tell you or stay behind."

"What year is it anyway? You never said."

"Assuming my calculations were correct, we should be in the early sixteenth century."

TWENTY-FIVE

Rowan stumbled back. The enormity of everything Keene said, the chase through the tower, a second dead body, transported to a different location, and men fighting with swords finally smacked her in the face. They were six hundred years in the past? She found a chair and collapsed, feeling light-headed.

Keene knelt in front of her again and gripped one of her hands. "Are you sure you couldn't use a bag?"

She glared at him until he finally stood. If he laughed, she'd have to kick him.

"I'm sorry to have done this to you." His sheepish expression seemed genuine. "There really wasn't any other way. You just need a little time to adjust. I promise we won't be here more than a night. Two at the most."

She laughed. She couldn't help it, and Keene was sure to think she'd lost her mind. She ran a hand under her nose. "I suppose when we go home, you'll be able to drop us back at your AVU, albeit a few hours after the Spider's death with no one the wiser."

He chuckled with her. "I was thinking the bunker. Then

you can drive that ghastly AVU of yours and return me to my more impressive vehicle."

She shook her head and stared with disgust at the dress lying on the table. "Couldn't I wear pants?"

He gave it consideration. "It wouldn't be entirely improper if they saw you as a warrior. But that would come with its own problems. Some of the men might want to challenge you to a fight."

"Lovely time period. Almost like fight night in the Yards." She stood, picked up the clothes, then pointed at the tiny room she suspected to be a bathroom.

"Aye, that will do."

The dress was as Keene predicted. It fit well enough but was too short in the sleeves and length, and not one for wearing dresses, she felt constricted by the heavy skirt. Keene fixed the length of the dress by changing out the plain shoes for calf boots.

Keene's plain work clothes brought out his rugged features. The sleeves of his shirt were rolled up, showing off his strong arms and the edges of his tattoos. He must have rinsed his hair while she fussed with the underclothing and stockings. It hung loosely, touching his shoulders, and carried a natural look that would probably be more appropriate to this century. For an instant, she pictured him in that field, wearing one of those skirts, his arm raised with a sword as he ran to meet the enemy. She blinked and forced her gaze elsewhere.

He picked up their weapons and strode toward the sign for the armory. She was as eager as Keene to move out, ready to see what this century was all about. But she wasn't leaving without her weapons. Not after seeing the earlier, bloody fight.

"What are you doing with my sidearm?" She shadowed him to the large vault that required a retinal scan and passcode. What would the locals think if they ever found their way into the room? And maybe that was the reason for the extra security.

The heavy door opened to reveal a walk-in armory, and all she could do was gawk. Firearms, swords, shields, axes, and bows hung from the wall. Based on the metals used and their construction, the weapons must have been from different centuries. In the back corner was another locked vault, this one six-foot-by-two-foot. A palm print in addition to a second retinal scan and passcode was required. It was empty except for a pulse crossbow and two pulse rifles. He placed their sidearms and knives on a shelf. After closing the door, he went to the computer display just outside the walk-in.

"Come here. I want to add you to the security system for both vaults."

She couldn't imagine a situation where she'd be there without him, but she couldn't disagree with his logic. He ran through the process of adding her palm print and retinal image to the computer, then she entered a passcode. The more she saw, the longer her list of questions grew. She could attempt to grill him now rather than wait until they returned to the bunker, but she was antsy to get out of the cave.

She couldn't resist at least one question. "What powers all of this?" She waved to indicate more than just the armory.

"The same as the bunker. Geothermal energy."

Not knowing the science behind it, she just nodded and tucked the information away until she could speak with Lanis.

Before shutting the armory, he grabbed a sword and scabbard. Then he went to one of the cabinets and opened a drawer that held various knives and daggers. He selected one and shoved it in his boot. He put another one in a belt scabbard.

He waved her over to another set of cabinets. "Lanis prefers her own weapons."

Her eyes lit up when he opened a central drawer. A neat row of daggers lay on black velvet. The metal glistened.

He stepped back. "Take your pick. This is only for self-defense."

She nodded and picked up several before finding two with the right balance and comfortable grip. One fit perfectly in the sheath belted at her waist. She turned away from Keene and lifted her skirt, tying a second sheath around her thigh. When she was ready, he tossed her a stone. She glanced at it before lifting a brow. "What's this?"

"A whetstone."

"Uh-huh. And what do I do with it?"

"You use it to sharpen your blades."

She stared at it. In ISA, they used lasers to hone the edges.

"Just tuck it away. I'll have time to show you how it works later." He couldn't seem to stop grinning, and she was beginning to feel like the butt of a joke. She could hear it now as he added her to the list of stories to tell around the picnic table. Conall would laugh so hard, he'd probably fall off the bench. The imagined humiliation made her testy.

Keene led her out of the armory. "We need to fill a couple of skins, grab some food, and we'll be off."

She didn't want to ask what skins were, assuming she'd find out soon enough. But she wasn't quite ready to leave.

"You haven't told me why you chose this time period. You mentioned some business to take care of. Is this one of your clean-up jobs?"

"No." He rubbed the bridge of his nose. "I came to check on one of our team members."

"I thought I met your team."

"You haven't met everyone."

While it surprised her, it shouldn't have. The bunker had over two dozen living quarters on the third floor. It was silly to think only a handful of people lived in the massive building. It wasn't any of her business. Conall had told her that the first day they'd met. But time travel? After this trip, she would have the right to know more than they were telling her.

"So, we're here to check on someone who's been living among them?" She hadn't meant it to sound sarcastic, but Keene didn't seem to take offense.

"Aye." Keene picked up two pouches that appeared to be made out of animal hide, and the term skin became obvious. He filled them with water and tossed her one. "He's overdue on reporting in. I've been meaning to come check on him, but our GSM mission has gotten in the way." He stuffed food into a leather pouch that he slung over his shoulder. "He loses track of time, and we usually have to retrieve him."

"Sounds like someone who should be fired."

He opened the door that led to the cave, then turned to her. "It's hard to fire family. We'll be looking for my brother, Liam."

She walked into the tunnel, and everything went dark when he closed the door. A few seconds later, his beam of light lit up.

"You didn't tell me you had another brother."

"It never came up. And if it did, I'd have to answer the dozens of questions you always seem to have."

He had her there. Rather than respond, she focused on the route out of the cave. Though, without Keene, she'd never find the door or know how to open it. In fact, without him, she'd never get back to her century, and panic seized her as the walls seemed to close in. Before it turned into a full-on anxiety attack, natural light grew around them as they reached the cave entrance.

He stopped to survey the landscape, and she stepped next to him, fidgeting in her boots. They were a little too big, and if the village was five miles away, she was sure to earn a blister or two. She tugged at the dress. The rough fabric chafed under her arms and around her neck. Though the air was cool, the sun was out. She'd be sweating like a pig by the time they finished the hike.

"It's best we walk single file. If you walk in my footsteps, it will be more difficult for anyone to determine our numbers. It might prevent them from following us. We move swiftly and stay focused. After that skirmish, I doubt anyone is ready for another fight, but I don't want to take the risk." He pointed to the right. "We'll go to the river and follow it to the village. Keep your ears and eyes open for anyone coming from behind."

She nodded and followed his gaze. Nothing but grassy fields and rolling hills. She noted the river she'd heard earlier when they'd stopped to watch the battle. The sun had passed its zenith and was heading to the west, which she noted would be behind them.

Keene started off at a fast pace, occasionally stopping to listen. When satisfied they were still alone, he continued on. She stopped for a moment when they reached the bottom of the rocky hill, searching for the mouth of the cave. It wasn't visible from where she stood. She glanced around, searching for some-thing distinctive from everything else. It wasn't until they'd walked a fair distance that she stopped to look back.

"What is it?" Keene stood so close to her, she felt his breath on her neck. Goosebumps erupted, and she rubbed her arms to make them go away.

"I was trying to see if I could find my way back to the cave."

He pointed to the left. "See where the ridge meets the valley?"

She nodded.

"Follow it about five hundred yards to the south. The trail isn't used much, so it can be difficult to find. If you walk along the ridge, you'll have a better chance of finding it. The cave entrance is just below the top of the ridge." He pointed to the right. "See where that other ridge comes down and meets the first one? There's an odd rock formation where they meet."

She nodded again, trying to ignore the hand he placed on her hip.

"That's how you'll know you walked too far. The cave entrance is about halfway between the two markers." He squeezed her hip then turned to continue their march to the village.

They stopped when they reached the river. It was wider than she'd expected and, from where she stood, appeared knee deep.

"How are the boots?" Keene settled on a small boulder and handed her a piece of dried meat.

She sucked on it before trying to chew it, and it quieted her growling stomach. "I'll have blisters."

"I'll see if I can trade for better boots once we get to the village."

Her first glimpse of the village was after rounding a bend as they came out of a dense thicket. She stopped.

She hadn't known what to expect a village of this century might look like. But whatever she might have guessed, it would have been ten times larger than the couple dozen thatched-roof stone buildings that lay before her surrounded by a haze she contributed to the smoke rising from them. The village sat four hundred yards from the river they'd been following. She gazed beyond the hamlet and to the right. She heard what could be a larger river beyond a small stand of spindly trees. It would make sense for the smaller river to meet up with another.

Then the sounds of the village reached her ears. Livestock moving about in their pens, a horse nickering from somewhere, children playing and shouting. The smells were a mixture of pungent waste, manure, and savory cooking.

Keene stepped next to her. He must have read her growing anxiety because there was a bit of sympathy in his voice. "I know it wasn't what you were expecting, but you'll find it comfortable enough. It's a good thing we didn't arrive in the cold season."

She rubbed her arms, though she wasn't cold. Not after walking five miles, but the air was chilled. She couldn't imagine living in this place with snow on the ground.

"I should have given you a mantle. I wasn't thinking."

"A what?"

"It's a plaid. A wrap."

"I'll be fine. Let's find this brother of yours."

Keene hesitated. "About that."

She humphed out a breath but refrained from responding.

"He's a bit different than Conall and me."

"What does that mean?"

He tilted his head to one side and gave her a long stare as if seeing her for the first time. She shuffled her feet and pushed back her hair. Sweat dampened her brow.

"You'll see soon enough." Then he turned and strode into town, shouting something she didn't understand. Her anxiety blossomed to full-fledged panic. It never occurred to her she wouldn't understand the language.

TWENTY-SIX

When they reached the middle of the village, Rowan remained several steps behind Keene as shouts came from all directions. He was swarmed by a dozen men and women. As many children pushed their way past the adults, their own yells and laughter matching the adults in volume. Keene swept one child up in his arms as he patted the heads of the others who clamored for his attention. It wasn't an image she would have considered until she remembered the young boys in Galway Alley. Children loved him. When he slipped a handful of treats to the kids, she understood it wasn't just the sweets—but that he'd thought of them.

Before she could consider how that impacted her impression of him, several young women gathered close, running fingers over the edges of their hair and shifting their wraps. He greeted them with warm smiles as they grabbed his arms and led him to one of the gray stone buildings.

"It's hard to remain in Keene's light when the village swarms him."

She swung around at the comment, her hand resting on the hilt of her dagger.

Under a mop of auburn hair, the man's brows pinched as he studied her. Behind the short beard, he had a young face with laugh lines at the corners of his dark-blue eyes. Eyes that sparkled with the same humor she'd seen on Conall's and Keene's faces when they joked with each other.

He wore a skirt and a light-yellow shirt similar to Keene's with a tie in front, which didn't hide the fact there was a muscled chest and slim waist hidden beneath. His upper arms strained the sleeves, and he carried an axe in his belt.

He crossed his arms and lifted a brow. "And who might you be?" He gave her the full perusal, from her boots, that rubbed against her blisters, to her dress, pausing at her breasts, which weren't her best feature but were currently straining against the restricted bustline, before finally reaching her face. "This is the first time he's brought one of his women with him. Faye and Moira won't be pleased."

She narrowed her gaze, giving him her own more thorough appraisal, which he seemed to find amusing. "I'm not one of his women." She was going to elaborate, but his smile had grown wider, and she decided to let Keene correct the misunderstanding rather than punch him in the face. "I'm going to take a wild guess that you're Liam."

"So, my brother told you about me."

She shook her head. "No."

He threw back his head and laughed. It was a deep, warm sound, and she suddenly pictured the three brothers laughing over a mug of beer around a fire. Keene and Conall carried a month's worth of facial hair. The fire sparked in the darkness, lighting their faces. Other men and a few children sat with them. Then the brothers were up, mugs tossed, axes and swords out as they turned to face something in the darkness.

Rowan blinked. She didn't know where the image came from and considered it a simple trip down fantasy lane, brought on by the stress of learning about time travel and Keene's growing family tree. *It couldn't be a vision. It couldn't be a vision.* No headache. No falling to the ground in blinding pain. So, no, it couldn't be a vision. But the thought unnerved her and made her snappish.

"Well, I don't know who you are, lass, or why you're here, but no matter." He spread out an arm. "Welcome to Glen Dar, current home to a small portion of clan Gregor and their kin. Let's go in and meet Marta."

She walked beside him as she surveyed the surroundings. When the surprise of Keene's arrival wore off, the villagers turned to her, the strange woman walking with one of their own.

"Do you mind me asking your name since you already know mine?"

"Rowan."

Her response was greeted by silence, and when she glanced at him, his smile was gone, and his brow had furrowed in thought. An instant later, it was gone, replaced by his enchanting smile. "A fine name."

And that didn't make her feel weird at all.

When they reached the building where a crowd had formed around Keene, the group turned to stare at her. Several of the children surrounded her, though one young girl stood a few paces back, partially hidden behind a barrel. Her red hair, the color of sunshine, tangled about her face, and her gaze pierced Rowan with sparkling green eyes. A tiny finger pulled at her lip, revealing a mouth with a missing front tooth. She reminded Rowan of herself at that age, and she smiled at the child. Someone clapped and shouted words she didn't understand, causing the children to vanish as quickly as they'd come. Except for the little redhead. She strolled toward the river, and after several paces, glanced back over her shoulder. She gave Rowan a huge smile before racing off and disappearing into the low bushes.

"Rowan, I see you met Liam." Keene raised his arm and waved her over.

Two young women hovered close to him, and she assumed they must be Faye and Moira. They didn't appear friendly as they gave her the same perusal Liam had. While Liam's perusal made her want to add another layer or two of clothing, the assessment she received from the women made her feel lacking on so many levels.

"Faye and Moira. Off with the both of ye." The loud commanding voice, one gratefully spoken in English, came from a diminutive woman who couldn't have been more than five feet and a bare inch tall. She wasn't frail but appeared thinner than the other women surrounding her. Her age was impossible to tell. She looked older than Rowan's mother, but there were only a few streaks of gray in the reddish-brown hair she wore in a bun.

Faye and Moira didn't question the order, and they moved off to the fire ring, where a pot of something was cooking. She'd caught a whiff of it when they'd first entered the hamlet, and the strong scent had made her stomach growl. Now it made her nauseous, and she blamed it on the village's lackluster greeting. At least where she was concerned. Keene was the star of their little show.

Then the old woman focused her attention on Rowan, her expression as unwelcome as Keene's sweetheart club. "Come in so we can talk in peace."

"Marta." It was only one word, but Keene's tone was clearly a warning.

The old woman waved a hand at him. "I'll welcome your guest as I would any other." Then she turned and disappeared through the door of the building.

Keene gave her an apologetic shrug that didn't ease the raw nerves crawling up her spine. Then he gave Liam a long look as the two men stared at each other. "Liam."

"Brother. How nice of you to drop by."

"I wouldn't have to if you checked in."

Liam shook his head and appeared embarrassed. "I did it again?"

"Aye," Keene breathed out a long sigh. Then he took three long strides, and the two brothers hugged, arms wrapped around each other as they thumped each other on the back. When Keene pulled back, he held Liam at arm's length. "I'm happy to see you're in one piece."

Liam grumbled. "You know they won't let a bard fight."

Keene ruffled his hair, and she realized that Liam was a younger brother. Now it made sense and made her feel closer to Liam. She understood what it felt like to be the youngest.

Keene stepped back and pointed to the axe. "They let you carry one of those?"

Liam hefted the axe with a solid grip, twisting it around in perfect control. There was a junior guard in her old squad that could do the same thing with a katana blade. It was impressive to watch, but he was also the best in the Capital sector.

Keene grimaced as Liam twirled the axe, and she wondered what the odds were of him cutting off a body part. Then he stopped, twisted on his left foot as he brought his right leg around, ending in a lunge as he brought the axe up with both arms and threw it. Her breath caught as she watched it flip end over end in a blur before striking the planks of a barn with a dull thud.

Keene's brow lifted, and Liam, with hands on hips, grinned with satisfaction. The light breeze tugged at his skirt, and she couldn't help but notice the finely honed legs. For a split second, maybe five, she wondered if Keene's legs were as finely shaped.

Then she shook her head to catch up on Keene's commentary. "I thought they weren't letting you go on raids."

"I convinced them I should probably be trained to defend the village while they were gone. They always leave a few armed men behind, but one more couldn't hurt."

Keene slapped him on the back. "A singing bard and his axe. I can already hear the tales."

They chuckled as they turned toward the building, and Keene caught her arm on the way. "Don't let Marta trouble you. She doesn't like most, and never an outlander, which is what we call an outsider. If the women pick on you too much, we'll leave in the morning."

She pulled her arm from his grasp. "I can handle myself." The growl, while not intentional, drowned out the butterflies. Or maybe it was Keene's look of approval.

Before they entered the building, a small boy ran up and handed Liam his axe. Liam dug in his pocket and drew out a small wooden figure. The boy grasped it before she could make it out. Liam noticed her follow the boy back to a group who were all eager to see what he'd earned.

"It's a stag. One of the spirit animals of the Celts. Receiving a gift from a Druid, especially a spirit animal, is considered a great honor."

"Liam." Keene's stilted tone made Liam blush until his anger flared.

"You bring her through the portal but don't tell her why? Who we are?"

"It was an accident, and she knows enough for now. Let's go in before Marta gets her temper up."

"Too late for that, young Keene. I'll not wait much longer." The old woman's strong voice berated the men from inside the house.

They entered a house filled with scents—spices, baked

bread, and a pleasant aroma of smoke coming from the fireplace. The first room was larger than she expected, with multiple chairs and a long table. Stairs led to what she assumed were bedrooms. A door toward the back would lead to a kitchen from where most of the smells drifted. The warmth of the fire was welcoming if the host wasn't.

A young girl, no more than eight or ten, tended the fire, adding what looked like charcoal bricks. She scurried away when she was done, then another young girl, this one somewhere in her teens, carried in a tray with a pot and several cups, setting it on a low table in front of Marta.

The old woman sat in a wood chair surrounded by woven baskets piled with fabrics and mending notions. "Sit." She nodded to the empty chairs, and Keene motioned Rowan to a chair that put her between him and Liam. "Pour the tea."

Once the girl filled the cups, she rushed off as the other girl had. Rowan couldn't tell if it was to get away from the old biddy or because of the visitors—mostly likely her.

Marta gave Rowan a sharp look as if she'd been reading her thoughts, and heat rose in her cheeks. "Don't mind the girls. They're not used to strangers." Then she glanced at Keene. "You've been gone so long the young ones don't remember you."

Keene snorted. "They seemed to know me well enough to empty my pockets."

She waved her hand, dismissing him. "You spoil them." She sipped her tea then stared at them until they dutifully tasted the offering.

The tea was pleasant enough, with a bit of honey, but Rowan would have preferred a strong cup of coffee.

"Tell me, Keene Gregor, why is it we haven't seen you for so many months? And when you return, you're trailing a woman with you. Have you finally settled down?"

The timing of the question was unfortunate, as Rowan

spewed tea across her lap, causing Liam to laugh hard enough for him to choke on his own drink. But she hadn't missed the slight change in Keene's last name.

Keene growled at both of them. "Rowan is my apprentice."

Apprentice? She bit her tongue. Under the circumstances, it was probably the best answer that wouldn't require more questions.

Marta's calculating gaze turned toward her. "Rowan, is it?"

"Don't get caught up in the name, old woman." Keene's eyes narrowed, and he pointed a finger at her. "You know I respect you and our ways, but a name means nothing on its own."

Her lips puckered into a frown that would make Rowan's mother proud, but then she relaxed them along with her shoulders as she leaned back in her chair. "Agreed." But the quick glance she gave Rowan, the old woman's gaze still cold, made her think Keene hadn't won the argument. He'd only pushed it off for a later time. And what did her name have to do with anything?

"There has been trouble at home, and with a new apprentice…" Keene shrugged. "I've lost track of time."

Marta cackled. "The young always want a faster way. At least you're learning quicker than this one." She nodded toward Liam. "He still gets his runes confused."

Keene shook his head. "He's always been one for words, not writing."

She expected Liam to take offense, but he simply smiled and nodded.

Keene continued, "We're only here for a short while. A day, two at most. This land and customs are foreign to Rowan, so we apologize in advance for her manners."

When she bristled, Keene gave her a warning glare. It was easier to keep the peace, so she sipped the tea and let her gaze wander.

"Tell me what's been happening here. We narrowly escaped a raiding party near the ridge."

Liam answered for Marta. "The raiding parties have grown bolder as fall approaches. The hunting has been poor, and we've put extra guards on the cattle and sheep, but even so, the winter promises to be harsh." He tugged at his shirt as if already feeling the chill. "We run patrols several times a day, at different intervals, and it seems to keep most away. Things should settle once the snow falls."

"Perhaps it's best to move farther south until spring," Keene suggested.

Marta scowled. "And our homes will belong to someone else if we leave them. It's not like earlier years when a raiding party might steal before moving on. Now they take over the land as if it were their own." Marta picked up a dress that she must have been mending earlier because a needle and thread already hung from it. She laid it on her lap and began sewing as she spoke.

"The village is stronger than it looks. We took in a small clan last spring. They resettled on the edge of our land, protecting our northern borders and bringing food for the winter stores. We'll take in a few more before winter sets."

"How many men?" Keene asked.

Liam smiled. "We've doubled our number of fighting men. And we expect to double that number before Samhain."

Keene nodded, seeming satisfied. Rowan's ISA instincts made her want to ask about the raiding parties and the village's defenses. But she sat back, irritated by the knowledge the only thing these people would expect from her would be to mend clothes and cook. They'd all starve and go naked if they had to depend on her.

"How fair Lanis and Conall?" Marta asked.

"They're both hearty and miss you. They want to visit this spring if it's permissible."

Marta's eyes lit with joy and a smile that revealed the beauty she'd once been. But the frown was back soon enough. "It will be good to see them." She turned her gaze to Rowan. "So, girl, what is it you can do? Are you good with herbs, or is tanning a hide more your specialty?"

Girl? So, that was how it was going to be. Keene laid a hand on her arm, most likely to remind her where they were. But Marta needed to know she wasn't any lamb. "I don't cook or sew and know nothing of tanning. I know something of herbs and can fight."

Keene and Liam cringed, but Marta pinned her with a wicked stare, brows knit together in a frown. "You'll do best to mind your elders, young Rowan."

She sat back, properly chastised and somewhat sorry for her outburst, even though she needed to have her say. And behind the old woman's bluster, she caught a measure of respect but also mistrust.

Marta stood. "Faye, come gather Rowan so she can help prepare her room." She motioned for her to get up. "If Keene can't teach you the proper ways, and your parents haven't performed their responsibility, then let's see what we can make of you in the short time you're here."

"I thought Rowan could stay with Liam and me." Keene's tone was respectful.

She swatted him as she walked past. "She might only be an apprentice, but a young unmarried woman can't live in a house with two men. Not even for a day or two. Now out with the two of you. We can discuss more at the council meeting. It's apparent Rowan has some catching up to do."

TWENTY-SEVEN

Rowan rarely felt fear. Not in her time with the squad nor when running from bad guys with Keene. Even when they'd been pinned in the storage closet and forced to time travel, the adrenaline pumping through her system wouldn't allow fear to take hold. There had only been two times the cold tendrils of sheer terror had almost taken her down—the day a bullet ripped into her brother and the vision she had with Keene and Zach running across a barren landscape. A valley that looked exactly like the one Keene and her crossed that afternoon.

Now, as she stared up at the menacing eyes of Marta Gregor, an icy chill raced through her. Keene gave her a worried frown as Liam pushed him out the door. Somehow, she'd pay him back for this.

"Don't worry, girl, I don't bite. Much."

Marta cackled like one of the old flower hawkers Rowan avoided in Galway Alley as she led her to the kitchen. For the next two hours, she peeled and chopped carrots, toted buckets of water from the river, and added peat—what she'd thought were charcoal bricks—to the baskets by the fireplace and stone oven. After thinking she'd worked the fight out of her—silly woman—Marta took her to the herb garden to test her knowledge. While she knew many of the herbs, she had no clue about their medicinal properties.

"What kind of Druid are you that you don't know your herbs?" Marta's expression had been a strange mixture of wonderment, irritation, and exasperation. "How long have you been an apprentice?"

Since she had no idea what the first question meant, she focused on the second one. "Not quite a week."

"Oh, gad, no wonder." She squinted one eye as she pinned her with the other. "You're not lying to an old woman, are ye? That won't go unpunished."

"Why would I bother lying to someone I'll probably never see again?" Now that they were alone, it was time for the gloves to come off, and manners be damned, she was going to stand up for herself. She might play little miss subservient while Keene was around if only to avoid his anger, but she wasn't going to roll over for someone who clearly disliked her from the start.

"What's your lineage, girl? I don't remember Keene mentioning your surname."

Her lineage? She racked her brain for what Marta was talking about. "My last name is Lockwood."

The squint in her one eye didn't go away. "Is that so? Hmm." She leaned on the rock wall to help her stand then stretched her back. With both hands pressed to her lower back, she lifted her face to the hazy sun. "We need to get dinner on. Since you have no talent for herbs, let's see what you can do with fish."

They discovered her hidden talent. She'd never deboned a fish before, but her skill with knives came in handy. If she was expecting any words of praise from Marta, she'd have better luck waiting for the sky to turn green. After Tally, the young girl who'd served them tea, showed her how to perform the task on two fish, Rowan pushed the girl aside and went to work on the rest of them.

A large group must have been invited for dinner because the fish never seemed to stop. Marta watched her for a while, then turned away with a mild grunt, leaving her to speculate whether that was a positive or negative response. Since Marta would cut off both hands rather than give her one ounce of praise, she decided the grunts were signs of approval. Any spoken words would most likely remain unfavorable.

She was exhausted by the time dinner was ready, and guests began arriving. Voices increased in the outer room as she scraped fish bones and guts into a bucket. She washed her hands in cold water to get the stink of fish off her, then stood in a corner for another five minutes before Marta released her from her duties.

The outer room was crowded with people laughing and drinking, and she had to push her way through, ignoring the stares as the guests elbowed each other to signal an outsider in their midst. Keene was on the far side of the room, between the door and fireplace, and she jumped into his arms, catching him off-guard. Though startled, he gripped her waist and gathered her close as she threw her arms around his neck.

She might have made a mistake as his strong arms tightened, and the increased beating of his heart pounded against her chest. Without thinking, she pressed her face against his cheek, taking pleasure in his familiar scent of wildflowers and warm spring rain. What she would remember as the scent of Scotland. One hand slid up her back, pressing her closer while his other hand cradled her ass.

He was either taking advantage of the situation or was playing to the crowd. She decided it had to be the latter since it was what she'd hoped for.

She whispered in his ear so only he could hear. "Get me the hell out of here."

His response was a chuckle that warmed her and induced an involuntary flush. When he set her down, she buried her head in his chest so no one could see the heat in her cheeks.

"She's an eager one."

She turned to find a beefy red-headed man with a thick beard that hung several inches below his chin. His chiding produced laughter from most of the room as people stopped their discussions to watch her display.

"Aye," said Keene. "I had to leave her with Marta so I could get some rest."

Her face grew hotter, and since Keene made no move to get her out of the house, she turned to his brother.

"Liam. I have a short reprieve from the kitchen. Tell me something about yourself. Didn't you mention you were a bard? I'm not familiar with that term." She kept her voice low, but a few men around them heard, and soon the whispers made it around the room.

Another man, larger than Liam and Keene put together, shouted something in their strange foreign tongue, and everyone began to chant.

Keene rolled his eyes, his expression amused. "Now you've done it."

"What?" She stepped closer to him, unsure of what she'd done wrong. When she glanced at the crowd, she released her breath. All eyes were on Liam. Another shout, and the silence was more deafening than the earlier laughter.

She turned to Liam. "I'm sorry for whatever I just did."

He shrugged and grinned at her. "At least you've gotten yourself out of the spotlight."

She perked up. "So, I have. Sorry, it couldn't have been Keene."

Keene gave them a wounded look. "What did I do?"

Liam's laugh boomed around the room, forcing chuckles out of others. Then several men parted to reveal a chair with a stringed instrument leaning against it in a far corner.

When Liam picked it up and strummed the strings, she leaned over to Keene. "Is that a guitar?"

He shook his head. "A lute."

When the music started and Liam's voice filled the room, Rowan leaned against the wall and closed her eyes. It was a haunting melody, sung in the language she was beginning to recognize if not understand. When he finished the song and began something more uplifting, she opened her eyes to find everyone had moved back to create space for two couples who began to dance. They were cheered on, and she laughed with them, clapping to the beat.

She turned to Keene to find him staring at her, a ghost of a smile on his full lips but confusion in his gaze. Before she could analyze it further, someone grabbed her hand and whirled her into the middle of the room. She bounced off a big hulk of a man who spun a woman half his size around in circles, both of them smiling with glee.

Rowan's suitor was tall and wiry with a thin brown beard and bushy eyebrows. His smile was missing two front teeth, and after a few twirls, he stopped to perform some unique dance steps before setting them in motion again, somehow staying within the small, confined space.

When her head spun faster than her body, Keene rescued her and handed Moira off to her energetic partner. Moira must have jumped at the chance to grab Keene while Rowan had been spinning like a top. When the young woman glared at her as she passed by in a twirl, Rowan wondered why she wasn't glaring at Keene. He'd been the one to give her away.

Keene pushed her to the door and slipped out behind her.

The brisk night air cooled her cheeks and dried the sweat from dancing in the sweltering room.

She sucked in the fresh air and caught the scent of peat smoke, the remaining scents from dinner, and livestock. "This reminds me of the bonfires in the Yards." Every month, somewhere in the Yards, a community party would host a bonfire. Barbecue pits, cooking stoves, coolers of liquor, and music that played into the morning. "Do they do this every night?"

Keene stepped down the stairs and perched on the backside of a wooden cart. "No. They'd never get any work done. They'll sleep till noon. But it's a custom when greeting a guest, and the clan chief was due for an elders' meeting."

"Is that their form of government?"

"In a sense. Nothing so formal or deep as you'd find in England. This meeting will be mostly about food and security."

"The fundamentals of any society."

He nodded.

"So why did they meet on your arrival?"

He shrugged but didn't rush his answer. "Just good timing."

She let it go. Asking Keene a point-blank question on topics he didn't want to answer never worked. She had to take a different tact. Then she remembered something Liam and Marta had mentioned.

"What's a Druid?"

He didn't bat an eye, his expression bland, but she swore he was holding his breath. Then his brows knit together in a curious stare. "That's not something that should have been shared." He waved her away when she opened her mouth to speak. "And it's my fault for bringing you here and not forewarning Liam and Marta."

"So just tell me."

His gaze softened, and he shrugged. "You're not going to like it, but I'm going to ask you to wait until we're back in the bunker with Lanis and Conall. We might as well discuss it once."

She considered his situation. More secrets. This time, she had something to hang over his head if he backed out of his commitment. She nodded. "But you have to make me a promise."

Keene was saved when the door creaked open.

"Rowan, Tally needs help with the dishes." Marta stood by the door, and it appeared her comment wasn't a suggestion but a command.

She slumped her shoulders and scowled at Keene before following Marta inside. His apologetic smile gave her courage until she spotted the washtub filled with dirty dishes. She rolled up her sleeves, refusing to be intimidated, and almost shrieked when her hands hit scalding water. She glanced over at the other tub, where Tally focused on her own stack. Her hands were beet red against her pale skin. It was nothing less than sheer torture.

She endured the first round, but when it was time to bring more water, she took charge of the duty and added cold water to temper the fire-heated bucket, making it more tolerable. When Tally's gaze widened at the cooler water, Rowan shook her head, hoping the girl would keep quiet. Tally glanced at Marta, who was across the kitchen, then smiled and nodded her thanks before returning to her duties.

An hour later, Marta allowed them to sit and drink honeyed tea with the other girls before turning in. She wanted to go straight to bed, but Marta insisted she wait for the tea. It tasted different than what she'd been served earlier in the day, with a bitter aftertaste beneath the cloying sweetness of honey.

She finished the cup, and Marta nodded in approval. Everyone continued with a second cup while they chattered nonstop in a language she didn't understand, often breaking into giggles. The melodic rhythm of the words lulled her eyes closed, and she began to sway.

A flash of pain.

Blackness.

A barren landscape. A village—burned and ravaged. The dead lay scattered on the ground. Rowan recognized the hamlet. It was this one.

Three people ran through the village, checking bodies and searching inside buildings for survivors—Keene, Zach, and her. She jerked, staring down at herself as if she were seeing it through a bird's eyes.

Another stab of pain.

The landscape changed. Stark and wild. Three people running down a hill. Two men, Liam and Conall, dressed in what she instinctively knew to be belted plaid with a linen saffron tunic, swords still in their scabbards. In the middle, a woman kept pace. Her auburn hair was in a short braid, and she was dressed in trews; her sleeveless saffron tunic billowed in the wind. She held a crossbow in her right hand, a quiver hugged her back, and an axe hung on her belt. From the back, she couldn't swear it was herself, but an intense panic consumed her. She didn't know why, but time was running out.

Then everything went black as her head hit the hard stone floor.

"ROWAN. CAN YOU HEAR ME? ROWAN?"

Keene's voice came and went as if he called her name into the wind.

"I think she hit her head." A girl's voice. Tally?

"She'll be fine. Let's sit her up." The sound of Marta's voice made her curl into a ball.

"Give her another minute." Keene's voice held a note of bitterness. "I shouldn't have brought her here. I thought you'd treat a guest better."

"I treated her like any other guest in my home."

"By having her work in the kitchen? She's my apprentice, not your personal maid."

"I didn't ask you to bring her here in the first place."

"Enough." Liam's voice, harsh and hushed, broke through the griping. "This isn't Keene's fault, and you know it."

She couldn't wait out the silence and pried a lid open in time to catch Marta glance away.

Keene inspected something on the table. There were two of him, and she blinked several times to bring the two halves into a whole. He sniffed a cup and gave Marta a menacing look.

Had the old biddy doped her tea? Damn. She was good. She hadn't seen that coming.

Then she recalled the vision—both of them. She groaned and tried to sit up, reaching for a chair.

Keene put an arm around her waist and helped her into the seat. He squatted and pushed a strand of hair behind her ear. "Look at me." When she didn't comply, he lifted her chin with the crook of his tanned finger.

She stared at him. The candlelight softened his rugged features, and warmth flooded through her. His eyes, usually so stormy, were filled with concern.

"Blink."

She managed to squeak out, "What?"

"Never mind. You'll be okay in another minute or two. Take slow, deep breaths. It will help to clear your head."

Liam helped her stand as Keene stepped back. "We think the heat of the house, the chores, and all the dancing might have gotten the better of you. You've had a long day." He winked at her, and she darted a glance at Keene, the effort draining what little energy she had left. His concerned expression hadn't faded.

"Moira!" Marta's voice pierced the room and her skull. "Get over here, girl, and help Rowan to her room. It should be ready."

Great. Now she'd have to make sure she didn't end up with a knife in her back from a member of Keene's sweetheart club.

Moira swept her away with the speed of light, and she held her head with one hand as she was tugged up the stairs. The last thing she heard before moving out of earshot was Keene declaring he wouldn't talk to the elders without her.

That was good. And she shouldn't be worried at all that she couldn't remember why they had to talk to the elders.

TWENTY-EIGHT

The next morning, it was still dark when Rowan grabbed the fur blanket that covered her and, feeling her way along the walls, made it downstairs. A candle had been glowing when she fell face-first into bed, but she had no idea how to light it. Smoke and heat came from the smoldering fire but shed no light. A single candle burned on the mantel above it.

Her head was clear and other than a stiff neck from the uncomfortable bed, she was back to her old self. More acclimated to the temperate climate of Los Angeles, she was chilled to the bone but had to get out of the house.

In the kitchen, a dim light and sounds of early morning housemaids preparing for the day had her tiptoeing to the door. The last thing she needed was Marta putting her to work again. She almost tripped over two men who snored on the floor in front of the fireplace, and she cringed when the door scraped against the stone floor. But she squeezed through without interrupting their sleep and pulled the fur blanket tighter as the bite of the morning air nipped at her cheeks.

She found a spot under a thin tree to watch the sunrise and must have dozed off because the sun had crested the horizon when she opened her eyes. Though she'd missed the sight of dawn, the pink sky was worth it as it painted the landscape a rosy glow.

"I brought you tea."

She startled before glancing up to see Liam holding out a mug. When she nodded but didn't take it, he sat next to her and managed to keep the two mugs from dripping. "I promise there's nothing in it. I made it myself, but I'll warn you, I brew a stronger tea than Marta."

She took the offering, grateful for the warm liquid. It wasn't coffee but the closest she'd drunk since arriving.

"I miss coffee." Liam's melodic voice blended with the trilling of the morning birds.

"I've gone less than a day, and I'm already testy."

He laughed. "I'll tell you a secret if you don't tell Keene, though I think he already suspects."

Happy to know something, anything, that Keene didn't already know made her grin like a little girl willing to trade one secret for another. She nodded and huddled closer.

A fur cloak covered Liam's shoulders, though underneath, he wore nothing but his yellowed shirt and pants. A flashback from her vision made her rephrase the thought in her head to a saffron tunic over trews. How would she know that? She shivered, and Liam, most likely mistaking her physical response as being cold, moved a few inches closer.

He sipped his tea, then gave her an earnest look. "Not a word of this to anyone. Not Lanis or Conall."

She nodded, eager to hear what this young rebel was up to.

"My role in the village is one of a bard. I think you learned last night the term means a singer and teller of stories. Bards record events that are passed down through the ages and revive stories that came before us. We keep the lineage of the clan alive since very little is written."

"You have a beautiful voice."

She wasn't sure if it was the remaining effects of the rising sun or if a blush made his cheeks appear pink, but he smiled before he lowered his head to study his mug of tea.

"To be a true bard, one must travel to other friendly clans and learn their stories. One could be gone for weeks, even months, learning new stories to share around a fire. And I do a bit of that, though I don't travel farther than a handful of days. I don't have the skills of a true warrior, and with raiding clans, I have to be careful."

"No one goes with you?"

He leaned against a boulder and shrugged. "Sometimes. Visiting other villages is a good time to trade, and depending on what we have to offer, several of the clan will go. But most of the time, I head out on my own. Sometimes, I travel to other villages I know, but mostly, I walk back to the cave. I stay for about a week, drinking coffee and reading my favorite books." He chuckled. "Even sleeping in a hard bed has its benefits."

"Why don't you transport home? Is there something about how often you can travel?"

"And both of those questions are best saved for another time and shouldn't be discussed here." Keene's low voice startled both of them.

"Brother." Liam's surprised tone turned his cheeks pink again. "I thought you'd sleep in."

"You're right about the beds." Keene smiled at his brother's blush, and he slapped him on the back. "Don't worry. We all knew you were spending time in the cave."

Liam lowered his head and scratched the back of his neck. For a second, she pictured him as a small lad, doing something he'd been told not to, then getting caught by his big brother. When he lifted his head, a grin replaced his frown. "I thought I'd been careful."

Keene laughed. "You were. If it had been just Conall or me, your secret would be safe. But Lanis..." He let the statement fade.

"I should have known. Nobody can hide anything from that woman." Liam stood, then held out his hand to help her up.

Once standing, Keene grabbed her shoulders, holding her at arm's length. His eyes narrowed as he looked her over. "Are you all right?"

She pushed his arms away, somewhat embarrassed by his concern, though a warm flush spread through her. Disregarding both unwanted emotions, she flipped her hair back and pulled the fur tighter. "I'm fine." But she couldn't help smiling. "I have to agree with both of you about the beds. They're horrid."

They both laughed, but there was something in Keene's gaze that said he didn't quite believe everything was all right, and she internally cursed his perceptiveness. She wasn't fine. Not even close. After the remnants of Marta's special tea had worn off, she'd tossed half the night thinking about the visions. Then she stared at the dark ceiling for what seemed like hours, remembering Keene's burning question about what Marta had put in the tea. Had that induced her vision, or had it been a simple coincidence? And if the tea had brought on the visions, what made Marta even think to try?

After a breakfast of porridge and eggs, they gathered in the main room with four additional people. Two men and two women sat facing an empty chair. Liam pushed her into a corner with a signal to stay quiet while Keene took the seat in front of who Rowan assumed were the elders. She'd seen one of the men the previous night, and one of the women was Marta. The other two didn't look familiar.

"The clan chief left last night," Liam whispered from their corner. "The man on the right is the local chieftain, and the others are elders who keep the history to pass down to other generations."

She nodded, curious as to why Keene asked for the meeting.

"What is it you seek, young Keene, seeker of truth and fellow clansman?" The other woman asked the question. If Rowan had to guess, she was older than Marta by many years. But her sharp gaze didn't miss anything. She'd glanced at Rowan several times when she'd first arrived, though hadn't asked who she was or why Keene insisted she attend the meeting.

"I come only for your wisdom, and if so honored, perhaps a piece of our history," Keene spoke firmly but quietly, his head partially bowed in deference to the elders.

The four peered at each other before turning to Keene. The old woman responded with her own head partially bowed. "You may ask your question."

Keene reached into this pocket and drew out a small piece of paper. The page looked old and yellowed, and she leaned over Liam to look at it, but he pushed her back. Keene shifted the page as he handed it to the woman, allowing her to catch a glance. It was a hand-drawn picture of the Celtic tattoo they'd been chasing.

She stared at him as if he'd lost his mind, and he caught her gaze while the paper was passed around. He winked at her before refocusing on the elders. Had it been his intention all along to come to the past in search of an answer? Or was he taking advantage of the opportunity?

"Did he show you the drawing?" she whispered to Liam.

He nodded. "I haven't seen it before but thought the elders might have." Liam's response dashed her wild hope that they'd find an answer.

The younger of the two men shook his head while the other spoke in what she'd learned was Gaelic. The older woman listened, occasionally adding to the conversation. Marta appeared to be listening, but her gaze was unfocused as if trying to recall something.

When Marta stirred from wherever she'd been, she murmured a single word. The other three stared at her, looked at the paper she held in her hands, and the talk began again. Keene and Liam paid close attention, though I couldn't tell if they were getting anything out of the discussion.

It was Marta who turned to Keene after the other three nodded. "This is very old. Not seen in many years, and not by many. I only saw it once when I was but a young woman with my four wee young. Far west of here, by the sea. Fergus remembers it as well. It was carved on an old stone along with an ogham inscription. Even then, the carving had been weathered by time. I've not seen anything like it since. The knot refers to ath-bhreithe and the ogham to ruis."

Keene and Liam sat back. Liam appeared confused and Keene stunned. Before Keene recovered his typical blank expression, Rowan caught the tic in his jaw and a flash of irritation, or maybe anger, in his gaze. She chafed at not being able to ask questions, to understand the meaning of the Gaelic words. What would something written decades or centuries before this timeline have to do with murders in her century? It made no sense.

Although frowned upon by GSM, the Yards were filled with multi-cultural beliefs that went back centuries. The current troubles with the Underground began two years ago, and some in the Yards thought it was a fight for their dying cultures. Was it possible that the dead guy and the tattooed mystery man were connected to the Underground? How would they have known about it? She ignored the conversation between Keene and the elders as they continued in Gaelic and mentally listed several search parameters to give Hernandez.

She would still have access to the ISA files on past Underground activities. Maybe they could find a connection to the tattoo or maybe to the Spider. The woman might be dead, but that didn't mean she couldn't still provide some answers.

Keened suddenly stood, drawing her back to the present. He gave the elders a slight bow. "Thank you for your time. Tell me how I can repay your kindness."

The old man, who'd been the less vocal of the group, nodded as he considered Keene's words. "The winter will be hard this year, but we have enough stores to get us through. But we worry the following years will be harsher and that trade might be difficult. We seek divination."

Keene considered his words. "I'll study the runes for guidance. If I can't return myself to share their wisdom, I'll send a message to Liam." He held out a hand to Marta. "We thank you for your hospitality and your assistance with my apprentice."

"She has much to learn." Marta ignored her, making her feel two inches tall. She'd been in meetings with high-powered GSM officials who made her feel more comfortable.

Keene nodded. "She's still young."

Thanks for the vote of confidence.

As if he'd heard her thoughts, he added, "But she has many talents you have yet to witness."

Marta appeared to want to say something else but simply returned the nod.

Keene motioned for her to follow, and not knowing what the protocol was, she bowed her head to the elders, keeping her eyes downcast. Liam walked behind her as the three of them exited the house. Keene led them some distance away to a small stone structure that was Liam's home.

Liam ducked inside and returned with a journal he tucked into the leather pouch he wore around his waist. How did she know that was a sporran? Before she could give it more thought,

Keene guided them back to the trail where they'd entered the village the day before. The hike back to the cave was completed in silence, each of them in their own thoughts.

She'd wanted to know what happened with the elders, but Keene would only tell her to wait until they reached the cave. He seemed closed off, and once again, she decided not to push. More flies with honey and all that. So, she spent the time studying everything around her, keeping an eye out for danger. That was something she could do.

The day had warmed enough that their quick pace had them sweating by the time they'd reached the safe room. Keene filled a pitcher with water and set three mugs on the table. Liam started a pot of coffee, and the smell alone seemed to revive them.

She tugged at her neckline and pushed up the sleeves, preferring to change back into her own clothes. But between the sleepless night, anxiety around the elders, and the long walk back to the mountain, she barely had the energy to stand. More than that, she had to know what the elders had said.

"What did they say about the tattoo?" The quick glance Keene gave Liam wasn't one she could read, but she prepared herself to be disappointed by the answer.

"Two of the elders have seen it before—Marta and the chieftain. But it was long ago, and as she told us in English, the symbol was already weathered. Probably by centuries of harsh Highland conditions, especially if it was close to the sea." Keene finished off his glass of water before picking up the coffee. He stared into it like he could see something in the ripples. "Most of their discussion was trying to remember where they'd seen it though there was little doubt to what it meant."

Liam sipped his coffee in front of a bookcase as he studied the books. He ignored their discussion, occasionally pulling out a book then stuffing it back.

She gulped the coffee, feeling more like her old self. "If this symbol showed up in Scotland, shouldn't this be something you should know or, I don't know, have in your files?" If Keene and his group were anthropologists, it made sense.

He surprised her by nodding in agreement. "There are thousands of stones throughout Scotland that have runes on them in various combinations. Many are barely recognizable, even during this century. Weather and the type of stone dictate how long etchings remain. If even a portion has worn or broken away, it could be impossible to decipher the original symbol. And it isn't like we travel just to read rocks."

"It's here."

They both turned to Liam. When he realized they'd stopped speaking, he turned to them with a bemused grin. "I don't know where. I just know it's here. With enough time, I'll find it."

Keene nodded as if that made sense, then turned back to her to finish his thoughts. "Malcolm, the village's chieftain, believes it was on the cornerstone of an old church. Marta remembers seeing it on a stone where an oak grove used to be." He rubbed his face, suddenly appearing more tired than she'd ever seen him. Even when he was shot in the arm, his body weak from the drug-laced crossbow bolt, he seemed more alert. He must not have slept any better than her. And something had him worried. She hadn't known him long, but his tells were becoming clear. "We need to get this information to Lanis. With her direction, maybe Horatio will have better luck finding something in our archives. Lanis didn't find anything in her first search, but none of us noticed the ogham buried within the knot. With this added piece, she might be able to expand the search."

"It will be like searching through all the hieroglyphs in the Egyptian pyramids trying to find one symbol that is different than all the rest," Liam added.

The enormity of the situation hit home, and she felt as tired as Keene looked.

"Can you have Lanis send the complete set of Imani's genealogical references?" Liam asked.

"Who's Imani?" Rowan asked.

"Another team member," Keene answered without providing any further information.

"And I could use a new fusion block?" Liam pulled books from the shelves, double-checking the first few pages before setting them in one of three piles. "I'll tell Marta I want to travel to a few clans to ask about the symbol."

"Why don't you come home and help search the databases?" Keene's tone was encouraging, almost pleading.

Liam turned his head away, refocusing on the books, his words nothing more than a whisper. "I'm not ready."

"It's been long enough."

"I say when it's enough."

Keene let the silence hang between them, folding his arms across his chest and dropping the touchy subject. He gave her a warning glance when she opened her mouth, but she waved him off. She knew better than to get involved in their family issues, no matter how curious she was to understand what prevented Liam from returning home.

"Now that we know the symbol is old, was anyone able to tell us what it means?" A symbol, especially one tattooed, must signify something.

Liam stopped segmenting books long enough to wait for Keene's reply. He either wanted to validate what he'd heard in the rapid-fire Gaelic or perhaps would have a different interpretation. Based on the continual running of his fingers through this hair, she braced for the response.

Keene tapped his fingers on the table, refusing to meet her gaze. "The main part of the tattoo is a Celtic knot, as we assumed. But buried in the middle of the design is an ogham symbol. Ogham is an ancient Celtic alphabet used mostly by the Irish. These symbols can have varied meanings. The knot can translate to ath-bhreithe or rebirth. The ogham refers to ruis—regret or possibly retribution. The elders seemed to agree on a single combined interpretation."

She waited, but Keene seemed to have gone someplace else. His expression turned blank, which wasn't new for him, but for some reason, this time, it scared her. But she still needed to know what it all meant.

Liam finally responded. "Cunntadh. The reckoning."

TWENTY-NINE

Rowan dry heaved into the toilet for the third time. She ran the back of her hand over her mouth, almost gagging at the bile. Not that this wasn't a familiar scene for her. The difference was the man standing behind her, holding the hair out of her face. She was embarrassed beyond belief. This was the second time he'd seen her throw up.

When they'd left Scotland, Liam was relaxing on the bed, covered with layers of blankets and nestled between his stack of books, a fresh pot of coffee close at hand. He seemed content and had a smile on his face before the room went black.

After another trip of colorful symbols and the feeling of being sucked down a drainpipe, she landed on her feet. Red lights flashed, alarms beeped, and a computer voice continuously repeated "unexpected arrival."

They'd arrived in what Keene called the point of debarkation room, or POD, located on the second floor of the bunker. The room was typically used whenever someone traveled to a specific time and location, but they could leave from any point, as they had from the storage closet at Stoker. The trip home always ended in this room. Though they'd spent a full day in Scotland, Keene returned them to approximately the same date and time they'd originally departed.

"Couldn't we have arrived earlier, like before the Spider was killed?" It was too obvious, but she had to ask.

"We return to the current time in the POD, or as close as possible. The time continuum is a tricky master, and we try to stay within strict parameters."

She didn't know anything about the technicalities of time travel, but he was right about one thing. If they had returned anywhere near GSM around the time of their escape, ISA patrols would have been everywhere. And it probably wouldn't have mattered. The Spider was most likely killed the minute they checked into the front desk at Stoker. It was going to be difficult enough to explain how they got out of the storage closet, should anyone report the incident. Though, Keene believed the entire record of them being on site at the time of the murder would be erased. And while she agreed, neither of them understood why Stoker would keep it quiet. Just one more mystery.

The POD was similar to a sterile lab. Half the room was separated into three sections by transparent circular walls. She wasn't sure what the walls were made of, but something told her they'd be bulletproof, laser-proof, and bio-secure.

They'd arrived in the center circle next to a free-standing coms station. Keene typed into a data pad, and she peered over his shoulder.

"What are you doing?"

"First, shutting down the alarms." Seconds later, a peaceful silence descended, and the flashing lights stopped. "Next, I'm syncing up our original departure time and destination, then adding the purpose of our visit and who we interacted with. I'll add more details in my official report."

"Do you do that each time you travel?"

He nodded. "When you live with scientists, scholars, and engineers, you quickly learn that everything must be documented…"

"Or face the wrath of Lanis." The woman herself, her mirth casually covering a look of annoyance, stood at the entrance of the room. "And you always advise of transport before it happens." She strode to an imager that sprang to life with her verbal command. "I'll need all your weapons removed and anything metallic. Stack them in a pile. You can retrieve them after you're cleared. Step into the next section."

The transparent wall separating them from the next circle disappeared into the ceiling. Keene stepped forward and glanced back at her. She looked up and then down, noting the thin circle of vents that ran along the ceiling and floor. She assumed they were air vents and fell into line next to him as the wall dropped behind her. A yellow beam of light flickered to life above them. It slid down, and as it grew closer, she reflexively ducked.

"Hold still. It's checking for bio-contaminates. You won't feel anything."

His calm voice steadied her, and she closed her eyes as the beam passed over her.

"What if it finds something?" Lifting one eyelid to watch the yellow beam at their legs disappear into the floor.

"Depends on what it finds, but usually an inoculation of some type would be required."

"Could we have transmitted something to the villagers?" She hadn't even considered that.

"No. The inoculations you received at birth prevent your body from spreading contagions. Known ones anyway, even those that are considered fully eradicated like smallpox."

That was a relief, but Keene would have considered that

before transporting them. The MacGregors seemed to think of everything. Besides, if they time traveled as frequently as it sounded, they would have already considered the impacts to the places they visited. Though she knew little about her partner, he wouldn't have risked the villagers to save themselves.

"I imagine there's a good reason that you traveled with Rowan." Lanis stared at the imager, then nodded. "You're clean. You can proceed to the next section."

The next wall disappeared into the ceiling and Rowan stepped forward. She glanced up as the wall descended and noticed the vents were in this section, too. She'd never seen anything like this setup anywhere in GSM and assumed it was a prototype from one of Keene's connections.

"This can be intimidating the first time, but there's nothing to worry about." Keene's measured tone was more annoying than helpful.

Why did his voice sound like it was coming out of the speakers? She looked to her left, but Keene wasn't there. She turned around. He was behind her and beyond the divider.

"Why aren't you in here?" Her voice rose an octave, and she took a deep breath. She didn't need them to think she was going batshit crazy. Some time home alone to consider everything that happened over the last couple of days couldn't hurt, but, in her opinion, she'd been handling everything pretty well.

Before Keene could answer, blue spotlights lit up from the floor, and a light mist floated down from the vents. Her bare skin tingled at its touch, and her earlier concerns flared as she watched the floor vents suck the mist away.

"What's happening?" She kept her tone controlled and remained calm, though she wanted to rub off whatever she'd been misted with.

"Sorry." Lanis smiled, but Rowan didn't believe her. She seemed to enjoy playing with the rookie time traveler.

After a minute, the air dried, and the blue light extinguished. Then, with a soft woosh, all the walls lifted to the ceiling. When she turned around, Keene was collecting his weapons. She holstered her sidearm, stuck her knife in her boot, and tucked the old timepiece into a pocket.

"What did you spray me with?" The tingling on her skin had stopped once the mist dried.

"Trixcillian," Lanis answered.

"I've never heard of it."

"It's a compound that conditions your body to your normal time continuum. While you're in this bunker, you're not impacted by time shifts. But if you were to step outside without the conditioning, you could experience side effects. Think of it as being a second or two out of sync with everything around you. It's not something you would perceive but your body would notice the difference."

"Why was I the only one in the mist?"

"Because only a single dose is required."

"Why didn't I need this when we arrived in Scotland?"

Lanis gave Keene a curious glance, and Rowan assumed it was the mention of Scotland. "If you had stayed longer than three days, you would have needed a shot. The mist is simpler."

Rowan spun on Keene. "What would you have done if we'd been delayed?"

"Calm down." Keene directed her to the door. "There's plenty of trixcillian on hand in each safe house."

She bristled at his assertion she needed to settle down. It's not like anyone explained this before dowsing her.

Lanis followed behind them. "Since you've only been gone about thirty minutes from our perspective, Horatio and Hernandez won't have much to report, but we can check their status right after the mission interview."

They walked down a long hallway and made one turn

before arriving at the command center, but instead of going inside, Lanis walked to the next set of doors and led them into a conference room. The walls were the same pleasant green as the hallways without the murals. A single table with six chairs filled the room. A data pad, a wall imager, and a holo-monitor were the only features.

Lanis used a data pad to bring up the imager and placed her journal and pen next to it. Conall entered the room and gave Rowan a large grin as he took a seat at the far end of the table. Once Lanis nodded she was ready, Keene launched into their visit to Stoker, finding the Spider dead, their race through the tower in an attempt to evade unknown men with guns, and his decision to time travel. His only report regarding their time spent in Scotland was their meeting with the elders.

"Can we create search parameters with this new information on the tattoo?" Keene asked. "I don't know how I missed the ogham."

"We all missed it." Lanis tapped a finger on her chin as she stared at the tattoo that was circling on the holo-monitor. "It certainly stands out now that we know it's there. I'm not convinced we have anything in our databases, but we can ask Horatio to try. What do you know about the elder's interpretation of cunntadh? The reckoning."

Keene hesitated, then shrugged his shoulders. "Nothing."

He was lying. She wasn't sure how she knew because she'd never caught him in one before. There wasn't anything specific in his expression. It was more of a feeling. Something she couldn't quite define. Lanis didn't appear to notice anything peculiar, but she was busy making notes in her journal, only lifting her head to glance at the tattoo.

For a moment, the room seemed to tilt, and a cold sweat beaded her forehead. Her clothes stuck to her skin, and she wiped her brow as she fell back in her seat.

"Are you all right, Rowan?" Conall asked.

Keene and Lanis turned toward her at his question.

"Sure." She wiped her brow again, then rubbed her damp palm up and down her pants. "It just seems a little warm in here." She didn't have to look at them to know that wasn't good. The room had been on the cooler side when they'd entered.

Lanis was at her side in an instant. "You're flushed."

"A reaction to the trixcillian?" Keene asked.

"I don't see how." Lanis placed a hand on her forehead.

Rowan pushed her hand away and remembered the restroom across the hall. She moved like lightning and pushed her way out the door but fumbled with the bathroom handle. Her frustration rose when the door wouldn't open. Who would lock a restroom in this place? When she got a better grip on the handle, the door flung open, and she almost tumbled onto the floor. She raced for the toilet on the far side of the room. She dove for it, throwing up what was left of the coffee and, unfortunately, some of the morning's porridge.

Keene held her hair, having been quick enough to follow her and pull it back before she emptied the first load. He didn't say a word, but she thought she heard a light humming as she threw up twice more until there was nothing left but bile.

When her stomach settled, she sat back, pulling her knees against her chest. "I don't know where that came from. I guess the food didn't sit well." The floor wasn't tilting anymore, and the sweat had dried.

Keene leaned a shoulder against the wall. "I'll agree the porridge was disagreeable, but you were fine until we returned."

"Which seems like the perfect catalyst to shake up my stomach."

"Are you all right, lass?" Conall poked his head in but stopped at setting foot in the room. She couldn't blame him. The room smelled horrid.

"I don't need the fuss."

"Great." He boomed. "Then meet us in the command center. Hernandez is concerned for your welfare."

Keene gave her an assessing look before shaking his head. "Give her another five minutes."

She wanted to prove him wrong, but when she began to rise, the room spun, and she dropped against the wall. So embarrassing.

She gave it two minutes, waiting for the bile to settle, then pushed to a standing position, keeping her movements slow to prevent the dizziness from returning. God knew she had enough practice trying to look cool in the face of sheer idiocy from more than one drunken adventure.

Once standing, or at least leaning in an upright position, she took a few tentative steps that took her past Keene, whose brow still wrinkled with concern. She gave him a little wave of thanks and ran a hand through her hair, thankful it felt dry.

The low lights of the command center were a welcome relief, and Hernandez met her as soon as she entered.

"Hey boss, you don't look so good."

And coming from her, that was saying something. "I'm good. Something I ate earlier didn't sit well. I just need a few minutes, and I'll be back to normal."

"Why don't you sit while Horatio updates us." Lanis pointed to an empty seat where everyone waited at the conference table. Several stacks of books covered the table, and she slid a few out of the way before carrying the rest to a side table, returning them to their orderly condition.

Horatio's leg bounced with its usual enthusiasm. "We're almost finished copying everything over from the vault, and once that is completed, a second program will search for the meeting at Stoker. I set up specific search parameters that will take longer to run, but we'll have fewer results to sift through."

"Didn't you give it the date and time of the meeting?" Rowan asked.

He nodded but included an eye roll. "Do you know how many meetings occur at GSM or their contractors in a single day at the same hour?" When she shook her head, he continued. "Let's just say there are a lot. It won't take much longer. The more interesting thing is what Hernandez has found."

"More like didn't find." Hernandez tapped a few commands into her data pad, and the holo-monitor popped up with a list of thirty names. "These were the names registered for the meeting." She typed an additional command, which brought up entries to the right of the names. "I found financial records on eight of them."

"How could that be?" Conall's question had the rest of them nodding. "Everyone should have a security file along with their financial data."

He wasn't wrong. Financial records of employees and contractors were continually monitored to prevent bribes or other illegal activities. Any strange activity would be flagged and investigated.

"It's rare, but sometimes files are pulled for high-risk investigations." Rowan's stomach grumbled, but she ignored it, hoping it was just resettling. "Is it possible another organization could be investigating this group?"

"I thought of that." Hernandez brought up a file. "Here's one record we found." She used a pointer to highlight a section at the top of the page. "If the file was being reviewed in an investigation, a code number should be listed in the top right corner."

"If one or two were missing, we might consider them lost." Horatio scratched his head, his leg still bouncing. Did the kid ever settle down? "There are a couple more options to explore, but it's odd so many seem misplaced."

This was bad news. A glance at the others' frowns

confirmed her suspicions. Someone had been one step ahead of them.

"With the files missing, I assume you don't know when they disappeared." Rowan figured the answer would be no but had to ask. When Horatio and Hernandez scooted close to whisper, she became optimistic.

"You think someone began deleting files as soon as the Spider was terminated?" Keene's expression suggested he already knew the answer, but she nodded. "Damn it. We'll never find them."

"Maybe," Horatio responded. "Give us time to check the vault. If it's true they recently erased the files, they might not have wiped everything from the individual financial institutions."

"They probably wrote a program to do that." Hernandez typed on her data pad as she stared at the list. "But it would take a while to get through the individual security systems." She slapped Horatio on the arm. "Let's get started on that."

"Agreed." Lanis turned her attention to Rowan. "You still don't look good."

Rowan grimaced. "You need to work on your delivery."

Lanis smiled. "You probably just need rest. Why don't you go to the room we assigned you?"

"I'd feel better if I was home."

The three MacGregors looked at each other as if the decision was theirs to make. But they nodded in agreement, and she blew out a breath. She didn't have the energy for an argument. The nausea was barely under control, and the flight home would require her full attention.

"I'll take you home." Keene stood and waited at the door for her to join him.

"I can manage on my own." She made it five full steps before a headache slammed into her and took her to her knees.

She waited for the vision. What would it be this time? She heard voices—Keene, Lanis, then Hernandez. The sound of the ocean drowned them out. Waves battered the shore. A cool breeze tickled her nose. No images, just sensations—her hair blowing across her face, a rocking motion, then pleasant silence followed by darkness.

THIRTY

Apounding in Rowan's head and what she thought was the chiming of her alarm dragged her out of a deep sleep. She managed a low rough command, "Alarm off." When the brief melody came again, she swept her arm out and rolled over. The clank of bottles hitting each other made her wince. She waited for the sound of broken glass, but all she heard was a thud as they hit the rug.

The empty bottles explained the headache and probably the pounding. And that's when the previous day slammed into her. She covered her head with the pillow. It was a dream. It was all a bad dream. Time travel wasn't real. It couldn't be.

The pounding returned, this time more emphatic, and then another recollection slapped her, jarring her completely awake. Kendra. She would have left town yesterday with the kids, running away from Mother. That must be the pounding. Mother had come to rage—or worse—Father. He would demand she tell him everything she knew about their disappearance.

She hadn't checked messages when she'd returned from— okay, just say it—Scotland. That was when the crazy got worse. She'd gotten sick and collapsed before she made it to the garage.

Or, she'd assumed that was what happened when she woke in a dark, strange room. Her room at the bunker.

She'd stumbled her way out of the bunker, thankful Conall had shown her all the security protocols so she didn't trigger the alarms. She waved at the security guard in the garage, who just nodded. She was halfway home before she remembered Hernandez. But she had her own room at the bunker and was probably still hacking systems with Horatio.

When she sat up, her head spun. Three beer bottles lay at her feet. She had to think. Those weren't nearly enough to make her as hungover as she felt. Had Lanis slipped her something last night? How had she flown home on her own?

The pounding resumed. It could be anyone at the door. Mother, Father, or Hernandez wondering what the hell happened to her. Her gut clenched. Or it could be Keene, pissed off that she'd escaped. Fuck it. The pounding wasn't going to stop, and she had to face the music, whichever song was playing.

She stood and swayed, grabbing the edge of the bed until the floor stopped moving. Her throbbing headache turned into a stabbing pain. She'd slept in her clothes, which were wrinkled but clean. It was far from the first time she'd woken that way. She staggered down the hall using walls and doorjambs for support.

When she was within sight of the front door, she croaked, "I'm coming." She coughed to clear her throat and tried again. "I'm coming." The visitor either heard her or got tired of pounding. With any luck, they'd be gone by the time she made it to the door. She would have given a voice command to open it, but after spending the last couple of days being chased, she decided to play it safe. To use an old earth phrase, she wasn't running on all cylinders.

She glanced at the side table where she kept her sidearm, but it wasn't there. No amount of concentration was going to fix that. She let go of the wall so she could rub her temples when a stab of pain almost knocked her off her feet. If she had the energy, she'd punch whoever wouldn't go away and leave her in peace.

No longer caring if bad guys were on the other side, she fumbled for the door, grasping the latch and tugging it open. She fell back and clutched the door to prevent landing on her ass.

She froze.

"Christ, Mouse. What the hell took so long? We're going to be late."

Zach.

She rubbed her eyes. Now, she was hallucinating—and this was no longer funny.

But his image didn't go away. He was dressed as she last remembered him—in his uniform minus the armor. He smiled that million-dollar smile, his eyes lit with mischief that, on a normal day, would warn her of an upcoming prank.

He rocked back on his heels. "I see. Another all-nighter. When are you going to settle down?" His gaze turned serious. Wrinkles appeared on his forehead as he lurched forward to catch her as her legs went out from under her.

"Zach?" Her voice hitched. He hauled her up by her armpits until she grasped a wall. "What are you doing here?" Her head spun, nausea from the day before returning. She focused on one thing—staying upright. The rest would eventually work itself out. Except, why was Zach there?

"You must be out of it. I pick you up every morning, Mouse. We go to work together. Remember?" His expression grim, he stood with hands on hips, squinting as if he could somehow read beneath her layer of confusion.

She understood. She was freaking out. Had she cracked and lost her mind? Maybe Lanis slipped her a hallucinogen. She shook her head and was instantly sorry when the pain intensified.

He felt her forehead. "You feel a bit warm. Are you coming down with something?"

She nodded nice and slow.

Focus.

Afraid this wasn't a dream and terrified it was, she let go of the wall and stepped closer. She touched his face. He was warm, his skin damp with sweat, probably from running up the stairs. He laid a hand on her shoulder, and she felt the weight of it. "You're real."

"Okay. That's it. Back to bed, you go."

He guided her toward the bedroom, his hand still on her shoulder, attempting to keep her straight as she bumped into the walls, unable to maintain a straight line.

"This can't be real. You're dead. But you don't feel dead. And I'm happy you're not dead."

"Now you're worrying me. As soon as you get into bed, I'll call Cap and let him know you're sick. Maybe I should call Mother."

Her gut clenched, and the floor that had been stable a moment ago began to shift. The headache came back and, with it, a vision. Keene and Zach running across a vast expanse. Zach constantly looking over his shoulder. Keene grabbing his arm to move him faster. "Stop looking back. Just run." Keene's voice as strong and loud as if he were shouting at her rather than Zach.

Then everything went black.

———

THE NEXT TIME SHE WOKE, she kept her eyes closed. Listening. She remembered her earlier hallucination. Zach. The vision. Keene. Had she made it all up? Had the last six months been nothing but a dream? Some elaborate story she'd built in her head from her visions and guilt over Zach?

"I think she's waking up." Zach's concerned voice settled her.

She didn't care what the hell was wrong with her. Zach was alive, and that was all that mattered. They could lock her up in the psych ward if it meant Zach and Kendra would be together again. *Kendra.* Had her visit the other night been another false memory? *Wow.* She was surprised she hadn't already been locked up. Or was she still dreaming?

"She got a good hit to the head. She might still be a wee bit groggy." *Conall? What the fuck?*

She pried an eye open. It was too bright, and she tried to roll over but couldn't.

"Take it easy, Rowan. We're almost done." Keene's worried voice.

Now, she didn't want to open her eyes. Reality and hallucinations were living together in her head. Panic set in. Someone's arm grazed her, and she pushed it away. Something sharp made her whimper.

"Pull it out before she does," Keene snapped.

Her eyes popped open, and she squinted against the harsh light. "Too bright." A few seconds later, the mechanical whoosh of the shades closing convinced her she was in her own bed.

The bedside lamp turned on seconds before the floor lamp in the far corner. Keene stared down at her, his hand holding hers. "Take it easy, Rowan. You took a bad hit during a training exercise yesterday and had a bad reaction to the medication. My brother, Dr. MacGregor, is flushing them out."

What the hell was he talking about? And when she searched his expression, there was a tightness around his lips and a slight tic along his jaw.

"Is she all right?" Zach asked from the far corner of the room.

When she opened her mouth to call to him, Keene squeezed her hand until tears formed. He couldn't have been more clear. He wanted her to shut up. She turned her head toward Zach's voice, but Conall, who was dressed in the uniform of a professional medic, blocked her view as he rummaged through a field med kit. Keene had called him doctor.

What the hell was going on?

"She'll be all right." Keene stepped back, his gaze never leaving hers as Zach came into view.

He looked the same as the last time she'd seen him—except alive. His brows were drawn in concern, but she saw the tease in his eyes. "I told them your head was too hard to get damaged. I called Cap and told him I'd be late and would explain everything. He hadn't been told you were working with GSM. I think he was more irritated about that than anything else."

Keene slid a glance to Conall, who gave a brief nod as he packed up the medical supplies. They had put an IV in her. It was more than a flush. Nothing hurt, and she had the pleasant buzz of a couple beers.

She inched up until her back was against the wall and scratched her head as she gazed at her brother's face. It was so good to see him—to hear his voice and his teasing. Her head had cleared, and she remembered the last six months. Every horrible minute. Yet there he was, standing in front of her. She tried a grin. "I guess GSM screwed up the paperwork again."

"Yeah." Zach sat on the bed and held her hand. "Hey, what's this?" He reached up and cupped her cheek, then wiped under her eye.

She wiped her face and felt the moisture. Damn it. "It must be the drugs." She closed her eyes, trying to figure out how to get out of this. As much as she wanted to hug Zach, he'd think it strange. They'd never been a family that showed much emotion. She had to speak with Keene. He must have screwed up the timeline.

A stab of pain hit, and she squeezed her eyes shut as she grabbed her head.

"What's wrong, Mouse?" Then Zach's voice turned hard. "What's wrong with her?"

"A headache, most likely." Conall's reassuring voice seemed to calm Zach.

The pain left as quickly as it had come, just as it did with the visions, except this time, there wasn't one. "I'm okay." She squeezed Zach's arm. "Get to work. I just need some time."

Zach stared at Keene, then shook his head. "Maybe I should have Kendra come by."

"No. She's got her hands full with the kids." Her response was short and probably an octave too high. She smiled with as much reassurance as she could muster. "I just need some sleep." She slapped his arm. "You know how I am after an all-nighter."

That earned a smile, and his shoulders relaxed. "I'll check on you later." He stood and gave Keene a long look before glaring at Conall.

"I'll be fine. They're with GSM, right?" She needed Zach out of there, but if he left, would he still be real?

He grudgingly nodded, made it to the door, and glanced back. "Stay home and get rest. No leaving."

"Promise." And like the six-year-old she'd been when they'd first made promises, she held her fingers crossed behind her back. Stupid. But old habits brought a sense of normalcy. She conjured her most genuine smile.

With reluctance, he nodded, and with a last look at Keene, he slipped out the door. A few seconds later, the front door closed, and Keene left the room. She tried to stand and would have landed on her ass if Conall hadn't caught her.

"Steady, lass."

She tried to pull away, but he held on tight.

"We need to get you back to the bunker."

"What's happening?" That good feeling was slipping away. Her vision blurred, and she blinked several times to restore it.

"Keene?" Conall called. "You need to hurry."

Keene strolled back in, slipping a disc into his pocket. "I've got it. Let's go."

Conall slipped a jacket around her and added a hat that she tried to remove until he slapped her hand away. "Leave it until we get to the AVU."

"I don't want to go. I want to see Zach." She pulled back, though the struggles were in vain. Between the two brother's combined efforts and her weakened state, she was nothing more than one of those weighted dummies they used in drills. "What did you do? Why is Zach back?"

Keene's lips brushed her ear as if telling her a secret, and maybe he was. "You need to keep your voice down until we get to the AVU. Zach probably activated the housing unit's recorder before leaving. You can't say anything. Do you understand?"

Her vision blurred again, and her headache was back in full force as they jostled her toward the door.

"Nod if you understand."

She must have done what he asked because the only sound was her feet dragging across the floor and the opening of the door.

"They're going to have visuals on this," Conall whispered.

"Keep her arm around your neck. We'll just say her behavior concerned us, and we took her in. I'll have Horatio update records to show her being checked into GSM's infirmary, then checking out a couple hours later."

Her legs came alive as they rushed down the hall. But instead of taking the elevator, they took the stairs.

"Are you kidding? Do you know how many stairs we have to fumble?" She considered her word choice. "That didn't sound right." A giggle erupted.

She caught Keene's worried glance, and her momentary humor evaporated. She was in more trouble than she thought. Why couldn't she focus?

They stopped after a few flights.

"Can we give her another shot?" Keene asked.

"I'd rather not risk it." Conall didn't sound confident.

"This time continuum is tearing her apart. I'm not sure we're going to get her back to the bunker in time."

Her blood chilled. "What does that mean? Have I been drinking? I can drink a helluva lot more than three bottles. My head feels like it's splitting in two."

"We need to run." Keene's anxiety came through loud and clear.

Someone lifted her up, and the pounding of boots on stairs was the only indication they were on the move again. Her head lulled against someone's chest. The scent hit her—wildflowers and rain. Keene.

Suddenly, her senses were invaded by the smell of peat smoke, cooking meat, thick porridge, and a room full of laughing and shouting Scots. Then the eclectic aromas from the Yards and barbecues with Zach and Kendra. She squeezed her eyes shut as the door burst open, and they were met with blinding light. The force of an AVU lifting off. Keene running across the bunker's garage.

By the time they reached the first floor, her headache had diminished. When they reached the infirmary, she pushed at Keene's chest to get down. Her strength, at least part of it, had returned.

The difference in how she felt between her housing unit and the bunker was like a different world, a different day.

Horatio and Hernandez sat on exam tables, and Lanis removed patches from their arms.

Conall shut the door behind them and engaged the lock.

She turned on them, feeling somewhat feral. "You have ten seconds to start explaining, or I'll rip this place apart."

When everyone stared at her like she'd flipped, she screamed at them. "Tell me how the hell Zach is alive."

THIRTY-ONE

"Who's Zach?" Lanis asked.

"He was at Rowan's unit when we arrived. He's her brother." Keene moved to her left, Conall to her right, flanking her. They probably thought she'd gone nuts. The truth was closer than she cared to admit.

Hernandez stood slack-jawed. Her eyes were wide as saucers and glazed over. She stumbled against an exam cart, knocking it over before Horatio grabbed her. "Zach is alive?"

Everyone turned to Rowan, and she swiped at the tears that ran unwanted down her cheeks.

Hernandez's voice floated around them, her words putting not too fine a point on the macabre situation. "He died six months ago."

"Damn it all," Conall swore and slammed a fist into another cart, sending it toppling to the ground.

"This is your fault," Rowan yelled and swung out wildly, but Keene caught her arms and pushed her against an exam table.

"You need to calm down. You need treatment."

She kicked him. If he'd been expecting it, it would never

have worked. But neither of them had seen the other in hand-to-hand combat. He didn't know she fought dirty. When his hold loosened from the hit to his shin, she twisted and went limp, sliding out of his grip. She rolled and tried to rise to a standing position, fists raised, but her body, or more pointedly, her head, wouldn't comply. Only halfway up, her legs moved in an opposite direction from her upper half, and she toppled over.

Conall was on her in a hot minute, lifting her and dropping her on the table before she could register what happened. Lanis tossed straps over her that Conall quickly snapped into place. She fought back, but the straps tightened, making it impossible to thrash. She screamed, jerking her head around which did nothing but trigger a headache, turning her yells into shouts of pain.

"Easy, Rowan. Relax." Keene crooned the words, his voice deep and husky. "No one wants to harm you. We want to understand what's happening. Just like you."

She didn't believe him. He hadn't been honest from the beginning. And the last thing she needed was them pumping drugs into her. But it was too late. The sharp pinch of the injector was quick. And seconds later, a soothing warmth ran through her, and though she was aware of everything around her, her earlier rage dissipated. Great.

"Your fault," she slurred. "You messed up the jump."

Lanis removed the blood pressure cuff from her upper arm and made a note on her tablet then raised her brow at Keene. "What is she talking about?"

"It has nothing to do with this." Keene shrugged her off, his focus pinned on Rowan.

"Tell us anyway," Conall requested. "It couldn't hurt to have all the facts."

Hernandez shoved her way past Keene, Horatio right behind her, looking over her shoulder. "What did you give her?"

"A sedative." Conall picked up the tray and medical supplies he'd tipped over. "It will wear off soon. Before that, we gave her a binding agent. We started the procedure in her apartment, but her brother was suspicious. He made it clear he was an ISA guard, so we anticipated he'd override her security protocols and start the unit's recording device. We had to stop."

"A binding agent for whatever trixcillian is?" Hernandez tried to stay next to Rowan, but Keene pulled her away.

"Aye." Conall opened a new IV pack, and all Rowan could do was watch him. "She had a reaction to the dose, which is quite rare. The binding agent will collect the trixcillian, and the IV will flush it out."

Rowan couldn't stop the tears, and unable to wipe them away, she blinked furiously to keep her vision clear.

A cool cloth with a light mint scent was laid across her forehead. "Breathe deeply. The pain will begin to subside, and you'll get your equilibrium back." Keene's tone was calm, easing her anxiety. It might have been whatever they injected her with because her foggy mind began to clear. "What are we going to do?" Keene glanced at Lanis and then Conall. "She can't leave the bunker without conditioning." He brushed her damp hair back and used another cool cloth to wipe away the sweat.

"I'd like to try a modified version." Lanis moved to one of the displays. "I remember one of the other sects having a similar problem with one of their members."

"Do you think it might have something to do with the shift in the continuum?" Conall asked. Once he finished securing the IV, he patted her arm. "Just relax and enjoy the meds. You'll be back on your feet soon."

She strained to lift her head, wanting to see what everyone was doing, especially Lanis. Hernandez caught her gaze and whispered something to Lanis. Someone slipped a pillow underneath her head as the back of the med bed shifted up ten degrees.

"That should give your neck a rest. Can you see everything okay?" Keene's brows still scrunched with concern. Now that she was calmer and thinking straight, she no longer saw conspiracies behind their actions.

She nodded, not trusting her voice. Her curiosity crowded out her irrationality.

"This database holds our medical records, diagnoses, and treatments for our personnel." Lanis shifted to the right so Hernandez could get closer. "It also has our complete history of medical research." Lanis pointed to something on the screen. "This is the section where we might find our answer." She nodded to a second console. "I've transferred it to that workstation." She smiled at Hernandez. "It appears your security level has been increased by necessity. Can you help with the search?"

Hernandez, with Horatio following close behind her, stepped to the other console. "What am I looking for?"

"At this point, anything that discusses trixcillian as part of the symptom, cause, or cure for any malady. Horatio, can you come over here? I have another task for you."

He glanced at Hernandez, and she shrugged. Only a handful of days together, and he followed Hernandez like a puppy dog. One always watching over the other.

"See this wave?" Lanis pointed to an image Rowan could only see from an angle. A thick multicolored wave spread across the display. "I need an analysis of changes for the last twenty-four hours. No. Make it thirty-six, just to be sure. Document each time this blue wave reaches these red lines." She faced him. "Look at me, Horatio." When he did, she continued, "Your first instinct will be to ask a dozen questions. I'm asking you to focus on the specifics, then we'll discuss everything in detail. Can you do that?"

He didn't answer immediately, his focus on some distant point. From experience with other tech personnel, Hernandez included, he was mentally running a probability analysis. After a few seconds, he nodded and pushed her out of the way, fully immersing himself in the program.

That accomplished, Lanis turned back to Rowan, her teeth worrying her bottom lip. "Now tell me what Rowan was talking about with your travel."

Keene ran a hand through his hair. He looked disheveled in that hadn't-gotten-enough-sleep, sexy kind of way. She hated to admit it, but it was easier to acknowledge her attraction than ignore it. He hadn't shaved while in Scotland, nor would it seem, since they'd returned. It looked good on him. But there were shadows under his eyes, and his shirt was rumpled. He hadn't changed clothes either.

He pulled over a stool. The wheels made a soft squeak each time he pushed himself back and forth as he recalled the events. "We checked in with the front desk and were cleared to meet with the Spider."

"Without an appointment? Did they call up?" Conall asked.

"They gave us the office number and let us go." Keene shrugged. "We knew it could be a trap, but we didn't have a choice." He glanced at Rowan, and she agreed.

"We were on GSM security business. An appointment wasn't necessary."

"When we got to the office," Keene continued, "we found the Spider on the floor. She'd been stabbed, possibly with the same type of blade as Sodowski, our first murder victim. We decided it was best to leave but were confronted by a team dressed in black before we could exit the tower."

When he glanced at Conall, Keene's expression looked feral, an interesting combination with his beard and the intensity in his gaze. Now that she had time to analyze it, it wasn't much different than his look each time they ran for their lives. The eyes of someone who would have preferred running into battle, arms raised with sword and axe, screaming a war cry like those Scots they'd seen in the valley.

"We ran." Keene's laugh turned into a sneer. "They didn't announce themselves as ISA, and it didn't seem prudent to wait and ask."

"Because they probably weren't ISA." Conall removed his medic jacket and leaned back against the counter, his heavily muscled biceps reminding her these men weren't just anthropologists. "It's against GSM policy for Stoker to have their own security. Whoever they were, why did they come looking for you?"

Keene shook his head. "My first thought was that they'd followed us, but I wonder if it was simply bad luck on our part."

"You think you ran into the Spider's killers?" Conall's question was one they'd already considered.

Keene rolled the stool until his back rested against the wall. He braced a leg against a nearby table and leaned his head back. She thought he'd looked tired before, but now she wondered how he was staying upright. "It's a possibility. Either way, they had us cornered. It didn't feel safe, so I locked us in a storage closet and traveled."

"And that's when you screwed up," Rowan added, convinced that whatever happened to their timeline had to have been his fault. The timing was too coincidental.

"I admit I thought I'd entered an incorrect sequence when you bumped into me," Keene retorted, a scowl marring his earlier dreamy visage.

"And now you're blaming me?" Her tone might have risen.

"I didn't hear anybody blame anyone," Lanis soothed. "If you were in a supply closet, it's quite possible you both got jostled. But one sequence wouldn't have damaged the timeline."

Keene agreed. "At most, we would have ended up a couple of years on either side of my projected timeline. But we landed at the exact date I wanted."

Before she could respond, Lanis held up her hand. "Even if you had arrived at a different time, it wouldn't have caused a shift. This kind of change, so many centuries later, would have required a tremendous change in history. Even a change of some import would have smoothed out over time like a ripple in a pond."

Rowan wasn't sure whether to believe them or not, but their expressions told her Lanis had spoken the truth. If it wasn't Keene, then what happened?

Conall removed the straps that held her down. "Let's get that IV out of you."

She moved her arm to make it easier for Conall to reach while she glanced between Lanis and Keene. Her voice shook, and she must have looked pitiful. "So, why did my brother knock on my door this morning?"

"That presents an interesting question," Lanis said. "But it most likely explains the issues Keene had with the TTD." When Rowan furrowed her brow, she explained, "The temporal transition device. The handheld model."

She nodded. Giving the device a name made it seem more commonplace and, strangely, made her more comfortable that these people might know what they were doing.

Lanis tapped her chin, her gaze unfocused. "The time continuum was enough out of phase to make your connection more tenuous. You were lucky to have made it back home without a new equation." She shook her head and gave Rowan an odd smile. "Did you notice anything else that was different?"

She snorted. "I barely remember this morning."

"That's one of the first things we'll need to investigate. Exactly how much is different." Keene said.

"Why isn't Horatio or Hernandez affected? Or you and Conall?" She was surprised she hadn't thought of it sooner, but she was only now feeling like her old self.

"The bunker keeps us safe from changes within the continuum, similar to the safe room in the cave," Keene responded. "Horatio found an inconsistency in his research after our return. At first, we didn't think anything of it, but when I tried to contact you this morning, and your brother responded, I knew we had a problem. If Kai Li hadn't mentioned your brother's passing, I wouldn't have suspected anything, and we might not have gotten to you in time."

She glanced away, not wanting to see the worry in his gaze. He knew it was because of her brother that she didn't like talking about family. If he knew why, would he still look at her that way? Or would he be disgusted by her guilt?

Lanis swabbed her IV site with a pad of cooling ointment. "We decided it was best to give Horatio and Hernandez the trixcillian, even though we suspected you were having a reaction to it. Your symptoms wouldn't have been as bad had you stayed in the bunker."

"I guess I wasn't thinking. I just wanted to be home." She felt like an apologetic six-year-old.

Lanis patted her arm and motioned for her to sit up. "We should have prepared for that and locked you in your room."

Yep, a six-year-old. "And maybe kept me sedated."

She laughed. "The thought did occur to me, but it might have disguised the symptoms."

Conall finished putting the supplies away, then leaned against the counter, arms folded across his chest. "We're on new ground here. I can't remember anything like this happening before, though there have been studies done." Even with that admission, he exuded an air of confidence. "But time travel is based on mathematics. Complex mathematics but no different than the simpler versions; you only need to uncover the formula."

"You make it sound so easy." Rowan had a decent head for math, but not nearly enough for this discussion.

Lanis shrugged, her manner casual, but she hid her emotions well when it suited. "It's not easy, but with Horatio's help, we should be able to pinpoint the exact time in the continuum when the initiating event took place. From there, it should point us in the direction of what happened."

If they discovered what happened and were capable of fixing it, would Zach be dead again? Maybe it was some accidental, one-time shift, and they could leave well enough alone.

"Until then," she continued, "we need to find a different conditioning method for you, or you won't be able to leave the bunker." When Lanis caught her concern, Rowan thought for a moment she might lie to her. Sometimes she questioned whether her ability to read people was a good or bad thing.

"With the data Hernandez is pulling together, we'll find a modified compound for you."

She'd have to trust Lanis to do her best. It would be impossible to do her job stuck in the bunker all day. She checked her wrist unit. "Zach will be checking in soon." She turned to Keene. "Who did you tell Zach you were? He must have asked."

"Your partner."

"At GSM? The first thing he would have done was check the records."

Keene nodded. "As soon as I understood what Zach being alive meant, we had Horatio and Hernandez do a check on all three of your records and modify where we could. Horatio's original role was someone who moved from project to project, and fortunately, that hasn't changed. He's already assigned himself to a special project for the next two weeks."

Hernandez, who must have been listening while running

her program, jumped in. "I still have the same access as before with the same rank and assignment. I'm still in Cap's squad, but I've submitted transfer orders from GSM security reflecting the start of a two-week special training program starting this morning. Then I sent a belated apology to Cap from GSM headquarters for the late notice. I dated it yesterday." She seemed quite pleased with herself until she glanced at Rowan.

"What's wrong?" Her stomach flipped. This wasn't going to be good.

"They show you reporting to Zach."

She laughed. "That'll be the day."

When Hernandez shifted her gaze back to the imager, her laughter died.

"Just tell me."

"Cap still runs the same squad, but Zach is a major now and runs the unit."

Bravo for Zach, but her mouth went dry. "And what am I supposed to be doing?"

Hernandez refused to look at her. "Street detail."

Her heart sank. How was it possible she was an even worse screw-up in this timeline?

"If it helps, it's only temporary." She tried to make light of it. "Just a disciplinary action."

She knew Hernandez was trying, but it didn't make her feel any better.

"Don't worry, Rowan. I fixed it. I sent a second message to Zach, dated early yesterday, that shows you transferred to a special ops assignment. Your records show that you're an expert marksman and skilled at hand-to-hand, which makes you valuable for that type of assignment."

Well, that part was true enough.

"I also showed the assignment as dark ops, Security Office

eyes only. That should stop Zach from asking any questions. Am I good, or what?"

She forced a smile, but it didn't detract from Hernandez's skills. "You're the tops." She glanced at Keene. "What did you tell Zach about you showing up at my apartment with a medic?"

"That you had signed in last night for skills assessment. During a rather grueling drill, you collided with an unmovable object. When I didn't hear from you this morning, I suspected a possible concussion and hurried over with a medic." He gave her one of those mesmerizing smiles. "Just in the nick of time."

"Now what?" she asked. When he winked and gave her a wicked smile, she scowled in return, mostly to stop the unwanted heat coursing through every inch of her.

"We wait for Lanis's new miracle treatment."

THIRTY-TWO

An hour later, Hernandez found the data for an alternate trixcillian treatment. Lanis used it as a base to work from and developed a modified version, but considering Rowan's original reaction, decided to split the dose into a series of injections. The procedure would take four hours.

Rowan was desperate to leave the infirmary, and Conall agreed to run the procedure in one of the rec rooms. He set Rowan up on a couch in front of a series of imagers that played movies, news, and sports.

"How many people work here?" She was on her third dose and bored to tears.

Conall leaned back, a beer resting on his thigh. "There are twenty of us, including our small security force, though it's rare to have more than a dozen here at any given time." He chuckled. "This is the first time there's only been the three of us besides the security team, but it sometimes works out that way. Lanis and I have enjoyed having Horatio and Hernandez here."

She had so many questions, she didn't know where to begin. Conall always seemed more forthcoming than Keene, but she shouldn't have worried as he kicked off the conversation.

"So I hear you met Marta's clan." He sipped his beer. "Well, it's not really her clan, but she runs the village as if it were."

"Yeah. That sounds about right." Her grimace didn't go unnoticed.

"She didn't like you." He shook his head when she started to speak. "Keene didn't say anything. He didn't have to. Marta doesn't like outlanders." He scratched his chin and took a long swallow of beer as he studied her to the point she began to fidget. "I probably shouldn't tell you this, but Marta's clan is different than other Gregor clans. Well, different than all the clans of that time."

She considered his words and tried to make sense of them. They were the only clan she'd met and had no idea what he meant. Then she recalled something Liam and Marta had said. "What's a Druid?"

Conall ran a hand over his thick mane and took another long pull on his beer. "Where did you hear that?"

"Liam mentioned it. When I asked Keene about it, he didn't want to talk about it. Then Marta used the term when she was drilling me on my knowledge of herbs."

"Christ." He laughed. "Keene knew you'd be trouble the minute he discovered GSM had assigned him a partner."

She scowled. "I'm not the one with secrets about time travel."

His smile never faltered. "True enough."

"As much as I didn't want you to learn any of this, the mud just gets thicker and deeper." Keene strolled in with a bucket of iced beer in one hand and her next dose in the other. He set the bucket on the low table where Conall had set up his medical supplies, then handed the vial to his brother before dropping next to her on the couch. He leaned over, pulling a bottle out of the ice and opening it for Conall before lifting another toward her with a question in his gaze. "Lanis said it was okay for you to have one."

She nodded, and he handed it to her before opening one for himself. "It would be easier to just tell me and get it done."

"History gave them many names—teachers, philosophers, judges, scientists, prophets, and healers." Keene paused and stared at his beer. "They were connected to the power of the earth, and some say, bridged the relationship between man and their gods. Long before Marta's time, Druids were persecuted, and their oak groves burned until they faded from existence."

"Yet, Marta believes you and Liam to be these Druids."

Keene gave Conall a sidelong glance before nodding. "The clan you visited still believe, as I suppose others do as well. And they still practice the old ways, which was what my brother referred to as their clan being different."

She wondered how long he'd been listening to their conversation before making his presence known. "And you've played on that with your visits."

"Something like that."

She rolled her eyes. Never a complete answer with this one. She would have gotten more answers if he hadn't shown up. She glanced at Conall, not surprised he'd follow Keene's lead.

"Why were they persecuted?"

This time Conall answered. "Many believed the Druids to be a religious sect, and like so many other pagans, were driven to near extinction by the spread of Christianity. A single god rather than several gods and goddesses."

She nodded. "Yet, beliefs are difficult to rid completely, so they went underground." Something niggled at the edges of her memories, but it slipped away just as quickly.

"Which is why no one speaks of the Druids outside of the village." Conall checked his wrist unit and the injection site on her arm. "How are you feeling?"

"Fine. So why doesn't Liam come home?" As she expected, the brothers gave each another look and was surprised when Conall answered again.

"Liam is our youngest brother and a more gentle spirit. His relationship to those around him and the earth is more sensitive than most." He grimaced before polishing off his beer and grabbing another, tossing one to Keene. If there was one thing she'd do before they parted ways was to take these two to Duster's. Maybe a night of drinking would loosen their lips.

Conall locked his gaze with hers, his own pain reflected in his eyes. "Have you ever done something unintentional yet so grievous you were never able to forgive yourself?"

She couldn't speak, and she blinked before breaking contact to study her beer. The question hit too close to home, and when she got her emotions in check and glanced up, the brother's expressions told her they understood she had her own demons. All she could do was nod, unable to utter a simple yes.

"For most of us, we hide our pain and guilt. We bury it, sometimes too deeply, yet we know we must in order to carry on. But not our dear Liam. He's still learning to deal with the consequences, and though we've told him many times we love him, he's chosen his own path of absolution. One day, we hope he'll come home."

"Until then," Keene broke in. "We'll honor his wishes and give him the time he needs."

"The village seems to like him." She remembered the child who was so excited to be given one of his carvings.

"They're Scots," Conall boomed with pride. "They understand hardship."

After a moment, no longer interested in asking questions, and maybe that was what the MacGregor brothers hoped to accomplish, she fell silent. She still smarted from her guilt over Zach.

Lanis waltzed in and broke the silence, steering them to more important matters. "So, how's our patient?"

Conall grinned, the earlier conversation forgotten. "You can see for yourself she's fine."

Lanis stared down at her. "Any headaches?"

Rowan shook her head. "And no nausea."

"Let's see how you fare overnight. If you don't experience any negative reactions, we'll see how you do outside the bunker."

"A perfect time to see how much of the world has changed." Keene set his empty bottle aside and opened the bottle Conall had tossed him. It seemed he was trying to keep up with Conall, who'd had a head start on him. "Horatio is still working on pinning down the exact time of the change, but we need to understand its impact."

"How do you think it happened in the first place?" She patiently sat while Conall removed the injection patch then rubbed an herbal ointment over the spot.

"There is an endless list of possibilities, but I don't believe much in coincidences."

"You think this has to do with your tattooed man." Conall packed up the medical supplies and returned to his beer.

"It would be foolish to rule anything out so early in the game." Keene leaned farther into the cushions and rested his legs on the corner of the table. "But it was the lead we were working before the time shift, and based on the interest we'd garnered up to that point, I believe it's still a valid one."

"Do we go back to the Yards?" Rowan wasn't sure where to start. Maybe back to the African Quarter. For some reason, it seemed the best place for the tattooed man to hide.

"No. Back to the GSM campus."

Even Conall couldn't hold his surprise at Keene's suggestion.

She raised a brow, knowing where he was going and aligned with his thinking. "You believe the Spider might be alive?"

"I'm not ruling anything out. But if it was the tattooed man, and he believes he can improve his advantage by changing history, then the Spider might still be alive."

Lanis crossed her arms and thinned her lips. "We should have Hernandez review the current GSM and ISA security protocols. It would be dangerous walking in without more information."

Keene frowned but appeared to be considering the suggestion. "She was able to confirm I'm still a GSM consultant, so I should be able to get us in. But I understand the caution. She has the rest of the day to run the data and provide anything she deems useful."

"We should see what else appears different while we're there." Rowan agreed that going to GSM made sense. If they managed to get in without a lot of questions, they could assess any other changes. Would the major be there? And would she still hold the same fondness for Rowan as she had before, considering she appeared to be more of a fuckup in this new timeline?

Conall set down his empty bottle but didn't pick up another. "I'd like Horatio to start running possibilities on what could have created the shift once we can pinpoint when it happened."

"You mean the who," Keene muttered.

"We can't confirm this was a manufactured occurrence." Lanis didn't appear hopeful.

"The past was already written. A supernova didn't just happen to show up sometime in our past history to change our current timeline. There's no way that time or another dimension could have crossed on its own." Keene seemed adamant about his theory, but was his passionate view based on fact or his growing obsession with the tattooed man?

"Well, now, we don't know that for a fact." Conall rubbed his chin. "If some astrophysical phenomenon impacted the barrier between dimensions or caused a wave in the continuum, it would be possible that a fundamental change occurred."

Rowan looked to Lanis, who seemed doubtful. "I'm inclined to follow Keene's instincts on this one, but perhaps Horatio can run additional scenarios as possibilities."

Conall nodded, but whether he would ask Horatio to do that remained unanswered.

Rowan became lost in thought, not sure whether she cared why or how any of this could have happened. Her only concern was how to keep Zach alive once they figured it out and whether they had to fix it. When she glanced up at the silence, Keene was watching her. Now, what was he up to?

He stood and nudged Conall. "Let's show Rowan what else is hidden within the bunker."

THIRTY-THREE

Conall led Rowan and Keene down a long hall on the third floor that she recognized from the security tour. When they came to a set of double doors, he used the retinal scan and a passcode to open them. The door on the opposite wall was labeled Electrical.

"Isn't this part of the building's environmental systems?" She waited while Conall stepped into the room, the lights coming on automatically.

Keene pointed to the other door. "That is. You just assumed every room at this end of the building fit that description." He followed Conall in.

Conall's tour of the bunker had been extensive, and she'd been exhausted by the time they'd made it to this level. The various corridors, the walls painted with murals of trees, began looking like an actual forest. Without a guardian or a map, she'd spend hours finding her way around. When Conall had waved a vague hand in this direction, he'd implied that everything in this section was part of the environmental systems. These guys were great at misdirection.

Keene poked his head into the hall. "Are you coming?"

She followed him in, and he had to nudge her so he could shut the door behind them. All she could do was stare. The room went on forever, easily four times the size of the command center, with six aisles of storage racks taller than her, all filled with metal boxes and various objects. But what caught her eye were the walls. It was like walking into a museum. Weapons from years gone by decorated the walls from one end to the other: swords, lances, shields, traditional bows, axes, crossbows, mace, flintlocks, rifles, pistols, and other sidearms. Smaller weapons were mounted on velvet-backed displays—knives, daggers, throwing stars, nunchakus, and other items she couldn't name.

"What is this place?" She didn't bother hiding the wonderment in her tone.

"It's one of two artifact rooms." Conall strode down the aisle, staring up at the wall. "This one includes weapons and other historical objects from one thousand BCE to the sixteenth century. The second room, located on the other side of this level, holds everything from the seventeenth century to the current. Most of these weapons are rarely used, but we like to keep things handy."

She stepped toward the closest wall and eyed an ancient crossbow. One of her favorite weapons was the compound pulse bow. It worked like any crossbow but with laser GPS positioning and released either armor-piercing or explosive pulse bolts. These bows released good old-fashioned wooden or steel-tipped bolts. She was handy with traditional bows as well, but they required a deeper knowledge of distance and wind. Something she trained in regularly as part of her weapons specialty courses.

She crept down the wall, her hand hovering over different pieces, wanting to touch but not wanting to damage anything. And knowing Conall, he'd probably added another layer or two of security. She'd been to museums in several regional cities but hadn't seen anything close to the diversity of weapons displayed in this single room. The centuries of swords ran the gamut from bronze to iron to Damascus steel. She stopped in front of a sword labeled Broadsword. Both edges were sharpened to a fine edge and as shiny as the day it had been made.

"You never even mentioned this room." She glanced down the rest of the wall, but her gaze kept returning to the broadsword in front of her.

"And what would I have said?" Conall switched to a deeper brogue. "Well, Sergeant Rowan, don't mind the stuff in this wee room. We only use these weapons when we time travel."

She rolled her eyes. "Maybe you could have just said what it is—your anthropological artifact room."

"And how many more questions would I have had to answer to squelch your curiosity?" He folded his arms across his chest and raised a brow. He was right, but she wouldn't admit it. He would never have been able to show her this room without her running around like a kid in a candy shop, needing to pick up each weapon just to feel it in her hand.

"We'll provide a more in-depth explanation of our research projects, then the armory and artifact rooms will make more sense." Keene stepped next to her and reached for the broadsword. She placed a hand on his arm to stop him, then pulled back. Her instinctual move had nothing to do with protecting him from Conall's security measures. She simply didn't want him to damage such a beautiful weapon.

He grinned. "Don't worry. Conall turned off the entire security grid when he entered the room."

When he pulled the sword from the wall, she glimpsed etchings on the blade, but the light in the room reflected off the surface, masking the symbols. Keene turned the blade as he studied the sharp edges, then pointed to the carved designs.

"We call this blade Curaidh, or Champion. It was made three thousand years ago, forged with special steel." He ran a hand along the flat part of the sword. "These runes were etched by a Druid silversmith for protection and accuracy in its use." He held out the blade. "How does it feel?"

She reached for the sword, gliding her fingers an inch above its surface. A tingling sensation flowed through her hand, making her hand quiver. For just an instant, she thought the symbols lit with a blue glow. She shook her head, her imagination running wild with the history that surrounded her.

When she glanced at Keene, his expression appeared to be a mixture of confusion and curiosity. A strange combination of emotions for someone who knew more about the blade than she. He offered the sword hilt first, and she grasped it, turning the blade to watch the light dance across the surface. If she expected to see the blue glow again, she was disappointed.

She took a few steps back and swung with a light hand, first to the right and then left. The balance felt perfect, the weight less than she expected, and the hilt narrow enough to easily fit her grip. Then, without warning, something surged along the blade and into her arm like an electrical shock.

A sharp pain slammed into her head, and shadows darkened her sight. She stumbled, but before she could fall, strong arms caught her. She pushed them away, but when her legs gave out, the arms wrapped around her again. Someone laid her on the floor. The cool stone eased her headache.

Her vision cleared, and a man fell to the hard stone ground in front of her. He was dressed in leather and chain mail, his helmet rolling off from the impact of hitting the ground. He gripped a shield in one hand while a sword fell from his other. He squinted against the glare of the sun, but his defiance was unmistakable. Pure hatred. She placed a booted foot against his neck, noticing the protective thinly linked mesh that wrapped around her legs. She felt the weight of the broadsword as she brought it up. Thick, gold bracers covered her forearms, strengthening her wrists. She raised the sword above her head with both arms. The insolence never left his eyes, and fury coursed through her as she brought the blade down, removing his head from his shoulders. A scream wrenched from her throat.

"Rowan!"

She released the sword from her grip. "Dìon Tìr nan Òg."

"Rowan!" This time her name came with a shake of her shoulders.

She blinked. At first, the bright sunlight wouldn't go away, but at least she couldn't see the severed head anymore. She blinked again. This time the room came into focus. Weapons on the wall, a thin carpet underneath her, and two men staring at her with concern.

"Who owned that blade?"

Keene and Conall glanced at each other before turning questioning eyes in her direction. She pushed herself into a sitting position, swatting Conall's helpful hands away. "It was a woman, wasn't it?"

After a moment, Keene answered. "Aye. It belonged to Brìghde or Brigid. At one time, long ago, the queen of Tìr nan Òg."

She had no reference for either the queen or the place and assumed it had something to do with ancient Scotland.

"How did you know it belonged to a woman?" Keene asked.

She accepted their help to stand, and when her legs were stable enough to hold her, she took a step back. Let them wait for her answer. What could she tell them? That it was just another of her visions, but this time a woman chopped the head off some warrior. They'd shove her in her AVU and tell her to forget all about the bunker.

"Rowan?" Keene's soothing voice almost made her spill it all.

She shook it off like a wet cat, pulling herself together. "Just a guess. The blade is light, and the handle fits well." She shrugged. "It didn't seem made for a man." She noted their side glances, and though she'd swear neither believed a word of it, they eventually nodded.

"Let's get you back to your room. The treatment must have zapped your energy." Conall picked up the blade and placed it on the wall.

"Sure. I could use some sleep."

No one spoke on the way to her room. She promised them she was fine, closing the door on Keene's thoughtful expression. She leaned against the door and blew out a long sigh.

Keene knew something was wrong. Did he suspect visions? But how could he? And who was that woman? The queen of someplace called Tìr nan Òg. There was no doubt she'd been looking through the woman's eyes when she cut off the soldier's head. That was the first time she'd seen a vision through someone else. And it scared the hell out of her.

"I LEFT a dinner tray with Rowan. She seemed fine but looked haggard. A good night's sleep should help." Lanis closed the door to her spacious office of carved, dark-wood bookshelves. Each case was well-organized with books and artifacts from her several centuries of time jumps. "Hernandez and Horatio are eating in the kitchen, so we have some time to ourselves."

Keene and Conall were already seated in the stuffed chairs, an open bottle of Scotch whiskey on the table between them. Conall poured a glass and handed it to Lanis, who sat on the small divan. A roaring fire played on the imager, and a light scent of wood smoke mixed with pine floated in the air.

"I miss the campfires." Conall stared at the flames and nursed his scotch. "Did they have one while you were at Glen Dar?"

"Aye," Keene murmured, also caught by the dance of the fire. "The chief had just left, and everyone was pleased by his visit." He wished Rowan had seen it. She would have enjoyed it, seeing how similar it was to the bonfires in the Yards. He should have insisted they find another place for her to stay other than Marta's.

"Before the two of you get misty over the old days, let's discuss the issue before us." Lanis set her glass down and pulled out her journal. Always straight to business with her.

"And what issue aren't we already working?" Keene knew the answer and hoped to avoid it. But after Rowan's collapse in the artifacts room, that was no longer an option.

"Before we review what happened earlier, tell us about Rowan's visit with Marta." Lanis wasn't going to give it up.

Keene glanced at Conall, but he kept his gaze on the fire. No help from that quarter. Conall had always been a fence-sitter. Rarely taking sides, he saw himself as the level-headed one, the negotiator. But, after today, Keene suspected his brother would side with Lanis.

"There's nothing to tell. Marta was her usual disagreeable self and treated Rowan no better than a servant."

"Testing her as she should." Lanis scribbled something in her notebook. "Did Rowan have a vision?"

He hesitated, aware that Conall's gaze had now shifted to him, eager to hear the answer. Keene could deny what he'd seen, but for all he knew, Lanis had already sent a message to Liam to get his part of the story. She was persistent as well as exacting and would never let this go. He ran a hand through his hair. "I don't know."

"But she had some type of episode?"

So, she had contacted Liam. "Is that what we're calling them now? Episodes, not visions." He tried to keep his anger in check.

"Don't get your temper up with me, Keene MacGregor. You might want to ignore the prophecies, but we can't turn a blind eye to them. Especially now with the shift in time."

A cold dread ran down his spine. He could have ignored the signs without batting an eye, but Lanis was right. The time shift changed everything and not just the future of this world.

"Take it easy, Lanis." Conall finished his glass and poured another, topping off Keene's glass. "This isn't easy for any of us. You know Marta as well as the rest of us. An elder she might be, but she's been known to influence events. She could have easily put too much of her special herbs in Rowan's tea, forcing a hallucination instead of a true vision."

Lanis pursed her lips, unable to deny Marta's zealot behaviors. "All right. I'll concede to that point and note it as such. But did Rowan say anything when she came to?"

"No." Keene didn't want to remember her ashen face, her discomfort at being in such a vulnerable state around strangers. Around him. "She's not one to share much."

"Chances are, if she is having visions, she might not know what's happening. She could be terrified to tell anyone." Conall sat up, turning his back on the fire. "I think she's having headaches. I know we don't want to tell her anything she doesn't need to know, but we need answers."

"There's a simple way to decide whether to put this to rest or investigate further." Lanis set her journal aside and sipped her drink. "I can do a deeper analysis of her DNA."

"Absolutely not." Keene slammed down his glass.

"Keene," Conall soothed.

"No. I'm not going to be overruled on this. Rowan has rights. Did she give permission to have her blood tested?"

Neither Lanis nor Conall would look at him.

"Do you already have a blood sample?"

"I required a small amount to determine the best treatment with the trixcillian." Lanis pulled herself up straighter, clearly on the defensive. "Her reaction to the initial treatment was suspicious enough."

Keene didn't have an answer for that.

"What did she say to you?" Conall asked.

It took Keene a moment to realize the question had been directed to him. "When?"

"After she collapsed this evening. When she was holding Brìghde's sword."

Keene shook his head. "She said nothing." How he wished she'd said nothing.

"She said something. Her lips moved, but she spoke too softly for me to hear."

He'd tried to avoid this meeting, but Conall had insisted. Lanis's stare was unwavering, and he had to say something.

"I couldn't make any sense of it. It was barely a whisper." He refused to look at either of them. They would know he was lying, probably already suspicious of anything he said.

"But the sword triggered a reaction. She was white as a ghost," Conall explained to Lanis.

"It could have been a reaction to the newer treatment." Keene was thankful Conall didn't mention Rowan knew a woman had owned the sword. Maybe he believed her tale about the grip of the hilt. Keene hadn't. "She hadn't eaten for hours while being dosed."

Lanis shrugged. "I can't argue that reasoning." And while she appeared to be backing off, she was simply placating him.

He stood. "I need to run my own research. I want to see if Elton Sodowski might be alive in this new time."

"Your dead informant?" Conall scratched his head. "If he is, whatever he'd been involved in might no longer exist."

"And I'd feel better if Hernandez had more time to determine how extensive the changes might be in GSM." Lanis appeared as happy as Keene to move past the discussion of Rowan. "Maybe wait another day before going out."

Keene shook his head. "No. We all need to get out, even if it's a walk around the building. The time shift didn't impact Conall or me when we picked up Rowan." He nodded toward Lanis. "You should be fine as well as the security team, but we need to confirm if the trixcillian works on Hernandez and Horatio. We need to ensure they won't be impacted by this new timeline. We can't afford to lose any of us to this new continuum." When no one argued, he acquiesced to one point. "Keep Hernandez working on anything of note that Rowan and I might need to know about GSM. But we still go in the morning. We need firsthand knowledge of what's happening. And if the Spider is alive, we need to get to her before anyone considers her too high of a risk."

He strode to the door but turned to them before leaving. "I'll monitor Rowan. Try to get her to talk. But I won't permit any analysis of her blood. Not without her knowledge and permission. My word is final on this."

He rushed back to his room, needing solace from his kin. It wasn't their fault. He didn't know why he was being difficult. Would he have requested anyone else's permission to test blood they already had on hand? He knew the answer. The real question was whether he was protecting Rowan or himself.

THIRTY-FOUR

The following morning, Rowan followed her nose to the smell of bacon as she stumbled down the hallway in search of coffee. Everyone was already in the kitchen. Hernandez and Conall worked the grill where eggs and pancakes sizzled. Lanis danced between the kitchen and the dining area, setting the table, pouring coffee, and fishing freshly made biscuits out of the oven as if she were a server at one of those old-fashioned diners down in the Yards.

Horatio sat at a long table with Keene, both their heads lowered over display tablets, mumbling together. Lanis spotted her first and pointed toward the end of the counter, where a coffee pot and several mugs waited. She wiped her eyes as she made a beeline for it. She'd washed her face and brushed her hair before leaving her room, but she still felt like she'd just tumbled from bed. She noticed Keene's glance as she walked by.

His hair was still damp from a shower, and his black button-down shirt showed off his tanned skin and gray eyes. He gave her a slight nod, his eyes tracking her as she filled a mug. The warmth from his gentle perusal didn't mask her nerves. He'd witnessed one of her visions, and she didn't think he or Conall believed the episode to be a mere headache. Not when she'd spurted out some Gaelic words she'd never heard before and could never have known.

Not ready to deal with questions, she sipped the hot brew and slid down to the other end of the counter to watch the trio make breakfast.

Lanis, glowing as if she lived for mornings, sneaked a peek at the others before slipping Rowan a piece of bacon. She winked before turning to place another pan of biscuits in the oven. When she was done, she refilled a mug and grabbed a stool next to her.

"Are you one of those perky morning people?" Rowan asked.

Lanis nodded and patted her arm. "And that tells me you're a night owl. To be fair, I don't usually get up as early as I did this morning, but I was so excited." When Rowan didn't seem to get it, she continued, "Breakfast. It's my favorite meal and the only one when most of us can be together. It was an important time growing up. The bustling in the kitchen, the amazing aromas, and the men grumbling why it was all taking so long." She laughed, and it was infectious.

She glanced at the grill. "I kind of understand their point."

Still laughing, Lanis called out, "Conall, the masses have spoken. Will you be fiddling with the pancakes and eggs for much longer?"

After breakfast, they discussed the plans for the day. Horatio had narrowed down the timing of the shift but not close enough to determine a specific cause. He'd worked with Lanis to develop a program to fine-tune the parameters, but it would take hours to provide any usable data.

Hernandez would continue her analysis of the changes between the two timelines, focusing on the impacts to GSM and their original mission—who killed Keene's informant, and was it tied to the tattooed man?

Rowan already knew enough—her brother was alive. The question was how to dance around her supposed assignment and Zach's role in this timeline. More important, was their search for the tattooed man. Keene had become obsessed with believing their mystery man had something to do with the shift in time. She didn't see how that was possible, but if something fishy was going on at Stoker Industries they had to know—as if the Spider making deals with district leaders in the Yards wasn't enough to create suspicion. If the timeline had been artificially altered as the MacGregors believed, then Stoker would be her first choice of possibilities.

If she hoped for an easy lead, she was going to be disappointed.

Hernandez moved her empty breakfast plate to the side and placed a holo-monitor on the table. Elton Sodowski's face, their first murder victim, floated in the air like a phantom ghost. "I thought we were in luck until I found a news report that our dear Elton was killed in a freak AVU accident late yesterday."

"Well, that seems a bit coincidental." Conall picked up Hernandez's plate as well as his own. "Are we to believe that his destiny was to die regardless of the time shift?"

"Like hell," Keene growled. "What type of accident? AVU accidents are almost unheard of."

"It's still under investigation, but I'll stay on it." Hernandez sipped her coffee and pulled up another image. This time the face of Sheila Cross, aka the Spider, appeared.

"She's not dead, too?" Horatio's plaintive question matched Rowan's own thoughts.

Hernandez shook her head. "Not as far as I can tell. However, her exact location is a bit of a problem. Her assistant was in the office yesterday, but now, the Spider's meetings have been canceled for an emergency business trip. I was able to piece together a part of her transport trail. She visited GSM headquarters, but her destination in the building is unknown. I can only confirm she checked in. She left the tower four hours later, then disappeared in the transit system."

"She could be anywhere." Keene's frustration came through loud and clear. He shoved his plate aside in time for Conall to grab it before it landed on the ground.

Lanis placed a hand on his arm. "We'll continue digging while you and Rowan visit GSM. I think you should avoid Stoker for today. Visit your contact and see what you can glean from him. Then we'll determine our next steps."

He placed a hand over hers. "You're right. And before you get lost in your research, make sure everyone gets out of the bunker today. That includes everyone in security. We need to confirm we're all immune to the time shift."

"Are you expecting something?" Conall asked as he retrieved the remaining plates.

"I don't know. But until we rule out human intervention in the time shifts, we need to be prepared in case there's another one. Be sure any data collected from this timeline is appropriately documented. If there is another shift, we need to understand if there's a pattern to the changes. It might provide a clue to the reason behind them. And that might be the only way to track down who's responsible."

That tidbit created a deathly silence as they considered the ramifications.

Lanis picked up her journal. "I still have a few travelers who haven't checked in. I'll focus on that. We need to ensure they have the updated calculations for transport."

Keene stood and glanced at Rowan. "Meet me in the garage in thirty minutes."

———

AN HOUR LATER, they arrived at the GSM tower in Rowan's beat-up AVU. Keene's vehicle was still parked where he'd left it before they transported to Scotland. She parked a few spots over, feeling oddly strange that while her world turned in a different reality, Zach was performing his typical ISA routine. And based on his multiple messages, he was slightly annoyed by her non-committal responses to his inquiries. The simple sight of Keene's AVU filled her with a strange sense of comfort and sanity.

"Remember, this is just a quick recon. Focus on tech and weapons." Keene nudged her as they approached the doors of the center tower—the heart of GSM headquarters and the Security Council. "Do you know anyone other than the major who works in the building?"

"My father."

A line formed to gain entrance while ISA guards monitored the door.

"This is new," she said as they joined the queue. "Did everyone just wake up and magically remember a different life? A different job?"

"I wish I could provide an answer, but I haven't experienced a shift before. At least, not one of this magnitude. I suppose the good news is that we still remember the original timeline."

She sighed. "To simpler times."

"An old adage I've heard on more than one occasion."

After a few moments passed as the line slowly moved, she turned into Keene so her voice wouldn't carry. "The weapons look a couple of models behind our timeline."

"Security is obviously tighter." He stretched his neck, almost raising on tiptoes to watch the guards. "They're scanning the badges. They appear to be a different color."

She reached into her pocket to finger hers. "We're not going to get past that."

"I agree. And I don't want to risk what happens if we're pulled aside." He shoved his hands in the outside pockets of his jacket, then the inside ones, before checking his pants. He raised his voice. "I can't believe it. I think I left my badge in the AVU. I'll need to go get it."

"I'll walk back with you." And with a nod and a smile at the two women behind them, they gracefully departed the line and walked toward the parking area. After a few steps, Keene pulled her along a path that ran in front of the two towers.

They walked the length of the central tower, but before they reached the halfway point between the buildings, he pulled her down a narrow gravel path overgrown with hedges.

"Where are you going?" she whispered, then swore under her breath when a branch slapped her in the face.

"We need another way in."

She bumped into him when he stopped abruptly, then had to maneuver past the hedge to stand next to him. "The food court?" There were restaurants in each of the towers, but food courts were available between all the campus towers to accommodate outdoor seating. Colorful tents and canopies protected tables from the sun and occasional rain. This particular court held six hutch-style buildings spaced around the area's perimeter, but only two were open for breakfast. The others would open in the next hour for the early lunch crowd.

The entire area was fenced off so no one could enter without first going through security at the front entrance of either tower.

"Scaling the fence would be noticeable." She spotted several cameras, but there were probably sensors that couldn't be seen.

"Do you speak with the janitorial staff very often?" Keene asked.

"If I'm investigating a lead, and I thought they might have something to offer." She wasn't sure where he was going with this.

"They know where every camera and sensor is. The groundskeepers need to know where they're located so they don't continually trigger them."

"Don't tell me you happen to know one of them."

"Two, actually. And we're going to put something they once told me to the test." He moved to the middle of a large bush that had grown too close to the fence. "See that gate behind the blue food hut?"

She nodded, studying the back of the two huts that faced them and the third blue hut that sat kitty-corner to the fence. The gate allowed the food staff to carry their trash containers to a central reclamation unit. She still didn't understand Keene's intentions until a worker rushed to the gate with one of the containers. He swung it open then waited for it to close. After he dumped the trash, he returned to the gate and pulled it open without a card or scanner.

"You're kidding me. That's a major security breach."

Keene shrugged. "They consider the lock inconvenient with how often they have to go in and out of the gate, especially hauling containers. The first one to use the gate each morning jimmies the latch so it doesn't lock. My understanding is that someone makes sure it's locked when they leave each day. With the codes being changed nightly, or they used to be, they don't think they're doing anything wrong."

She rolled her eyes, somewhat incensed by the worker's laziness in breaking the rules, but for now, she agreed this was their best option. Security had to know what the workers were doing. The sensor would send a signal for the unlocked gate. "Security will have eyes on the camera."

"Yes. But they won't be watching continuously." He nodded

toward a stack of trash containers sitting next to the reclamation unit.

Keene removed his jacket and rolled up his sleeves, tucking his jacket under an arm. She copied his movements, grateful she'd worn a dark sleeveless shirt that made her look less like a government agent. They each grabbed a trash container, and keeping his head down, Keene held the gate open for her, his posture relaxed as if they had every right to be there. He left the gate as he found it, and they walked behind the huts like any other worker. She followed him to the yellow hut on the opposite side of the court, where they placed the containers near the back door before stopping to put their jackets back on. He led them around to the front of the building, surprising her by stopping at the end of the waiting line of customers.

He ordered two coffees and paid for them with his credit chip that miraculously still worked.

"You're a scary guy. Were you a criminal at some point?" she asked as they sipped coffee and headed for the doors leading back to the tower.

He just smiled and took a long drink as they passed through the door with two bored security guards. She kept her head down and fiddled with her badge, but the guards ignored her with the number of people coming and going. They dumped their cups at the first reclamation unit they found.

Keene stopped at a directory kiosk and punched in a name. "I'd rather not split up, but it would look more suspicious with two of us poking around together. Keep your badge on but in a difficult spot to read. With any luck, the different color won't trigger a response."

"I don't see any security in the halls. They probably assume the checks at the doors are sufficient."

"Okay, my contact is still here. I suggest we each try to contact one person. Try to get a sense of the current climate in

GSM. Keep your eyes open for tech or anything else that stands out. Be obtuse about anything they ask you. Dark ops, remember?"

"I'm an ISA agent. I know the drill." She pushed down her irritation, remembering they hadn't been partners long enough to assume the little details. So, why did it feel like they'd been doing this for years? It must have been the time travel.

"Sorry. I'm not used to working with a partner."

"No problem." She shrugged it off but suspected it was more than that. Was he as nervous as she was? If they got caught, she wasn't convinced his contact would be of much help.

"You said your father worked in the building. Give me his name, and I'll see if he still works here."

Her chuckle wasn't a happy one. "If I showed up in my father's office, he'd call security and have me hauled to medical to see if I cracked. I doubt a time shift would change our relationship."

"You don't get along?"

"Not even a bit."

He punched in another name. "The major is still here, but it looks like she's in a different office."

"Does it say which department?"

"Weapons development."

That was interesting but not worth further speculation. Maybe she wasn't in ISA anymore. If necessary, Hernandez could confirm her new job and whether it created consequences to their current dilemma. She'd forgotten to ask for the information before they'd left the bunker. "I'll just say I was in the neighborhood and thought I'd look her up."

Keene checked his wrist unit. "Let's meet back here in an hour." When she started to walk away, he pulled her back. "Wait. Let me see your wrist unit."

"Why?"

"Don't be stubborn. I want to set two additional backup trackers. If either of us is more than fifteen minutes late in returning, we need to find each other. Security will automatically turn off your tracker, but they probably won't suspect more than one. Someone bucking for a promotion might catch a second one but won't think to check for a third."

She studied him for a moment. "Someday, the two of us are going to do some serious drinking, and you're going to tell me all the things you're hiding from me."

He didn't turn away from her scrutiny and appeared to be doing his own. She refused to squirm as his gaze moved from her eyes to her lips then back. "That goes both ways, Rowan."

She turned away from him, ignoring the heat that ran through her from his perusal. She wasn't sure they were talking about the same thing at all.

"Remember to act like nothing has changed for you."

She heard the humor in his voice and, with her back to him, she waved her middle finger above her head. Some things transcended time.

THIRTY-FIVE

Rowan spent most of the allotted time Keene had given her trying to find the major's office. The headquarters tower was massive, and each floor had dozens of corridors. One would think an organization specializing in science and math would have a more efficient way of numbering their offices. After the third wrong corridor, she finally found the right office. When she stepped into the reception area, the major's assistant, a corporal she'd never seen before, waved her through with barely a glance.

That seemed odd, and her fledgling paranoia wondered if someone had been tracking her on the security cameras. The major always had a bulldog blocking visitors from disturbing her, and an open door to her office was not her standard practice. She swallowed her nerves and knocked once on the doorframe as she entered.

The major faced the wide window that overlooked the campus. When she turned, Rowan saw the earbuds and waited for her to end her conversation, which she did almost immediately. The major's wide smile made her sigh in relief until

Rowan got a closer look at her eyes. She held her smile in place while all her warning bells began ringing.

The major didn't move from her spot, her arms folded across her chest. Rowan remained standing, wanting to stay on equal footing.

"Of all the luck to have you pop through my door." Her honey-voiced seemed too agreeable, too sincere. "First, your brother called, asking if I knew why you'd been pulled from his unit." She glanced down at the coms system. "Now your father is demanding to know what's going on."

Ice filled her spine, and it was all she could do to keep the smile plastered on her face. If the major was now in weapons development, why would everyone call her about Rowan's temporary assignment with the Security Office?

"I've never known either of them to care about my interests." It was true enough, and if the major was as close to her family as she appeared to be, which was a lot more than before the time shift, she would know her father thought little of her.

"They only care for your well-being."

"More like their own reputation, being related to a trouble-maker and all." She chuckled, hoping the major would join in her self-deprecation.

The major's smile turned predatory. "You know I don't like secrets, Rowan."

She shrugged, taking a wrapped mint candy from the crystal dish on the major's desk. "I wish there was something I could tell you. The Security Office offered, and it was a way out of my disciplinary assignment." She stuffed the candy in her pocket, something she'd always done since the major had run her ISA unit in the Yards. "I happened to be in the building and wanted to stop by to say hello." That was as far as she was willing to take their chat. Something else was going on. When had the major become so chummy with her family? Zach maybe. But not her father. Without knowing more, she could easily walk into a trap of wordplay.

The major clicked a nail against her front teeth, the sound grating. Rowan never remembered her to be shark-like. Was this a manifestation of the alternate reality, or was she reading too much into it? "Something doesn't feel right about this."

"If it helps, they promised I could return to my old squad once I was finished." She figured that was true enough, assuming not too much had changed in the Security Office. She checked her wrist unit. "Look, I have to run. Like I said, I was in the neighborhood. I didn't want you to hear I'd been in the building and didn't take the time to say hello." She backed up, wanting to put some distance between them before turning around.

"For now, Rowan."

She bolted. Or it seemed that way as she forced a casual pace out of the office, down the hall, and to the nearest stairwell. Inside her head, she was screaming, wanting to run like hounds were after her. The major was going to be a problem, and while she second-guessed visiting her, it was better to know who she could trust. She never thought she'd have to put the major's name in the same column as her father.

The only thing that mattered now was getting out of the building, but it wouldn't hurt to make one more stop since it was on her way out. Sort of. She took the stairs to the basement where the main armory was located.

She pried the door open to scan the area. Two people in lab coats strolled by discussing the merits of one restaurant over another. She had to smile. Simpler times and some assurance that some things hadn't changed much. There should be dozens of labs, storage facilities, and a lounge in addition to housing for the security details, who worked seventy-two-hour shifts.

Though this floor wouldn't be as busy as the upper floors, it wouldn't be odd for her to be there.

The armory wasn't just for the tower's security forces. It was one of many locations where GSM and ISA field agents could get weapons. She was a betting woman and assumed that was still the case. The farther she marched down the hall, checking door signs to ensure she was heading in the right direction, an increasing amount of people roamed the halls. Most were dressed in lab coats, but she was more concerned with the number of security forces.

She could count on one hand the number of times she'd seen this many security personnel in the tower, and they'd all been for drills except for one high-security alert. She kept her expression neutral, like she belonged in the group, and nudged her badge an inch forward, just enough to see she had one. Dressed in civilian clothes, the armory personnel should assume she was undercover or special ops.

When she turned down the corridor for the armory, it appeared she wouldn't have to test her theory. While in the building, the security team would carry minimum weapons—a sidearm and one or two knives. In an actual emergency, the forces would be equipped with pulse guns or long rifles within minutes. But now, dozens of guards swapped stories as they checked their weapons and loaded rounds. They must be running drills. Her luck had finally changed. This was better than trying to get into the armory. She studied the weapons as she walked by. They were a few years older than those of her timeline. She didn't see the automated targeting sensors they relied on, but it was possible they had a different design.

Over the chatter, she heard the approach of marching boots. They were still a distance away, but based on the uniformity of tempo, it sounded like at least a dozen of them. Sweat broke down her spine and dampened the hair at her temples. She ignored it as she considered her options. She knew the general layout of the tower but hadn't been in the building often and only once on this level.

She racked her brain for possible exits as the voices around her became murmurs as the security detail grew closer. Then she saw the sign for the shooting range. That would lead to two areas—an indoor and an outdoor range. Most doors wouldn't require a code or passkey to get out, especially around the armory, where the guards would need quick access. Of course, that wouldn't be true in the case of a security lockdown. She had to get out before that happened. Her first thought was of Keene. Had he been caught and now they were searching for her?

She turned down the hall leading to the ranges, thankful they were empty. She was a quarter of the way down the corridor when a door opened behind her. Before she could turn, an arm grabbed her around the waist as a hand covered her mouth. She was dragged through the door and pressed up against a hard chest. A warm breath tickled her neck as the arm around her waist loosened.

"It's me."

She relaxed against Keene, grateful she wasn't alone anymore. His hand dropped, and he stepped back. When she turned, he was already moving up the stairs. She raced after him.

"Are they looking for you?" If they were, a lockdown would be coming before they made it to an outer door.

He stopped when they reached ground level. His expression was grave, but there was a gleam in his gaze. The memory of the valley in Scotland rushed back. Danger invigorated him. "It seems a General Lockwood is in charge of security. He heard his misfit daughter was in the building, and irritated by not knowing about her dark ops mission, wants her found."

Frustration dried her earlier sweat. "Damn him. Always sticking his nose in things." Then his words hit her. "You said he was in charge of security. You mean for this tower or the campus?"

His look of unease told her what she didn't want to hear. "All of GSM for the Los Angeles region."

She would have sunk to the floor, but Keene dragged her out the door to blinding sunshine. She was surprised her father hadn't had the outer doors locked. They were one-way doors— exit only. But even the head of security would answer to the GSM Council if he freaked out the civilians by locking them in the building just to find his errant daughter. Besides, it wasn't like he didn't know where she lived.

She stopped, unable to get her feet to move. Would she be able to go home again?

Keene slowed and glanced back. "Rowan, we need to go."

When she didn't move, he strode back and grabbed her arm, glancing around to see if anyone was watching them.

He kept his voice low. "I don't know what's going on in that head, but we need to deal with it later."

That snapped her back, and she kept pace with him to their AVUs, each of them heading to their own without another word. They were in the air in less than a minute, each taking a different route back to the bunker. She circled the campus once, watching for anyone following them. All she could think about was her father's new position at GSM. He'd always held high appointments, but the head of GSM Security? No matter how many ways she looked at it—they were screwed.

———

"THIS IS SO MESSED UP!" Horatio grasped his blue hair as

he paced in front of the oak tree. Hernandez stayed close, whispering words that did little to ease him.

Lanis thought a meeting in the garden would provide a calmer setting to discuss said mess. Rowan had experience dealing with complex ops, especially when they weren't going as planned, and a new environment gave everyone a different perspective. Unfortunately, the garden didn't have the positive impact Lanis hoped for, but it had been a great idea.

On the drive back from GSM, she'd had time to assess their situation. This was her element. Something she'd been trained for, and Horatio was right about one thing—they were in trouble. But with careful planning and limited interactions with the outside, the team had the right skill sets to figure out what had happened. Whether they could fix it was a different story—but one step at a time.

"Horatio, get your ass over here." She'd had enough of his fragile outbursts. "Have you been taking your meds?"

He turned on her, a flare of anger confirming she'd hit the mark. Hernandez glared at her, but only for a second until she realized what Rowan was doing. "Yes, Mother," rolled out of his mouth with pure venom, but with his blue hair and lime-green sneakers, the overall effect didn't even dent her armor.

"Then get over here and help walk us through our next steps. Just because someone has their knickers in a knot because they can't find you isn't the end of the world. And a missing person's report is easy to remedy. You're on a special assignment. Blast your network and tell them to leave you alone. You're trying to focus and can't with all the interruptions, which is why you went offline."

Years of worry drained from his young face, and he trudged back to the table with a chagrined expression. "There are so many things that seem to tie back to me, I might have gotten overwhelmed." He dropped onto the bench and slouched, his hair sticking up at odd angles.

Hernandez perched next to him. "We'll work through it." Her rhythmic voice continued to calm, and he blew out a sigh.

Keene leaned forward, a beer in his hand. "Let's go through each of our issues one by one and see how truly bad it is."

Lanis set the holo-monitor in the middle of the table and expanded its size to be readable by everyone. "As you can see, I've already made notes on what Keene and Rowan discovered at GSM."

Keene took the first item. "My contact took some convincing of the situation—" he gave Rowan a quick glance then continued, "but he can give us cover for at least two weeks, maybe more. But it will depend on one factor."

"My father," she broke in. "As the head of the Security Office for the Los Angeles region, it gives him plenty of rein over the guards and most of the networks. Fortunately, Keene's contact is on the Global Security Council, which definitely gives us cover. But my father is a bulldog who won't let this go."

"I take it this isn't something you can smooth over with him." Lanis thumped a pen against her journal, her expression telling Rowan she already knew the answer but felt the need to ask.

"Not easily."

Hernandez snorted in response. "He's not called the Grizzly for nothing."

"Let's hold that piece for now. It will tie in with something Rowan and I discussed." Keene dropped ID badges on the table. "My contact was able to provide new badges." He tossed one to Hernandez. "I don't know that you'll need it, but just in case."

"Okay." Conall finished a cracker, wiping his hands on his pants before picking up his beer. "Everyone has a cover in place for the next couple of weeks. But we'll need to keep an eye on transmissions to ensure they stick. I'll have our security team monitor the daily news, security outlets, and the emergency net. Let's discuss the timeline."

Lanis sat back and referred to her journal. "We've been able to narrow the impact to sometime during the twentieth century, but we can't get any closer than that." She glanced at Conall. "I've called in Nathan to help, but he hasn't responded." She turned to the rest of the team. "He's our continuum expert. I'll give him another day, then send another message."

Keene nodded. "We need a list of all major and minor events from that century—political, economic, and sociological. I know that will be a long list, but nothing Horatio can't handle. Right?" He glanced at the kid.

"Easy enough." Horatio ran his hands through his hair and glanced at Hernandez, who nodded reassurance. "We might have found a problem in the GSM council."

"A larger problem than my father in charge of the Security Office?" This day was just getting better.

Hernandez sat up. "The GSM and ISA Council members are all the same with one exception. There's a new member on the GSM side. Someone that—" She glanced at Horatio, who just nodded before lowering his gaze to his hands, which now rested in his lap. Hernandez shifted in her seat and restarted. "Do you remember Horatio talking about his project moving people from the Yards to better jobs Topside?"

They all nodded, and Conall groaned. Everyone understood where this was headed.

Hernandez tapped her tablet and a face appeared on the holo-monitor. "Well, one of them, a woman by the name Tilani LeCroix, is now on the GSM council for the Los Angeles Region."

Conall scratched his head. "So, she replaced Greg Fischer. Not sure if that's a bad thing, but we'll have to watch her. I'll search public records for what she's been up to since she's been on council in addition to where she worked on her move upward. It wouldn't hurt to see how Greg lost his seat or if he simply retired. If I find anything fishy, I'll get Horatio to dig further."

"Okay." Lanis scribbled in her journal. "This brings us to a perplexing issue."

Rowan gave Keene a questioning look, but he shook his head and shrugged. They must have missed something important while they'd been running around GSM.

Lanis made them wait as she drank a slow sip of lemonade.

Rowan suspected she probably wished she'd spiked it and followed suit with a long pull on her beer. Everyone was going to need something stronger before the day was out.

"Horatio believes we can't pinpoint the exact time of the shift because someone else is traveling."

She expected an uproar after that bombshell, but the only sound was the trill of birds that had been imported into the garden. It was apparent Keene and her were the only two who hadn't known.

"And how do you know that?" Keene pinned his gaze on Horatio, who didn't seem bothered by his intense stare.

"The power you use for traveling is generated from the earth, similar to the power you use to operate and mask the bunker."

Conall and Lanis nodded in agreement.

Horatio's leg bounced with nervous energy. "But it's not exactly the same. I don't know how this all works, but there's a definite difference in the power signature. It probably has something to do with how it connects with the continuum and the impact of temporal conversions. When I tried to narrow down the exact moment of the shift, I kept getting interference. I can't be positive, but whatever is impeding my queries looks similar to the power source you use for travel, but again, not quite the same.

"At first, I thought it might be coming from some off-site GSM lab that experiments with different power sources." He tugged at his ear as the bounce in his leg increased. "But the signal carries a temporal signature, so I asked Lanis and Conall to check my findings."

"He's right," Lanis added. "I can't explain it, and we could be wrong, but I don't think so."

"How could that be?" Rowan asked. "Could it be GSM?"

Conall's brows furrowed. "I don't see how. They're decades away from time travel." He shrugged. "And centuries from using our method."

Keene had paled. Lanis placed a hand on his arm as she explained what they knew. "We know it's coming from this sector. The closest we can get is that it's someplace in the Yards or the Barrens."

"The tattooed man." Keene's response sounded so positive, yet Rowan had to question whether it was his obsession with the mystery man or deductive reasoning.

"That's a stretch." Conall appeared to have the same doubt, but his expression wasn't as convincing.

"Maybe," Keene admitted. "We need to know what has changed, if anything, with the relationship between Topside and the Yards. Is the Underground still active?" He glanced at Horatio and Hernandez.

Hernandez seemed uncomfortable. "I haven't spent time in that area, but I did notice Zach's unit has two active missions connected to the Underground. So they're around, though I don't know if they're typical contraband runs or something more substantial."

"Dig deeper." Rowan waited for Hernandez's nod then turned to the group. "So far, we have an unexplained time shift, someone outside of the bunker time traveling, someone from the Yards now on the GSM Council, and a possible increase in Underground activity. Are these just individual incidents, or are they connected?"

Her theory was met with a cacophony of voices as everyone chimed in at once.

Keene thumped the table for silence. "Rowan's question deserves a deeper discussion, but we need more information or it's all guesswork. If there's a connection between events, let's find it rather than speculate. But let me add one more thing." He ran a hand through his hair, and that telltale tic along his jaw didn't bode well. "I received a message from Kai Li just before this meeting."

"He's one of the council members in Asia Town," Hernandez said.

"Aye. Kai has been contacted by our tattooed mystery man, who has asked for a meeting."

"Kai remembers our discussion before the shift?" Rowan was dumbfounded that someone outside the bunker remembered a meeting from their original timeline.

Keene glanced at Conall and Lanis before responding. "It would appear so. I find the timing, pardon the irony, to be questionable."

Lanis added it to the list. "So, where does that leave us?"

"Rowan and I need to spend time in the Yards. We need to see how widespread the Underground has grown." His glance was all business when he turned to her. "This won't be an issue for me, but our investigation will put a spotlight on you. I suspect your father and brother will hound you for answers."

She considered this latest bombshell. Could this day get any worse? And though she wasn't superstitious, she wanted to kick herself for even thinking the question. While it added one more mystery to their already full plate, it also validated Keene's obsession with the tattooed man. This was the first lead they'd received that the man was still out there, and it was an obvious string to pull. That didn't even begin to answer the question of why Kai Li had been impervious to the time shift. Did the tattooed man know this? She also had an itch growing ever since Lanis mentioned the Barrens.

"They know I've been assigned to a dark ops assignment, but Zach will push back if he thinks it's related to the Underground, which he would consider a connection to his missions. But he also knows he can't ask. It will make him irritable at best." Her stomach churned. The best place to gather intel on GSM and ISA was at a family dinner, assuming they still happened and that she was still invited. But knowing her father, he'd be as eager as her to see how much he could weasel out of a dinner conversation. As far as she was concerned—game on. Zach would be a different matter, but she had a plan for that as well.

"I think we've had enough for one day." Lanis shut down the holo-monitor. "Rowan, I assume you'll be staying at your place?"

She nodded. "It would be suspicious otherwise. I can make a few exceptions without drawing attention, but I need to leave the impression everything outside of work is normal."

Lanis nodded. "Try to make it here in time for breakfast. I'd like to have two daily meetings to keep us all updated."

Everyone nodded as they began their walk back to the elevator.

Keene stopped her. "Are you going to be okay going back to your place?"

She studied him. His brows furrowed with concern, and his gray eyes were less stormy. "Worry for your partner?"

He relaxed and grinned. "Who would have thought it?"

She patted his chest before moving away. "Don't go soft on

me, Keene. We're headed into troubled waters. I need to know you can handle it."

He barked out a laugh and kept pace with her as they followed the team. "Before you get too sassy, just remember, I can always send you to Marta for additional training."

Shivers ran down her spine. "Now you're just being spiteful." And she increased her speed to catch up with Hernandez. His chuckle should have irritated her. Instead, it filled her with a warmth she couldn't explain and a sense that she wouldn't want anyone else watching her back for whatever was to come.

THIRTY-SIX

Keene hadn't intended to follow Rowan, but he didn't see the harm ensuring she arrived home without incident. He monitored the neighborhood, studying each AVU and commercial cargo unit, satisfied none of them appeared suspicious. Other than their quick tour of GSM, they hadn't done anything to warrant the Security Office tracking them, but who knew what trouble Rowan might have created in this timeline. She'd been transferred for disciplinary action, which, based on her file, could mean anything.

She'd been through a lot in the last six months, but that had been the old timeline when she had to work through her brother's death. Based on her personnel records before and after the shift, she'd always been a troubled soul. But, after pulling the files on her father, General Thaddeus Lockwood, he understood something of what made Rowan the rebel she was. Her father was a hard-ass, and a person didn't just shrug that off when he got home. Keene knew something about growing up in a household like that.

To add to her complicated life, Conall believed Rowan was having headaches. Lanis was convinced they were visions.

Keene had doubted it, had pushed it from his thoughts. The old prophecies were stories his ancestors had weaved to give the people something to believe in. Something that would make their miserable struggles more tolerable. But Lanis and Conall still believed. Had they been away from home for so long, they'd fallen into the same trap of needing something larger to believe? That their work, monitoring and tracking human evolution, wasn't enough?

Then the time continuum shifted, and Lanis and Conall had their first sign the prophecy was real. Keene admitted that something, or more likely, *someone* was trying to change the future. The question was why. Power. Love. Vengeance. He considered the meaning of the tattoo—a reckoning.

When Conall had given Rowan the tour of the artifacts room, she'd stopped at Brìghde's sword. Keene brushed it off as another coincidence. It meant nothing. It was a beautiful work of craftsmanship, and Rowan was a modern-day warrior who appreciated the old. But when she collapsed after holding it, then woke knowing the blade belonged to a woman, a cold breeze had raced up his neck. A quick glance at Conall told Keene his brother was even more convinced that Rowan was the woman prophesied centuries before.

The only problem was that two people had been foretold in the Druid Prophecies—one righteous, the other chaos. At least, that was the knowledge his family had passed down to each generation. If she was a prophecy, which of the two was she?

The tattoo had to be the key. It was an ancient symbol. While someone might have mistakenly come across it and resurrected it for their own purposes, it was sufficient to bring back ghosts from the past. And he wouldn't stop searching until he found the tattooed man.

Keene surveyed the neighborhood one last time, but before he started the AVU, he spotted Rowan leaving the tower. She'd changed into black camo pants, a thin sweater, and a light jacket. She glanced up and down the street before strolling in the direction of the public transport station.

Without a second thought, Keene left the AVU and followed. Whatever his little minx was up to, he wanted to know. And he'd convinced himself he was simply keeping an eye on his partner. When she entered the monorail, he waited until the last call was sounded, then jumped through the door of the second car down from hers.

At first, he thought she'd head for the Yards and was surprised when she exited while still in the Edges. Two blocks later, she ducked into a bar called Safety Zone. He stepped next to the large display window, glancing inside like the outsider he was. She approached a table where Zach was drinking with three other people. He surveyed the rest of the bar. If he had to guess, this was an ISA hangout. She seemed to enjoy walking into possible trouble.

Was she meeting with Zach as part of her cover or for some other reason? He'd been dead, and now he was resurrected. Who could blame her for wanting to spend time with him? But if they fixed the timeline, her brother would very likely be lost again. Would the love for her brother lead her to keep the continuum as it was now? Would she eventually work against them?

When a beer was placed in front of her, Keene began to step away until Rowan shouted something and jumped up. A grizzled old man, a scar running down one side of his face, placed a hand on her shoulder, forcing her to sit down. Then he pulled a chair over from another table and sat between Rowan and Zach. He said something, and brother and sister stared at the table, both mumbling. That was easy enough to interpret—a forced apology. He smiled. Family.

Once the conversation began again with frowns turning to

laughter, Keene crossed the street and found a comfortable place to sit in the shadows. He would wait until she got back home, telling himself it was because he didn't trust this timeline. And weren't partners supposed to look out for each other?

As the hour passed, one memory kept resurfacing, once more making him question his own beliefs. When Rowan had woken after holding Brìghde's sword, he'd heard her say something. Something he denied hearing when Conall had asked. He believed it had been his imagination, but he couldn't deny it any longer. She'd spoken the words "Dìon Tìr nan Òg" which meant "Protect Tìr nan Òg." How would Rowan have known that call to arms, let alone say the words in Gaelic?

Too many mysteries. Too many questions. He pulled a flask from his pocket, one he rarely carried in this century, but the woman was driving him to drink. He laughed at the memory of once warning someone else of getting involved with a redhead. He toasted to his Scottish brethren and waited.

———

ROWAN SENSED the tail minutes after leaving the tower. She'd only stopped at home long enough to see what, if anything, had changed. Her housing unit was starker than usual. Not one potted plant. Her mother had bought them for her in their original timeline. Was her relationship with the woman even worse in this time period that she didn't warrant a little greenery? She didn't think it was possible, yet, there they were.

The fridge and shelves were as barren as usual with the exception of three brown beers. She grabbed one and sipped it as she strolled through the unit, finding nothing to connect her to who she was—whether this timeline or the one before the shift.

It had barely been a week, if that, and the bunker felt more like a home than any other she'd ever had. There was some underlying connection between her and the MacGregors that she couldn't explain. And she wasn't sure she wanted to look too deeply. They were in the shit with this new timeline, and Keene's words of this not being the only shift they might have to contend with blew a cold winter storm through her. She shivered as an image of the Scotland landscape covered in snow flashed by. Not a vision, and she shook her head to dispel it.

Her last stop was her coms station. She blew out a breath, dropped into the chair, and took a long swig of the beer before hitting the button to replay her messages. From the date on the recordings, she'd last checked them the previous afternoon. Whoever she was in this timeline, it surprised her to find two dozen unread messages. Most from that day.

Two from her mother, one from the day before and one that morning. Neither held anything more than a stern tone to call her. With the turmoil from the time shift, she'd forgotten about her father's birthday. It irritated her that she was curious about her mother's plans for the event. Were they the same as before? Or was she such a mess in this world that her mother simply wanted to advise her that she wasn't invited to the party?

She took two long sips of beer before checking the next message. Kendra wanted to meet for lunch the following day. She saved that one. Maybe her sister-in-law would be the best one to fill her in on what was happening without Rowan having to ask too many questions.

There was one from her father's aide. He was a cookie-cutter of her father's hard-as-nails attitude, giving her notice that her attendance was required to meet with the Grizzly at the Strand Hotel the following afternoon. Interesting. Not GSM, but his favorite watering hole. That request in itself was scarier than dealing with the time shift. She saved that message too.

The rest of the messages were from Zach. They started with a worried tone as he checked on her health. The next several skipped straight to irritation at ignoring his calls before swiftly returning to concern. The last six or so were plain rage at her selfishness. But underneath it all, she heard the same worry in his tone. He sensed the change in her, and he had to be dying to understand how she ended up in a dark ops mission with a partner.

She glanced at her watch. It was still early enough that Zach might be at Safety Zone. It couldn't hurt to stop by. If he wasn't there, it wasn't far from the Yards if she wanted to check the crowd at Duster's. Both places were perfect for gathering information about the Underground with little effort—assuming the group was as troublesome now as it was in her time period.

She took the monorail because if she had to run from anyone, it would be easier to evade them on foot. If she took her AVU and was forced to leave it behind, she didn't want to have to retrieve it before her morning meeting at the bunker.

Once she found a seat on the monorail, she glanced through the window to the next car but didn't see her tail. Maybe she lost him, though she doubted it. He was better than that. She leaned her head against the window and closed her eyes, waiting for her announced stop.

After leaving the transport station, she stood at the edge of the park across the street from the Zone. The bar was busy, and though it had a large front window, she couldn't tell if Zach was there, but she did see a couple guards she knew. This would be easier if Hernandez was with her, but she heaved a breath and marched across the street, pulling open the front door like it was a normal end of her day—like it used to be.

The place was warm from the crush of the crowd, and she pushed her way through to get a better view of the room. It only took a moment to hear Dozer's shout through the boisterous voices.

"Lockwood, get your ass over here."

She wasn't sure if he was talking to her or Zach, but when she spotted the table, Zach was already there, his gaze catching hers immediately. He appeared a bit surly. That wasn't his normal expression, and it was a toss-up whether she or his job had put that look on his face.

Dozer took that moment to head for the bar, so she put on a brave face, smiled at the group, and took the open chair next to Zach. She responded to the hearty welcomes and typical rowdy comments before looking at her brother.

"Sorry, I haven't had a chance to catch up. You know how it is."

Zach stared at her. "The last time I saw you, your partner..." he said the word as if he suspected it was all a ruse, "well, he made it sound like you had a concussion. If that had been me in the bed, you wouldn't have let it go without tracing my movements all day."

She shrugged, unwilling to acknowledge the truth of his statement. After the worst six months of her life, she couldn't seem to find the common ground that once came so easily between them.

"Is it because I put you on a disciplinary assignment? You call a friend and have them get you reassigned."

Ah. So that was it. He was feeling guilty. Well, she knew all about that—tenfold. She found herself caught between wanting to hug him, promising everything would be all right even though he wouldn't have a clue what she was talking about, or punching him.

A mug of beer was pushed in front of her, but before she took a swig, she simply said, "Contrary to your beliefs, the world doesn't revolve around you, and you know I take care of myself."

Then she took a long swallow before she said something she might regret. She shouldn't be mad at him, yet her anger at the situation they found themselves in needed a release. Maybe laying it at his feet, which he seemed so willing to assume, would be best all around. She didn't want to admit that getting close to him again and then having him ripped away when they fixed the timeline would crush her.

"Christ, Mouse, the least you could do is let me know you were okay."

"Well, now you can see I'm just fine." She glanced across the table. "Hey, Schroeder, how's it going?"

The young skinny guard stared at them as if he were watching the Jonga ball finals. Probably waiting to see which of them would blow first. The kid's Adam's apple bobbed as he tried to find the right words. "It's good to see you again, Sergeant." He glanced down. "I mean corporal."

Rowan turned and rose so fast, her chair almost tipped over. "Corporal? You demoted me?"

Before Zach could say anything, Dozer pulled over a chair and pushed it between them. "Sit down, Rowan. This is an old argument. And Zach, you know better than to push. You've been at each other's throats for the last two months. Enough is enough. Now apologize and let's put the job away for one night."

She lowered her head and pulled her beer closer as she mumbled a quick apology that didn't sound like she meant it. And she held back a grin when Zach's sounded as lame as hers.

Then Dozer took over the conversation, talking about one of their snitches getting mixed up in the middle of a contraband run, thinking he was getting a joyride to the other side of the Yards. While the conversation reset to a normal night at the Zone, and though this wasn't her timeline, the fact she'd lost her rank continued to rankle. And Zach had done that? He seemed amiable when she'd answered the door the morning after her time travel, so she must have forgiven him. Or she'd done something so stupid she knew she'd earned the punishment. It was still hard to take.

She glanced toward the window and saw Keene searching the crowd, avoiding making eye contact with her. Was he going to stand outside all night? After a painful hour, the camaraderie she'd hoped to feel with the team wasn't there, and though Zach laughed with the group, she felt his tension, his need to get whatever was eating at him out.

She finished her beer and stood. "Sorry for the quick drink, but my mornings start earlier than normal." She got the expected boos and calls of lightweight and sore loser, the last one hitting home harder than she expected. But she grinned like it meant nothing, gave Dozer a slap on the back and Zach a quick nod before she stormed through the room and out the door, grateful for the light fog that brought the cool sea air.

Keene stood in the shadow of a tree where the streetlights couldn't reach. She was on her way across the street to him when an arm pulled her around.

Zach stood there, his hands clenching into fists. "Come out with it, Mouse. What the hell is going on?"

"What do you mean?"

"This new assignment. Father doesn't know anything about it."

"Did you call him, or did he call you? And for that matter, how do you both have enough time in your busy schedules to follow my every move? The continual babysitting? Is it just because I'm a screwup or because it will somehow ruin your reputation? Did it ever occur to either of you, that maybe I'm a fuckup because of the constant smothering? You need to give me the space to let me be who I am."

She panted, trying to catch her breath after her rant. She

hadn't meant to let it all out, but why was everything always her fault?

Zach stared at her. His hands weren't clenching into fists anymore. But his mind was whirling with all the words he wanted to say but wasn't sure where to start. She'd seen it a dozen times growing up. It wasn't the first time she'd gone off on a tirade, leaving him in the same whirlwind of mixed emotions.

"When are you going to trust me? Let me make my own mistakes. Stop judging me."

"Mouse..." He glanced past her, and she closed her eyes.

She didn't have to turn to know Keene was coming. What was it with the men in her life?

"Rowan." Keene stepped next to her. "We have to go. Something is coming, and I don't think we want to be here." He glanced at Zach. "None of us."

"What are you talking about?" She stared at him as if he'd lost his senses. Then her mind cleared when she noted his hunched shoulders and wrinkled brows.

She felt it more than heard it. A deep rumbling beneath her feet.

Zach turned at the same time she did to glance down the street.

Rammers. Four of them.

And they were coming fast.

THIRTY-SEVEN

Zach reacted first, pushing Rowan out of the way.

"Rammers!" Zach's shout was aimed at the Zone, his arms waving at anyone who might see him.

Keene caught Rowan before she fell and pulled her away. She reached for Zach and clutched his shirt, dragging him with them.

Zach tried to pull away, but she held on tight as the rammers closed in on them.

Rapid gunfire sprayed the buildings, most of the businesses closed for the day, with bullets that ripped holes through the cement. Pinkies. Small arms pulse grenades. They didn't leave holes as big as the standard-issue pulse grenades did, but they were just as deadly. And they were heavily regulated, even within ISA.

Zach continued to wave, and now Rowan joined his screaming, hoping to catch the eye of at least one of the guards in the bar.

Then she was rolling as Keene tugged her to the ground before he reached out for Zach and pulled him down on top of her.

When the rammers reached them, Keene ran for the lead vehicle.

Was he out of his mind?

Then Zach was up, chasing after him. She didn't have any choice but to follow.

Glass shattered from the barrage of bullets. What were rammers doing in the Edges? This was unheard of. And more than one? Destroying businesses didn't make sense.

Then it hit her.

Their intent was the Safety Zone at a time when they knew it would be filled with ISA guards. Some of them might be carrying, but many wouldn't be. They were having a good time after a long day at work. They were sitting ducks.

Keene had wrenched open the passenger side door of the lead rammer and pulled someone out. He tossed them to the ground before moving deeper into the cab of the vehicle. But the man he'd dragged out managed to turn and grab Keene's leg. Gravity did the rest as Keene fell on top of him.

Then the two of them were throwing punches.

Keene easily had the size and weight, but the other guy was scrappy, a leaner version of Hernandez. If she wondered what Keene would be like in a hand-to-hand fight, she didn't any longer. He was as dirty a fighter as she was. He poked a finger in the guy's eye before rolling him over. But the smaller man recovered quickly, punching wildly and getting in a couple of good hits in Keene's stomach and kidneys.

She ripped her gaze away long enough to see where Zach was. He stood on the runner that ran alongside the cab, holding on to the open door. Then he was kicked off as the rammer picked up speed. He rolled when he hit the ground, landing in the bushes.

The other rammers followed the lead vehicle but kept

shooting toward the Zone and the buildings on the far side before they disappeared into the night.

Zach scrambled out of the bushes, gave a glance toward the bar, then dove after Keene and the scrawny dude who kept slipping out of Keene's grip.

The guy grabbed Keene as if purposely holding him in a bear hug. Keene pushed him away, but his jacket was pulled off in the process. Then Zach was on top of both of them.

Rowan reached for Zach until she saw him pull out his flex cuffs. Their flexibility made them easy to store, but once in place, they tightened automatically and required a security code to release them. Of course, her brother would be carrying cuffs even when off the job. One reason he was a major now.

She would typically just grab the closest thing near her to bust over someone's head. A personal choice. She grinned as she waited until the green light lit the cuffs then reached out to grab the guy's arm when he twisted back, knocking her over.

Keene, who was at the bottom of the pile, had pushed hard enough to get the stack on top of him to shift. He had the muscles to do it. The problem was that the bad guy took advantage and swung his head back, hitting Zach square on the forehead.

Zach rolled to the ground, and the bad guy crawled away on his knees. With his hands cuffed behind him, he wouldn't get far, assuming he didn't get on his feet.

She went after him, assuming Zach was just dazed, and she didn't want to lose the one man who could explain what had just happened. The guy was making a good attempt at standing when she reached him, and she kicked him hard on the back of the thigh. He stumbled, falling on his chin in the soft grass. She took out her own cuffs and grinned as she tied the guy's ankles together.

The apple didn't fall far from the tree. Their father had beaten certain life-saving measures into their thick skulls while growing up. And even though her father hated the fact she'd signed up for ISA, he'd instilled the same values in her—always carry a sidearm or knife and have your cuffs tucked away. That advice had never steered her wrong. And while the cuffs weren't the first thing she reached for, they came in handy once the criminal was down.

She stood and brushed off her knees then turned to find Zach and Keene several feet apart staring at each other.

"Just drop it, Zach." Keene had his hands up, his forehead wrinkled as he took a step forward.

Rowan's heart skipped a beat as panic rose.

Zach held Keene's TTD. The damn time travel device. Why was Keene even carrying it? The logical side of her brain knew why, but she was working on pure instincts and, for the moment, couldn't give a flip to his reasoning.

"I'll explain what it is, but it's critical that you drop it now." Keene's took on a tone of desperation.

"Listen to him, Zach. Please, drop it. For me. Drop it for me."

Zach didn't seem to be listening to either of them, more mesmerized by the device's flashing multi-colored lights.

The lights turned to a single blue color and the flashing stopped.

"Zach, drop it and run." Keene had taken a couple of steps toward him then fell into a sprint.

She glanced back at Zach. His form shimmered.

Then he was gone.

Keene had been seconds away. He fell on the spot where Zach had been standing.

All she could do was stare. She had no words.

Then cackling broke through the fog, and she looked to her left.

The bad guy was rolling on the ground, his chuckles ringing through the night air. "That's cracken." He almost choked and sounded half-mad. "Man, oh man, I bet you didn't see that coming." Then nothing but hysterical laughter.

She hadn't seen Keene get up, and she sighed with relief when he swung his fist and knocked the guy out.

Then everything came to her in some crazy slow-motion reel. She turned toward the Zone. She didn't know how much time had passed during the struggle with the bad guy—it seemed a long time but would only have been a few minutes.

But it was long enough for ISA to storm the area. Blue, red, and yellow lights flashed, lighting up the dark streets, their reflection bouncing off the shards of broken glass. People stumbled out of the building, weaving as they tried to find their footing, dazed and confused by what had just happened. Most were stained with fresh blood. One man dropped a few feet from the door and didn't move.

Then the med units arrived. ISA on-duty guards sifted through the rubble, walking some people out, and carrying others on stretchers. They had arrived quickly. Since this was the Edges, ISA would have picked up the rammers on the security net. They hadn't been able to get there in time, but they were fast enough to get med units rolling.

Her gaze lit on Dozer, who was inside the building, next to the blown-out windows. He took several steps then stopped and bent over before moving on. Searching for live victims. At least he was alive. There had to be massive casualties, and she turned her back on the scene.

Keene held the bad guy in a standing position. The man's ankles were still bound, and he would topple without the support. But he was still laughing. She stalked over and punched him in the nose. Blood squirted, and he toppled back, either from the hit or Keene letting him go. She assumed it was both.

Then she dropped to her knees and sobbed. She couldn't hold it back. Where the hell had Zach gone?

Keene's arms were around her, and he rocked her back and forth. He hummed softly, and for the barest of moments, she recognized the tune though she didn't know its name. Then the grief consumed her.

Zach was gone again.

"We'll find him, Rowan. I know where he went. He's not gone."

She gripped his arm, holding on as if he were a lifeboat.

"We need to get back to the bunker." When she didn't move, he added, "We can't be found here."

That got her attention, and she glanced at the man rolling around in the grass next to them.

She slowly nodded. "Where did he go?"

"Scotland. Conall has us running emergency protocols. I had the TTD primed to go back to the cave about a month after we left. We don't know what's going on here, and we don't have the time to be caught in GSM or ISA lockdowns."

She glanced over at the scene of destruction. How many of the guards had she known? What the hell was going on? Then her gaze pinned on the bound man.

"What do we do with him?"

"As much as I'd like to take him to the bunker, we need to leave him for ISA. At least for now. Can you run over and grab an ISA guard? Tell them you were leaving for home when the rammers came. You couldn't get to the bar in time, but you managed to pull this guy out."

She stared back at the bar.

"Rowan. Time is of the essence. Are you listening to me? Zach needs us."

That did the trick. She nodded.

She wanted to grab the first ISA guard she came upon, but she didn't recognize anyone and didn't want to hand the guy over to someone she didn't know. Cap would be there soon enough, but she spotted Dozer carrying out a woman and handing her off to one of the medics. Knowing everyone was in rescue mode, she took the chance of not being noticed, and pushed her way through, grabbing Dozer's arm.

He was surprised when he saw her. "Are you injured?"

She shook her head. "I caught one of them. I need you."

He pushed her away from the crowd. "Where?" That scary look he got that made others run the other way was already stamped on his face, but now it turned darker.

They ran across the street to find Keene sitting on top of the guy, who was still trying to inch his way to freedom. The guy had strong survival instincts.

If Dozer questioned who Keene was, he shoved it away once he saw the bound man.

"Striker." Dozer stared down at the man. "Now, why doesn't this surprise me? Guess you're in the thick of it, after all."

"I need to go." Rowan tugged on Dozer's arm. "I can't be seen here."

Dozer stared at her, then glanced at Keene, giving him a quick once over. "Have you seen Zach?"

She didn't know what to say. What could she say? He was here, helping out, then accidentally time-traveled?

"He chased after another one on foot." Keene grabbed her arm. "Rowan's right. If we get pulled into this, it will destroy our dark ops mission."

Dozer nodded. "I'll tell them Zach bound him before chasing after the other one."

Rowan gripped Dozer's hand. "I'll check with you in the morning. I'll need a full recap."

Dozer gave her an odd look then nodded before picking up the bound man's feet. Without another word, he dragged the man toward the closest ISA vehicle, letting the man's head drag and bounce behind him.

The man screamed. At least he wasn't laughing anymore.

Keene pulled her away, and they ran for the monorail, but halfway there, she collapsed to her knees. He sat down next to her and pulled her into his arms. She couldn't hold it in anymore, and she beat her fists on his back, her cries of frustration turning to sobs. The scene ran over and over in her mind. Everything had happened so quickly.

Then he was rocking her again, humming that same damn song she'd heard in Galway Alley. It was soothing, and his voice was deep and melodic. She closed her eyes, her sobs turning into hiccups.

"We'll find him. But we need to get to the bunker. I need you to pull yourself together. You're an ISA agent, and we have a missing man. Get your head in the game."

She pulled back and ran a hand under her nose before wiping her eyes. "How long do we have?"

"If we hurry, we can get close to the time I'd originally set. If this was our normal time, I wouldn't question it. But the shift has made the calculations trickier. The faster we get back, the better chance we have of getting to him before he leaves the cave."

"What's going on, Keene? That man didn't seem surprised when Zach disappeared."

"I don't know. We can have Horatio and Hernandez monitor the net while we're gone."

She stood before Keene did and glanced back toward the bar. All she could see were the flashing lights and shadows of people moving about. Keene's arms wrapped around her, and she closed her eyes for the briefest moment. As comforting as his arms were, she pushed them away.

She straightened her shoulders and gave the scene a last glance like the ISA agent she was. Then she turned and strode toward the monorail. Keene's boots kept pace with her, following a step behind. It gave her almost as much comfort as his arms had. He didn't ask questions. He didn't doubt her purpose, her resolve, or her abilities.

Whatever had occurred with the rammers would have to wait. Her only mission now—bring Zach home. Then find out what the hell was happening to her world.

―――――

Thank You For Reading!

The story continues with **Children of the Mist**, book two in the **Time Renegades** series.

Nothing made sense.
Time shifts.

Time travel.
Visions.

Six months ago, Sgt. Rowan Lockwood's life was simple—catch smugglers, seize contraband, make arrests, then hit the bar to swap stories with the other ISA guards. Maybe take someone home if the night called for it.

Now? She was drowning in problems she had no idea how to solve. The visions were coming faster, pressing on her, demanding attention she wasn't ready to give them. Then there was her brother, Zach—who she saw die—alive again, resurrected by a time shift she couldn't begin to understand.

But there was no time to process any of it. Someone was behind these shifts, pulling the strings, warping reality—and if they weren't stopped, it would happen again.

To fight back, she needed answers. Fast. And the only person she could trust to help her get them? Her reluctant, infuriatingly moody partner—Keene MacGregor.

And now a glimpse...

CHILDREN OF THE MIST

BOOK TWO

Sergeant Rowan Lockwood gripped the door handle as Keene MacGregor, her reluctant partner, lifted the AVU off the ground and sped to Zone 3 airspace so quickly they were almost vertical. She kept her mouth shut. No one wanted to get back to the bunker faster than she did.

Keene touched a screen, and after a few seconds, Conall's face appeared.

"What's up, brother?" Conall's brows scrunched together as he took in Keene's irritated expression and Rowan's somber one. If he was surprised to see her in the AVU, he didn't show it.

"We need to get to Scotland. Get the POD system booted up for a trip as soon as we arrive. ETA is ten minutes."

Conall didn't say anything, but when he looked to Rowan, and noted her panic or, perhaps, her readiness to kick someone's ass, he nodded. "I'll inform Lanis." The screen went dark.

Keene glanced at her momentarily, then turned back without a word to focus on his piloting. He could have set the AVU for automatic flight, which most people did, but he was old-school and preferred manual controls, even at this time of night when traffic was light. Though, she suspected most of his silence came from replaying the last hour of madness.

She didn't know why Keene had followed her to the Safety Zone, the local bar where most ISA guards spent their off hours. But it wasn't unusual for partners when trouble was brewing. She'd once followed Zach home after a particularly difficult raid just to make sure he hadn't picked up a trail. What were little sisters for other than ensuring their big brother's family was kept safe?

She'd been mired in trouble ever since meeting Keene. She turned her head to watch the lights of Los Angeles, Earth's capital, diminish as they grew closer to the outer edges of the district. If she was honest with herself, she couldn't blame him. The last six months had been nothing but trouble for her. All of it her own making.

It all began when she'd lost Zach in a raid. Shot in the line of duty. It should have been her, and now, because of some weird time shift that had messed up Earth's history, she fought an internal battle on whether to restore the natural order or just leave it alone so Zach could stay alive. So that Kendra and their two children didn't have to live with her mistake.

But something sinister was going on in this new timeline. Someone with enough money and influence owned four fully-weaponized rammers and had them driven through the Edges to open fire on the Safety Zone at a time when it was packed with off-duty ISA guards. That was serious business.

If the mass murders, something unheard of in their original timeline, even in the Yards, weren't bad enough, Zach had to do something stupid. While she couldn't blame him for his curious nature, why hadn't he just dropped the TTD, Keene's time travel box, when he'd been warned? Because he was a major in the ISA Guard and considered the device a possible threat. Now, he was lost somewhere in sixteenth-century Scotland.

She glanced at Keene and noted the stiff jaw, his focus on the screen in front of him, and his casual scan of the occasional cargo transport they passed. Before she could bounce her knee with impatience, the AVU dropped into Zone 2 and the lights of the silo, a mile to the west of the bunker, came into sight. Keene circled the silo before lowering to Zone 1 and then touched wheels down a couple hundred yards from the gate that automatically opened as the AVU approached.

There was little outdoor lighting, and the bunker remained dark until the dock-style loading doors opened to the garage. Rowan jumped out before Keene shut down the AVU and ran for the elevator, where Thomas, the night security guard, waited by the doors, holding them open. Keene was seconds behind her before the doors shut.

When the doors opened on the second subbasement floor, eighty feet below ground level, alarms blared at an almost intolerable level. Red lights mounted in the halls, their housing painted to blend into the forest murals that covered the walls, lit the corridor.

Keene turned right but came to an abrupt stop when Conall raced down the hallway toward them.

"We need you in the Command Center."

Keene shook his head. "We need to get to the POD."

"This emergency is impacting our time travel protocols." Conall grabbed Keene's arm and turned him around, forcing Rowan to turn with them.

"There wasn't an emergency when Keene called you." Rowan's heart pounded with the delay. What was happening in Scotland while they were screwing around here? Zach most likely arrived in the cave's safe room, but what if he'd landed out in the countryside like she and Keene had? She clearly remembered the axes the clansmen wore on their belts. If he'd arrived in the safe room as expected, he could be lost in the cave's extensive tunnel system.

Conall stormed through the double doors that led to the Command Center. Rowan was expecting to see the remains of a destroyed room, similar to the first time she'd seen one of Horatio's tantrums. To her surprise, other than the red lighting and the alarms that seemed to be growing louder, the room was in its same orderly condition.

Except for Lanis.

This time, rather than Horatio, she was the one pacing and wringing her hands while glancing over at him and Hernandez, who stood at their consoles, their hands frantically moving over keyboards and imagers.

"Can someone shut the damn alarms off?" Keene yelled.

Conall ran to a console on the other side of the room while Lanis turned to them.

"There you are." Lanis's face was red, and based on her wrinkled forehead and grim set of lips, she was angry as she stormed over. Rowan couldn't remember seeing her this angry. "You didn't report leaving the building."

Keene ignored her admonishment. "Four rammers hit the Safety Zone."

"In the Edges?" The news drained Lanis's anger, and she fell onto a stool and shook her head.

Without warning, the alarms stopped. Instead of silence, a buzzing filled Rowan's ears, and she rubbed their base to dispel the pressure. She hadn't been the only one affected.

"That's not the only problem." Keene continued rubbing his ear as he explained how he'd followed Rowan back to her housing unit to ensure no one had tailed her, then to the bar, and the nightmare that had ensued when the rammers arrived.

"I managed to pull someone out of the lead rammer, but things got sticky after that."

"In what way?" Conall asked.

"We had a hard time taking this guy down..." Keene started.

"Striker." Rowan gave them the man's name. "Dozer, an ISA guard, recognized him, so he must have a record or evidence of surveillance on file."

Keene nodded, seeming to assimilate the information before continuing. "During the fight, my TTD fell out." He ran a hand through his hair. "It was primed to our emergency protocols, but then Zach picked it up...it happened so fast. Zach was gone."

"Zach?" Lanis asked, then turned to Rowan. "You're brother?"

All Rowan could do was nod. Pressure was building behind her eyes, and she feared she'd either start yelling orders or break out in tears. She had to pull herself together. She would not lose Zach a second time.

"By Dagda's blood," Conall fell against a wall and stared at them, his face paling. "You mean Zach traveled back to Scotland?"

"It gets worse," Keene said. "Striker watched it happen and didn't seem surprised by Zach's disappearance."

Conall slammed a fist on a nearby console. "You're telling us that someone or, more likely, more than one person knows about time travel? This isn't good."

"That's why we need to reprogram the coordinates from my TTD so we can retrieve Zach. Once we return, we'll attempt to get access to Striker or at least dig up information on him and his cohorts."

Rowan, tired of the delay, focused on Hernandez, the one person with whom she had some control. The corporal was immersed in her actions, but someone needed to start explaining what the alarms were about.

"What's going on that's preventing us from following Zach?" Rowan demanded, but when a mere second passed with no response, she turned on Keene.

His hands were already raised. "Don't set your sights on me. I just got here, too." His angry tone was softened by his concerned glance. He was just as confused as her.

"Ha. Got ya." Horatio stepped back from the console and pumped his fist while Hernandez did what Rowan could only describe as a poor attempt at a jig.

The red lights, which hadn't disappeared when the alarms had been shut down, died as the room lights brightened, forcing squints while their eyes adjusted.

"I knew we could do it." Hernandez noticed the others in the room for the first time. When her gaze lit on Rowan, who now stood with hands on hips, her foot tapping with the beating of her heart, her smile vanished. "Sorry, boss. Everything should be back to normal now."

"What happened?" Keene asked. "And be quick about it. We need to make a time jump."

Horatio shook his head. "We should wait until all the systems are back online before you try that." He glanced at Lanis. "And maybe run a diagnostic, too."

"Again. What the hell happened?" Keene's words came out slow, as if speaking to toddlers

When Horatio couldn't seem to spit it out, Rowan turned her glare back to Hernandez. "Corporal, report."

Hernandez came to full attention and provided a crisp report. "At approximately twenty-two hundred hours, we received an alarm on a trace Horatio developed to monitor the time fluctuations. The alarm identified a return trace, which we assumed was an automated response to a breach in their security protocols. Horatio wrote a program in anticipation of this, and the return trace was diverted to several fake locations. The alarm was designed to notify us of this type of cyberattack. The trail Horatio set up sent the return trace through various jumps before directing it to the GSM Security Council. The trail requires fifteen minutes to complete, and we initiated manual monitoring in case adjustments were required." She broke from her report to give Horatio an adoring smile. "I'm pleased to report that the diversion program worked like a charm, with nothing tying Horatio's trace to the bunker."

"At ease, Corporal. Thank you for the report." Rowan turned to Horatio. "Why is this preventing us from a time jump?"

Horatio glanced at Lanis, who sighed. "If you remember, we traced the issue with the time shift to a signal somewhere in the Barrens. Horatio and I were both concerned that whoever, or whatever, was creating that signal might also detect our time travel signature. We've added a layer of security, similar to Horatio's trace, that would bounce evidence of our travels to another location."

"Actually, several locations," Horatio added. "Each time a trace is detected trying to breach our time travel protocols, the trace is diverted to one of two hundred rotating locations."

"Two hundred?" Rowan's eyes widened, though she doubted she was grasping the larger picture. "Which locations?"

Hernandez grinned. "A variety of GSM locations in various Earth regions."

"Let me see if I'm understanding." Keene sat on the edge of a desk, his arms crossed over his chest. Rowan didn't believe for a minute that he was confused. This was his way of organizing the information into smaller bites. "Horatio tracked down what we believe to be the source of the time shift somewhere in the Barrens. To secure his trace, he added a layer of security that prevented anyone from returning their own trace back to the bunker. He did this by diverting those return traces to a variable loop of different GSM locations." He shook his head, but not in disgust. His smile said everything Rowan needed to know, and she couldn't argue—it was brilliant.

"And the alarms go off when that happens?" Rowan asked. When Horatio nodded, she looked to Conall. "Isn't there a way to provide a notification that doesn't sound physical alarms or dim the halls with red light like some old horror flick? I mean, it's critical no one discovers the bunker, but there has to be a quieter way."

"I agree." Conall gave Horatio an irritated glance. "Apparently, as head of security, I wasn't informed of this update."

Horatio looked sheepish as he stuffed his hands in his pockets and shrugged. "Sorry. I forgot your security protocols." His gaze turned confused. "Though, I'm surprised we didn't get a hack sooner." Then his eyes brightened, and he pointed at Conall. "It came in right after you received Keene's call about the rammers. I wonder if the two are related."

"I don't see how," Lanis replied. "But perhaps we should do a more thorough review now that the emergency is over."

"I don't understand. Why is this preventing us from traveling if you've already set up a trace?" Rowan began bouncing on her toes. Now that the emergency was over, her focus returned to Zach.

Lanis sighed. "When the return trace is diverted, the time jump system is locked down to ensure no one is searching for the POD's temporal signature at the same time. Once the system validates the trace bounced to a new location, the system is brought back online, but it takes some time to reboot."

"What if they decide to run their own continuous loop?" Keene asked. "That could permanently shut down our system."

Horatio and Hernandez nodded like synchronized robots. "We're working on that next. We should have something set up to deflect our temporal signature by tomorrow. I suggest not using the system until then."

Rowan shook her head. "That's unacceptable. We can't let Zach wander around in sixteenth-century Scotland. He could get himself killed." And she wouldn't be able to handle that. She turned away, blinking rapidly while taking a calming breath.

"Rowan's right." Keene stood. "We can't stop travel on the hunch someone might be tracing us. We'll have to go to the Barrens to see what's out there, but we have to retrieve Zach first. You can work on your program after we've left." He pointed a finger at Horatio. "You've got one day after we leave, and you better get your program right, kid. We don't want to get stuck in Scotland."

THANK YOU FOR READING

Children of the Mist - Time Renegades - Book 2

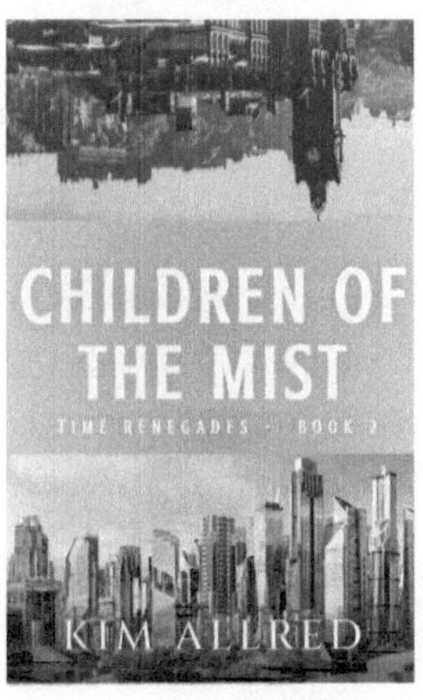

Coming early 2026!

Make sure you never miss a new release!

Join my FB Readers Group - Kim Allred's Heart Racing Romance

Join my newsletter...I'm pretty much unobtrusive.

Follow me at Amazon, Goodreads, or Bookbub

If you can't wait and want to check out my other series, visit my website.

DON'T MISS THIS!

Here's a **FREE** first book in my vampire urban fantasy series, *Of Blood & Dreams*. A touch of mystery...with just a pinch of spice.

Seduction in Blood, Of Blood and Dreams
Book 1

A thief. A vamp. A dangerous temptation.

Cressa Langtry is the most elusive cat burglar on the West Coast—fearless, clever, and always one step ahead. But when a debt comes due, she's forced into the shadows of a world she's tried to avoid. Her only chance at survival? Steal for the city's most dangerous and ancient vampire—Devon Trelane.

Devon has waited a century to settle a score, and the vampire who betrayed him remains on the Vampire Council. Now, he has the perfect weapon—a cunning thief with nothing left to lose, offering the perfect chance at revenge.

But what starts as a cold-blooded business arrangement soon ignites into something neither of them expected. Cressa and Devon find themselves tangled in a game where every move is deadly—and shared dreams turn dangerously prescient.

Grab your copy now!

ABOUT THE AUTHOR

Kim Allred grew up in California but now enjoys the quiet life in an old timb

er town in the Pacific Northwest where she raises alpacas, llamas, and an undetermined number of free-range chickens. Like her characters, Kim loves sharing stories while sipping a glass of wine or slurping a strong cup of brew.

Her spirit of adventure has taken her on a ten-day dogsledding trip in northern Alaska and found her sleeping under the stars on the savannas of eastern Africa.

Kim is currently making up stories while shooing cats and dogs away from her lap, and Willow, the parrot, from her keyboard. Willow can peel the keys from the board in fifteen seconds flat.

Kim's current works include her time travel romance series, the *Mórdha Stone Chronicles* and *The Swan Syndicate*, the urban fantasy romance series, *Of Blood & Dreams*, and a time travel sci-fi and fantasy adventure series, *Time Renegades*.

———